NORTH TO ALASKA

JOHN THOMPSON

ARCHWAY PUBLISHING

Archway Publishing books may be ordered through booksellers or by contacting:

Archway Publishing
1663 Liberty Drive
Bloomington, IN 47403
www.archwaypublishing.com
1 (888) 242-5904

Interior Image Credit: John Thompson, Mary Parker (Image 2)

ISBN: 978-1-4808-9191-3 (sc)
ISBN: 978-1-4808-9192-0 (e)

Library of Congress Control Number: 2020911103

Print information available on the last page.

Archway Publishing rev. date: 07/14/2020

AUTHOR'S NOTE

This is a completely fictional story. However, the Race to Alaska is very real. It was dreamed up by the good folks at the Northwest Maritime Center in Port Townsend and the inaugural race was held in 2015. I completed the race in 2016 aboard a 38' catamaran on *Team Golden Oldies meets Team Ghost Rider*. We finished the race in six days in tenth place. The 2018 race was completed well before this novel was written, and I chose to deviate from the actual events of that race. That gave me the leeway to create whatever events I wanted to include, in whatever order I saw fit, without having to worry about historical accuracy. I hope any readers who participated in the actual race in 2018 will forgive me. The events described are typical of each race without being specific or historically accurate. The intent is to give the reader an accurate sense of what the race is like, described by someone who has participated. I have also cruised up the inside passage in my cruising boat, a Nonsuch 30 (which happens to be the model for the wishboom rig on our subject's little boat) and I have a growing knowledge of the waters. Please enjoy this novel for what it is, pure fiction. The named restaurants are actual establishments. I have eaten in all of them and recommend them all. The characters are all fictional except for Karch Kiraly. Karch is a very real and beloved U.S. Olympic hero, winning several golds in both indoor and beach volleyball and is now (at the time this book was written) running the Team USA Women's Volleyball Association.

This story is a fantasy of mine, which likely will never come true. I did build a ten-foot cedar strip dinghy and often wondered what it would take to build the perfect dinghy for the Race to Alaska. My criteria, like Gerald's, is that I want to do it solo and I want to do it in the smallest boat ever to finish the race. I've put a lot of thought into the ideal design, and our subject's little boat is the result. We can argue the pros and cons all day long. You supply the margaritas, and I'll engage in that discussion. Will I ever build her? Who knows? It's still a dream.

CONTENTS

TROUBLES

1

Bobby groaned as he slowly extracted himself from his truck, dumping the pillows that he had to sit on to the floorboards. About two hours behind the wheel was all he could tolerate without a break these days. His tailbone ached, and the evening sun in his eyes gave him headaches. His head throbbed and his ears were still ringing from the road noise. His hotrod truck wasn't built for creature comforts. Without air conditioning, Bobby was getting used to driving with the windows down even at highway speeds. At twenty-four years old, he felt more like an old man as he stretched and tried to loosen up his banged-up body. Finally, his legs were limber enough to get him to the rest-stop bathroom. He'd already logged 500 miles today down Interstate 70 and he was done. Only a year ago he would scoff at anything less than a thousand miles in a day. He yearned for a decent hot meal in a restaurant, but with precious little money and a huge credit card bill, it was out of the question. For the third straight day, he would spend the night at a rest stop sleeping on the bunk in his toy-hauler trailer amongst all the endlessly idling big rigs, eating carrot sticks and hopefully a sandwich if he had any luncheon meat left. He took a long walk around the entire rest area four or five times until his legs were tired, then slowly climbed into his trailer, careful to protect his broken right wrist. He'd had a hard transition losing his dominant hand, even though he knew it was just for a short period. Writing left-handed was one thing, but how about simple things like trying to turn the truck's ignition key with his left hand? He ended up having to almost lie over on the seat as he reached under and around the steering column with his left hand. And shifting gears? He could do it barely. He wouldn't be winning any races any time soon. How about brushing his teeth or even worse his long unruly hair? Ha! He could do one side okay. The other side, well, not so good. The hated cast would come off in another month. His body was slowly mending, but his career on the Motocross Pro Circuit was over. At least for now. The wreck was over two months ago now. The broken pelvis and collarbone were almost healed though he still felt sore from sitting or standing in one position too long. The doctors weren't overly concerned with those. They'd heal in their own good time. The soreness would pass. They were far more concerned with the severe concussion and broken wrist. Those kept Bobby in the hospital for two weeks as the medical charges piled up and his credit went to hell.

His buddy Frankie Ross (aka Gearhead) claims the Kid wrecked him on purpose, but Bobby didn't really believe him. He remembered the wreck vividly. He was attempting a pass on the outside, both he and the Kid were sliding their bikes almost sideways as they negotiated the turn. He remembered the dirt flinging off the Kid's rear tires all over him and thinking that maybe this wasn't such a good idea. He clearly recalled the Kid's front tire hitting a rut, jamming the rear out into his front wheel. Both riders tumbled to the ground at about thirty-five miles per hour. The memory of impacting the ground on the back of his head, then being run over by two other riders who couldn't stop in time was burned indelibly into his psyche. He had nightmares for weeks. In total, four riders went down. All hopped back up and continued the race except Bobby. He tried to stand, but the world wouldn't stop spinning and his body screamed in agony. He wanted to get back on his bike, but he couldn't even find it. Everything was a blur. He tried to shake it off, but the pain wouldn't go away. All he managed to do before the EMTs got there was to stand up very unsteadily.

He'd been on the pro circuit for almost three years, and this past year he was finally nationally ranked. Okay, so it was at the bottom of the list, but it was still in the top 100. Gearhead kept kidding him that there were only about a hundred riders on the circuit. Some friend! He was ranked forty-four, but then he'd been riding since he was sixteen. Bobby usually beat him when they raced each other. And he was improving every year. This year he had even managed three top ten finishes. That brought in a tiny amount of earnings. He usually just had to make do with sponsorship money and some extra money made on the side modeling motorcycle accessories. His gangly frame, crooked smile and long brown, unruly hair made him an interesting and popular model. He figured he needed another year on the circuit before he could start to count on race winnings. But now he was sidelined for at least six months, if not nine. That was a career killer. Could he stage a comeback? Was it even worth it? He had contemplated quitting the tour in the past, but it was Piper who had kept him going.

Piper rode on the women's Pro Circuit, and she was his first love. Sure, he'd dated other girls before, but he'd lost his virginity at the ancient age of twenty-two with Piper. She was far more experienced than he was and proved to be an outstanding teacher of the fine art of making love. He was a rapt student, taking to heart everything she taught him. They had an unusual relationship. Piper and Bobby saw each other generally for a few days each month, never more than a week. They made no commitments to each other. Rather, they just enjoyed each other's company whenever they could. Sometimes their races aligned, but most often they didn't. Piper was doing well on the circuit, and had a lot of sponsorship money coming in. It enabled her to go to every race no matter where it was located. Bobby had to carefully pick his events to minimize travel. That alone hurt his standings more than anything else. He was finishing consistently in the tenth through fifteenth positions and was slowly moving up. But many of his races were unsanctioned events that earned him no points and little in the way of winnings. Piper had nursed him through the first two weeks after he left the hospital, but then had to return to the circuit. When they parted ways, they mutually agreed to go live their own lives with no ties. If fate brought them back together, then great. Breaking up with Piper was the hardest thing Bobby had ever done, and he'd been in a funk ever since. And now he had to return home with his tail between his legs to recover. As much as Bobby hated the idea, he had already concluded that his racing career was over.

He ate his sandwich and baby carrots slowly, washing the meager meal down with the last of his water. He contemplated whether it was worth the effort to refill his bottles in the rest area bathroom. With a wrist in a cast, he found it no simple task just getting the top off the bottles. But he discovered that a strap wrench makes it possible with only the tips of his fingers and the half a thumb that stuck out of the cast. If he didn't fill them tonight, he'd have to in the morning and the job wouldn't get any easier. Groaning, Bobby finally gathered up all the empty bottles and the strap wrench and clambered clumsily out of the trailer. He managed to get himself thoroughly wet and only succeeded in getting each about three-quarters full. The damn photo sensor in the sink kept turning the water off prematurely. Totally frustrated, Bobby finally crawled back into the trailer, dropped the bottles on the floor and slumped to the bunk. Time to tune out the world. He found his ear buds and fumbled with them with his left hand. Finally succeeding, he turned on his rock playbook and settled back as *Skillet* blared as loud as he could tolerate. And then the phone rang.

Hoping it was Piper but knowing it wasn't, Bobby looked at the caller ID. It was Mom. He had to take this one.

"Hi, Mom. How's everything back home?"

Her voice was shaky, as if she'd been crying. "Bobby, Gerald's in the hospital. I think he had a stroke. I'm here now in the waiting room with Jessie. The doctors haven't told us anything yet. We've been here for over three hours and we still don't know his status."

"Oh, my God! What happened?" I was on my feet now, heart pumping.

"Ohhh... He went out for a run after lunch. I wasn't there when it happened. I was told a stranger driving by saw him stagger and then fall. He called 911 and the EMTs got there in a couple of minutes. A police officer came to the house a little later and took me to the hospital. I haven't been able to see him. He's in surgery right now."

"Surgery? For a stroke? What for?"

"I don't know. I haven't been able to speak to a doctor. The nurses tried to reassure me by saying that since he got here so quickly, he should be okay. But they couldn't give me anything specific to Gerald's case."

"Oh shit, Mom! Shit! I wish I could be there with you right now. I'm in Missouri now, just outside of Columbia. But I'm on my way. I'll be home as soon as I can. I can't drive more than seven or eight hours a day. I'll be there in a couple of days. Just keep me updated, please.

"Of course, Dear. What are your plans?"

"Well, first off, to recover. Then I need to earn some money and pay off my debts. After that, I don't know. I'm not sure I want to go back to racing."

"That would make Gerald incredibly happy. Frank won't approve, though,"

"I'm hoping he'll hire me again. I'm flat broke with a huge credit card bill. I just need to settle down for a while and re-evaluate my life."

"It does my heart good to hear you say that, Bobby. That's the first good news I've heard all day. And your room is ready for you. We turned it into a guest room. You can stay as long as you like."

"Thanks, Mom. I love you guys. Give Jessie a kiss and a hug for me. I'll be there as soon as I can."

"We love you too, Bobby. And I'm looking forward to having you home again for a while."

Bobby hung up, turned off the music and settled back to contemplate the news. How could this happen? His Dad was so healthy! He was still running and still competing. He had just finished his third marathon last year! And he's only, what 61? 62? That's way too young to have a stroke! Hell, Grampa LaRoche is still going strong at 93. Grandma Rosie died at 88, but that was due to an accident. She was still walking two or three miles a day and living alone. Grandma Martha died at 89, but she had chain-smoked all her life, so it wasn't unexpected. LaRoches are supposed to live well into their nineties! Gerald was fit and happy, a true outdoorsman, and highly active in society. He did enjoy a fine cigar from time to time, and was a connoisseur of fine wines and micro brews, but would that kill him? Bobby thought about all the weed and coke he'd used over the last five years, and the heavy drinking he'd done ever since he was sixteen. His fearless recklessness on the racetrack won him a lot of respect from his fellow racers, but he should have been dead many times over. But somehow, he always seemed to get away with things, at least until his last wreck. Maybe his Dad's stroke was a sign. Maybe it was time to grow up.

Gerald LaRoche owned three huge auto dealerships in Edmonds, Lynnwood and Everett which made him a very wealthy man. He still had all his golden years ahead of him. Could he really die so young? Would God do that? Bobby moped all evening trying to make sense of this, but at least he wasn't focused on his own troubles. About eight, he clambered clumsily out of the trailer and took another walk trying to clear his head. Forty-five minutes later, he returned with a clearer vision of his future.

His Dad had always intended for him to take over the family business when he retired. Bobby had studied business management in college for nine quarters before he ran off to race motorcycles. He always knew he would return one day when his riding career was over to take up where he left off, but he wanted desperately to compete while he was still young enough to be great. His Dad was supposed to live forever! There would always be time to settle down and learn the ropes of the automotive retail world. But now... well, maybe not... He just prayed that his Dad would survive this. But the signs were clear. It was time for Bobby to put his nose to the grindstone and finish his degree.

He grabbed his toiletry kit and went over to the restrooms to clean up a little as best he could with one hand. When he returned, the big rigs that had been on either side of him were gone, and the next two closest were turned off and silent. Maybe, just maybe, he would get some sleep tonight. But first, he called his Mom back.

"Hi Mom. Any news?"

"Yes. Thanks for calling. We were just about to call you. We just talked to the surgeon a few minutes ago. Gerald's out of surgery now and in ICU. They had to relieve the pressure in his head and find the cause of the bleeding. He's in a drug-induced coma right now. They said he will be that way for at least two days, and then they'll try to bring him back. Bobby, it was a dreadfully serious stroke. Most people wouldn't have survived it. If they hadn't gotten him to the hospital so quickly, he would have died right there on the street. As it is, they say he has a decent chance of recovery, but they won't know the ramifications for a while yet. There's no reason for us to stay, so we're heading home to get some rest. It's been a long day. I'm exhausted. I'm sure Jessie is also."

"Good idea, Mom. Listen, I've been doing some thinking. I think it's time I finished college and started working with Dad. Assuming he survives that is. What do you think?"

"Oh Honey, I am so happy to hear you say that! And Gerald will be also. He'll be okay, I just know it. You know your college is already paid for. That's great news!"

"Well, I'm happy to bring some good news then. I guess you won't know anything else about Dad for a couple of days then, right?"

"That's what they're telling me. He's in good hands, but please pray for him anyway."

"Oh, I will, and for you also. Be strong, Mom. He'll be okay. I'll see you both in a couple of days."

"Okay. I love you, Dear."

"Love ya, Mom. And Jessie too. I wish I were there."

"Bye, Bobby. See you soon."

"Bye, Mom."

Bobby settled back into the bunk in the trailer and tried to find a comfortable position. He still missed Piper, but he had a mission now, a path forward. For the first time in weeks, he wasn't morose. Quite the opposite, in fact. He was getting more and more excited to get on with it. Go get that degree. Take over the family business. Become independently wealthy by the time he was forty. That was his path. He could always do some racing on the side. With those happy thoughts, Bobby drifted off to the best sleep he had since before the wreck.

HOME AGAIN

2

Three days later, late in the afternoon, Bobby arrived at the Swedish Hospital in Edmonds. Of course, there was no parking, especially for a truck with a large trailer. He had to park over a mile away and walk in. It felt great to get out and stretch his legs, but his pelvis was sore when he eventually arrived. Trying to find his Dad was the next great challenge. The ER staff directed him to the admissions office. But after walking completely across the campus, admissions found him back in the ICU. The ER should have known that. The next chore was finding the ICU, and his pelvis was starting to ache more and more. He followed the directions provided and got to the right floor easy enough. As he exited the elevator, Bobby found a couple of wheelchairs parked along the hallway and snagged one. Sitting down gave him immediate relief. Off he rolled presumably in the right direction. Within minutes he was lost again in the labyrinth, but a nurse, or maybe a nurse's aide, was able to get him pointed in the right direction. Finally, he arrived at the nurse's station and introduced himself. The nurse, an older woman who was not one to mince words with, checked his name against the visitor list, then wheeled him into a room that more closely resembled a laboratory than a hospital room. On leaving, she cautioned him to be quiet and to keep the visit to a minimum. Bobby's Mom, Annette, was there sitting in a chair next to his Dad's bed. Bobby didn't recognize him at all. His head, except for his face, was completely bandaged and his mouth and nose were covered with some sort of mask. There were all sorts of tubes and wires attached to him and a big machine with several screens monitoring his vitals. A nurse was just leaving after administering some drugs into his IV drip. He had a hard time even recognizing his Mom.

Her face was drawn and lined with fatigue and concern. Her eyes were bloodshot. There was no sign of the jolly, plump woman who brought such joy into every occasion.

Bobby rolled over alongside his Mom, and they embraced. She had been crying and now she burst out crying all over again.

"How's he doing?"

"Shhh! I'll bring you up to date in a few minutes outside. They want silence in here."

So, for the next fifteen minutes or so, they sat holding each other's hands and gazing at the lifeless form of the great man. But eventually they made our way back out to the nurse's station where they could talk.

"The doctors stopped giving him the drugs to induce the coma yesterday morning. For now, it's a waiting game. The sooner he comes around, the better the situation. The doctor guessed that he would most likely come around this evening. But he also admitted that there was still a very real but very minor risk that he might not ever come out of it at all. They have no idea how much damage has been done by the stroke or collateral damage by the surgery. He'll be weaned off the ventilator soon. If he breathes on his own immediately, that's a great sign. So, I'm here for the night."

"I'll stay with you, tonight. You shouldn't be alone."

"No, they only allow one person. When he comes around, then he can have more visitors. Jessie will be here tomorrow morning so I can get some rest. Here's a key to the house. Go home. You've been driving all day. You need some time to unwind and unpack. And I bet the hot tub might do you some good in your present condition."

"I've been looking forward to that hot tub for a long time. I'll be in it before I even get unpacked."

She finally smiled. A very tired smile. "Bobby, I'm so happy you're back. I hope you stay for a while."

"Well, that's the present plan. I can commute into Seattle for classes. I can't afford an apartment."

"I'd love to keep you around the house, Dear, but if an apartment makes more sense then go ahead and plan on it. If you are truly determined to follow your Dad's footsteps, then don't you worry about money. He will sponsor you no matter the cost. He can't take it with him. Assuming that he survives this stroke, it's a big wake-up call to all of us. Now, go home! I expect to see you comfortably settled in when I get home in the morning."

Bobby kissed her. "Good night, Mom. Keep your fingers crossed. I think he'll pull through. Bring me some good news in the morning."

"Oh, I do hope I can do that. Good night, dear."

The house was north of Edmonds right on the coast overlooking Puget Sound. It was a two-story Spanish-styled hacienda with peach colored stucco walls and an earthy red ceramic tile roof. The front yard had a circular drive, and a fountain. The entire two-acre lot was surrounded by a very tall stucco privacy wall inlaid with Spanish tile. Except for some raised gardens and a large fountain, the back yard was hardscaped with decorative pavers and stained concrete. A huge garage dominated the back yard. Bobby's Mom and Dad designed the house together and had built it back in 2003. It didn't really fit in with the neighborhood. But then the neighborhood was an eclectic mix of wild styles, mostly all ostentatious. They were all large houses, and this one was no exception. It featured two master bedroom suites, one on the ground floor and one upstairs, plus four other bedrooms. Mom and Dad slept in the upstairs suite and used the downstairs one as a game room with an antique pool table and a shuffleboard.

Bobby's older sister, Jessie had moved out long ago when she got married, but his younger brother Davie still lived there. And he came running out when he heard Bobby maneuvering his rig alongside the big garage and waited impatiently until Bobby finally shut down the motor and stepped out. Then he ran over and embraced him.

"Hiya, Bobby! I missed you! Are you back to stay this time?"

"I missed you too, Davie. It's been, what? A year now since I was home? I'll be staying for a while this time."

"Oh good! I want to show you my pictures... and read you a new poem!"

"I look forward to that, Davie. How about we wait a few minutes until I get my stuff inside, okay? Can you help me carry some stuff in?"

"Sure, Bobby! I'll help you. Then we'll go see my art?"

"Absolutely! Come over here and take a load. I'll be in my old room, I think."

Davie had Down syndrome and had the intellect of a nine or ten-year old. But he was always happy and remarkably self-sufficient. With a huge struggle, he had made it through high school, and could take care of all his personal needs and even do some simple cooking for himself. He loved to help in the kitchen and be in the middle of any crowd. Everybody loved Davie. It was impossible not to. He was so enthusiastic about everything. He didn't understand sports or politics or religion, but he took great pride in everything he did. Davie worked at the Cadillac dealership detailing cars. No one was more thorough than Davie. Just don't hurry him along. That just doesn't work. Davie even sold a Caddy every now and then when repeat customers by-passed the sales staff and came directly to him for their next purchase. So, he was making decent money all by himself. He took great pride in his watercolor paintings which were very primitive but very charming. Mom and Dad encouraged him by framing his best pieces and hanging them throughout the house. But it was Davie's poetry that got most people's attention. He used a very simply rhythmic pattern and his limited vocabulary never held him back. He just made up nonsense words as needed, much in the same style as Lewis Carroll. When read out loud, they were all highly amusing, and the local paper had even published several of them.

Bobby knew that he would have to wait to unload the trailer, but that was to be expected. Not only was Davie not to be put off, but the hot tub was also calling his name. So, he and Davie grabbed all his bags including the dirty laundry and tramped back into the house, dropping the laundry by the washer, and toting the rest up to his old room. He didn't recognize the room. The old furniture was gone. His trophies and posters were gone. A queen-sized bed with an ornate headboard and throw-pillows took up most of the room. The dresser and a small desk took up the remainder, leaving just enough room to comfortably walk around the room to the closet. Davie's framed art, much that Bobby had never seen before, filled the walls. It reminded him of some of the nicer hotel rooms he'd been in. The frames really made the watercolors look great. Most of the art were rural scenic views copied out of one of many magazines, but with a childish two-dimensional style and bold, vibrant colors. If you stepped back a bit, they looked like colorful abstract art. Subtlety was not Davie's style. Some people really liked his work, and the local framing shop had a large painting up on their wall. Dumping his bags on the bed, Bobby followed Davie to his room and spent a good hour with him and his art.

Finally, Bobby broke free leaving Davie working on another watercolor, and headed downstairs. First stop, laundry. He ducked inside to grab a towel, then stripped off his clothes and started the wash. Once that was going, he headed outside to the back porch and the hot tub. Thankfully, it was turned on and ready for him. He slowly sank into the hot water. He was in the mood to just soak for an hour or more, but the water was way too hot for that. After ten minutes, he dragged himself out on steaming, rubbery legs and plopped down in a lawn chair to let the evening air dry him off. This was Bobby's home. This is where he grew up. He was comfortable here. It would be nice to buy this place from his Dad someday, but that would have to be far in the future. He had a lot of schooling to do first. He felt at ease sitting outside in the late afternoon sun naked as the day he was born. Sure, his Dad was in critical condition, but Bobby had no real doubt that he would bounce back and be running again in no time. Yes, he missed riding and the thrill of competition. He would just have to find a new outlet for that. He was an avid sailor, a rock climber, and a diver, amongst other things. There were possibilities. Yes, he missed Piper, really missed Piper, but that was all in his past now. Someday, there would be someone new. In the meantime, he had a mission. He'd finish his degree, maybe go on to get an MBA, then join his Dad's management team at LaRoche Auto Group. And once his Dad retired, maybe he would be named the next CEO. That's what his Dad wanted, but only if he was ready for it. Mr. Gerald LaRoche was an astute businessman and wasn't about to let his baby be run into the ground by incompetence. Bobby would have to prove himself worthy. Jessie had the hard job there. She ran the Financial and Administrative Departments, but she had no desire to run the entire operation. She wanted kids and plenty of them. At least she could perform most of her current duties at home once she started having kids. Annette thought Jessie might already be pregnant. She could see it in her eyes. Maybe she was just waiting for a better time to make the announcement.

Bobby wrapped the towel around himself and went inside, stopping by the laundry room to put in the second load, and went upstairs to dress and put away his things. The room would take some getting used to. Maybe if he could find some of his old trophies, he could personalize it a bit. He put everything away then went outside to continue unloading the trailer. He had one bay all to himself, isolated from the other bays. The sailboat had to come out first so he could fit the bikes and the ATV in against the back wall. His two kayaks hung from the rafters, and the shelves on the wall held boxes full of camping, climbing, diving and motorcycle gear. There were a couple of new boxes on the shelves that he suspected held his trophies. He had built a small workbench in the very back. He wheeled the bikes and the four-wheel ATV to the rear, along with his tools, leathers, and other gear. It took about half an hour to drain the fuel tanks and the carburetors. It could be years before he used them again. He finally pushed the sailboat back into the garage and turned off the lights.

He looked forward to getting out on the boat again. It was a gift for his fourteenth birthday, and it had changed his life. Up until then, he had been sailing an ancient O'Day Mariner designed in the 1950s. He and his Dad raced it weekly in the summer against the newer, lighter dinghies. He was used to coming in dead last, but he still came out to race diligently every week. The handicap helped a lot, putting him typically in the middle of the fleet once the times were scored. The new sailboat was a Laser, a light, high performance racing sailboat. What a thrill! Overnight, Bobby became uber competitive. He read everything about sailboat racing and studied the racing rules. He started working out, especially his abs so that he could hike[1] out hard to keep the boat from capsizing. At first, no amount of hiking seemed to prevent capsizes. But he learned, some by watching the other sailors, some by asking directly, and some by reading every book on racing Lasers and small dinghies that he could find. By the end of his fourteenth summer, he had moved to the front of the local mixed dinghy fleet and was totally hooked on racing. He joined the US Laser Association and started traveling further to regattas, but suddenly found himself at the back of the fleet again with no handicap to help him. These guys were much more aggressive sailors than in the mixed fleet. Bobby was discouraged at first, but his Dad reminded him that you don't improve by surrounding yourself with lessor sailors. Sail against the best and watch what they do. He enrolled in the local youth sailing program in Edmonds and had an honest to goodness coach teaching him the skills that he would need to compete against the best. He put away the Laser for a while and sailed the two-person Flying Juniors. He learned to roll-tack[2], to roll-gybe[3] and starting line strategy. He learned to read the wind ripples on the water and how to play the waves. He learned race strategy and even team racing, which was a thrill. But Bobby yearned for the solo experience, so he got the Laser out whenever he could convince his Mom to tow the boat to the marina for him. The problem is that at fourteen, he was just too light for it. He had to race with a smaller sail, while the other guys used the standard

---

[1] Hiking – hanging the skipper's weight over the side to counterbalance the force of the wind trying to overturn the sailboat

[2] Roll Tack – Tacking is turning the sailboat through the wind when sailing against the wind. A sailboat can only sail against the wind to about 45 degrees off the wind and progresses to windward on a zig-zag course. On light wind days, a skilled skipper can roll the boat as the boat turns onto the new course then flatten her out quickly, thus whipping the sail through the still air producing a spurt of forward propulsion to compensate for the speed lost in the turn.

[3] Roll Gybe – Gybing is the process of turning a sailboat from one broad reach to the other going down wind. Most light dinghies sail faster on a broad reach rather than straight down wind, so they steer a zig zag course from one broad reach to the other. Roll-gybing means throwing a roll into the turn which helps steer the boat through the turn and then accelerates the boat again as the sail is whipped through the still air. It is only used in light wind.

sail. But on light wind days, he would break out the larger standard sail and sail head to head with the Laser fleet. And on those days, his light weight paid dividends. He found himself mixing things up with the fleet at the start and at the turning marks. And now he was confident in his abilities and his knowledge of the rules. He could yell at the other sailors just as loud as they were yelling at him. On light wind days, he began moving up in the fleet. There were still three or four sailors in the Seattle Laser fleet who were unbeatable, but he joined the large group that were always nipping at their heels. He just needed another twenty to twenty-five pounds to be competitive, and that would come with time.

Bobby shut the garage door, drained his ice chest, and brought all the remaining food into the kitchen. There wasn't much left after his trip. It was going on eight o'clock. Davie was still upstairs happily working on his latest watercolor, not even thinking about supper. Bobby dragged him downstairs and together they prepared four hamburgers for the grill. Davie helped with everything. That was his style. He loved to help. He knew how to make his supper, but he was often too focused on his art or his poetry to prepare anything for himself. He just needed some supervision and direction. There was always peanut butter and jelly in the house if his hunger ever overcame his enthusiasm for his art. He wouldn't starve. But he liked to help make dinner and was reasonably useful if you had enough patience. Together, they made up some macaroni and cheese from scratch using every kind of cheese in the house but mostly sharp cheddar. While that was baking, Bobby sent Davie out to grill the patties. This wasn't his forte and Bobby had to keep a close eye on him to make sure he didn't burn himself or kill the patties. But his supervision was discreet allowing Davie to think he was on his own. Bobby really loved Davie and knew that one day he would end up being Davie's caregiver once Mom and Dad got too old. And that was how it should be. Jessie didn't have the patience and generally just did everything herself rather than letting Davie help. Hopefully, she wouldn't have any Down syndrome kids. The burgers were perfect, and Davie brought them in with a great big smile that lit up the whole room. Bobby slipped out to clean the grill and turn it off, little details that Davie couldn't think to do.

They chattered about everything over supper. Bobby told him about his races, and even about Piper. Davie was heart-broken that they had broken up and that he would never get to meet her. He actually cried, and Bobby had to console him though he felt like crying also. Davie spoke about his job at the dealership and the people he'd met recently. He never really went anywhere other than to work, but he seemed to have a very full and happy life. He was a big help cleaning up after supper. Davie knows how to clean. Just be patient with him. The dishes and cups have to go in the washer just right; the spoons have to be separated and facing one to the front and one to the rear; same with the forks with all tines up, and the knives go sharp end down. Don't try to change anything. That's just the way it is, and that's the way Davie does it. Bobby took care of putting all the food away, and wiping the counters, but Davie did the rest. It took over an hour, but Davie was happy, and Bobby was exhausted. He finally dragged himself off to the shower at ten and to bed by ten-thirty. The new mattress was incredibly comfortable compared to the bunk of his trailer, and he was asleep in minutes.

The phone rang at a little after six, spoiling an erotic dream for Bobby. It was his Mom.

"Hi, Mom. I hope you have good news. I was having a great dream."

"Sorry to wake you so early. Jessie just showed up and I'll be home soon, but I just wanted to talk to you now. I'm a walking corpse. I'll be asleep within a minute of getting home."

"That's okay, Mom. I'm awake now. How's Dad?"

"He came out of the coma last night a couple of hours after you left. He's still out of it, though. But he did wake up briefly and acknowledged me. He's really confused. He doesn't know what happened to him. One minute he's running, the next he's waking up in the hospital. But he moved his hands and he felt it when the nurse pricked his toes, so I think he's going to be okay. The doctor will be in later today to give him a complete test, but it may be later this week before we know the full scope of the damage. I'm exhausted and just can't stay any longer. Jessie will stay today and let me know of any developments."

"Mom, I can stay with him as well. Jessie has a job and a husband to take care of."

"That would be nice. Speak to Jessie about it. I'm too tired to think straight. And take Davie to work at seven-thirty, would you?"

"Okay, Mom. I'll do that. I'll call Jessie now and see if she wants me to come over now or maybe a little later."

Hanging up, Bobby suddenly realized that his solo life was over. He was the newest attraction in the LaRoche family circus. Time to get out of bed and get dressed. There was work to be done.

A NEW DIRECTION

3

Bobby spent the next week sorting out his life. His Uncle Frank welcomed him back to town and was happy to rehire him. He'd have to take a pay cut for six weeks to regain his proficiency with the equipment, and he'd have to wait until his cast was removed. He needed a clean bill of health from a doctor and clean urinalysis before he could work in the factory. The piss test was the biggest challenge. Bobby had been using weed regularly since the accident to dull the pain. He hoped that six weeks would be enough to clear his system. Frank owned a unionized sheet metal factory that employed several hundred and they took safety and drug use very seriously. Bobby had worked there from the day he graduated high school until he ran off to join the pro circuit at twenty-one. It was hard, physical work, but Bobby enjoyed it and moved up to Operator One in only two years. He set several production records just to prove himself, lest anyone try to claim that he got promoted through nepotism. Now, he'd have to start as an OP2 for a while, but he had no doubt that he would be an OP1 within six months.

It was Uncle Frank who gave him his truck, a decrepit 1966 Chevy with no engine, when he was 16. And it was Uncle Frank who taught him how and helped him to restore it. Frank had an old 396 motor lying around the shop that had been in his own truck, and together they rebuilt it. When the engine was installed, it barely resembled the power plant that Chevrolet had produced. Bored, stroked, balanced and blueprinted, it now produced over 500 horsepower and drove the big truck to twelve-second quarter miles. Frank's truck ran sub-ten second quarters, but it was a true race car. Bobby didn't want the roll cage, fuel cell, fire extinguishers and all the other things required to race at that level. From the beginning, he planned to drive it on the street, so Frank found a used six-speed manual transmission with double overdrive and installed it. Bobby learned to paint the hard way, by trial and error. Fortunately, every time he screwed up a coat of paint and had to sand it off, it was just inexpensive primer. He painted it eight times and sanded six coats back off before he was ready for the color coat. And he did a great job on that. The only flaws were well hidden between the cab and the bed. The truck was gorgeous in opalescent white paint, especially when Frank produced the custom wheels and tires. It took another six months to get all the chrome work back from the shop, and in the meantime, Bobby learned how to do upholstery work and installed custom electronics and audio. The truck was complete just in time for homecoming on his senior year. Frank had covered all the expenses, and Bobby had the dream ride all the kids dreamed about. Well, maybe not all the kids. Most of the girls didn't even notice. But the guys did. And Bobby was instantly as popular as if he was a jock.

It was Frank who encouraged him to join the Motocross Pro Circuit. Bobby had been racing bikes locally since he was eighteen and tearing up the tracks. He scarcely ever finished worse than third and won far more than his fair share. Bobby was fearless on a motorcycle and took abundant risks, which usually worked out for him. He drove right past the more cautious riders and he always rode clean. He never stooped to the bumping and shoving on the track that the lesser riders did. Frank taught him how to tune the little two-stroke motors, and how to build them for reliability. It was Frank who toured with him locally and coached him as he learned to race, and it was Frank who germinated the dream of going professional. Frank had been a professional motocross rider when he was a kid, and later a drag racer for a decade before settling down, and he still raced locally just for fun. And it was Frank's toy-hauler that Bobby had been living in for the last three years. Bobby's Dad didn't encourage his riding but didn't dissuade him either. Personally, he preferred for Bobby to stay racing Lasers or to race with him on his Beneteau 36 sailboat.

But he let Bobby go down his own path. Even if he succeeded as a pro rider, his career was most likely to be short. Plenty of time for him to come back home to take over the family business. As it turned out, it was especially short. And now it was over.

Shortly after returning home, Bobby visited Frank's personal shop and discovered that Frank had shifted to collectible cars rather than building race cars. Besides Frank's race truck and two older race cars that hadn't seen a track in decades, there were three cars in various stages of assembly or disassembly. Almost complete was a 1970 Hemi Charger Daytona, every collector's dream car. It was worth a fortune, and Frank had painstakingly restored it to show standards. Finding the correct parts was an excruciating process, and that's why the car sat unfinished for over two years since it was restored. There was what appeared to be a first-generation Corvette on the rotisserie, though it was hard to iden- tify it stripped as completely as it was. In the paint booth was a 1967 Pontiac GTO. That wasn't Frank's car. It belonged to Jerry, a buddy of his who did all his painting for him and who had taught Bobby how to paint. Frank and Jerry were like brothers. Frank's latest acquisition was a 1973 De Tomaso Pantera. The Ford 351 cubic inch engine and transmission were removed, but the body was still intact. The car looked like it was going a hundred miles an hour just sitting still in the shop. The mechanicals were at a machine shop. Frank wasn't sure if this was going to be a show car, or maybe a vintage race car, so he wasn't ready to jump into it until he made up his mind. In the meantime, he had a Corvette to restore. When Bobby wasn't sailing with the youth sailing team, he had spent every afternoon after school in the shop since he was sixteen. It was like his second home and Frank was like his second Dad. But things were different now. All these incredible cars fascinated him but seemed alien to him in a strange way. This wasn't his life now. Since he had given up riding, the urge to tinker just wasn't there anymore. He could go appreciate the work that Jerry and Frank were doing, but it wasn't calling him. Possibly, being broke had something to do with it.

Bobby spent time at home with Davie, or at the hospital with his Dad. His Dad was improving very slowly. There was no paralysis at all, but he did have severe weakness and lack of muscle control on his entire right side. He had been in intensive care for over two weeks before moving to a recovery room. He had a hard time talking, but he could listen well enough and understand completely. Bobby spent hours with him telling him about his racing. He told him about Piper and how much he missed her. She was doing great on the pro circuit now. Bobby hadn't contacted her since they split up, but her name was showing up more and more in the race results near the top of the list and he checked the list constantly. She won her first race against real talent the day Bobby had returned home. This moved her up in the national rankings to fourteen. Without having to ask, Bobby knew that it meant major sponsorship money. Her financial worries were over for the time being. Bobby was happy for her, but still missed her terribly. His Dad just smiled and didn't try to say anything. It wouldn't have come out well anyway. The last thing Gerald would want is for him to marry another rider and not come home. He was genuinely happy when Bobby told him of his plans to return to school and to continue working at Frank's for a while. Jessie was also happy to have him home again. She seemed relieved that he had decided to take up the path that Dad had laid out for him. Jessie would have taken over the business. She owed it to their Dad to keep it going. But it would be a burden since she wanted lots of kids. And she did announce her pregnancy when Dad was moved to the recovery room. That brought tears to Dad's eyes. I'd never seen him cry before. I'm sure he was incredibly happy, but he just could not express it. Dad still couldn't walk, though he could, with a lot of help, get himself into a wheelchair to go use the toilet. He was fiercely independent and supremely stubborn, and he insisted on doing this for himself. He wasn't allowed to bathe himself, so using the toilet was the only time he ever got out of bed for the first two weeks. The physical therapists worked his muscles in the bed. Everything seemed fully functional, he just didn't seem to have much control of his right side. Recovery was going to be a long process.

Bobby went down to Seattle to meet with the University of Washington guidance counselors about restarting his collegiate career. Unfortunately, he had been away from school so long that his original course catalog had expired. His classes would have to be re-evaluated for credit and reapplied using the new catalog. But it wasn't a long process, and everything he had already taken still applied. The route forward from here on was different, but not that much so. He had six full quarters ahead of him, with summers open. Generally, there were no upper level classes offered then, but it was a good time to do project work or independent study. He also intended to intern at his father's dealerships over the summer. His degree required a senior project, though it was usually done in the last two quarters. Fortunately, it was too late to register for fall classes. Bobby wasn't quite ready to jump into a full course load, and there was too much going on at home to focus on school. And the classes he needed weren't available in winter either, but he could do some online classes and start full time in spring. Bobby got himself registered again as a student and signed up for an accounting class.

The cast came off the first week of September. Six weeks of physical therapy followed, and he could finally go to the gym again, albeit very carefully. The muscles in his right forearm had atrophied amazingly, but the arm was fully functional. Range of motion was normal. He could finally brush his teeth and hair properly again. His signature was a bit unusual, so he took some time and developed a whole new one with big loopy letters, kind of like John Hancock's. Bobby's pelvis no longer ached unless he over did it on the treadmill or the elliptical trainer. He no longer got headaches from bright sunlight and the collarbone break was completely forgotten. The wrist was the only daily reminder of his wreck, and that was getting stronger every week. Little by little, life was getting back to normal. Only his yearnings for Piper remained to take him back to his prior life. When he went to bed, Bobby often thought of laying with Piper, usually in her rig which was a lot bigger than his. He could feel her smooth skin against his, her breath on his cheek as he toyed with her, teasing her, and ever so slowly bringing her to a climax. He always tried to bring her off before he entered her. It was a lesson that he learned well. Women often don't climax with intercourse alone, and so they often get left out when it comes to sex. Once the guy climaxes, it's generally all over. So, Bobby went out of his way to make sure Piper climaxed first. And then sometimes, she would climax a second time as he made love to her. He knew that he should stop thinking of her, but he enjoyed the memories and occasionally used them to pleasure himself. Someday another woman would replace Piper, but for now, memories were all he had.

A NEW PROJECT 4

Bobby started working full time at the factory on the first of October. Six weeks was plenty of time to flush out any remaining THC from his system. His wrist was stronger, but he still had to be careful with it. In the factory, sometimes he had to lift a lot of metal, which previously had been no problem. Now he had to do it in multiple, lighter loads, which technically complies with the factory's safety guidelines. But you don't set production records by doing things in multiple steps. It's all about working hard, working fast and multi-tasking where possible. Within a week, Bobby was back in the swing and producing as much as or more than the other guys. Frank had hired a bunch of new kids since Bobby left, and they liked to talk more than work. Setting records wasn't even a thing for them. They just came to work, mostly on time, did their job for eight hours, then fled. No pride in their work at all. There were several new machines that Bobby had to learn, and he noted that the records for each were easily within his reach. So, he set that as a goal by the end of the month. Bobby worked from six in the morning until two-thirty every day, got home by three-fifteen usually and studied for at least an hour every day, occasionally two.

One evening in early-October, Bobby wandered out to the garage looking for something to do. His Dad had bought a lathe back when Bobby was seventeen, and he and Jessie were always fighting over it. He suspected that Jessie may have taken it with her when she moved out since his Dad never used it. The garage was huge, with five bays and a carport on either end, the middle bay being an RV bay. His Dad's massive diesel-pusher barely fit inside. The two end bays were isolated by walls from the adjacent bay. The wood shop was at the opposite end from Bobby's personal bay. It was locked of course, but the house key opened it. Flipping on the lights, Bobby was surprised to see a big mess. His Dad was organized to a fault. Everything had a place, and everything was expected to be in that place. But now there was wood everywhere, and boxes full of God knows what along the walls. There was a long beam set up on sawhorses taking up the middle of the room, and a portable work bench piled high with pieces of wood, with more surrounding it on the floor. At least all the tools were hanging on the peg board where they belong. And the floor was swept clean, though the trash can was full to the top with wood dust and offcuts. Bobby looked at the wood parts on the workbench. Particle board. Who builds with particle board? It's heavy, absorbs water like a sponge and has no intrinsic strength. Generally, a poor building material, except maybe for floor underlayment. Bobby held up one of the shapes and rotated it trying to figure out what it was. It was vaguely mushroom-shaped. Puzzling. Looking around for the lathe, he found it behind several sheets of plywood, some whole, some partial. He did recognize a new North sail bag in the corner with battens sticking out. And there was a carbon-fiber mast wrapped in bubble wrap along the wall. That caught Bobby's attention. He went over to the work bench and looked around. There was a pile of paper on the bench. Looking through the papers, he realized that he was looking at a set of plans for a sailboat. That's what his Dad was building! Unfolding and laying them out on the workbench, he studied the drawings. It was a sixteen-foot sailing dinghy with a single mast and a single sail. Remarkably simple. No jib. No spinnaker. A cat boat rig. Not much different than his Laser, just larger in every dimension, especially freeboard[4]. She had elegant lines with a nice sheer line[5] and much higher freeboard than a typical sailing skiff. The rig was high tech with a fully battened mainsail and a flexible unstayed carbon-fiber mast. It had an

---

[4] Freeboard – The sides of a boat from the waterline to the deck
[5] Sheer line – The line of a sailboat's deck. Modern racing sailboats have a flat, purposeful deck. Traditional designs have a graceful curving deck that raises towards the ends.

unusual wishboom[6]instead of a conventional boom, similar to a sailboard. When he found the section views, he recognized the wooden shapes on the bench. They were like ribs. But who makes ribs for a boat out of particle board? What was his Dad thinking? Obviously, he was not going to be able to use the lathe, buried as it was. So, he picked up the plans and took them back into the house.

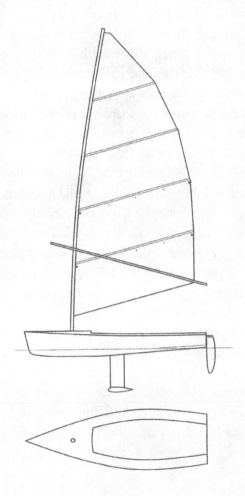

[6] Wishboom rigs – Unlike a traditional mainsail with a boom that supports the bottom of the sail, the wishboom surrounds the sail and is aligned diagonally downwards from the mast. It is commonly seen on sailboards.

His Mom was at the recovery center in Lynnwood with Dad. At least he was out of the hospital now. He was learning to walk again with much assistance by either a physical therapist or an occupational therapist. His talking was improved, though he still had little feeling on one side of his face. He kept biting his tongue and his cheek as he ate, so they were feeding him soft foods that he didn't need to chew. He was determined to improve and used the exercise bands diligently even when the therapists had left. He was confined to a wheelchair still, and probably would be for another month or maybe two. Until he could take care of his daily needs of everyday living, he would be at the recovery center. Bobby planned to take the plans with him next time he visited his Dad. So many questions. The boat was totally cool. And his Dad had already spent a lot of money getting the rig built, so he was obviously serious about building this thing. It was the construction technique that puzzled him. Particle board? Really?

Davie was dropped off by Jessie at a little after five, but Jessie didn't stay other than to say hi and exchange hugs. Davie was hungry as usual, so Bobby put him to work mashing the potatoes that he had just boiled. He usually cooked the pork chops on the grill, but today he just broiled them with a lot of Cajun seasoning. They ate their supper to Davie's incessant chatter. Bobby got to know the details of every minute of Davie's day. He'd met another couple today with young children and he was completely taken with them. He'd given their car special attention and they were thrilled. They even gave him a twenty-dollar tip! Bobby asked him about the boat that their Dad was building, but he didn't know much about it other than Dad was spending a lot of time in the shop lately.

After cleaning up from supper and sending Davie off to take a bath and get ready for bed, Bobby wandered off to his Dad's office to see if he could find any clues as to how this boat was going to be built. Being a life-long sailor, it wasn't surprising to find a whole collection of books on boat building and boat maintenance. But thumbing through them revealed nothing at all about using particle board for ribs. Wooden boats used hardwood ribs either steamed to the proper shape or cut into the proper shape. Maybe the particle board ribs are forms that his

Dad intended to bend the ribs around? That was a possibility. Seemed like a lot of work, though. He found a couple of books about building canoes and kayaks and passed those up. He found another on building paddles. That was kind of interesting. Could be a fun project. He didn't find the answer he was seeking. He'd have to go speak to his Dad. On his way out, he did grab the book on building kayaks to take back to his room. He had to wait until Davie got out of the bath, which could be an hour, and this book would kill some time. He wasn't really interested in building a kayak; his were still in perfectly good condition in the garage out of the sun. But the picture on the cover showed a very artistic wooden kayak built with several different shades of wood. It intrigued him to know how it was done. Bobby settled onto his bed and thumbed through the book quickly.

Suddenly he sat bolt upright. There was the answer right in the book! The kayak was built out of thin cedar strips bent around a set of particle board forms. The frame was discarded after the boat was built, so particle board was perfectly acceptable! The kayak forms were remarkably similar to those that his Dad had cut out in the garage. He paged through the book looking closely at all the pictures as the kayak progressed. That's what that big beam in the garage was for! The boat was to be built on it to keep everything properly aligned. It was getting late and he needed to be asleep by ten since he had to get up at five in the morning. He desperately wanted to go out to the garage and set up the forms on the beam and see what it looked like, but it was shower time. So, he called out to Davie to finish up in the bathroom. Davie took another ten minutes before Bobby could finally use the bathroom, so he perused the book again. Now it all made sense. And the process didn't seem difficult at all. The kayak was far more difficult to build than the sailboat would be since it had a top and a bottom and they had to match exactly. And the boat in the book was being built in a very artistic manner, the strips swooping over the frames in large leaf-like shapes, rather than simply running longitudinally over the forms. Leave out the artistic stuff and the top deck and the cockpit coaming, and Dad's boat seemed like an extremely easy project.

It was three days later, on Saturday, before Bobby found himself in the garage again. He went through all the boxes and parts lying around. Seems like his Dad had bought everything, and just needed to build the boat now. The cedar strips were lying on the floor beside the beam wrapped in bubble plastic, along with a shipping tube that was full of fiberglass cloth. There was a large cardboard box full of epoxy resin, mixing cups, squeegees, dispensers and what-not. Another box was full of new tools, most notably several dozen small clamps. The plans didn't show how to build the boat, just what the finished product should look like. There were fourteen particle board forms cut out and one made of nice plywood. Each was numbered with a sharpie except the plywood one. It also didn't have the stem of the mushroom shape, like the other frames. But it did have two oval cutouts on it for some reason. It didn't take much intelligence to figure out that the forms were numbered from the bow, and that the nice plywood form is the transom, part of the finished boat. Bobby carefully laid them out on the beam, noting that there was already a center line and lateral lines every foot marked in sharpie on the top of the beam. Obviously, the forms aligned with the lateral lines. Looking around, he found a pile of triangular wooden brackets, and quickly determined that they were to be used to mount the forms to the beam. Bobby spent the next two hours carefully clamping the forms onto the beam in their designated spot, making sure each was aligned as perfectly as possible. When he got done, he had used up all the clamps. Maybe he should just use deck screws instead and save the clamps. His Dad had no shortage of deck screws. He stepped back and looked at the forms. The shape and size of the boat was obvious in the negative space between the forms. She would be much larger than the Laser in every dimension, most notably the freeboard. And she had hard chines[7] in the stern, which would make her quick to plane and very stable once on a plane. But even Bobby realized that those presented an incredibly unique challenge for construction. Pondering the shape, Bobby wondered what

---

[7] Chines – The area of a sailboat's hull where the bottom meets the sides. A boat with soft chines has a nice graceful curve between the bottom and sides. A boat with hard chines has hard corners between the bottom and the sides.

his Dad was thinking when he came up with this design. Why not use a jib and an A-sail[8] like most modern skiffs? Why bother with a super high performance main with a flexible mast, and forgo the spinnaker? And why the high freeboard? Most skiffs are designed to be sailed wet these days. Wipe-outs are part of the draw to white-knuckle sailing. Yet this boat was designed very conservatively with lots of volume, a bluff bow for maximum waterline length and high freeboard to stay dry. It also uses a fixed high aspect ballasted keel, which is unheard of in sixteen-foot dinghies. That would make trailering it a pain in the ass and require a special trailer. And for some reason, his Dad had designed oarlocks and a sliding seat in the middle of the cockpit. Why? Why not just put a tiny outboard on the transom? His Dad wasn't particularly noted for thinking outside the box and taking risks, which is why he proved to be such a mediocre sailboat racer but an extraordinarily successful businessman. But this design was unlike any that Bobby had ever seen before. He finally shut off the lights, locked up the garage and went indoors as his Mom came home. It was his turn to go visit his Dad in time for the Huskies game. They were playing Stanford and both teams had a perfect record so far at five wins each.

He kissed his Mom in the kitchen as she made herself a salad and lingered to talk to her for a while. She seemed in a good mood.

"So, how's Dad doing?"

"I left when lunch was served, but he seems upbeat today. He's looking forward to the game and looking forward to watching it with you. He's getting stronger. He's still confined to the wheelchair, but he's walking with assistance for quite a long way. He can only do laps in the recovery center, but he probably does a mile or so. You'll have to measure the length of one lap for us. They won't give him a walker yet because they know he'd be out walking without assistance. He'd most likely end up on the floor and he can't get up by himself yet. And his arm isn't strong enough yet for the walker. But he's talking better. You can actually understand him these days. He can't bathe himself yet, or use the toilet without help, so he'll be at the recovery center for a few more months."

---

[8] A-Sail – Sailors lingo for Asymmetrical Spinnaker, an exceptionally large sail used off-wind.

"I was hoping we'd have him back before Christmas."

"I think I can borrow him for Christmas day. He may be confined to the wheelchair still, but we can make that work. That's still a couple of months off, so we'll cross that bridge when we get there. I'm thinking more of Thanksgiving. I'm keeping my fingers crossed that maybe we can bring him home then. The therapist wasn't optimistic about that, though. But your Dad's a fighter. He's making the therapists earn their salary. He works out constantly with his bands and his ball of clay. I just know he'll recover completely. It's just going to take some time."

"Look, Mom. I've been out in the shop puzzling over Dad's sailboat design. It's a really cool design, but I can't figure out what he was thinking when he designed it."

"Oh that…. He's been obsessed with that boat for the last six months."

"Well, it's an unusual design. Do you have any idea what he was thinking? And I thought he was done with sailing when he bought the Grand Banks."

"He was planning on doing the Race to Alaska solo in it. So, it's designed to be sailed easily by one person with enough room for supplies for three weeks."

"Ohhhh…. That explains the high freeboard. And the single sail, though I think I would have added a spinnaker."

"I think his original plan did include a spinnaker, but then he decided to simplify it as much as possible for reliability and so it doesn't exhaust the sailor. You sail all day and night whenever you can. You only get to rest when the wind dies and the current is against you. After the first day, you'd be too exhausted to use the spinnaker and it takes up too much space in the boat. He was planning on sleeping in the boat, so the deck needs to be clear."

"That explains a lot. I'll have to look at the plans again with that filter. Pity he won't get to do the race. He's already made quite the commitment."

"There's always next year."

Bobby spent the afternoon at the recovery center watching the Huskies barely squeak out a victory over a determined Stanford squad. The final score was 33-34, and only settled in the last few seconds when the Stanford kicker missed a 58-yard field goal attempt. He almost made it. He would have been famous had he made it. But there's only one letter difference between champ and chump. Today, the Huskies were the champs. Bobby didn't mention the boat once, and just focused on college football. They watched part of the Ducks game against ASU, both rooting for ASU. But supper was served at halftime with ASU handily in control of the game, so Bobby decided to go home for his own supper. He kissed his Dad good-bye and drove home still consumed by the boat. He found his supper almost ready when he walked in. He sat down and silently contemplated the boat for a while, until his Mom served up dinner and sat down. Davie was already eating.

"You're quiet, Bobby. Is everything okay?"

"Yeah… I'm just thinking of Dad. You said that you expect a full recovery. How long?"

"God only knows that answer, Dear. Maybe six months? He expects to go back to work after the New Year, even if he's still in the wheelchair."

"You think he'll be back to normal by May?"

"I hope so. Maybe not 100 percent, but close enough."

"I'm just thinking…. what if I built his boat for him? Maybe then he could still do the Race?"

"Really? You think you can do that? That would be wonderful! Did you talk to your Dad about it?"

"No. I hadn't made up my mind. And if I do build it, I want it to be a surprise. I want to see his face when we show him the finished boat."

His Mom laughed. "But can you do it?"

"I think so. I've been reading his books on building canoes and kayaks. The process is the same. I think my workmanship is better than his as well, so if he can build it, so can I."

"Well, that would be wonderful if you can. He's already entered in the race, and he's really bummed that he can't participate this year. His was the very first entry once they opened registration. He was so excited about doing it. For the last two years we've been going to Port Townsend and Victoria to see them off. He's been talking about it ever since."

That clinched it. "Okay. I'll do it. But don't tell Dad. I'm not ready for that yet. I'm not 100 percent sure I can even build it yet."

CONSTRUCTION 5

It took two weeks of studying the plans and reading every page of the books on canoe and kayak construction before Bobby felt confident enough to start building. The process was straightforward, *except* for the hard chine and the keel. Bobby puzzled over those for a while, and eventually resolved the chine issue well enough that he was ready to just give it a try. The keel was still a puzzle with its ballast bulb on the end. How do you make that out of wood and make it strong enough to support the ballast? It was about five feet long with a thin cross-section. Bobby thought about laminating it out of plywood sandwiching a layer of carbon fiber inside, but he doubted even that would even be strong enough. He guessed the lead bulb weighed maybe one hundred pounds. That's a lot of weight on a thin wooden keel. Finally, Bobby decided to leave that part for later. He'd have to get online and search for another solution. He had a boat to build. But, between work and school, he also only had about two hours per day during the week that he could dedicate to the boat. And Saturdays were now spent working over-time since the construction season was in full swing probably through the beginning of December.

Bobby's answer to the hard chine was to simply to start there and work out on both sides. That way he could ensure that he got the right fit at the corner. The transition from a hard chine aft to a soft chine forward would be interesting. The thin cedar strips were edge glued to the adjacent strip and temporarily stapled to the forms. Once the forms are completely covered, the staples are pulled out, the boat sanded smooth and the whole thing covered in fiberglass to hold it all together. Simple? Well not quite, as Bobby would soon to find out. Starting at the chine,

Bobby glued and stapled the strips to the form working towards the gunwale, alternatively working port side then starboard. Within two hours, he was done. Pleased, he stepped back and admired his work. The shape of the boat was clearly visible. With a lot of imagination, he could tell she was going to be gorgeous. Very elegant lines. Enough for one day. Energized, Bobby went inside for supper with his Mom and Davie.

"How's the boat coming?"

"So far so good. I've got about nine inches of strips on the sides and they went on fairly easily. I can see the final shape now. She's going to be a very pretty boat."

"Wonderful! I'll have to come out and see it sometime."

"Anytime. Just don't tell Dad about it."

"Oh, I won't. Davie, how's your latest project going?"

Davie talked on and on about his latest masterpiece. He did spend a lot of time on each piece, completely filling the scene with the minutest little details. They may be a bit flat and bold colored, but there were certainly lots things to find hidden in his art. One could spend an hour staring and still not find all the little details.

Bobby skipped a day from working on the boat and researched various techniques for building the keel. The solution did not present itself, but one conclusion was eminently clear – wood was not the answer. Somehow, he was going to have to figure out how to build it out of carbon fiber. He wasn't looking forward to that. He went back to work on the boat on Friday night, when most guys his age were out drinking and raising hell. Bobby had totally lost track of his fraternity brothers by now. He didn't really have many close friends nearby. He did miss the hell-raising fraternity parties that continued onto the racing circuit years. In fact, the racers could generally drink a fraternity brother under the table. Piper was no exception. So, the boat would have to suffice as his Friday night date. So far, it had been a fun project. That was about to change.

Adding strips now meant working from the chine towards the center line. The problem presented itself immediately. The strip not only had to be bent around the forms, but also had to be twisted ninety degrees toward the stern. The wood resisted. Bobby fought the strip, but only had two hands and the job required four. The first strip snapped due to a minute knot in the wood, so Bobby carefully went through the stack seeking those that were perfectly straight grain and hoping that he had enough to finish the project. Davie was a little resistant to help, but after thirty minutes of talking with him about his art, he finally reached a quitting point and came out to the garage. Between the two of them, they wrestled a strip into place and stapled it down. That took fifteen minutes alone. The strip on the other side only took about ten minutes. Another half an hour and they had another two strips in place. And that was all the time Bobby could give. Two hours and he only got on four more strips. Obviously, this was going to take far longer than he thought.

Two more weeks, and the strips had progressed excruciatingly slowly towards the center line maybe two or three per side in a day, and ultimately met at both bow and stern leaving a football shaped opening. If the stripping had gone slowly before, now it basically came to a standstill. One of the books suggested a solution of just applying the strips fore and aft from this point on. Bobby didn't like the look, so he plowed on ahead. But now each strip had to be fitted exactly at both ends, all while being held in place against the will of the wood. Bobby broke several strips, even though there were no knots.

It was time to start steaming the strips to loosen up the fibers, but he didn't happen to have a steamer. That cost him another two days and a few trips out to the thrift stores and the hardware stores. A camping stove with an old kettle produced the steam, which was routed via tubing to the middle of a long piece of sewer pipe which contained the wood to be steamed. It worked but presented another problem. The wood came out wet. Bobby was using carpenter's water-soluble wood glue. So, the wood had to dry out before he could install it. That meant that he had to clamp it temporarily in place until it dried, then take it off, glue it and staple it in place once dried out. Giving the wood fifteen minutes to steam, then clamp it in place and let it dry for another fifteen minutes, then take it off, glue it and staple it in place took forty-five minutes for the first one, and about half an hour for the second since it was already in the steamer. At least he didn't need Davie for this work. Bobby was only working one side at this point. His intention was to close one half of the football not worrying about the fit at the centerline, then trim the ends all at once along the centerline. The second half would be far more difficult than the first. With all the difficulties of steaming the wood as in the first half, now both ends would also have to be exactly fitted while the plank was being wrestled into place. The first side was complete by mid-November. Bobby spent one workday just admiring the boat's one complete side, not looking forward to working the second side. She was a truly pretty boat, and Bobby knew the true beauty of the cedar wouldn't show up until he applied the fiberglass.

By the first week of December, the stripping was done. The hard chines had come out perfectly. Bobby sighed a huge sigh of relief. Stripping was so much more difficult than he had ever realized. But he had accomplished it without any significant woodworking experience. His goal now was to get her covered with fiberglass by Christmas. But there was a lot of sanding to be done, and thousands of staples to remove. Davie was especially useful pulling the staples. That was the kind of repetitive job he excelled at. He would hum the same song over and over, making Bobby finally put in ear plugs, and work away diligently. Shaping the bow and chines, then sanding the boat was a labor of love, even if did take over a week, two hours at a time. Bobby now had Saturdays off again and was flush with cash. The credit card bill was finally paid off thanks to all the overtime. By this time, he had set all the production records for the new equipment. And he'd set them so high, they would stand for some time. Frank promised to promote him to OP1 as soon as a position opened, probably by the first of the year.

A week before Christmas, Bobby glassed the hull. This was a huge step. He decided to use three layers of fiberglass, two six-ounce layers and one fine three-ounce layer for smoothness. He cut the cloth such that the first layer had the weave aligned with the center line and the second was shifted by forty-five degrees off the center line. It turns out that he used up all the cloth, forcing him to order more for the inside. His Dad had obviously planned on one layer on each side, as the books recommended.

But this boat was to be sailed into danger, and Bobby wanted it to be strong. Being careful to keep the cloth clean, he smoothed the first layer out over the hull. The epoxy resin, catalyst, mixing containers and what-not were all laid out neatly on the portable workbench. He had laid plastic sheeting out on the floor and taped it down so he wouldn't have to take crap from his Dad for making a mess on his nice clean floor. This was a messy job. He donned painter's coveralls complete with booties and a respirator since it was too cold to open the garage door.

Taking a deep breath, which was a challenge with the respirator, Bobby started mixing the resin a few ounces at a time. He had heard that since epoxy generates heat as it is mixed, it could boil over if you mix too much at one time ending with a mass of useless resin. Better to mix many small batches than one big one. Once he started applying the resin, the magic began. He simply poured the resin over the boat and used a squeegee to spread it around towards the sides. The cloth instantly disappeared, leaving glossy cedar behind, much more beautiful than the newly sanded wood. He had to work very quickly, mixing epoxy, and spreading it around. A second person would have been especially useful, but he couldn't trust Davie with the work. After twenty minutes, he had to go back and squeegee off all the excess which dripped all over the floor despite his best efforts to catch it in a waste jug. So, he slowly progressed from the stern towards the bow, applying new resin, then going back to squeegee out the older stuff until he was finally complete with the first layer of cloth.

He couldn't rest here. Now he had to add the second layer of cloth while the epoxy is still wet. Again, a second person would have been particularly useful. Laying the cloth over wet resin was a real challenge. It basically had to be laid out in the correct place the first time since it wouldn't slide over the sticky first layer. Frustrating. Maddingly frustrating. But eventually Bobby succeeded. Just that step alone took well over an hour. Fortunately, Bobby was using a slow setting catalyst in the resin. The second layer absorbed resin out of the first layer, especially with a little help from an epoxy roller. Bobby had to paint on a thin coat of epoxy to get the weave completely saturated and invisible, then again squeegeed off the excess. The final thin coat of cloth was a nightmare to apply. Several times Bobby almost quit in disgust. But with a lot of cursing and tugging and pulling, he finally got the cloth laid down smoothly. The roller alone was all he needed to get it to saturate completely. There was plenty of resin remaining after the second layer despite his efforts to squeegee off the excess.

Stepping back, Bobby admired his work. The weave of the cloth was still visible which hid the true beauty of the cedar. The edges of the cloth hung down below the gunwales dripping resin. It looked like a real mess, but he could see the beauty of the final project. In six hours, he would paint on another thin coat of epoxy to fill the weave. It was important to apply each layer of epoxy before the previous layer had cured for the layers to combine and bond chemically. He would be back out at midnight to apply the last coat. Bobby had skipped lunch and only eaten a light breakfast before he started work, so he was famished. But he still had to clean up before he could go seek supper. There was no way to shortcut this process, other than maybe to use only one layer of cloth. It's just a long, exhausting process.

The fiberglass had to cure completely before the boat could be taken off the forms, which was the next big step. So, Bobby spent a week researching methods to build the keel. Eventually, he settled on building one out of wood, including the bulb, and using that as a male mold. He'd make a mold of each side, then build a carbon fiber keel in two halves. He'd cast the lead directly into the bottom of the bulb, making sure that the carbon fiber surrounded and supported the lead. Bobby wasn't looking forward to it, but that's the only solution he could find other than ordering one custom made for him. He was sorely tempted and kept that option in his back pocket. Plan B. With that settled, Bobby went back to work on the boat. He trimmed off the excess cloth along the gunwales, marked out the final sheer line, and trimmed the excess cedar strips to that line. What a difference that made! It finally looked like a finished boat. Then he laminated up a series of cedar strips to form the rub rail and glued them in place making sure he followed the sheer line exactly. In a day, it was time to take the boat off the forms. He needed both his Mom and Davie for this step. They hadn't been out to see the boat yet. This was going to be a big day. She agreed to help the following day, three days before Christmas.

Bobby had made up some slings to set the boat down in once she was off the forms. He shoved the beam, boat and all, over to one side of the shop and set up the slings in the middle ready for the boat. He unscrewed all but two of the forms from the braces and, by wiggling them, got most of them to fall out. His Mom came in and stopped, her mouth agape.

"My God, Bobby! She's gorgeous! You did such a good job!"

"Thanks, Mom. I'm pleased with her so far. But she's got a long way to go."

"Your Dad will be so happy when he sees her."

"I sure hope so. Please let's keep it a secret until she's done. Or maybe until he walks out here on his own account after he comes home. Any news on that?"

"The doctors won't release him for a while yet. His arm is still so weak that he can't use a walker and can't get in and out of the wheelchair alone. It'll probably be February before he comes home."

"Do you think he'll be ready by May? So, he can do the race, I mean?"

"I hope so. He's working out diligently all the time. He's getting better. The therapists think he'll eventually get to one hundred percent again given enough time. We'll just have to wait and see."

"I wonder if seeing the boat would inspire him to get better faster?"

"No! He already works out harder than the therapists want. When they aren't there, he's working the bands continuously. I don't want him working any harder. He might have a set-back."

Davie finally came in and stared at the boat for a long time. He hadn't seen her since he pulled out all the staples.

"Come on, Davie. You and Mom take the stern. I've got the bow. Let me unscrew this one last brace and we'll be ready. We're just going to lift her up and roll her over and set her in these slings here. Just another few seconds..."

Even with the extra layers of fiberglass, the boat was much lighter than Bobby expected. It lifted off the beam easily, two forms dropping out as it rose. Davie was in the way and not much help. But just with Bobby and his Mom, they rolled her easily and set her down in the slings. The inside was a mess of glue drips despite all the efforts Bobby had made to reach inside and wipe them off as he added each new strip. It would take some work to get it smoothed out. The inside would never be visible due to the deck and side chambers. But Bobby wanted it to be perfect, and any drips left behind would interfere with the fiberglass cloth laying down flat. He wiggled the last remaining form out, the one in the bow that he couldn't get to while it was on the beam. A scraper made short work of the glue drips. Sanding and glassing would have to wait until after Christmas.

The family, except for Dad, went to services on Christmas Eve, and to Christmas Mass in the morning. It wasn't until after noon that Dad was ready to be picked up. It proved difficult to get Dad into Mom's *Escalade,* but Jessie and Bobby finally succeeded. Mom had gone all out as usual for Christmas. She and Davie had bought and decorated a tree in the living room a week ago and had been listening to and singing carols for a week before that. The family had stopped giving gifts once Bobby and Jessie had grown up and moved out. But it was still a very solemn religious celebration, and a celebration of family. Mom always cooked way too much food, and often had friends over for supper. Today, it was just the LaRoche family, plus Jessie's husband Ralph. Jessie was already showing off her significant baby-bump, and that was the topic of conversation for much of the afternoon. Bobby's Mom and Dad relived all the horrors of childbirth and pregnancy supposedly just to reassure Jessie and Ralph. Then they brought out all the old family albums and relived the baby years for an hour or more. Bobby was relieved that the conversation was going any direction but towards the boat. And Davie was itching to show his Dad his recent art pieces. There were a couple of college football games on, and Bobby, Ralph and Gerald really wanted to watch. Finally, the ladies went off to the kitchen to get supper going leaving the men to cheer and groan over the game. They only made it to half time before they were called to the dining room. Once seated,

Gerald said a very poignant grace and they dug into a perfect turkey with every side imaginable. Conversation lagged for a while as they ate. After supper, Davie dominated his Dad for a while, and Bobby snuck Jessie and Ralph out to the shop. They were amazed when they saw the boat.

"She's beautiful, Bobby. I didn't know you were going to build a boat."

"It's a secret. It's Dad's boat for the Race to Alaska. He designed it over the past year and is already registered to race this year. But with his recovery, he can't work on her, so he's given up on that dream. I haven't told him that I'm building it for him. I'll spring that on him when it's done. I want him to race this June."

She looked dubious. "I'm not sure he'll be physically able to do the race this year. He's recovering very slowly. And that's an awfully small boat."

"Maybe not. But it won't be for the lack of a boat that he doesn't go. And there's always next year. The boat is large enough to hold all the supplies he needs for one person and to sleep on the deck. It's a remarkably simple, but high tech and manageable rig. It should sail fast but be easy to sail solo. It's a dry design, and unsinkable and self-draining. I think he can do it in this boat."

Ralph spoke up. "You've done an outstanding job on her. The stripping is just about perfect. Can I see the plans?"

"Thanks. Sure! They're on the workbench over there. I'm hoping to have her done by the end of February."

"So, she's going to be completely decked over I see. Lots of watertight compartments for gear. I'm not sure about this rowing gear though. You said he's going to sleep on the deck? The tracks are in the way. Mighty uncomfortable."

"Got a better idea?"

"Yeah... I do. I've got a Hobie kayak with the Mirage pedal drive unit. That's the way to go. The drive unit pulls out and is a lot smaller than oars and riggers. And far more efficient. And you're facing forward as you pedal. You can try my kayak if you want. It's surprisingly fast. You just need to make a hole for the drive unit and a plug to seal it when you're sailing. That should be easy enough. You can borrow my kayak for a while if you want and copy the design. You'll have to get your own drive unit, though."

"Hmm... Then Dad maybe could pedal and sail at the same time in the light stuff. Good thought, Ralph!"

"Exactly! You'll have to come up with some design for a seat. But I'm thinking that you could use that seat when you're sailing as well. It's a long way to Alaska. Mount the seat on either side and kick back and sail comfortably."

"Another great idea! My back hurts when I get off the Laser after just a few hours. I usually go soak in the hot tub after I sail. This boat will have a trapeze[9], and I hear those are comfortable enough. But when it's not windy, I can see where a seat that offers good back support would be really useful."

"Okay. I've made my contribution. I'll bring the kayak over sometime next week. Keep it as long as you need it. I won't need it until spring."

"Thanks, Ralph. And, please don't mention this to Dad yet. If I can pull this off and surprise Dad with a finished boat, I'll invite you guys over for the celebration. Mom says he may be able to come home in February. I'm racing to have the boat done in time."

Jessie came back over from examining the boat. "Let's get back inside before he misses us. Nice job on the boat, and it's awful sweet of you to do that for him. I know he'll appreciate it."

"Thanks, Jessie."

They came back to the house separately, and the conversation eventually turned to their Dad's recovery and his future plans. Despite the doctor's orders, he was determined to go back to work at least for a few hours per day starting in January. And he was ready to come home now. Knowing that his Dad couldn't make it up the stairs, Bobby volunteered to move all their bedroom furniture from the upstairs master bedroom

---

[9] Trapeze – A line running to the top of the mast that the crew connects to a harness so that he can stand on the edge of the boat out over the water. It's used to get the crew weight as far outboard as possible on windy days.

to the downstairs suite, which was a bit larger. They all agreed that was a good idea, and Jessie and Ralph volunteered to help next weekend. The house was designed with their old age in mind, which is why they built the downstairs master suite. The pool table would come out to the den, and Jessie would take the shuffleboard table. The rest of the various seats and the sofa would just be absorbed elsewhere in the house. With the plans finalized, it was time to get their Dad back to the recovery center. Jessie and Ralph took him in Annette's *Escalade* again, leaving Bobby and Davie to do the cleanup. Bobby was able to get all the food packaged up, the dishes washed, and the counters wiped by the time Davie got the dishwasher loaded just perfectly.

DISTRACTION

6

Bobby had to wait on applying fiberglass to the inside of the boat for a couple of weeks into January since he needed a full weekend. The first weekend was spent with Jessie, Ralph, Davie, and his Mom moving everything out of the upstairs master suite and down to the first-floor suite. He was tempted to ask if he could move into the upstairs suite but decided that he just needed to focus on the boat and school right now. If he did, he would have to buy all new bedroom furniture and he was enjoying not having any debt. It could wait. He spent the two weeks working on the keel, building a non-functional but exact size keel out of plywood with a wood bulb on the end. His Dad had drawn a specific foil shape, so he had to build a template to use as he shaped the wood. It took a lot of time, but by the end of two weeks he had what looked like a finished keel in varnished plywood and maple. And it really looked sweet made from wood. Pity it wasn't strong enough to use. It was too flexible, so he would have to make sure that was perfectly flat when he covered it with fiberglass to make the female molds.

Fiberglassing the inside of the hull took much less time than he ever imagined. He started by filleting the hard chine for strength and to allow the cloth to wrap around the inner corner. He realized that he didn't have gravity to help scrape the excess resin off the hull, so he decided to add a second layer to the very bottom of the boat just to soak up all the excess resin. Within eight hours, it was complete. No need for a second coat of resin to fill the weave. No one would see it, and, besides, if it *were* exposed it would make good non-skid. The shell of the boat was complete. He could put it in the water and paddle it around if he were so inclined.

That evening, as Bobby showered, he discovered a great glob of epoxy in his hair from leaning over the side of the boat to epoxy the bottom. Epoxy might not stick to plastic well, but it sticks quite well to hair. And the epoxy was completely dry. No amount of combing would pull all the epoxy out. He redressed and went out to the garage and tried some acetone. Some of the epoxy dissolved, but the bulk remained doggedly attached. Bobby ended up cutting off a good four inches of his long ponytail, bringing it up to his shoulders.

The deck was the next step. It was about six inches below the gunwale and about a foot above the bottom of the hull at the deepest section of the boat. Bobby had to rent a rotating laser level to mark the deck line from bow to stern. Under the deck was a series of waterproof compartments, and braces to support the mast and the keel. And now Bobby had to add a compartment for the Hobie pedal drive. He had redesigned the rig a bit with the help of Traci, a naval architect that he knew. It just so happened that his Dad had used the same architect to help design the boat. She was already familiar with the design. Bobby shifted the keel ten inches further aft to make room for the pedal drive unit in front of it. To compensate for moving the center of lateral resistance aft, he had to rake the mast a bit more. That was the extent of it. He wanted the pedal drive forward of the keel so the skipper's weight would be centered when he pedaled. He used some cheap one eighth inch plywood as templates, which turned out to be a good idea since he made so many mistakes that he had to buy additional plywood. But little by little it came together, and towards by the end of January, it was complete. All seams had a good fillet of epoxy with a strip of fiberglass on top to completely seal each compartment. All the plywood below deck was protected with a layer of epoxy resin, and the exposed deck had a layer of cloth as well for abrasion resistance and non-skid. Each compartment had a watertight hatch with quarter turn recessed latches. The batteries and anchor chain were to be mounted next to the keel, where their weight would help as ballast. Bladders of drinking water were to be stored on either side of the Mirage pedal drive for the same reason. The lighter food and camping gear could be stored under the deck aft. All that remained now was the side and bow decks. Bobby had ordered some more cedar strips for the deck and side decks. The plans didn't specify the materials to use and Bobby decided to just keep the same theme going by using the cedar strips. The hull was built of light yellow Western Red Cedar, so he ordered darker brown strips of the same material for the deck. The side decks were about ten inches wide and extended all the way up to and merged with the bow deck. The watertight compartments in the coamings would be used for the things that needed to be readily available as his Dad sailed north. The bow deck extended aft five feet from the bow, and the edge was reinforced to take the load of the sail control cleats.

By mid-February, construction of the hull was complete. Ralph had found an ergonomic, exceptionally light seat made of aluminum tubing and nylon mesh that came off a recumbent bicycle. Bobby took it to a welding shop and had a bracket welded on that consisted simply of two posts that fit into two holes in the deck. While that was being completed, Bobby started the varnishing process for the boat. The entire hull inside and out needed to be thoroughly sanded to remove all the surface imperfections. A tedious task, but one that would result in the glass-like finish Bobby was after. It was a long, exacting process with at least four coats of good quality two-part varnish. Two days of drying time and then each coat had to be sanded lightly before the next was applied. At this rate, it would take until mid-March to complete.

His Dad was also released in mid-February but had not yet come out to the shop. He was using a walker relatively well now and was cleared to drive. So, every morning he would walk out to the garage to go to work, and never once realized that there was a finished boat on the other side of the wall. He was way behind at work, and that was his primary focus. He had a brand-new Cadillac dealership facility being built, and the old one was slated for reconstruction and then repurposed into a used car dealership. He had long wanted a Ford dealership, but Ford wasn't willing to grant a franchise to a competitor. Bobby had some thoughts on that in the back of his mind. But time was ticking down before eventually his Dad would go into the shop for some reason. He had to get the boat finished secretly. But then the unthinkable happened and progress came to almost a complete stop. Bobby fell in love.

Hali left Lynnwood promptly at two so she could be down in Lacey before the infamous Seattle Friday evening rush hour traffic set in. But she had barely gotten on the interstate when traffic came to a complete standstill. After an hour of fuming, she was still in Seattle and the rush hour traffic she had been trying to avoid was upon her. Her indoor volleyball team, the Strikers, were meeting at a restaurant in Lacey at six and it was looking more and more like she would need a miracle to get there. Without traffic, she had done this drive in little more than an hour. With typical Friday evening rush-hour traffic, maybe three hours for the same drive. But this wasn't typical. Something was stopping the traffic up ahead. She had originally decided to forego the team dinner and just go down early on Saturday and Sunday mornings and skip the hotel room. She was always just one step ahead of the collection agency and she could scarcely afford the luxury of a hotel. But her teammates had pressured her to stay with them in Lacey. It would be one big party all weekend. At least, they'd be paying for the beer. She'd have to share a room with three other girls, but she was finally on the way and looking forward to it. And now the interstate was backed up. Completely choked. She shut her engine off to keep the old Honda from overheating and just waited and fumed.

By four, she was sitting in her parked car staring at Boeing Field and starting to get hungry. Another hour and she was ravenous and was approaching the I-405 interchange. The interstate south was stopped dead. At least I-405 was moving, though it would take her the opposite direction. She obviously wasn't going to make the team dinner, so she followed her stomach. There was a restaurant just off the interchange called the *Bahama Breeze* and it was calling her name. She worked her way across two lanes of traffic to take the I-405 exit, then got off at the first exit and weaved her way along the frontage roads to the restaurant. Even though it was early, lots of other motorists had the same idea. The restaurant was packed. The hostess took her name and told her to expect a thirty to forty-minute wait. And so, she waited, her hunger growing more acute by the minute.

Some thirty minutes later, her attention was captured by a cute guy talking to the host. His clothes and build were blue-collar labor force. His leather work boots were scuffed and worn. He wore heavy duty Carhartt denim work jeans and jacket, both black with a white tee shirt. He wore them well. He certainly wasn't GQ or even handsome in the Clark Gable sort of sense. In fact, it was his imperfections that made him so attractive to her. His crooked smile and unruly long brown hair tied back in a ponytail mainly, but those eyes! My, my! Baby blue eyes that could melt a woman's heart! Hali's heart beat faster just looking at him even though her brother's voice was screaming at her in the dark recesses of her mind. He had warned her numerous times to never get involved with white guys. And her previous experience had proven him correct. Hali was African American, though she had exceptionally light brown skin, straight black hair pulled back into a ponytail and facial features that many white guys found attractive if not a little exotic. The guy left the host and headed slowly towards her on his way presumably to the bar. Impulsively, she called out "You're welcome to join me. I should be called any time now." He stopped and glanced at her and his face lit up immediately. God! Those eyes! And now the smile! How could she ever think that he wasn't handsome?

"I'd be happy to join you. I'm Bobby. And you are?"

"I'm Halima. My friends call my Hali."

"That's a pretty name. My friends call me the Roach."

She laughed. "Really? The Roach? Why?"

"Ohhh... My last name is LaRoche. I hung out with some rowdy friends for a while, and we all had stupid nicknames. Hardly anyone went by their real names."

"Mind if I just use Bobby?"

"Not at all. I'm actually on track to the business world. I'll probably have to become Mr. Robert LaRoche one day. But Bobby is good for friends."

About that time, Hali was called for a table so off they went following the Hostess to the heated porch area and were seated at a nice table big enough for four. Hali just ordered water, but she noticed that he ordered a large flavored margarita.

"So, what brings you here all alone?" He asked.

"I'm heading to Lacey and got stuck in traffic. I was supposed to meet a bunch of friends for dinner in Lacey right about now. I needed a break and I was getting hungry. This place was convenient, so here I am."

"No shit? I'm also heading to Lacey, and I was in the same frickin' traffic. I got off work at two-thirty, and I haven't had anything to eat since ten and that was just a sandwich. What are you doing in Lacey? Is that your home?"

"Oh no! I live in Lynnwood. I'm going down to Lacey just for the weekend for a volleyball tournament at Saint Martin's University."

He laughed out loud. "No shit! I'm going down for the same tournament!"

"Really? Do you play?"

"Not really. Just pick-up games. I have some friends who are in a volleyball club and I'm going to cheer them on. I suppose I could get dragged onto the court if they needed someone, but they'd be at the bottom of the barrel. I can serve decently and maybe pass, but that's about the limit of my abilities."

"Are your friends serious about it?"

"Naw... They're far more serious about drinking. Volleyball is just a thing they do between drinks. They're serious enough about it when they're on the court, but they're not really that good. They may win a couple of rounds if they're on their game, but they won't make it to the playoffs. It's just a good chance to get away from home and drink heavily."

"Ohhh... I guess I'm in a different league. It's been my focus since my sophomore year in high school. I played for the Huskies on a scholarship for four years. I'm trying to get on the national team and go to the Olympics in Tokyo in 2020."

"Wow! Good for you! I'll follow your progress. I used to ride motocross professionally until I got hurt, and I'm still tracking my friends. I should go out and watch them race when they're in town, but I know it'll just inspire me to want to race again. I think I'm at that point in my life when I just need to grow up and start a career. Hard for me to admit that, though. Makes me feel old."

She laughed. "I know what you mean. I'm studying to become a lawyer. But I have this one chance, and I want to see how far I can take this before I have to grow up."

"Growing up sucks. But, good for you. Follow your dreams while they're still realistic. What's your plan for getting there?"

"Getting noticed right now. Karch Kiraly will be in Lacey this weekend. He's in charge of the USA Women's Volleyball Association. I want to meet him and let him know I want to be selected for the team. Hopefully, he'll come watch me play."

"Indoors or beach ball?"

"I play both. Beach volleyball is mostly in the summer and most often down in California. I drive down there seven or eight times a year for competitions. My partner, Courtney and I are the team to beat. We have a streak of five straight victories going. My club in Lynnwood plays indoor volleyball. We do a lot of traveling to meets around the west coast. It's breaking my budget. We've done this meet several times. It's a fun tournament for us. The Saint Martin's team is hosting, and they may put a team or two on the court. UDub could be there. One or two other serious clubs may show up and give us a fight, so winning is never taken for granted. But we've won it for the last two years. My club is fairly good, but there is only one other girl as good as I am. She and I were at UDub together. She got team MVP in 2013 and 2014. I got it in 2015 and 2016, just because she graduated before me."

"Well, I'll certainly come over and watch you play and cheer you on. What's the team?"

"I train at Puget Sound Regional Volleyball. It's close to home. But my team is at Washington Elite Volleyball. The team name is the Strikers. Courtney and I play beach volleyball for the Beachballers Volleyball Club."

"Are you sponsored yet?"

"Barely. I get a tiny bit of money that helps me get to the tournaments in California. I get more by modeling volleyball outfits and gear.

And we get some money from our winnings, but not enough. I need to travel internationally, but I can't afford it."

Bobby laughed. "That's my story! I got a bit more sponsorship money than you and that kept me going since I wasn't getting much in winnings. But I was still living in my toy-hauler and staying for free on BLM land. I made more money modeling motorcycle gear than I ever did racing."

"Really? So, you understand where I'm at."

"Exactly. I was consumed with racing just as you are for volleyball. I gave it a shot. Did three years on the circuit. You need to give it a shot. You'll never forgive yourself if you don't at least give it a try. What do you think of your chances?"

"I'm hopeful, especially in beach ball. I have the qualifications and the wins. We've been seeded in the top twenty for the last two years. We're seeded number six right now. We're the defending national champions. We have a better record than the current Team USA beach volleyball teams. We've beaten them both several times lately. *And...* we've beaten the Japanese and the Chinese national teams. Of course, they've beaten us as well, but not in the last year. Indoor volleyball is a little more difficult to get noticed since you're just one of six. I like to play the net, but someone my height would typically play back as a setter. I can do that well enough, but I like to block and attack. It's my thing. I feel like I'm starting to reach my peak and it's just at the right time. If I don't get selected this time, then I think I'm done. I don't think I could maintain this kind of intensity for that much longer."

"The defending national champions, huh? Good for you! Don't you think Karch already knows who you are?"

"Very probably. But I want to look him in the eye and get him to acknowledge me. It's different being black. You wouldn't understand."

"Really? I'd think at the elite level performance is really all that counts."

"In my world it is. But I'm still the underdog when I play in California despite having a winning streak of five against the best in the country. And people always cheer for my opponent. I've just kind of grown to expect it. But I like being the underdog. It inspires me to play harder. My partner, Courtney is white, and she gets more than twice the sponsorship money than I do. She knows it's unfair and often covers our travel expenses."

"I'm sorry to hear that. But I'll be cheering for you. And I'll bring over a bunch of my rowdy friends to give you a personal cheering squad. How's that?"

Hali laughed. "I like you, Bobby. Are you single?"

He grimaced. "Yeah... I had a girlfriend while I was racing, but we split up when I got hurt and came home to recover. She's still racing. Haven't seen her in nine months. You?"

"Yeah. Occasional dates, but nothing serious. I have too much focus on my volleyball for a relationship right now."

"I live in Edmonds right now. I hate to admit it, but I'm actually living with my parents. How embarrassing is that?"

"I wish I had that option. My apartment in Lynnwood is costing me twelve hundred a month, and I still need to pay for utilities and internet. I work as a paralegal, and it's using up all my money."

He sat up straight. "Well then, today I treat! I make decent money working for my Uncle Frank, and I have absolutely no expenses other than gas. I paid off my last debts back before New Year and I'm flush with cash. Let's order grub."

"Oh, you don't have to do that! I have money."

"Keep it. You need it far more than I do. I insist."

"Well, thanks, Bobby."

They ordered food and chatted for the next couple of hours as rush hour came and went. As they departed, Hali could not get those deep blue eyes out of her mind. It was after eight when she merged on the interstate again. Traffic was still stop and go, but at least go was an option now. As Hali headed south at no more than twenty miles an hour on the interstate, she called her Mom.

"Hey Mommy! Guess what?"

"What? Don't make me start guessing, Baby."

"I stopped at a restaurant in Tukwila because traffic was completely backed up and I met a guy! A really sweet guy! We had dinner together. He's going to the same tournament that I am!"

Hali could hear her Mom laughing. "Baby, I thought you were going to stay away from guys for a while!"

"Ohhh... Mommy, it was his eyes! He's got these incredible big blue eyes that are just so deep. It's like he can look right into your soul. I couldn't resist him."

"Un huh. And a white guy at that. You've been burned before, Baby. Be careful."

"Well, chances are I won't ever see him again, though he is going to the same tournament and he did say that he would come over and cheer for me. We talked for a long time, and... I don't know, he's different from all the other guys that I've been with. I was only with him for a couple of hours and I don't know him that well, but I trust him. He wasn't trying to come on to me or anything. We just had a really nice dinner together."

"Baby, like I said, just be careful, especially around white guys. Kellan won't be happy if you start dating a white guy."

"I'm not planning on dating him and I really don't give a damn what Kellan thinks. But I'll be careful and protect my heart. I was just so happy to have someone to share my table with. I was feeling blue until he came along. Made my day! And he did pick up the tab for both of us. Wouldn't even consider letting me pay."

"Well, Baby, he sounds like a real gentleman and I'm happy that you had a nice meal with him. Hopefully, he won't break your heart in the future. Now, you drive safely and focus on your tournament. I love you, Baby Girl!"

"I love you, too, Mommy!"

Traffic started moving again and she finally made it up to forty-five miles an hour all the way through Federal Way, WA, and by the time she got to Tacoma she was doing the speed limit. As she drove through Hawks Prairie, her car began to shudder a little bit and seemed to have less power. The hotel was on Pacific Avenue and she got off at the College Way exit. Her car was not right. It was struggling to accelerate and had a new shake. Great! She didn't have any cash reserves to fix it or buy a new one. If the car died, she had no idea how she'd continue her quest. The tired old Honda made it the last mile or so into the hotel parking lot by ten. It was too late to call anyone other than her Mom and she wasn't quite ready to do that. She'd have it towed tomorrow before the tournament and get a quote to repair it. Then she'd have to decide whether to tell her Mom. Her parents didn't have a lot of money, but they would help her if she asked. She just hated to ask.

Bobby arrived at his buddy John's house close to ten. The party was well underway, music blaring. There were twelve drunk guys and no chicks. Bobby hadn't done a guy's night out since he left the circuit, and he had time to make up. First stop was one of the two kegs. Supper here consisted of pretzels, chips, and peanuts. Out of consideration for his job, he did skip the weed, but there was so much smoke in the air that he was high by midnight. The house was already trashed, just like the good old days in college. He knew most of the guys and they all wanted to hear about his racing. As a professional racer, he was kind of a hero to them all. He told them about Hali and her quest for the Olympics, and that he wanted to form a cheering squad for her. They were all over that. Eventually, in the wee hours of morning, the party waned. People started crashing wherever. Bobby found a recliner and passed out.

The venue was at St. Martin's University. The girls were playing in the gym and the guys in the Marcus Pavilion across campus. As expected, despite their hangovers, the Sharks clobbered their first opponent, which was just a pick-up team from a local bank. It wasn't even close. But it did serve to sober them up. They had to play five on six several times as players dashed off to the men's rooms in the middle of the game. It didn't matter. They won handily even short-handed. They won their second match just as handily as they began to sober up and get serious. Their second opponent was a decent volleyball club from Olympia, four men and two women. But they couldn't withstand the assault of aces and slams fired by the Sharks. Surprisingly, they won their last match as well, but Bobby had already gone over to find Hali's team. They were smoking! They were playing another Seattle volleyball club, but the Strikers were dominating. Hali wasn't that tall at maybe 5'6", but she could jump like a kangaroo. When she played the net, she was spiking balls left and right and batting the opponents spikes right back at them. Bobby hooted and hollered for her, and she gave him a smile. He was the only one rooting for her. She looked hot in her skin-tight uniform, and that fact didn't go unnoticed by Bobby. There was no sign of the Team USA blokes, though.

That night, the party continued. Bobby didn't even think to invite Hali over. This was a guy thing. Chicks would have spoiled it. Hali was probably doing the same thing with the girls in a hotel room somewhere. They relived every spike, every serve, every missed opportunity all evening. This was one of the few times they had ever made it to the second day. They were one of eight teams left in the men's bracket. Bobby dared to take a shower in the filthy shower stall, hoping that his tetanus shot was up to date. But he was drunk by ten and passed out by one. The tournament started at ten on Sunday, and he slept until seven. The guys, many still severely hung-over visited Denny's for breakfast. Food and a lot of coffee helped most of them, but a couple visited the men's room and puked. Just another typical guy's night out. The Sharks met their fate on their very first match. Their opponent was another Seattle volleyball club that was well-rested and well-trained. It was a blood bath. The Sharks lost both games badly. Bobby normally would have driven home at this point, but Hali was still playing. So, off he went across campus to find her team trailed by his buddies. They found her amid a fierce battle with a team that had come up from Oregon, mostly Ducks alumni. The guys behaved themselves for a few minutes at least, but once the Strikers started a run of three straight points to take the lead, the guys lost their restraint. With every point earned, with every block, with every spike, they cheered, yelled, screamed, chanted. And the Strikers responded with more as they finally pulled ahead. They ended the match with the guys chanting "Hali! Hali! Hali!" Hali was thrilled and gave Bobby a big hug. They still had the finals to go, and the guys weren't going anywhere. As they walked over to the last court, Hali pulled Bobby aside.

"Bobby, can you give me a ride home tonight?"

"I'd love to. What's up with your car?"

"It started acting up on the way down here. It started shuddering and then just lost power as I drove into Lacey. I made it to the hotel, but it wouldn't start yesterday morning. I had to get it towed. The service guy said it had a blown head gasket. I'm not sure if it's worth fixing, but I can't afford another car. So, I told him that I'd think about the repairs. He could junk it if that's what I decide."

"What kind of car do you have?"

"It's an old Honda Accord, 1990. It was my Dad's car and he passed it on to me. It has well over two hundred thousand miles on it."

"Yeah, but it's a Honda. Replace the head gasket and it'll go for another two hundred thousand. How much did he want to change the gasket?"

"Nine hundred just for the gasket change. If there was anything else, it would be more."

"There's always more... like a new timing belt, serpentine belt, hoses, etc., etc. Okay... Tell you what... just tell him to pull it outside. I'll bring a trailer down next week and haul it up to Frank's place. I can change the gasket myself. I'll only charge you for the gasket. Maybe fifty bucks."

"You can do that? Are you sure?"

"Easy. And Frank or his buddy can steer me clear of any issues. When you see my ride, you'll understand my capabilities. Engines are easy. I've never worked on a Honda before, but I'll go get the Haynes manual and we'll knock it out. You can help."

"Thank you, Bobby! That would be so great!"

"Oh, and one other thing.... You need to go out to eat with me tonight on our way home. My treat again. We'll stop in Tacoma unless you have a favorite place here."

"You drive a hard bargain, Bobby. But you're on."

"You could have gotten a ride with your team-mates, right?"

"Yeah, but I liked talking to you. So, I'd rather go with you and get to know you a little more."

"I like the sound of that, Hali" Bobby said giving her that crooked smile. "I'm looking forward to getting to know you too."

He hugged her and she went off to find her team. This was the finals, and this court had bleachers set up around it. Their opponent was a serious looking team that had come all the way up from California. Two of their players had been in the Olympics before, but as a group they were older and past their prime. Late forties mostly with a couple that were over fifty. The Strikers were a young group, all under thirty except one and all in their prime fitness. Youth and fitness versus experience. Best two of three games.

The first game was fierce, but Bobby and the guys made it fun with their hooting and hollering, especially when Hali spiked the ball. She was always under-estimated due to her height, but she made them pay for the slight. It didn't take long before the other team figured out not to test her. On the other side of the court were the Team USA guys watching intently. And Bobby noticed them talking every time Hali spiked the ball or blocked a slam. The two teams tied at twenty apiece, and the game went on. Each team trading points until finally the Californians scored two in a row and won the first game 27 to 25.

They had done their damage in the first game and were quickly running out of steam. The Strikers scored early and went on a five-point run before losing serve. But they won the serve right back and scored four more. The guys were getting completely obnoxious in the stands, louder with every point. And when Hali scored, everyone in the gym knew it. And she was killing it! At one point, the Strikers were up twelve to four and Hali had scored six of the points alone and assisted on three more. The second game ended at 21 to 10. The Californians were done. But they rested a bit and showed up gamely for the final game. It was a slaughter. The final score was 15 to 6. The Strikers had won it all. After the two teams had shaken hands, the guys, less Bobby, ran out and grabbed Hali, hoisting her to their shoulders and marched around the court pumping their fists and chanting "Hali! Hali! Hali!" The rest of the crowd cheered as well, while the Team USA guys looked on amused. The guys finally marched her over to Bobby and dumped her into his arms. He hugged her and congratulated her. If the Team USA guys were looking for anything special, Hali certainly had delivered. They were nowhere to be seen.

Bobby held her hand as she retrieved her duffle bag from a teammate's car. She was amazed when she saw his hot rod truck.

"You really built this?"

"With a lot of help from my uncle. He gave it to me as my sixteenth birthday present, then helped me restore it and rebuild the mechanicals. It makes about 500 horsepower. It'll pass anything on the road except a gas station. I painted it myself. I even did the upholstery myself. He paid for everything."

"That's amazing, and it's a really cool truck. So, you really think you can fix the Honda?"

"I think so. Should be relatively easy. I need to get it apart and just see exactly what happened. Hopefully, it's just a gasket. Every engine is different, so it'll be a learning experience. What are you going to do for a car while we're working on it?"

"Well, I can take the bus to work. I often do that since parking is a hassle. I can also take a bus to the volleyball club for practice, so I can live without it for a little while. I have a beachball tournament in two weeks in California. It would be nice to have it back by then."

"We'll see what we can do. If not, you can always rent a car or go with Courtney. Or I could always give you a ride..."

"Mmmm... I think I like that option best."

Bobby smiled. "Do you want to change before we go out to eat?"

"Yeah. I'm all sweaty. I'd like a shower also, but I can live without one. Do you have a place? We checked out of the hotel this morning."

"I think so. We'll see if anyone's home over at my buddy John's house. Just lower your expectations all the way down to the floor. We just had a guy's night of heavy drinking. You might not want to breathe too deeply either. Lots of weed. The house was trashed when we left, and the shower is filthy. You can change there, but don't bother with a shower. You still smell nice. I'd like to get on the road soon, and we still have to eat."

"Do you do that often?"

"What's that?"

"Drinking binges. Pot, that kind of stuff."

"No... not much anymore. I used to all the time back at UDub when I lived in the frat house. Even tried coke a few times. It was, like, every week back then. It was fun at first. Getting shit-faced and trying to get the sisters naked, that was what life was all about back then. After a couple of years of that, it started to get old. Kind of juvenile, actually. That was one of the reasons I left school. Not only just to go racing and follow that dream, but because I had no direction in my studies other than just getting drunk all the time. Since then, I've been out drinking from time to time with my rowdy racing buddies, or with my volleyball buddies, but now it's rare. This is the first time out in a year. And I never use pot or coke any more. My employer does urinalyses. I hate to admit it, but I think I'm slowly growing up. I have focus in school now, and I'm trying to get my GPA back up and staying away from the frat house."

"Did you ever succeed in getting the sisters naked?"

Bobby laughed. "Oh, no, not me. But I witnessed a lot of crazy shit at our parties. I'm sworn to secrecy. Can I tell you a personal secret? For all my bravado back then, I was still a virgin all through college."

Hali laughed. "No way!!! God... I lost my virginity on my sixteenth birthday."

"Really? You're a beautiful girl, Hali. I'll bet you had lots of guys chasing after you."

"Yeah... I did. My brother Kellan did a good job chasing them off. And if they made the mistake of calling my house, my parents would give them the third degree. But I still had lots of boyfriends."

"I don't doubt you. Hungry?"

"Yeah... Oh, my friends suggested the Spar Restaurant downtown."

"You're on. Let's get you presentable and we're off."

They spent the next four hours getting to know each other, their family life, their scholastic experiences, their futures, their likes, and dislikes, and they were holding hands the whole time. Bobby told her about the boat and that he was building it for his Dad so he could race it in the Race to Alaska. He had to explain that it was a 750 mile non-motored race from Port Townsend to Ketchikan, Alaska through some incredibly treacherous waters. Ten grand to the winner, a set of steak knives for the runner-up and no rules. You took your life in your own hands if you went ashore with all the grizzlies. And there were orcas in the water keeping an eye on you. She shivered noticeably when he mentioned the bears and the orcas. And he had to explain that his Dad had a stroke and was unable to build it for himself, so he was building it for him as a surprise. That kind of melted Hali's heart. When Bobby kissed her goodnight on her doorstep, they were a couple. Bobby didn't get much sleep that night. And the boat wasn't on his mind.

BOBBY AND HALI 7

The boat didn't languish forgotten. Though Bobby would have much preferred to go visit with Hali every day, she was either working or training all day until late. He wasn't even able to meet her for lunch since he only got half an hour off for lunch at the factory. So, Bobby focused his energy on the project. He went out after work every day and lightly sanded the boat, before wiping it down thoroughly and varnishing it again. He still needed to build the rudder and tiller, but he didn't want to create any dust. He did get the keel molds done, but he couldn't trim the excess cloth or do any sanding while the varnish was wet.

On Saturday, he borrowed Frank's race car trailer after carefully backing his quarter of a million-dollar race truck off it. Picking up Hali, they set off to Olympia to fetch her car. The trip down was unusually fast, never getting below the speed limit, and they arrived around noon. It didn't take long to get the trailer loaded, so they stopped at the Fifth Street Sandwich Shop before heading north. This was one of his Dad's favorite restaurants in Olympia, and he wasn't disappointed. They split a Hot-Oly Prime sandwich and got side salads each. The trip back was slow. There was an accident just past Nisqually River, a backup at Joint Base Lewis-McChord, and the perpetual road construction in Tacoma. They reached Frank's shop at about five to unload the car. Bobby didn't dare try to reload the race truck. Hali had already been to the dealership and had purchased a new head gasket, which they conveniently had in stock, and a repair manual for her year Honda. While she was there, she asked them how much they would charge for the gasket replacement and they verified the Olympia shop's quote. They did suggest a new timing belt, exhaust, intake and valve cover gaskets and a kit for setting the valve lash. Might as well do it right while the engine was apart. Hali bought them all. Apart from the engine issue, the Accord was in decent shape for a twenty-eight-year old car. Together, they went to an auto parts place and bought new oil, filter, plugs, antifreeze, hoses, and sealant.

Frank was in the shop on Sunday morning working on a big block engine for Jerry's car, when Bobby and Hali showed up at eight. Hali had on old clothes, but still looked far too cute to be getting dirty. They lifted the hood of the Honda and discussed the plan of attack with Frank. Hali had put tabs in all the relevant pages of the manual. Her job was going to be to read the instructions since guys weren't particularly good at that. And maybe fetch a tool or two. Bobby drained the oil and antifreeze, then started disassembly with Hali reading the step by step. With the radiator out of the way, the four-cylinder engine came apart easily with a minimum of cursing and bruised knuckles. Frank kept coming over to check on the progress and jest about them reading the instructions. By noon, the top of the engine was apart down to the bare block, and it was time for lunch. They cleaned up and went off to Dick's Drive-in for burgers.

"Bobby, you've got to stop spending money on me."

"Uh... no, I don't, and I won't. I like being with you. And I have money to spare right now. I'd take you over to my house for lunch, but that would take too long. You'd have to meet my parents and Davie and we'd be there all day. They'd want to know all about you."

"I'd like to meet your family."

"And I'll take you home soon so you can meet everyone. I'd like to meet yours as well."

"Okay. That'll be interesting. We'll just have to see how my Daddy takes to me dating a white guy. And especially my brother Kellan."

"You think it'll be an issue?"

"Who knows? Probably not. Dad tries to be open-minded, but he lived through the sixties and seventies. Sometimes things slip out. Like when a white police officer shoots an unarmed black man. You can tell that he still has some anger. And Kellan... he'll be a challenge. He's an outspoken activist for equal rights. He already told me that I was making a huge mistake. He has a lot of anger against whites, which is strange since he never lived through any race riots or anything like that. He keeps preaching about how I should live my life, but he flits from job to job, never completed college and seems to be going nowhere. It's a sensitive subject."

"Okay… well, we won't talk about that kind of stuff. I suspect blacks are more open to mixed relations than white people are. But I'm quite sure my parents will be cool with it. My Dad does a lot for minorities and tries to be a voice at the Chamber for minorities."

"Ohhhh... Now I'm making the connection! Your family owns LaRoche Chevrolet!"

"And La Roche Cadillac. And LaRoche Ram Trucks. And LaRoche Pre-owned Vehicles. My Dad is very wealthy. And I'm supposed to get my business degree and take over the business."

"Sounds like you have your future all planned out!"

"Yeah. I kind of resent that he gets to tell me exactly what I'll do with my life. That's partially why I ran off and joined the Motocross Pro Circuit. But he's willing to pay for my schooling, including my MBA, and leave me a very lucrative business ensuring that I'll be wealthy as well. How do you complain about that?"

"Don't complain. Take the schooling. Take the job. Be happy. I wouldn't have been able to go to school if not for the athletic scholarship. And even then, I had to tutor on the side for any spending money. I made it, but it was hard. Now I'm trying to get into law school at UDub and I have no idea how I'm going to pay for it. My paralegal work barely pays for my apartment and volleyball expenses."

He sighed. "You're right, of course. I just want to do something for myself instead of being handed a silver platter, you know?"

"Yeah, I know exactly what you mean, Bobby. But take the silver platter and make it your own. You can personalize this business once your Daddy retires."

"What I'm thinking about doing, and I'll let my Dad in on this before I do anything, is starting a Ford dealership on my own. Dad always wanted a Ford dealership as well, but Ford won't give a franchise to a competitor. It's Ford versus Chevrolet, like the good ol' sixties from what I've heard. So, I'm thinking of starting a Ford franchise myself before I work for Dad, then later I can merge it into the LaRoche Auto Group. That way, I accomplish something on my own *and* fulfill my Dad's wishes to have a Ford dealership *and* I get to take over Dad's business. I'll bet Dad can arrange the financing for me. I just need to complete my MBA first."

"Wow, Bobby, that sounds like a great plan. I don't have anything figured out yet other than to become a lawyer, and that's only if I can get accepted into law school."

"You'll do it, and you'll be a great lawyer. Or, who knows? You could be a professional volleyball player... Or a coach. Make the Olympics and you'll have all the sponsorship money you can handle. Lots of options! Don't even think about it. It'll happen if you want it to. Right now, you just need to focus on volleyball."

She smiled shyly. "I'm kind of having a hard time doing that right now being with you."

"Yeah, that feeling is mutual. I think you might just have a personal cheerleader! And if you make it to Tokyo, I promise I'll come cheer you on. And if you need more support, I'll bring along all my rowdy friends!"

She laughed for a long time. "Yeah... That was great! Especially when they picked me up! I felt like a champion. I never get that from white people."

"Well, get used to it. I think you'll get that more and more once you get on the national team. And I'll always be cheering for you."

"Thanks, Bobby. You're so sweet. I love being with you."

"Whoa! Careful there! There's something I haven't told you. *Don't* go falling in love with me until you know what you're getting yourself into. I'm a package deal. Fall in love with me and you've got to fall in love with my brother Davie as well. Two for the price of one."

"What?! What do you mean?"

"My brother Davie. You have to love him also, not just me."

"That sounds kinky..."

Bobby laughed. "Nah... I just wanted to get a reaction from you.

Davie has Down syndrome. He has the mind of an eight to ten-year old. Mom takes care of him now, but it will be my job before that long. I'll be his caregiver. But don't worry. Everybody, and I do mean everybody loves Davie. He's the happiest person I know. Doesn't know anything about politics, doesn't even know how to lie, doesn't know race or religion. He just goes through life happy all the time. He works at the Cadi dealership detailing cars. So, he's surprisingly very functional. He can take care of himself for the most part. It's easy. You just need a lot of patience with him. He does art and poetry, and you just need to make time to let him show you his stuff. He's quite charming. You'll see."

"Oh... And you've taken it upon yourself to look after him? That's so sweet of you! I'll have to meet him, but I don't think I'll have any problems loving him. From what you say, I love him already."

"Yeah... If everyone were like Davie, there would be no wars and the world would live in peace. I look at Davie and I just think how stupid we all are. Happiness is so easy if you just let go of all your petty greed and need for power and money and status, and just live in the moment and notice all the pretty flowers and the butterflies. We could all learn a lot from Davie."

"Now I'm really looking forward to meeting him. And your family."

"We'll do it soon. Maybe after your California trip."

"Speaking of that, do you think the car will be ready?"

"Not if we keep chatting all afternoon. C'mon, let's get back to work."

While they had been out eating, Frank had been checking the parts. The head and the top of the block showed no signs of warpage, a common cause for head gasket failure. Good news there. And there was no leakage of antifreeze into the cylinders. More good news. There was a distinct lip around the top of each cylinder, but Frank decided that it was good enough for a street car. It would run with that just fine. To fix it would require new cylinder liners and rings, and that would mean complete disassembly. The pistons were in decent shape. Bobby scraped off all the carbon and vacuumed up the debris. Hali did the same with the head and the manifolds. Reassembly was a more exacting and time-consuming process than disassembly, but it went together slowly with minimal complaint. By six, it was time to add fluids and crank her up. It started on the second try and sounded healthy. Frank came over when he heard the engine start and Hali clapping her hands. High fives all around. No fluids leaking, no smoke. Just a smooth-running Honda. Bobby finished buttoning it up and closed the hood.

"Got any plans for supper?"

"No. Want to come to my place and I'll fix you something?"

Bobby smiled. "Now, that's a hard invitation to turn down. But I was thinking of bringing you home for supper to meet my folks."

"Oh, I'm not ready for that yet! But I do want to meet them soon, just not tonight. Maybe after my trip to California. Okay?"

Bobby sighed. "Okay. Then it's off to your place. I'll follow you in my truck."

Hali's apartment was a nice complex with a large pool and a community center complete with a fitness room. Her apartment was on the second floor overlooking the pool area. Her furniture was an eclectic mix of thrift store cast-offs, plus bookshelves made of concrete blocks and planks of wood. The art was mostly posters or cheap prints. But it was neat and clean, with little colorful doodads like polished stones and peacock feathers, scattered all over for decoration. Definitely a girl's place. Bobby didn't spend the night and Hali didn't ask. They enjoyed a meal of baked chicken thighs and steamed vegetables, and a couple of beers. But they did cuddle on the sofa for a while and talk. Bobby did agree to go with Hali to California next week and share the driving. Courtney would also be with them. They could take the Honda, or Courtney's battered old Mazda, but one of the courtesy cars from the dealership would be far more comfortable. He left at nine and was asleep in his own bed by ten-thirty ready for work the next day.

BEACH VOLLEYBALL

8

Bobby was able to get the last coat of varnish on the inside and decks of the boat on Monday evening. The boat was no longer on his mind much, so he almost grudgingly went out to work on her. He spent Wednesday fitting the deck hardware. There was far more to do than he could accomplish in one night, but he got the deck cleats mounted and the mainsheet block mounted. He also mounted the gudgeons[10] on the transom and laid out the two solar panels that would mount to the deck. They were flexible panels that were held in place by snaps. The electrical system was still a bit of a puzzle. Two batteries, an autopilot, and lights to connect somehow. The navigation lights were nicely recessed into the bow on either side, but the anchor light was at the top of the mast and needed some sort of waterproof disconnect fitting.

It was mid-March now, and the deadline to withdraw from the Race to Alaska was a month away. Bobby's Dad had made a remarkable recovery over the winter. He went to therapy daily, then straight to the gym where he had a trainer helping him. He still used a cane and walked with a noticeably strange gait, but he walked with purpose. His arm was stronger and his speaking clearer. He still stuttered a bit, and sometimes was at a loss for words. But his brain was at 100 percent. He could write out his thoughts very clearly and made sure he did so in critical situations. But could he sail a small boat to Alaska and handle

---

[10] Gudgeons – the female half of a set of hinges for the rudder. The pintle is the male half that includes the pin.

whatever storms Mother Nature threw at him? Not yet. Definitely not yet. The boat would be ready by mid-April at the latest. Would he be?

Bobby, Hali, and Courtney were leaving for Santa Cruz on Thursday night, having both taken Friday and Monday off. The plan was to switch drivers and drive straight through, sixteen hours if traffic cooperated. Same on the return trip. This tournament was critical for Hali and Courtney. Not only was it a qualifier for the nationals, but Team USA would be there. That meant that Karch would most likely be there. If the girls could defeat Team USA, Hali had a real good chance of getting selected to the national team. Courtney wasn't quite as good and she knew it, but she was determined not to let Hali down.

Bobby grabbed a brand-new silver Cadillac CTS courtesy car from the dealership and went over to pick up Hali at four. She was impressed. Then they picked up Courtney, who was likewise impressed. Courtney, like Hali, was a real looker. Tall, thin, and tanned with bleach-blond hair pulled back in a ponytail, the typical California surfer girl. She took the first turn at the wheel and drove for four hours. Dinner was sand-wiches, carrot sticks and sliced apples that Annette had prepared. The girls drank water while Bobby drank caffeine-rich cola. His was the night shift while the girls slept. He wore his earbuds as he drove and listened to his hard rock mix to keep him wired. Hali tried sleeping on the front seat propping a pillow across the console and laying her head in Bobby's lap, but she tossed and turned and finally just put her seat all the way back and slept with the pillow against the window. Courtney crashed in the back seat and slept well. Neither awoke when Bobby stopped for gas in Oregon. And not again when he stopped for gas in California. Hali finally woke up and took her turn at the wheel before the sun rose. Bobby was a zombie. He just dozed off and on for the remainder of the trip to Santa Cruz. He awoke to find Courtney driving. She and Hali were awake and singing along quietly to Lizzo's *Truth Hurts*. They were wide awake and ready to stop for breakfast. Once Bobby was roused, they googled restaurants and found a Denny's not far off their path. Coffee was heavenly, and roused Bobby, though he was glad he wasn't playing.

They had about three hours to go to get to their hotel. The sandwiches for supper hadn't done much for Bobby, and he was ravenous.

March in Santa Cruz is pretty cool, as in temperature. But the forecast called for sunshine the whole weekend with highs in the low sixties. Perfect for athletic competition, but Bobby needed a sweatshirt. The girls had a practice day starting at noon with courts open until four. They were looking forward to meeting another team or two to spar with in the usual fashion. They arrived at the hotel at noon, checked into their two rooms and did a quick change before dashing out to the courts on the beach a few blocks away. Bobby lagged as he was dead tired again. There were literally dozens of courts set up and each one taken up by teams practicing. Some were six on six and some were two on two, both men and women's teams. There were team awnings all over the beach representing all the major universities and clubs on the west coast, and crowds of players, coaches and followers filling the beach. There was no prize money for this tournament, so the pros hadn't shown up. Bobby's pale skin stood out against the tanned beach bodies. It had been at least six months since he last wore shorts. Bobby walked up and down the string of courts without finding his girls. Finally, he sat down at a picnic table adjacent to a court with four attractive girls in very revealing bikinis battling it out. The girls held his attention for a whole five minutes before he dozed off. Hali roused him some hours later. Her and Courtney's bikinis were far more conservative than many of the girls, and obviously designed for sports. To Bobby, they still looked sexy, but they looked like true athletes. That alone is pretty darn sexy.

"I've been looking all over for you. How long have you been here?"

"Uh... I don't know" Bobby stammered. "What time is it?"

"It's after four. I thought maybe you went back to the room to take a nap. We've been looking for you for the last half hour."

"I couldn't find you, so I found some girls in really skimpy bikinis playing right there and fell right asleep."

She and Courtney laughed. "You guys are all the same!"

"We played a Greek team once" Courtney said, "and they wore

thongs and tiny little bras. Nipples kept popping out every other play. They were by far the crowd favorite, but we skunked them twice."

"We're not worried about the girls in skimpy bikinis" Hai said. "The serious girls wear this kind." She pointed to her own.

"Well, you look pretty hot in that, if you don't mind my saying."

"Coming from you, I don't mind it at all."

"How was practice?"

"Great. We played two games, won both. One was against UC Berkeley. They've got a good team this year. And one was a mixed guy and girl team from UCLA. The guy was really tall and played up front thinking he'd spike me to death. Was he surprised when I jammed it down his throat! We beat them both handily. We observed some of the top teams just to get a feel for them. We're ready. Thanks for driving through the night, Bobby. It makes a big difference to get here wide awake and ready to play."

"Ohhhh.... I expect great things from you for my sacrifice. Just tell me where to find you. I was lost in the crowd."

"We'll know tomorrow. We need to go out and get some sports drinks for tomorrow and some ice. And maybe some Power Bars to keep us going. Are you hungry yet?"

"I don't know. I'm not quite awake yet. Ask me again once I get moving around. Alright... back to the hotel?"

"Yeah. Give us a minute or two to change and we'll be off."

They found a small Mexican restaurant away from the beach and away from the crowds and each ordered the tacos special and a margarita. Bobby was starting to wake up and listened to the girls chattering about the tournament. He didn't really understand the language. They were comparing notes about each team. Which teams to attack, and which ones to play defensively. It was kind of against Hali's nature to drop back and play defense, but she recognized the need. Bobby realized these girls were playing on a whole different level than the pick-up games he played. They tried to explain the secret hand signals they used, but their explanations went over his head. What did they mean by 'cross-court block' or 'line block'? He figured out what ball block was all about. That was Hali's specialty. He finally tuned out completely when they started talking about different serving strategies for different teams. Leaving the restaurant, they bought drinks and ice for tomorrow, stashed them in the hotel refrigerator and went back out on the town looking for the nightlife. They found a great little bar with live music, stayed for a couple of drinks and maybe an hour of dancing until the floor got way too crowded. Dancing with two attractive girls was a lot of fun for Bobby. All the other joints were packed, so they ended up in a pool hall drinking beer and playing shuffleboard. At ten, Bobby was done and begged off. He could walk back to the hotel from there. He took a quick shower and was sound asleep by eleven.

He was completely dead to the world when his alarm went off at seven. Groaning and fumbling for his phone to silence the alarm, he almost fell out of bed. Eventually, he gathered himself together and got up to use the toilet. Stretching, he suddenly sensed he wasn't alone. Turning, he discovered Hali in his bed just waking up. He stood there clad only in his underwear trying to figure out how she'd gotten into his room.

"Uh... Good morning. Did I let you in last night?"

"Mmmm... No. But you slipped me the second key when we checked in. I interpreted that as an invitation."

"Jeez... I don't even remember doing that. I guess I'm pretty smooth when my brain is dead... What time did you get back?"

"Ohhh... probably not long after you went to bed. We stayed for another game and then came back."

"Soooo... Let me get this straight.... we slept together in a hotel room and we didn't have sex? Don't let any of my friends find out."

She laughed. "Yep, no sex. Just some scrumptious snuggling. I like your tattoo." She was looking at the fierce tiger upon his chest.

"Thanks. My pals on the circuit all had tattoos and were pressuring me to get one. They wanted me to get a roach, or maybe a trail of roaches since it's my nickname. Thank God I was sober enough at the time to pick something I could be proud of. I picked the tiger because I'm so fierce on the track. You got any tats?"

She smiled. "You've seen me in a bikini. No tattoos."

"There are other places you could hide a tattoo. I see no piercings either, right?"

"Only my ears. I've been way too focused on volleyball and way too broke for frivolities."

He turned and used the bathroom. She was just getting up when he returned, dressed only in her panties and a faded and very worn purple Huskies T-shirt.

"You're really a beautiful girl, Hali."

She walked into the bathroom. "Thanks. And you're really cute yourself."

Together, they ate breakfast at a nearby Shari's early enough for the meal to settle before the games began. Bobby was ravenous and ate a big breakfast, while the girls only had a high protein meal of two eggs and a piece of Canadian bacon. The games started at ten, though they didn't know if they'd be playing right off. The team pairings were handed out at nine, round-robin single games to establish the seeds starting at ten, then sudden death matches start in the afternoon. Those were best of three. No point in sandbagging the seeding or you play the best first in sudden death. Hali and Courtney easily won four in a row in the round robin without even breaking a sweat. The fifth was a real struggle. This was Team USA, the B team. They were young, skilled, and well-coached. But eventually Hali and Courtney overpowered them, winning 21 to 18. They would meet again.

Hali and Courtney were seeded number three despite being the defending champions and despite being undefeated in the round-robin games. With one loss, Team USA B Team was seeded number one. There was a definite bias there, as Hali had predicted. Their first two opponents in the sudden death rounds put up little resistance, falling in only two quick games each. Both were college teams, coached adequately, but very new to beach volleyball. They wore indoor uniforms rather than bikinis, suggesting that they had just been recruited from the indoor squad for this tournament. They did have a great cheering section though that Bobby couldn't match as much as he tried. The third match was tougher, and the girls dropped the first game. But they came back in game two and put it away in game three with a decisive victory. And that was all for Saturday. Sixteen teams would play on Sunday for the championship. Team USA-A Team didn't make it. But the B Team did. And they'd be out for revenge against Hali and Courtney.

That night, they again went out to sample the nightlife, and once again danced until the floors became packed. They headed back to the same pool hall they had found last night and played pool for a couple of hours. Courtney was a phenomenal pool player. Hali wasn't. But she laughed a lot and hung all over Bobby. Later that night, she came back to his room to find him wide awake and showered. And this time, they didn't go straight to sleep. Bobby made love to her slowly, driving her mad with desire and making sure she climaxed before slipping on a condom and entering her missionary style. They moved together slowly at first, each getting used to the feel of the other, then more urgently as the need increased until both climaxed almost together. Then it was time for snuggling as Hali fell asleep contentedly in his arms.

Sunday was bright and warm for a March day. The remaining teams were already warming up when Bobby and the girls arrived. All the teams were hard-core at this point. Their first opponent was from ASU. Arizona's entire volleyball program was top notch, and several Olympic athletes had come out of their program. This pair was particularly good. Courtney served first, and promptly lost serve after a lengthy volley. ASU served and scored an ace right off the bat when Hali mishandled it. But they lost the serve, and Hali turned it into three quick points. ASU fought back and they traded serves for over ten minutes. Fifteen minutes into the first game and the score was only 5 to 1. It was going to be a long game. But Hali and Courtney kept the pressure on and slowly they extended their lead. 8 to 4. Ten minutes later it was 12 to 10 as ASU kept fighting. They tied the score at 16 each, then Hali served for four unanswered points. She had a wicked curveball serve, and when the opposition got used to that, she'd send a hard floater right at the passer. ASU eventually won back the serve, then promptly scored twice. That's all they'd get. Courtney served deep, the ball was slammed back, and Hali spiked it with one of her signature jumping blocks. Game over.

Bobby was jubilant. But that was only the first of three. Game two was not as close. The ASU team was as fit as Hali and Courtney, but they had lost their confidence. At first it looked like Hali and Courtney would run away with it, but ASU finally got themselves together and scored five unanswered points to bring the score to 10 to 7. But a couple of Hali's spikes put the game away, and they cruised to an easy victory in game two, 21 to 12.

As the girls were resting, drinking, and wiping off all the sand, Bobby went to check the master bracket board to see who their next competition would be. Same court. Team USA. This was the must-win game for Hali. And each team knew their opponents. The Team USA coaching staff would be there, watching intently. Hali served first and promptly lost the serve. But they won it right back only to lose it again. Five minutes into the game and not a point scored. Team USA scored first after an exceptionally long rally that had the crowd on their feet, but Hali spiked the next ball to win back the serve. That spike shook Team USA and they dropped three quick points. But they came back with a spike of their own. Courtney saved the point with an excellent dig, which Hali set for her to slam back. They were very gradually pulling ahead and scored two more unanswered points. 5 to 1, then 7 to 1. Team USA got it together and put up a string of three points for themselves to make it closer. But Hali and Courtney were determined and would not be denied. They scored two more, then both teams traded points until the score was 17 to 14. Two more Hali spikes and a long rally put them at game point, but Team USA came back to score 5 in a row. Courtney served up a hard floater right down the line between the defenders for an ace to finish the game. Both teams were tired and sweaty. Hali and Courtney took a few minutes to brush off the sand and sweat, drink a small amount of Gatorade and psych themselves up for game 2. They controlled the game from the onset. Team USA put up a good fight, but Hali and Courtney answered every point scored with at least one if not two of their own. The game lasted thirty-two minutes but was never close. The final score was 21 to 14. The dejection on Team USA's faces was completely understandable, as they knew that they weren't the best team the USA had to offer. Bobby could see that both Hali and Courtney were both tired. They washed off, ate a Power Bar washed down with Gatorade, donned their sweats, and sought shelter in the shade while Bobby went off to see who their next opponent would be. He was pleased to see that the other semifinal match was just getting under way, Huskies against UCLA, so the girls had some rest time. That's one big advantage to the girls. The winner of this match wouldn't be fresh. He wandered back and told them the news.

The final match started late in the afternoon. The tournament should have been over by five, but their match didn't even start until five-fifteen. Most of the crowds had dispersed by then and the courts and awnings were being taken down elsewhere, but there was still a sizable audience for the final. The Huskies had prevailed, so the final was Huskies varsity against Huskies alumni. Both teams were young and well-conditioned, but Hali and Courtney had the advantage of an hour of rest and some nourishment. They also had been playing elite level volleyball, especially beach volleyball, a lot longer than their opponents. The entire Team USA coaching staff were in the stands. Hali started the game with an ace but lost serve immediately after. The Huskies scored twice after some incredibly long rallies that had the crowd cheering. But Courtney won the serve back with a fake slam that ended up being a light dink shot over the net. Finesse and serving were her fortes. Hali and Courtney went on to score four unanswered points, and the rout was on. The Huskies tried to keep up, but Hali and Courtney scored two points for every point the Huskies scored and cruised to an easy 21 to 11 victory. The second game wasn't as close. Hali and Courtney drubbed them. Starting with six unanswered points to start the game, they never gave the Huskies any respite. One spectacular spike after another, Hali and Courtney were playing to the crowd at the Huskies expense. Completely dejected, they barely stayed in the game. The final score was 21 to 7.

Hali and Courtney were the repeat champions and had put on a stellar performance in front of the Team USA coaches. There wasn't much more they could do to earn their way onto the national team. Only time would tell. Bobby thought that Courtney should go as well and keep the team together. She showed incredible poise along with 22 aces in the tournament. She had a wicked serve that she could place accurately anywhere on the court, especially up close to the net if the opposition were playing back. Her signature move was the fake spike to drive the opponents back from the net and then a light dink shot to drop the ball over the net. Hali was a power player with an unusually strong serve and incredible blocking and spiking abilities due to her jumping talent. She was also an excellent passer. Both girls had an endless supply of competitive spirit and were extremely fit. The national team coaches all came over to congratulate the girls but said nothing as far as the team selection.

Even Bobby was exhausted from watching the games in the sun all day. The girls were toast. And now they had to drive sixteen hours to get home. The girls washed off at the beach showers and changed clothes in the car while Bobby turned his back. They found a restaurant on their way out to Interstate 5, and Bobby treated them all to a big supper. The girls were famished. By nine, they were on the interstate heading north with Bobby driving and listening to hard rock again, both girls dead to the world. Neither woke up at the first fueling stop, nor the second. But Courtney finally woke up and took the wheel around four in the morning giving Bobby some much-needed rest in the back seat. Hali didn't wake up until they were entering Portland around eight in the morning, and they decided to take a break for breakfast. She would drive the rest of the way to Edmonds.

SPONSORSHIP

9

April first was fast approaching. This was the day that Bobby had selected for the unveiling, but he still had to turn the boat over and varnish the bottom. Hali came over to help and met Davie, Jessie, and their Mom. They all accepted her warmly with big hugs as if she were a long lost relative. Hali was particularly taken with Davie, and, after they helped Bobby roll the boat, spent the afternoon with Jessie, Annette and Davie reviewing his art and listening to Jessie read his poetry out loud. Jessie was a master at this and had everyone laughing uproariously at her expressions and Davie's words. Bobby got the boat lightly sanded, and the first coat of varnish on before his Dad came home. He was also quite accepting of Hali, though he didn't give her a hug. At dinner, Annette wanted to know all about Hali and how they had met. She could see that Bobby was obviously head over heels in love with her.

Looking at Hali, she asked "How long have you and Bobby been dating?"

"A little over a month. We met at the tournament in Lacey."

"Oh, so this is all pretty new, huh? Exciting times!"

Hali smiled bashfully. "Yeah, it is. I think I fell for him the first day we met."

Jessie spoke up. "Oh, I want to hear this! I just can't think of Bobby as a Casanova... Tell us how you guys met."

It was Bobby who answered. "We met by accident at *Bahama Breeze* in Tukwila. We were both heading down to Lacey for the volleyball tournament, and we both got stuck in the same traffic jam that put us right in the thick of the Friday evening rush hour. So, we both finally got off the road and ended up at the same restaurant. She was a few minutes ahead of me and there was a long wait for a table. She didn't want to eat alone so she asked me to join her. And I did. And I was attracted to her immediately. We stayed and talked until eight o'clock."

"And then my car broke down in Olympia" Hali chimed in. "And it was going to be too expensive to repair. But Bobby offered to fix it for me for nothing but cost. I couldn't pass that offer up. And it gave us lots of time together to get to know each other. We had to drive up here to get a trailer, then back down the following week to get the car. Then he took it apart and fixed it in Frank's shop and now it runs as good as new. Every time I drive it, I think of Bobby. I probably would have junked it if he hadn't fixed it for me. And I can't afford a new car. It's almost as good as new!"

"Bobby's an excellent mechanic. If the car could be fixed, he could do it. There's not much he can't do, especially with Frank there to help" Annette said. "As far as you two meeting like that, sounds like a lot of coincidences to me. Maybe you guys were fated to find each other."

Bobby and Hali just looked at each other and smiled.

"I still can't figure out how he could be single, but I'm not complaining. Bobby is really special. I saw that immediately. I just thank God I found him before someone else. I wasn't in the market for a guy, but then he came along. I'm training for the Olympics and the last thing I need is a guy in my life right now. But I couldn't pass him up."

"Really? The Olympics? What sport?" Gerald suddenly perked up and took interest in the conversation.

"Volleyball. Probably beach volleyball, but I'll take either sport." Hali replied.

"You're a bit too short for beach volleyball" Gerald observed. You could play the backfield in indoor ball though."

Bobby laughed. "That's exactly what everyone thinks. But you should see her jump! She plays the net better than any of the tall players. Her opponents try to spike the ball on her, and she jumps up and jams it down their throats. Absolutely amazing! And she is incredibly quick in the back field. Nothing gets by her." Bobby told them all about the tournament in Santa Cruz, and how dominant Hali and Courtney were.

"You know, I had Olympic aspirations when I was a kid. Played basketball in high school and was red-hot. Made the all-star team twice" Gerald said. "I got recruited by maybe a dozen colleges, but they wouldn't offer me a full scholarship. I was considered too short. I was penniless back then, so I needed a full ride if I were to go anywhere out of town. The University of Washington wouldn't give me anything at all. I went there just because I could live at home. I had to work my way through school. On a whim, I tried out for the indoor volleyball team and loved it. And they gave me a partial scholarship after my first year. I needed that just to get by. I still wanted to go to the Olympics, but I wasn't quite good enough. I trained hard with that dream and got to be a damn good setter. I was a starter on the varsity team in my junior and senior year. I had a full scholarship on my senior year. We came in second in the nationals that year. We had three guys who were on the national team and one would have gone to the Olympics except that USA boycotted in 1980."

"Really? How cool!" Hali replied. "You know the dream, then. I played with UDub for all four years. Full ride scholarship in both beach and indoor ball."

"Both sports? That's impressive. I'd love to see you play up front. I'll always root for the short guys. That was my downfall. But, there's a couple of guys playing in the NBA that are shorter than me. I'm sure I could've made it. It's all about heart. And skill. And jumping ability. I had all that. The problem is that I didn't have the money to go to one of the schools that recruited me so I could prove myself. I'm sure I could've gotten a scholarship after my first year. Anyway… what's the plan to get to the Olympics, Hali?"

"Well, I have to get on the national team first. I think I took some big steps towards that by beating Team USA in Santa Cruz. And the national team coaches watched me play in Lacey, also. I spoke to Karch Kiraly after the game in Santa Cruz, and he invited me to train with the team this June. I get the feeling that he was looking for quality opponents to work out his players against. But, if I can beat his teams consistently, maybe I can get selected. I may be short by volleyball standards, but I can out-jump just about anyone. I love playing the net so I can block their feeble attacks. Courtney and I have a tournament in Florida later in April and then the nationals are in July in California. Those are must-dos. Courtney and I are the defending national champions. That's beach volleyball. The bigger mystery is indoor volleyball. Somehow, I've got to convince my whole team to travel to wherever the national team is playing. Most of them will do it just to support me, but not all. We don't have to win. I just need exposure to the national team coaches. I've sent them videos already. They know who I am. They know I was the UDub women's MVP on the indoor team both in my junior and senior year, but I haven't heard anything from them. In Lacey, right after I met Bobby, he made sure that the Team USA coaches noticed me by bringing over a bunch of rowdy friends and cheering me on personally. After the game, they picked me up and marched me around the gym like I was the champion. The coaches all noticed that. That was fun, and Bobby won my heart with that move. No one had ever noticed me before that. There're a few black girls playing indoor volleyball, but hardly any in beach ball. All the girls are blue-eyed and blond. So, I'm always the underdog."

"Defending national champs, huh? So, you really are top-notch. Repeat that and you should be a shoo-in for the national team. But unless you're independently wealthy, you'll need a lot of money to make it to the Olympics. Are you sponsored yet?"

"No. And I'm certainly not wealthy. Occasionally I'll get some travel money thrown my way so I can make a meet, but no commitment. We earn a bit for winning in the professional events, but it's not enough to go to the international tournaments which are key."

"So, how are you going to afford it?"

"Well, if I get selected to the national team, they'll cover a lot of the expenses. At least the travel and entry fees. I'm hoping to land some sponsors, but I need that breakout performance to really get myself noticed. We'll start focusing on the professional tournaments to maximize the winnings. I think we can beat all those teams. We've beaten Team USA several times, and they represent the best from that circuit. And if we can start winning some international tournaments, the winnings are a lot larger. Some teams earn over a million a year, though they spend almost all of that just participating. We just need a boost now to reach the national team and get into the circuit. Does your company sponsor athletes?"

Gerald paused for a while before answering. "Well... we sponsor six Little League baseball teams, three scout troops, a cheerleader squad, a dance team and two car racing programs. I would have sponsored Bobby if he'd only asked. But he's too mule headed." He paused for a while contemplating Hali. Finally, he made up his mind. "Okay, yes. I'd like to get involved with your quest. Maybe I can live my own Olympic dream vicariously through you. I can probably get you some sponsorship money, some from my company, more from some others. I could introduce you and Courtney to the Chamber of Commerce and make a plea on your behalf. Tell you what, why don't you just leave the fund-raising to me? You focus on your training. I'll need your cooperation, signing autographs and what not, but I think I can get you some money to get you started."

"That would be great, Mr. LaRoche! I'm just about broke right now!"

"It's nothing. And call me Gerald. Are you working right now?"

"Yeah, I'm a paralegal. The best part about the job is the flexible hours. The owner was an Olympic biker. Didn't medal but he understands the drive."

"Making much money?"

"No, and my apartment uses up most of what I earn. I'm really scraping by. Courtney covers a lot of my expenses since she gets way more sponsorship money than I do."

Gerald paused for a while considering. "Okay. Here's the plan. The apartment is a waste! First step is to get rid of it. That'll probably save you fifteen, twenty grand right off the bat!"

"Uhhh... yeah, it would, but I have to live somewhere."

"You can have the master suite upstairs. Room and board for free. How's that for a start?"

Bobby looked up just as surprised as Hali. "Really?! With Bobby?"

"Bobby has his own room. But if you guys want to share a room, that's fine also."

"That so sweet of you, Gerald! I'll take you up on it. I look forward to living with you guys. You're all so nice to me."

Annette clapped her hands. "Oh, Hali! I'd love to have you stay with us! It's been so long since I had a girl in the house!"

"Hali, you know what the most sure-fire way to derail your Olympic career is?"

"No, what?"

"Get yourself pregnant! Poof! Olympics are over! You're using protection, aren't you?"

Jessie almost choked. Hali laughed and looked at Bobby. "Yes, we're using protection."

"And the second most sure-fire way to derail your Olympic career is to fall in love! I may be a little late on that little piece of advice. A brand-new romance is a huge distraction, and you need to focus on your training. You've got one chance at this, Hali. You blow it and you'll regret it for the rest of your life. You need to let go of everything in your life and train, train, train. At least you and Bobby have a year to let the giddiness fade. And you, Bobby, you need to set her free and let her soar. Catch her when she falls and cheer her when she flies. Her Olympic dream must become your Olympic dream. You can't hold her back. You've got to keep pushing her harder and harder. When she's tired, she'll come back to roost. But you won't be seeing her that much and that's got to be okay with you. It's tough, but 2020 is not far away. You have the rest of your lives together to catch up. Can you both commit to that? Bobby?"

Bobby and Hali both nodded. Then Hali spoke up. "You're right, Gerald. I've been avoiding dating for precisely this reason. But I just couldn't pass Bobby up. He's one in a million. I'll never meet another guy like him. But if it's okay with you, Bobby, let's sleep separately for a while. I do need to focus, but that doesn't mean I don't love you, too. You need to go to sleep early and get up early for work. I tend to go to bed late and get up later. We can sleep together on weekends. We've only been together for a month now, and all of this is taking some getting used to."

Bobby smiled. "I'm happy just to have you in the same house. I'll commit right now to supporting your dream one hundred percent. You can have all the space you need."

His Dad spoke up again. "Good, I'm glad you saw my point. Now, I'll have Jessie create an account for you so we can claim all funds we provide, like use of the CTS last week. Got that, Jessie? Good. I'd like you and Courtney to come to the next Edmonds Chamber meeting in April. I think it's the 3rd, but it's the first Monday of the month. Can you do that? And the chamber meeting in Everette is the following week on Monday. I need to get some photos of you two in action. I want to do a very quick Power Point, and I want you to have a stack of five by sevens that you can autograph. We'll hit up the Lynwood Chambers as well. I'll make sure the press is there. I want your pictures in every newspaper in the northwest. There's a great story here and I'm confident they'll print it. We'll set you up a GoFundMe site also so your fans can contribute."

"I've got some killer shots of them in action that we can use! Mostly Hali, but I have some of Courtney as well and some of both. They're just smart phone shots, but they're surprisingly good."

"And Courtney's husband is a professional photographer, so I'm sure that he has plenty of shots of us in action" Hali said.

"Good. And one more thing, Hali. You've got to get better. You and Courtney both. Better endurance. Better strategy. Better reflexes. Better skills in every aspect."

"Better? I'm just about at my peak."

"No, you're not. You're not anywhere even close. That's exactly my point. If you think you're the best you can be, you stop pushing yourself to get better. Look at Michael Phelps. Best in the world, right? But he hasn't been out of the circuit that long, and each one of his world records are falling one by one. There's always some young buck out to knock you off your pedestal. Did you know that some guy just broke the two-hour marathon? They said it was physically impossible. The human body just couldn't do that. That's about four-thirty per mile! For twenty-six miles, for God's sake! You've got to keep training, Hali, and train hard. Train in the humidity. Train at high altitude. Find the best coach in the country and train with him or her. Find the best volleyball team in the country and go train with them. Surround yourself with people who are better than you and rise to their level. Then go find someone even better. Go to Europe and see how they train. Study video of the best and note their strategy. There is always room to improve. You want to be the best in the world, Hali? You've barely started. I'll get you the funding. You do the training. How bad do you want this? Are you willing to do the work? You know eventually you'll have to quit working right?"

Hali nodded. "I'm ready if Bobby will wait for me. I'll do the work. I'll get better. I want the Olympics. I want the gold medal. But I want Bobby to wait for me."

Bobby hugged her. "You don't have to worry about me, Sweetheart. I'll be waiting for you and I'll support you all the way, Hali."

Gerald looked at Hali, then back to Bobby. "You picked well, son."

ROOM MATES

10

Hali was off training almost every night, leaving Bobby to work diligently on the boat in the evenings through the end of the month. The keel was a chore. But it got done. Bobby was no structural engineer, but he knew it had to be strong and stiff to withstand the lateral forces. The shell was pure carbon fiber, about an eighth of an inch thick. Then Bobby fashioned a thick carbon fiber beam that ran down the center to resist the lateral bending forces. He finally filled up the bulb and the lower part of the keel with lead birdshot mixed with epoxy. The remainder was filled with spray-in-place foam. Getting the two halves to fit together neatly took an entire evening, a lot of grinding and a lot of test-fitting. But when that was accomplished and the two halves were joined, he had created a sexy smooth carbon fiber keel that looked very professional. It weighed about ninety-five pounds give or take a little. Mounting it would be a chore since it would have to be slid up into the hull from below, then a cap installed to keep it in place. Other than the carbon fiber, it was exactly as his Dad had designed it. The rudder was easy, and he finished it in a week, while he was also building the wishbone boom and tiller. The wishboom was laminated Sitka Spruce, bent around a form that Bobby had built atop the now useless beam.

Apart from rigging the boat, and doing the wiring, the boat was ready for the water by March 28th. Bobby bought a trailer and spent an evening modifying it to allow for ramp launching the boat with the keel raised, but the bulb still protruding. He had to brainstorm some sort of tripod lifting gear with a block and tackle under it that could be temporarily set up in the cockpit when launching and retrieving to hold the keel up. Once on the trailer, the keel could be lowered gently into the

cradle that he had built. He built the lifting gear of wood using some old
two by fours that was purely functional, then designed a nice aluminum
version which Frank promised to build for him for free.

The unveiling was scheduled for Sunday, April first, 2018. April
Fool's Day. Fitting. Bobby and his Mom planned on doing a big cookout
as the excuse to have a crowd there, and they easily got commitments
from Jessie and Ralph, even Frank and Jerry. Both naval architects that
had helped design the boat promised to come, though they agreed to
show up late so Gerald wouldn't suspect anything. Hali had a meet in
Kingston on the weekend and would be home after four on Sunday. So,
the unveiling would be when Hali got there. Frank and Jerry agreed to
come over on Friday afternoon to help put the boat on the trailer and
get the keel installed. Everything was just about ready.

On Saturday, the last day of March while Hali was off at her tournament, Annette, Jessie, and Bobby raided Hali's apartment and stripped
it bare. Everything was brought over to the LaRoche house and set up in
the upstairs master suite. There really wasn't that much stuff. The brass
bed was a twin, and an old one at that. But they brought it all over and set
it up just as it had been. The master suite was so big that the dinette set,
living room furniture and bed barely made a dent in it. Annette collected
up all her toiletries and food, all the girlie decorations, everything and
brought it all over. Then, while Annette and Jessie were setting up her
room, Bobby spent two hours cleaning the refrigerator, stove, bathroom
and finally vacuuming the carpets. And just before he left, he turned over
the keys to the office after a brief walk-through. They promised to send
her a check at her new address for the security deposit. Hali came to her
new home in time for supper, so Davie gave her a quick tour of her new
digs. Bobby was still setting out her toiletries and her decorations.

"Oh my God, Bobby! Is this all for me? It's huge!"

"All yours, Sweetheart. Davie's room is all the way down the hall,
and I'm right next door. And I never lock my door, by the way."

She hugged him. "I think I'll join you tonight. Show me your room."

They both went next door into his room and threw themselves onto
the bed hugging and laughing.

"Your bed is so comfortable! I think I'll be visiting you often."

"It is. And next week you and I are going shopping for a big bed for you. If I'm going to sneak into your bed at night, there better be room for me."

"Oh, don't spend any money on me! I can sleep here with you."

"By buying you a bed, I'm spending money on us. Not just you. Your bed is really old and completely worn out. It's going to the dump."

"I like my bed! I've had it my whole life! Since I was three, at least. It is pretty worn out, though. And it wasn't a particularly good mattress when my Dad bought it."

"Time to grow up, Hali. Adults don't sleep on twins. We'll get you a king-size mattress with a nice bed frame to put it on. When it comes to beds, I believe in spending a lot and getting the best since you spend so much time on it. That's one place where you shouldn't skimp. And I want you to sleep well. It's part of your training."

Just then Davie came in. "Mom sent me to fetch you guys. Supper's on the table." So, they disengaged and followed Davie downstairs.

"Welcome to the household, Hali! I hope you like the room. It served us well for all these years. Gerald and I only just moved downstairs last month, when he was released from the recovery center."

"Thanks, Annette. You guys are wonderful! The room is incredible! It's huge! I really feel so special since I met Bobby."

"You are special, Hali" Gerald said. "Bobby wouldn't have been attracted to you if you weren't, and you certainly wouldn't be living with us if you weren't. Bobby's an incredibly lucky guy to have met you. Fortunately, he didn't scare you away as he usually does."

"Usually? Is there a story there?"

"Well, he's generally not very smooth with the ladies, are you son?"

"Maybe not, I just had to find the right ladies. I was comfortable with Piper, and now I'm comfortable with Hali. I felt at ease with her from the moment we met."

"Was Piper your last girlfriend? The one who's still riding?"

"Yeah... She was my very first girlfriend. Met her when I was twenty-one. Dated on and off until my accident last May. She's still riding. Last I heard, she started doing really well since we split up."

"You never had any girlfriends in high school? Or even in college?"

"No. I had a lot of dates that never went anywhere. I had plenty of friends who were women, but no girlfriends."

"Really?! Why? I bet the girls were all interested in you. You're a good-looking guy!"

"I suppose I can blame Dad. He never taught me the come-on lines. I was always too bashful to smooth-talk a girl."

Gerald laughed. "Blame it on me, then. I'm glad you didn't become a lady's man. You'd have run off and married some bimbo and divorced her a couple of years later. That seems to be the theme these days. You just had to meet the right girl to be comfortable."

"Yeah... And my mind was full of my truck, and riding. Girls aren't into that stuff."

"Maybe not" Hali said. "But now that I know you built it yourself, I love your truck. When you build something like that all by yourself, a bit of your heart and your personality goes into it. It's not the same when you just go out and buy a snazzy car. I couldn't care less about fancy cars, except that I know you built this one from scratch. And seeing you rebuild my Honda gave me a real appreciation for your mechanical talent. I feel a little of you in my car whenever I drive it now. If you hadn't fixed it for me, I probably would have junked it. You've got a real gift, Bobby. I can't wait to see what you build next."

"Maybe I'll build you a custom rod next when you're an Olympic champion. How about that? What would it be? A sports car? A sixties hot rod? Hmmm?"

"Only if I get to help you build it. If it's going to be mine, I need my personality in it."

"So, Hali" Annette broke in. "Tell us about the tournament today."

"Yeah, it was fun. We had four teams, three of them local and one from Portland. The Strikers would have won easily."

"But?" Gerald asked.

"Well, since the winner was pretty much already determined before the tournament started, we all decided to do something different. So, we broke up all the teams and formed new teams randomly. We were playing with people we've never played with before, and against our own team-mates. It was a blast! But it was still uber competitive once the games started. And in the end, it didn't matter who won or lost. We all had a great time. We're doing it again tomorrow, but with all new teams. In a way it's kind of like a pick-up game but with serious players. I found it particularly useful to play with strangers and against my own teammates. It was a good learning experience. And I played great, even better than on my own team. I had to carry a bit more of the weight. We didn't win all the time, but I did great and had a blast. It injected fun back into the equation, without any loss of competitiveness."

"Mom and I were talking earlier, Hali" Bobby said. "We think we should consult a nutritionist about your diet. I suggested a high protein, low carb diet, lots of vegetables and lean meat. That's what I was on when I was riding. We won't mention all the beer. But I don't know if that's right for you. Your diet is a big part of your training."

"I think that's a splendid idea" Gerald said. "We could all probably use adjusting our own diets a little, as long as I still get to eat some of your pie, Annette."

"I'm okay with that" Hali replied. "But I need to be in on that conversation. My only concern is that the diet is too strict. I need calories, lots of calories. But good, healthy calories. Courtney was a vegan for several years, and she agrees that she missed out on a lot. She lost weight but didn't have enough energy to compete well. And when I'm on the road eating at a restaurant, it's difficult to find healthy foods. I generally eat fairly healthy now, but I like some sweets from time to time."

"Speaking of food..." Bobby said, "Dad, we're having a cookout tomorrow afternoon for April Fool's Day. Frank and Jerry are coming over. Jessie and Ralph will be here if she hasn't had her baby yet. She's already late. Hali, you'll be here right?"

"I'm planning on it. As soon as the tournament is over, I'll be on my way. But there's a ferry to take that could slow me down."

"Well, I'll be grilling tri-tip and chicken. We decided to forego the burgers and brats in the spirit of healthier eating. Let's say we plan to eat at five, five-thirty."

"Well..." Gerald said. "If you're cooking tri-tip, I'll be there. It's not like I have anything else to do on a Sunday. The weather is supposed to be decent tomorrow afternoon. I have some books I need to go over in the morning."

After dinner, while Bobby and Davie were cleaning up the kitchen, Hali went up to her new room and tried to make heads or tails of her new digs. The bathroom was huge with a large jetted tub and a walk-in shower stall with not one, but three shower heads. The walk-in closet was almost as large as her previous bedroom. Jessie and Annette had carefully hung up her clothes which barely made a dent in the capacity. Her old twin mattress on the old rickety brass bed looked puny against the wall, but Jessie and Annette had made the bed for her. It still beckoned her after all these years. That was her safe spot. She'd had that bed just about her entire life. Her little dinette set with four mis-matched chairs was set up in the corner looking completely out of place. Even her dresser, her one piece of furniture that was still in decent shape, looked small and puny against the wall. Her bookshelves were set up and her book collection was neatly laid out. Someone had taken the time to organize it so that her school text books that she'd probably never crack open again were on the bottom shelf, her non-fiction books were on the middle shelf and her favorite romance novels were on the top. There were three totes with all her posters and decorations that she started to go through.

She turned as Bobby entered.

"I would have hung your posters for you, but I thought you might move your furniture around. The posters should go up last."

"You're sure you got everything?"

"Yep. If you're missing something now, it'll show up. I scoured your apartment thoroughly as I cleaned it out. I admit that I did snoop a little though. You have a severe lack of lingerie. All you have is practical stuff. What's up with that?" He had an adorable crooked smile on his face and his eyes twinkled.

Hali laughed. "Then I guess I know what I'm getting for birthdays and Christmas from now on, don't I?"

"Count on it. Not that you don't look sexy in plain cotton panties." He walked over to Hali and put his arms around her.

"I've been too broke for girlie stuff. And I've been focused on volleyball for the last seven years. I haven't had interest or time for guys. And then you came along..."

"Well, sorry about that" Bobby chuckled. "I'll try hard not to interfere with your volleyball, but you know every now and then you can let your hair down and be a woman."

Hali kissed him as they embraced. "I can be your woman tonight..."

"Speaking of that," Bobby broke the embrace, took her hand, and led her out the door. "Part of your training regimen that you need to get to work on."

"Where are we going?" She asked as she followed him down the stairs.

"Ohhh... Outside."

"It's cold out there at night."

"Don't worry. You won't be cold." Still holding Bobby's hand, Hali followed him through the laundry where he grabbed a couple of beach towels, then out to the back deck where the hot tub was. Lifting the cover, he said "C'mon, get undressed."

Hali looked around. "Really? What about your folks? And Davie?"

"Davie's in the tub, probably for the next forty-five minutes. And then he'll go straight to his room as he has done every day of his entire life. Mom and Dad never use the tub anymore, and they know I usually soak naked, so they give me my privacy. If they hear us out here, they'll assume that we're both naked and they'll leave us alone. In fact, they've gone to their room already. They're getting ready for bed. They usually go to bed around nine-thirty to ten. That leaves only me to spy on you." He was already naked and waiting for her.

"I don't know..." She looked back at the house. The curtains were all closed.

"C'mon. The longer you take, the colder you'll get. Just strip and hop in. Once you're in, if anyone looks out, they won't see anything. I'm the only one who ever uses the tub anymore. And now you're here. And your muscles could use some relaxing after your workout."

That was true. She did feel tight from her workout. Hali quickly slipped out of her clothes and climbed up on to the edge of the tub covered with goose bumps. She slipped into the hot water slowly letting her body get used to it bit by bit. Bobby was watching her with that coy little lopsided grin of his. She finally settled in and relaxed for a few minutes opposite Bobby, then crossed over to his waiting arms. Bobby had set the temperature a little lower, so they were able to stay in for a while. They cuddled quietly in the hot water for twenty minutes or more before deciding to get out.

"Bobby, this is all going to take some getting used to. I love you. I really do. I love your family. I love your lifestyle. I love the way you and your Dad support me in my quest for the Olympics. I love everything since I met you. I love this hot tub. I love Davie and Jessie and your parents. I feel like I have a whole new family. It's like a dream. But it's all so sudden, it's overwhelming. I just need time to assimilate it all."

"Sweetheart, you take as much time as you need. I'm here for you whenever you need me."

He was earnest, she knew it. She lay her head against his chest and listened to his heartbeat. There was something very soothing about it. "Bobby, can I sleep with you tonight?"

He half snorted and half chuckled. "Really?! Like you really think you ever need to ask? My door is always unlocked for you, Hali. If you want to make love, I'm your guy. If you just want to cuddle, I'm still your guy. If you just want to be alone for a while, that's okay too."

Hali pulled him closer. "I think I would really like to make love with you tonight. You have such a special way of doing it."

Bobby lifted her head to his and they kissed passionately for a few minutes. She could feel a heat that wasn't coming from the tub. "Then let's get out and go get cleaned up. I want to shower with you since Davie is probably still in the bath. C'mon."

She stood up as he did. "I've never showered with anyone before."

"You've never had a shower like this one. It's a waste to shower alone."

Hali took his hand as she climbed out of the tub. Her muscles were so relaxed that she needed his support. Her body was steaming in the cold night air, so she wrapped the big beach towel around herself quickly. She bundled up her clothes and went upstairs as Bobby locked up downstairs. Hali found all her shampoos and soaps already laid out in the shower alongside Bobby's. He'd been using this shower ever since his parents had moved downstairs. It saved having to wait for Davie. She found her toothbrush and hairbrush by the sink, and all her ponytail holders and barrettes in a little drawer by the sink. Hali followed Bobby into the shower and just held him as the warm water flowed over their bodies. He finally broke the embrace, lathered up the washcloth and proceeded to wash her body everywhere. She smiled as he focused so intently on her body. Then it was her turn. He was already semi-erect, and it only took a little teasing with the washcloth to finish the job. They didn't bother washing their hair, but spent many long minutes embracing again once they were clean. Stepping out of the shower, Bobby wrapped Hali in an incredibly soft towel and dried her off.

"I've never been washed since I was a baby" Hali said. "It feels nice to be pampered." She went over to the dresser and put on some ragged shorts and a T-shirt for pajamas.

"Sweetheart, you're going to get a lot more of that. Get used to it. Okay.... Your first gift from me will be some new pajamas to wear while you're training. After that, you probably won't be needing pajamas."

Hali grinned. "You're such a distraction! I look forward to that day. But right now, new pajamas would be much appreciated." She noticed that he was still quite naked, his erection had waned a tiny bit. She could fix that.

They walked over to Bobby's room hand in hand and locked the door. Bobby dimmed the lights, put on some easy listening soul music while she stood by the bed. When he came to her, she raised her arms and let him slip the tee-shirt over her head. He kissed her breasts, tickling the nipples to erection as his hands worked her shorts down. Once again naked, Hali turned, pulled back the covers of the queen-sized bed and climbed in followed by Bobby who laid down right beside her enveloping her in his arms. It didn't take long for both to become fully aroused, and their kisses quickly became more passionate. Hali returned his kisses passionately until she felt his lips move down to her neck, her breasts, her belly and finally to her special place. She stroked his hair as he teased her, feeling the passionate energy beginning to swell within her. She felt her hips thrusting in response to his kisses as the passion built in intensity until it finally exploded in a mind-numbing climax. She heard herself moaning and tried to stifle herself but failed. Bobby kept at it even after the climax passed until she had to pull his head back up to her face. She couldn't take any more. After a few minutes of cuddling to recover, he gave her a condom. Now it was her turn. Hali moved down to his semi-erect member and kissed and licked the sensitive tip bringing it to full glory within minutes. Sliding the prophylactic over his shaft and kissing it again to ensure that it stayed fully erect, Hali moved back up. She kissed him again deeply, then shifted her body and slid down, taking him quickly inside of her. He held her there on top of him, neither moving, just enjoying the sensual feeling of their naked flesh, his breath on her cheek. She wanted more. The passion was building again, but he held her motionless. Finally, she felt him start to push a little deeper into her and she responded. She tried to flex the muscles around her vagina, to grip him tightly. She felt him thrust deeply and slowly into her and tried to match him as much as her limited degree of freedom allowed. Her passion was getting intense now until she was squirming and trying to get more of him. He finally released her, and she sat up and began vigorously riding his erection, taking him as deep inside her as he could reach, then almost out of her. She felt her climax coming as she focused on the feeling in her loins, lost to the outside world. As her climax began to build, her thrusting became faster and faster until she finally exploded loudly, shudders running through her body, and then collapsed on top of him. She lay on him for several minutes trying to catch her breath. Bobby hadn't climaxed yet. She felt him rolling her over onto her back without disengaging. She gazed lovingly at his face as he made love to her. He was so focused, so intent, so damn good-looking and all hers! His thrusts were slow and deep at first, then faster as his climax approached. Hali's own passion hadn't waned much, and she met every thrust with her own. He groaned loudly as he exploded into her, paused for a minute or two to catch his breath, then continued slowly thrusting as his erection waned. He held her tightly as they recovered, and then withdrew, taking no chances that the condom might spill over. No pregnancies allowed. After disposing of the soiled condom and wiping up, Bobby settled on his back and pulled Hali onto his shoulder. They were both breathing hard.

It took Hali over ten minutes to catch her breath. "Oh my God, Baby! That was wonderful! You do that so well."

"I love you, Hali. You know that, right?" He said between deep breaths.

"Oh... I do. I've never felt so loved. By you and your whole family. I feel safe here in your arms. I know you'll always look after me. For some reason, I trusted you right from the start. It's not easy for a black girl to trust a white guy. Hell, it's not easy for any girl to trust any guy. But I trust you completely. I love you, Bobby LaRoche. I do. I just pray that you'll wait for me while I'm chasing my dream."

"I will, I promise you that. And hopefully, I'll be able to help you chase those dreams."

Hali felt tears in her eyes. "God, Bobby! You've already done so much for me. And your Dad is going to sponsor me. Suddenly I feel that the Olympics are within reach."

"They may be. They may not be. But we'll try to remove the roadblocks and open the doors, and if it was meant to be, then it'll happen. And if it doesn't work out, I'll still be immensely proud of you just for giving it your best shot. And I'll be looking forward to a lot more of this. You've got to take this opportunity, Hali. Very few people ever have a legitimate shot at the Olympics. It's up to you now."

"I know that. And I'll do everything I can possibly do. And I'll be happy when I come back to you, either way. For I have the best guy in the whole world. And I'll know I tried my best for the Olympics. And I have a bright future with you. I love you, Bobby LaRoche."

"I love you too, Hali. Good night, Sweetheart."

THE UNVEILING

11

Hali left at eight in the morning after a quick breakfast. She laughed when she discovered that Annette had made a lunch for her and even left a little note expressing her love. Just like home! Bobby was left with nothing to do until the unveiling in the afternoon. Moping around the house for a while, he finally decided to take the Laser out for a few hours. It had been almost five years since it last got wet. Out in his garage bay, he had to move all the stuff that had gotten placed on the boat and find all the parts. They were all there ready for him. He had two dry suits and a wet suit hanging in the back of the garage bay, but he had to climb over the ATV and the bikes to reach them. The wet suit was a men's size small and one of the dry suits was a medium. They wouldn't fit. They had been given to him back when he was in the youth sailing program. The dry suit might fit Hali. The other dry suit was a man's large, and he hoped he could still get into it. With a lot of trouble, he retrieved both dry suits, then tried on the larger one. It fit if he didn't wear the thick fleece body suit that came with it. The weather was gray and cool, and normally he would want the fleece. But maybe just some thermals would suffice.

By eleven, the Laser was floating and rigged, ready to push off. Having not touched a Laser in years, Bobby was a little apprehensive and overly cautious. But once he cleared the marina, he threw together a quick series of roll tacks, each one more aggressive than the last. Then he reversed course and tried the more dangerous roll gybes. After half a dozen, his confidence was back. Just like old times! He sailed out into Puget Sound loving the ten to twelve knot winds and the mild chop. Just enough wind to bring the boat to life and not enough to make it a work-out. Hiking hard, he made his way south against the wind, playing

the small waves and looking for someone, anyone to race against. There
were many sailboats out on Puget Sound, which was a bit surprising
considering the gray sky and the cool temperatures. As he worked south,
toward Ballard, he could see a race getting ready to start. But these were
bigger yachts, and way too far away to get there in time. Within an hour,
his abs were reminding him that he hadn't been sailing in years. When
he was sixteen and had been sailing every day for two years, he'd developed the perfect six-pack. He still had a flat stomach, but his six-pack
had fallen victim to way too many six-packs and not enough work. He
made a vow to get back into the Laser racing scene now that the boat was
done. He finally turned back towards Edmonds and ran with the wind.
There wasn't quite enough wind to plane, but by catching what waves
there were, ooching[11] his body and pumping the sheet[12] with each wave,
he was able to get the boat to break into an occasional surf. Working
the waves was one of his specialties, both upwind and down. He really
excelled when the wind and the waves were up. Or, at least he used to
back when he was fit. Just as he was approaching the marina, another
Laser and a Force Five came out to play. He sailed over and said hi, but
it was obvious that both sailors were new and not worthy opponents. The
Force Five was ancient and decrepit. So, he sailed on into the marina. It
would normally take only fifteen minutes to derig the boat and put her
on the trailer. But Bobby liked hanging around the marina, and so he
dawdled, chatted with some other sailors, and finally headed home a bit
before three. The sun finally broke out just as he arrived.

There wasn't much to do to set up for the cookout. The tables and
chairs were all kept at the ready out on the big back veranda, along with
the built-in grill. After rinsing off and putting away the Laser and hanging up the dry suit, he checked in with his Mom about any preparations
that needed his help. As usual, she had the situation well under control

---

[11] Ooching – using your body weight to propel the boat forward. Technically
illegal, the rules allow you to do it three times on order to catch a wave. It involves
shifting your weight forward slowly, then suddenly aft which throws the boat
forward.
[12] Sheet – The primary control rope used to haul the sail in closer to the centerline,
or to pay it out when running off wind.

and had even secretly made a carrot cake with a crude representation of the new boat inscribed in the icing. There were two ice chests full of beer and soda on the deck already. Hali texted him at three-thirty saying she was just off the ferry and would be there on time at four, traffic permitting. Bobby decided to take a quick dip in the hot tub, but with a suit on this time since the guests were due to arrive at any time. And they did arrive while he was still in the tub. Jessie and Ralph came over first. Jessie was well over-due now and was feeling every bit of it. She waddled over to a seat on the deck to rest her aching back. Ralph dutifully fetched her a wine cooler and stood by to fill any other needs or desires. She and Annette were talking about the upcoming birth, and names for the baby and preparations around the house. Annette was really looking forward to becoming a Grandma and intended to attend the birth. Bobby and Ralph listened in on the girl talk silently until Frank and Jerry came over together. That brought Gerald out. Immediately, the beers started popping and man-chatter ensued. It was time for Bobby to go up and get dressed. When he returned, he pulled everyone aside one by one to tell them about how he had planned the unveiling. Hali was the last to arrive, still in her sweats. Bobby embraced her and they kissed, upon which he heard Annette comment "It warms my heart to see Bobby with Hali. That's a side of him that I've never seen before." Everyone chatted, nibbled on chips and pretzels, and just chatted for a while waiting for Bobby's cue, which came shortly after four-thirty. He made his way over to his Dad who had been chatting with Frank about his latest projects. Frank shut up as Bobby approached and wandered slowly off towards the garage with Jerry.

"Hey, Dad. A while ago I went out to the shop to use the lathe and I found it buried under a lot of wood. So, I checked out what you were building, and I eventually found your plans for the boat. It's an interesting design."

Gerald looked pained. "Yeah… I wanted to do the Race to Alaska with it. Maybe next year."

"That's what Mom told me. I've been looking at the plans for a while, and I have some suggestions for changes."

"Really?" Gerald smiled. "I've worked on those plans for well over a year, consulted two different naval architects, and you think you can do better? Just like that?"

"Well, they're only suggestions. Can I show them to you before you diss them completely?"

"Okay, but let's make it quick. I'm hungry and we have guests."

As if on cue, a man and a woman appeared walking up the driveway into the back yard. They were the two naval architects that had helped design the boat.

"Arch! Traci! What are you guys doing here?"

"Well, we were in the neighborhood and decided to stop by and see your progress on the boat."

"Oh... You hadn't heard" Gerald replied. "Sorry to disappoint you, but I didn't build it. I had a stroke and was in recovery all fall and winter. I haven't gotten back to it yet. Maybe I'll start this summer. But you're welcome to stay for some beer and some tri-tip. Hey, everyone! I'd like to introduce some friends of mine who helped me design my sailboat. This is Archie Wilson and Traci Dougherty, both naval architects."

Beers were handed out as everyone was introduced. Frank and Jerry were missing though.

"I'm sorry to hear about your stroke" Archie said. "But I'm damned happy to see you up and about and mostly fully recovered. You're looking really good for what you've been through."

"Thanks. I've been working out every single day to some degree. I'm almost back to one hundred percent" Gerald replied. "So, this young whipper-snapper here thinks he has some improvements on our design. He thinks he can do better than two professional naval architects."

"Well, yes I do" Bobby said. "And I don't think you'll argue my point. Let's go out to the shop and I'll show you what I mean."

The four of them started walking towards the garage, with everyone else trailing a few steps back, knowing exactly what to expect. Gerald didn't notice. As they neared the shop, Frank suddenly threw open the garage door, and a moment later the finished boat emerged from the shop being pushed out on her trailer by Jerry. Her polished woodwork gleamed in the sunshine and everybody clapped. Everyone except Gerald and the naval architects had already seen the boat indoors. But in the sunshine, everyone's refection was mirrored in the polished varnish. Gerald was stunned. The crowd surrounded it and admired the beautiful cedar hull. Everyone was commenting about how gorgeous it was.

"What?!! What the Hell?! That's my boat! What did you do, Bobby?"

"Well, I built her for you, Dad. Mom said that you had your heart set on doing the Race to Alaska, so I built you a boat. Your own boat. You couldn't very well build it yourself while you were recovering. And now it's too late to get started. So, here's your ride. You can still do the race this year."

"Oh, shit! Bobby! Shit! This is too much! And you did such a great job on her. How'd you ever learn to build cedar strip boats?"

"The same way you did. I read the books in your office. I just figured it out. It wasn't really that hard, except for a few areas."

"This is stupendous, Bobby! And she's incredibly beautiful! You did a wonderful job on her. I couldn't have done half as good a job as you did."

"Well, that's definitely true" Bobby said, to much laughter. "Take a good look at her, then we'll talk about my modifications."

Gerald walked around the boat lovingly caressing her almost like a new baby. He lifted the hatches and peered inside. He noted the pedal drive unit and the recumbent seat. He caressed the carbon fiber keel and looked underneath at the bulb.

"You did not make this keel. That's obviously professional. Nor this seat."

"I did make the keel. That was one of the hardest parts. Took me a lot of research online. The seat came off a recumbent bike, and I had the mount custom fabricated. It mounts on the sides as well so you can sail comfortably all day. That's one of my modifications. The pedal drive is another."

"That's thinking. Good for you. What the hell is this?" He was pointing to a black mark on the edge of the deck.

"That's a roach. It's my symbol. That's what they called me on the circuit. I built her, so I put my mark on her."

He laughed. "Fair enough, though I wish it were something else, like an orca or a seal. Roaches are a nuisance."

"Yeah... but I bet I fit that description when I was younger." Everyone laughed again. "I put the pedal drive unit up front of the keel so your weight would be centered as you pedal, and you can still use the rudder. But I had to move the keel aft by ten inches to do it, and that meant that I had to rake the mast a bit to compensate. Traci helped me and she said more rake might make the boat go to weather a little better. I made a plug to fill up the hole for the drive unit, so it doesn't create any drag at all when you're sailing. And I have a dodger with a removable cockpit cover being made for her so you can get out of the rain at night. It'll have windows so you can pedal in the rain without getting wet. And I took the sail back to North and had the bolt rope[13] removed and replaced with nylon slides. That way it stays attached to the mast when you reef or lower the sail. Easier to manage that way."

"Good idea. All of them. God, Bobby! You did such a good job! I wish I had been able to help you."

"I talked to Mom about that and she said that you were already working out too much. She just wanted you to focus on getting better. She said that you'd probably play hooky if you had a boat to work on."

He laughed. "Well, she knows me too well. What's left to be done?"

"Not that much. I just finished the rudder. I need to mount the pintles[14] and the tiller. I need to rig the wishboom. Connect the lights, autopilot, solar panels. Just a lot of little things. I'll finish the boat. You need to start planning the trip."

"Do you know how much she weighs?" Traci asked.

"Just the hull alone is a 130 pounds. Add the ninety-five-pound keel and you have 225."

"That's close to the design weight" she commented. "The keel is a few pounds heavier, but the hull is right on."

---

[13] Bolt rope – A piece of rope that is sewn into the hem of a sail along the leading edge. It slides into a groove in the mast to hold the sail against the mast.

[14] Pintles – One half of the rudder hinge system, the other half being the gudgeons. The pintles have the hinge pins.

"When can we splash her?" His Dad asked.

"Well, let's plan for next week and see where we are."

"I'd like to help you do the final rigging. I need to get to know my baby."

"Sure. I'd like that."

"And... Bobby, what you did... I can't find the words. It's just so... just so special, so tremendous. I can't thank you enough."

Clutching Hali to his side, he responded "You already did by offering to help Hali in her Olympic dream. That means more to me and to her than we can ever express. We're even."

"Bobby, I'm so immensely proud of you. And I love Hali, too. You are both incredibly special and you deserve each other." He had tears in his eyes as he hugged them both in a great big bear hug, then turned away to examine the boat with Traci and Archie. His boat. They raised the mast, and then the sail after fussing with the battens for a while. The wishboom wasn't rigged, so they just held the sail out and looked at it from all angles. Bobby and Hali backed away, watching him lovingly play with his new toy, then turned and headed for the grill. They had work to do and hungry mouths to feed. The rest were already back to their beers.

"Everybody, thanks for coming today, and thanks for helping me pull this off. I think Dad's moved."

"Moved?!" Annette said. "That's an understatement!"

"I wouldn't have missed this for the world, Bobby" Frank said. "You're a real craftsman. Are you sure you want to go into business?"

"The boat is gorgeous, Bobby" Jessie chimed in. "She's a work of art."

"It is that" said Annette. "Bobby did a wonderful thing by building it for Gerald, and he did an incredible job on it."

"Good job, Bobby" Jerry said, clapping him on the back. "A hell of a good job. You're a good son."

"Thank you again, everyone. It means so much to me to see his eyes light up like that. He's done so much for me, and now for Hali. It's just a small token. But now I have tri-tip to cook. Someone pass me a Coors, would you? And one for Hali. Unless you'd rather have a wine cooler?" He asked her. She took the beer.

As Hali and Bobby stood by the grill searing the meat and drinking their beer, Hali put her arms around him and held him tightly. "I've never met anyone like you, Bobby. What you did for your Dad is just so incredible. And what you are doing for me... well, I can't even describe it. I am so in love with you, Bobby. I just can't hold myself back. You're everything to me. Next week I want you to meet my parents, okay? I'm so excited, I just can't contain myself. Please say you'll come over."

"Of course I will, Hali. I'm really looking forward to it. Have you talked to them about me?"

"Oh, yeah! At least with Mommy. And I'm sure she talked to Daddy. From day one. Before we were a couple even. On the way down to Lacey. I was so excited even back then about meeting you. And it's only gotten better ever since. And I've been telling Mommy the blow by blow. She laughs at me for being so out of control over a guy. At first, she cautioned me about dating a white guy. Same with Dad. They thought that you would just use me and leave me. And I suppose that's what I thought of all guys, but especially white guys before I met you. But you're special, Bobby. I knew it the night we met. I trusted you completely. I don't even trust my own brother that much."

He smiled. "I knew you were special that night myself. I didn't know it would blossom to this. I certainly wasn't looking for it. But I was drawn to you. We talk so well. I'm starting to think we were fated for each other. I love you, Hali. And I'll be happy to meet your parents. And if that goes well, then I'd like to invite them over here. Do they know you're living here now?"

"Yeah. I told them. I told them we each had our own rooms, but Mommy just laughed. She knows."

That night they went upstairs early, around eight-thirty, while Jessie and Ralph were still talking in the living room with Annette about the baby. Davie was already in the tub, chanting or singing or just talking to himself pleasantly. One was never quite sure. Bobby and Hali went up to her room and showered together. Once clean, they just embraced under the hot water.

"This is so decadent, Bobby."

"Wealth has its rewards. I love this house. I'm hoping to inherit it when my parents are gone, though hopefully that's a long way off."

"Bobby, can I sleep with you again tonight?"

"I have to get up at four forty-five. You should sleep in your own bed tonight. We have Fridays and Saturdays together."

"Alright, but can I just snuggle with you for a while?"

"You never have to ask, Hali. My door it always unlocked unless you're with me. Are you sure snuggling is all you want?"

"No, I'm not. I want you to make love to me like you did last night. You are just so incredible, and you make me feel so special."

"You are special, Hali. I couldn't make love to any other woman the way I make love to you. But don't worry, I won't be making love to any other women. You're it for me. I'm totally smitten with you."

They both dried off and went to Bobby's room naked and locked the door. Their passion was even greater than yesterday, and they made love with much more intensity. They didn't even try to stifle their moans and groans as they climaxed. Hali snuggled in Bobby's arms until he started to doze off, then reluctantly went back to her own familiar bed. Once settled in, she realized just how bad her mattress really was. Bobby was right. She needed a new mattress. She wanted to buy it herself, but she had far more debt than cash. And Bobby seemed to like to buy her things. This next weekend......

NEW FRIENDS

12

Over the next week, Hali's schedule started to settle down and become more routine. She would get up around six-thirty, long after Bobby had started his workday, then eat a hearty breakfast with the family. Off to work at seven-thirty with a bag lunch lovingly packed by Annette, then back home by four-fifteen for a special high protein supper again prepared by Annette. She'd get maybe an hour or so with Bobby as she ate, then off to work out from six to nine every day. By the time she got home at nine-thirty or later, Bobby was already in bed. Most often, she'd behave and just go shower and go to bed. But occasionally she would sneak into Bobby's bed for some snuggles. Sometimes, Bobby didn't even wake up.

Bobby had some catching up to do with his schoolwork due to the recent focus on completing the boat. He had decided to just stay with online classes for the spring, and maybe an independent project over the summer, then start real classes in the Fall. He had done very well in his fall and winter online classes. His new focus on getting his degree and starting work with his Dad suddenly made accounting classes less boring. He got A's in both classes, which is good because he had to raise his GPA if he wanted any chance of being accepted into the MBA program at the University of Washington. And he had an idea about his independent project. It involved researching what it would take to start a Ford dealership.

He worked through the week with his Dad to finish up the boat. The big day was Friday when they finally stepped the mast and raised the sail. They spent all evening rigging the reefing points, attaching all the last blocks now that the final position could be determined and cutting all the control lines off to the correct length. By the time Hali came home, the boat was back in the shop buttoned up and ready to launch. Bobby would be the test skipper, and since he was busy on Saturday, the splash day would be Sunday, the eighth. Dad was excited to get the boat on the water. Bobby was also excited because this was Friday night and he'd get to spend the night with Hali. And, because this was the big weekend.

Hali awoke much earlier than she wanted to on Saturday morning when Bobby stirred beside her. Bobby was used to waking up early. She shifted herself closer to his warm body and pulled his arm around her. She felt safe in his arms as she spooned with him and loved to feel his hand lovingly caressing her breast. He was awake. She could tell by his breathing. He just lay quietly next to her holding her gently. Hali had never felt this securely in love before. There was no doubt that she was loved in return. Further sleep wasn't going to happen, but she just lay there and dozed contentedly in the comfort of his arms. This was heaven for her. Eventually, her bladder reminded her that it was time to get up. She sat up on the side of Bobby's incredibly comfortable bed and looked down at him. He was wide awake and just gazed back at her with his big soulful blue eyes and a coy little smile. God, he was such an irresistible guy! She bent over and kissed him, a nice long passionate good morning kiss, then stood up. She hadn't worn anything when she came directly from the shower to his bed, but now the family was up and about. She thought briefly about borrowing one of Bobby's tee-shirts, but then just dismissed that idea. It was only a few steps down the hall to her room. She cracked open the door and saw no one. She stuck her head out of the door and saw no one. No problem. She quickly stepped out of Bobby's room stark naked and walked quickly towards her door. She almost made it. As she crossed the stairway, there was Annette coming up the stairs. Busted!

"Good morning, Hali! Go get some clothes on. We're going shopping today."

"Uhhh... Shopping? For what?".

"Furniture, Dear! We're going to fix your room up really nice!"

"Annette, you're such a sweetheart! But you don't need to spend money on me. I'm used to old stuff."

"Hush, Dear! We were going to have to buy furniture for that room sooner or later anyway. This way you and I get to go shopping together and we can set it up just the way you like. Hurry up, Hali, and get dressed. You can't go out like that! I'll have your breakfast on the table in ten minutes. And get that lazy guy of yours out of bed also!"

Hali laughed. "Does Bobby get to come as well?"

"If you insist. But this is a me and you shopping trip. He can keep his trap closed and just carry our purchases."

"Okay, Annette. I'll be down in a minute or two."

After a hearty breakfast of a Denver omelet and Canadian bacon washed down with coffee and cranberry juice, Hali and Annette set off to go shopping hand in hand with Bobby trailing behind. Hali essentially had to part with all her worldly possessions. It was all second-hand stuff anyway, things she'd collected while a student at the University of Washington. Some of it was left in the apartment by the previous renters, some of it given to her by friends who were moving on. Other than her bed, which had been hers for her entire life, she had been given all of it. It had sentimental value, but that was the extent of it all. They shopped for a mattress first, and Hali was shocked by how much a good quality box spring and mattress cost. They were so comfortable, though! She argued that a queen-size like the one in Bobby's room was perfectly adequate, but Annette insisted on a king. She kept hiding the price tags from Hali so she wouldn't focus on the cost. After lying on seven or eight mattresses, Hali finally selected a soft pillow top set. Annette paid for it without telling her that the cost was well over 2500 dollars. And that was a discounted price. They didn't have a sale going on, but Bobby had talked the salesman into giving them a fifteen percent discount. The salesman didn't blink at the offer. Bobby felt like he should have asked for more. It would be delivered on Tuesday and they would even dispose of the old mattress for them. That whole process had only used up two hours, so off they went to shop for furniture.

With Annette still holding Hali's hand and Bobby trailing behind, they cruised through three different furniture stores without seeing anything that caught their eye. But right after grabbing a sandwich at Subway, they found a store that had a style of bedroom furniture that appealed to both Hali and Annette. They picked out a sleigh bed. Not exactly what Bobby would have chosen, but it was Hali's room after all. Annette bought the whole room full of matching furniture. This included two end tables with lamps, a big dresser with a large wall-hung mirror, a chest of drawers (for Bobby's clothes whenever they get a chance to live together), a desk and chair, two large bookshelves and even a leather recliner with a reading lamp. It would all be delivered and set up this week.

The next stop was Macy's for sheets, blankets, pillows, and a comforter. Annette had plenty to spare, but Bobby wanted Hali to have fresh new stuff and a pattern to fit her own taste, and Annette didn't argue. Hali needed a place she could call her own. Annette had her own reasons to make sure Hali was comfortable living with them. Hali picked a gold and brown and deep red earth tone motif with a faintly Aztec pattern for the comforter and matching gold sheets, again not what Bobby would have chosen. It came with the bed skirt and two throw pillow covers, and they selected matching drapes to complete the look. Hali was finally getting over the cost of nice furnishings, and she and Annette were having a great time shopping together. They loaded everything up into a cart, then Bobby dragged her and Annette upstairs to the women's department and made her pick out four sets of comfortable, yet very feminine pajamas. Nothing sexy like lingerie, but just nice comfortable pajamas that looked very feminine and pretty. They loaded it all into Annette's *Escalade* and she drove off back home. With about an hour to spare, they stopped at a frame shop and went through all the wall art that was available. But Hali, after looking through the available prints, decided against getting any. She wanted to commission Davie to do some large original paintings for her room. She'd pick the photographs for him to copy, buy him a couple of huge canvasses and turn him loose. Then they dashed off to Hali's folk's place.

The Abara's owned a small but nice condominium in Lynnhaven, a short drive away. They found a parking stall in the underground lot and took the steps up four flights to the third floor. Hali knocked instead of just walking in. They were greeted at the door by both of Hali's parents and great big toothy grins. Hali's Mom, a very stout woman, wrapped them both in a huge bear hug.

"Halima! So good to see you, Honey! And you must be Bobby! My, what a good lookin' fellow you are! Don't just stand there! Come on in! Get outta their way, Zane!"

"Pleasure meeting you, Mrs. and Mr. Abara."

"Psshht... Stop that right now! My name is Asha, and this here is Zane. Now that we're retired, we don't use surnames much anymore. Kellan will be here shortly. He's always late. Come sit down here in the living room."

"Daddy was a Master-Chief in the Navy" Hali said. "He served for twenty-two years before he retired, then worked as a contracting officer for another twenty years before he retired for good last year."

"Really? Thanks for your service. Should I call you Master-Chief?" Bobby replied.

Zane laughed. "If you like. Once a Chief, always a Chief, I suppose. But you'd be about the only one that still calls me that. Zane will do fine. Hali tells me that you're in school at the U. Whatcha studying?"

"Ohhh... business. Dad's paying for it and he wants me to take over the family business. It's really kind of boring, but he's done really well and it's a straight shot for me to do really well also."

Kellan came in without knocking and sauntered into the living room. Bobby stood up, shook hands, and introduced himself. Hali gave him a big hug.

"Kelly, I want you to get to know my guy here. He's the best!" Kellan eyed Bobby suspiciously but nodded and sat down."

"Bobby just finished building a sailboat for his Dad!" Hali gushed. "It was a surprise and we just had the unveiling last Sunday. He was so thrilled!"

"What Hali left out is that my Dad had a stroke last August. He was laid up in the hospital and the recovery center for almost six months. He was planning on building the boat himself so he could race it to Alaska this June. He's been dreaming of it for over a year. So, when he was hospitalized, I decided to build it for him so it would be ready when he recovered. I took some pictures of it... here check these out." He handed them his phone.

"Hali told me all about it. I was hoping you'd bring some photos. This is beautiful, Bobby! You're a real craftsman. Very thoughtful of you. What a good son! What do you think of that, Zane?"

"Nice! And you said he plans to race it to Alaska?"

"Yes sir. It's the Race to Alaska, from Port Townsend to Ketchikan with no motors or outside support allowed. It's 750 miles altogether. Mostly sail boats, but some kayaks and rowboats. Last year a guy made it all the way on a paddle board. This boat is self-bailing, has watertight compartments for gear, and room on the deck to sleep. There's a cockpit cover coming that will allow the skipper to get out of the rain. The race starts this June."

"You said he had a stroke? Has he recovered completely?"

"Almost. He's getting there. He still has some weakness on his right side, but he's getting stronger every day. Hasn't affected his thinking, and he can talk clearly, finally. He'll get to sail the boat tomorrow, so we'll see how well he does."

"Well, wish him luck from us" Zane said. "I'd never do that unless it was painted Hades gray and at least 400 feet long."

Bobby smiled. "I'll do that. Even if he doesn't race, building the boat was a blast. Since I built her for him, it won't be the lack of a boat that stops him. I did what I could."

"You're a good son" Asha said again. "I'm sure he appreciates it dearly."

"Oh, he does. Brought tears to his eyes, and I almost never see him cry."

"And now he's going to sponsor my Halima? What a great man!"

"Hali is special. He recognized that right off the bat. I saw it when I watched her play and she defeated Team USA. She's fierce! And she can jump higher than I've ever seen anyone jump. It's so much fun watching other players underestimate her and try to slam the ball at her only to have it smacked right back in their face. My Dad had his own Olympic aspirations that never gained traction. By sponsoring Hali, he's living his dreams vicariously. He's going to line up sponsors for her. He knows everyone in the business world around here. And just about every business sponsors some sports team, even if it's only Little Leaguers."

"Yeah, but Hali's black" Kellan spoke up for the first time. "No one around here is going to donate to her. White people don't give a shit about black athletes."

"Well, sadly, there's an element of truth to that. I think blacks only make up about, what, maybe ten percent of the population in the northwest?" Bobby replied. "Maybe some people won't contribute just because she's black. And maybe she wouldn't want their money anyway. But my Dad's betting that he can get enough people that care more about performance than skin color to donate. Beating Team USA, not once but twice now speaks volumes. Hali's the defending National Champion and she's earned a berth again this year. She and Courtney beat the Japanese and the Chinese last year and those were the top-ranked teams in the world. And my Dad can be very persuasive. He's a car salesman after all."

"Your Dad sells cars?" Kellan asked. "I thought he was rich."

"He owns LaRoche Auto Group" Bobby replied. "He's doing really well. He's got Cadillac, Ram truck and Chevrolet dealerships, not to mention his used car business. Yeah, he's wealthy. But he didn't start out wealthy. He had to work his way through college to get his business degree, then opened a little shop detailing cars. That turned into a used car lot. And that turned into a dealership. Then two more. It took him thirty years, but now he can do whatever he wants."

"I bet he wouldn't hire a black man like me" Kellan said.

"Well... Not with that attitude he wouldn't. But if you were a well-dressed, free-thinking black man with a smooth tongue and a knowledge of cars, he certainly would. He has several black and Hispanic salesmen. He has a lot of black and Hispanic technicians. He even has a program where he will sponsor you through trade school, but you've got to agree to work for him for five years afterwards. At a decent salary, mind you. It's a program targeting under-privileged youth, mostly blacks and Hispanics. He's trying to get other businesses to do likewise. A couple of other dealerships have similar programs because of him. So, don't go calling him bigoted, or prejudiced. He's done a lot for minorities. And they end up becoming his most loyal employees since they appreciate what he's done for them. He's not color-blind at all. He sees the challenges minorities face and he's doing his share to help. He's a good man. Same with my Uncle Frank. He didn't even go to college. He started working at a factory when he got out of high school, rose through the ranks into management and eventually bought the factory when it was in a down phase and about to go under. Turned it around and made a fortune. He also hires a lot of minorities. I bet half his employees are minorities. I work there. When you work in a factory, skin color doesn't matter at all. It's all about production numbers. I happen to own a lot of the production records. If you're looking for work, and you're willing to bust your ass and you can check the attitude at the door, I'll bet he would hire you. Especially if I recommend you."

"You'd do that? You don't even know me."

"You just need to promise me that you'll check the attitude. Not all white folk are bigots. My folks love Hali like a daughter."

"Yeah, Annette makes me lunch every day" Hali cut in, "and puts little notes of affirmation in with my sandwich. The LaRoche's are the most loving and caring people I ever met. I feel like I'm part of the family living with them."

"And are you behaving yourself, Honey?" Asha asked jovially.

Hali blushed. "Occasionally. Bobby's bed is so much more comfortable than mine."

They all laughed. "My Mom took Hali out on a shopping spree and bought all new bedroom furniture for her room today" Bobby said. "I had a great time watching them. Mom was like a little girl on Christmas day. They got a big sleigh bed and nice quality mattress. Comforter, pillows, sheets, even matching drapes. Dressers, end tables, lamps, desk, bookshelves, the whole works. Mom had a great time shopping with

Hali. I think she's found a new daughter. Her room is going to be really nice when it's all delivered and set up."

"But I bet she'll still be sneaking off to your room..." Asha laughed.

Bobby blushed a bit, looking at Hali. "Or vice-versa. Usually, we only get to sleep together on Friday and Saturday. I've got to get up at five-fifteen during the week and go to bed at nine. So, she just leaves me alone."

"That's what he thinks! Sometimes I sneak in and snuggle and most times he doesn't even wake up!"

They all laughed.

"My brother hogs the bathroom right when I need to use it, so I've been using the shower in her room. It's usually before she comes home, though.

"Oh, I love Davie" Hali gushed. "He's so funny. He has Down syndrome. He's so innocent and child-like even though he's all grown up. He's an artist and a poet and he does incredible stuff."

"That's what everyone says," Bobby said "and he's even had some poems published in the paper. Personally, I just think they're silly, but they're funny when you first read them. You've got to read them out loud to get the full effect. He just makes up words. His art is very childish and two-dimensional, but unbelievably detailed and he uses very bold, primary colors. I've seen a lot worse in art museums worth tens of thousands of dollars. I suspect that one day, he'll be discovered as an art savant or something. They'll name a whole new style after him."

"I take it your Mom is his care-giver? So, she doesn't work?" Asha asked.

"Yes, ma'am. She used to work with my Dad until Davie was born. That's when she decided that his care was more important than the extra money. Funny thing is, right about the time she stopped working, my Dad started to get successful. They didn't need the additional earnings after all."

"God has a plan for all of us. Do you go to church, Bobby?"

"Yes ma'am. Maybe not as much as I should. We belong to a Lutheran church in Edmonds. I have a bad habit of finding excuses not to go. Building the boat gave me plenty of excuses. But my parents go just about every week. You guys are Baptist, right?"

"Yes. You're welcome to come to services with us some day."

"I'm guessing that Hali will make that happen before much longer."

"So, tell me" Zane said. "How much money is Hali going to need to get to the Olympics?"

"I have no idea... Maybe several hundred thousand. But once she gets selected to the national team, they'll cover a lot of her expenses. We need to get her sponsored until then and fill in the gaps that the national team doesn't cover. I'm thinking fifty to seventy-five thousand roughly to get her started. Maybe a hundred. Maybe even more. Maybe less. Sponsorships will start rolling in when she gets better known. She needs to start winning international tournaments."

"And your Dad is willing to give this to her?"

"Yes and no" Bobby answered. "His company is sponsoring her and committing to the full cost whatever that may be. But they are going to get assistance from a lot of other businesses. Hali will be busy traveling around the city, talking on the radio and TV, and signing autographs. She'll have to stop working before too much longer. I'll bet that Dad's company will front maybe half of the total. By letting her stay with us for free, she just freed up maybe twenty grand that she can use towards her career. But she still must earn her way into the Olympics. Dad's opening the doors that need to be opened, but Hali still must defeat the best in the world. That's a tall order. But this is the only chance she'll ever get. And she'll regret it for the rest of her life if she doesn't go for it. She may not make it, and that's okay. At least she'll know she gave it her best shot. She can worry about her professional career later."

"Bobby used to be a professional motorcycle rider until he got hurt and had to retire" Hali said. "Now he's back in school focused on his professional career."

"What kind of bikes?" Kellan asked.

"Motocross. Dirt bikes. 125s and 250s. Both of mine are Kawasaki's. They sponsored me. I just raced in the US. The big money is in Europe, but I never got that kind of sponsorship."

"That's cool, man. I'd like learn to ride."

"Well, I have two bikes and an ATV. The ATV is super easy to learn. I can have you riding that in five minutes. The bikes are super high performance two strokes, so you need to be careful when the power band comes on. My 250 needs some minor repairs after my wreck, but if you and Hali want to go out riding, I'll get it fixed and we can go out to a field somewhere. Somewhere where you won't drive into a tree."

"Kellan, you should see his ride" Hali cut in. "I don't even like fancy cars, but he built this one himself, so I love it. It has his personality in it everywhere. He even painted it himself."

"You can do that?" Kellan answered. "Let's go check it out."

"That'll have to be another day" Bobby answered grinning. "We left it at home and brought the Honda, gets better gas mileage than the truck. I'll bring it over the next time I come over."

"It's a truck? That's cool, man. I got a turbo Honda Civic."

"Honda's are hot. And, easy to work on as we found out when we rebuilt Hali's car. The truck is a 1966 with a big 396 pumping 500 horsepower. It'll pass everything on the freeway except a gas station. I painted it opal white. It's a cool ride. My uncle Frank taught me how to restore it and build the engine. I should probably get something like a Civic that gets better gas mileage and just show the truck."

They talked on through dinner and all evening, and when Hali and Bobby got home at nine-thirty, they went straight to the hot tub without worrying about suits. Bobby's Mom and Dad were still up and about, but the curtains were closed, and they didn't really care that much anyway. After showering, they made love gently and quietly before falling asleep in each other's arms.

SPLASH DAY

13

Sunday was the big day for the boat. After a big breakfast, Hali and Bobby pulled out the boat and hooked it up to the truck. Hali tried on Bobby's old dry suit, and it fit well enough, even with the fleece liner. Being a man's suit, it didn't enhance her female form in any way, but it would keep her warm and dry. Since the temperature wouldn't likely exceed sixty, Hali wore the fleece. Bobby just had to make do with thermals. Eventually, all was loaded by nine and they were off. Annette and Gerald were off at church. The ride to the marina was uneventful, as was the launch. There was only one other boater ahead of them at the ramp, which was a bit unusual. By the time they had paid their launch fee, the ramp was clear. The boat slipped off the trailer with no fuss and waited expectantly for them to drop the keel and raise the mast. They did that quickly before taking the trailer and truck away to the parking lot. There were already several boats waiting to launch. The first test was the pedal drive unit. So, Bobby threw the sail bag into the boat, and rigged the rudder, tiller, and the steering ropes that he had devised so the skipper can steer while pedaling. Once all was set, he sat Hali in the seat, pushed off and let her pedal away. She drove off quickly, turned down the length of the marina and disappeared. Bobby paced impatiently on the dock for her expecting her only to make a quick trial trip. It was a long twenty minutes later before she was back, and Bobby waved her over to a spot on the guest dock. She was grinning.

"That was fun, Bobby. I got a lot of looks as I went by all the boats."

"Probably at you as much as at the boat. You were going really fast. You didn't have to pedal that hard."

"I wasn't. I could have kept that up for hours. The pedal drive is amazing! It's almost silent. And so fast!"

"So, in your opinion, did the pedal drive pass the test?"

"Oh, hell yes! It would be fun just to go out without the mast and cruise around."

"Are you ready to try sailing?"

"You'll do the sailing! I'm just along for the ride."

"I wish the wind were stronger. But I suppose it's good for my Dad if it stays like this later on."

They walked the boat along the dock to a spot where she was head to wind, fumbled with the full-length battens[15] trying to get them into their individual pockets, then raised the sail. They didn't bother with the reef pennants[16] since the wind was less than ten knots. They simply lashed the clew[17] to the end of the wishboom, adjusted the choker[18] and they were ready. The wishboom rig did away with a traveler[19] and the boomvang[20], leaving the cockpit completely uncluttered. Hali climbed aboard carefully first, clutching the sides as the boat rocked under her weight, followed by Bobby as he pushed off from the dock. He hauled in the sheet, and the boat heeled slightly and gathered momentum. Within moments, Bobby had her up to speed and flying down the marina fairway heading for open water beyond.

"Damn, Bobby! We're going so fast! And this is just from the wind?"

---

[15] Battens – Fiberglass (usually) sticks which are inserted into pockets sewn into the sail to help support the sail and maintain a good air foil shape.

[16] Reef Pennants – ropes that are used to reduce the size of the sail when the wind gets too high. The sail is lowered a bit and the extra sail cloth along the bottom is bundled up making the overall sail smaller.

[17] Clew – outer corner of the sail furthest from the mast

[18] Choker – a rope that is used to push the wishbone aft, thereby stretching the sail and making it flatter. Boats with conventional booms have outhauls instead.

[19] Traveler – A track running transversely across the cockpit that the main sheet block mounts to. Adjusting the traveler allows the skipper to adjust the angle of the sail relative to the wind (angle of attack) without having to adjust the sheet.

[20] Boomvang – a control, often just a block and tackle on small boats, that runs between the base of the mast and the boom to keep the boom from rising as wind fills the sail.

"Yep! Just the wind, and she'll go a lot faster than this when the wind comes up stronger. This is good for your first ride, though. I don't want to scare you away. But I've been out in some pretty gnarly stuff."

"What do you do when the wind gets too strong?"

"Well, we can reef the sail. See those grommets on the sail? We can lower the sail and bundle up the bottom making the sail smaller. Notice there's two rows of grommets? We can do it twice. That would make the sail tiny. I think we're probably good for up to thirty knots."

"And what do you do when the wind gets higher than that?"

"A prudent mariner would seek shelter."

"What would you do?"

"Depends on the boat I'm sailing and the location. I used to travel all the way down to the Columbia River Gorge just so I could practice in heavy air. It's often well over thirty knots down there. It's fun, especially down wind. But it's exhausting and you break things. You don't do that when your life depends on your boat."

"What would you do then?"

"Hopefully avoid it by checking the weather forecast. If I got caught, hopefully I'll recognize what was coming and seek shelter before it gets to me. And if I were totally out of touch with the weather and I got slammed, then I'd reef twice and run downwind until I found shelter. If I had one, I could always lower all my sails and throw out a sea anchor and just wait it out."

"What's a sea anchor?"

"It's kind of like a bucket tied to the end of your anchor line. It fills with water as the wind blows your boat downwind and just holds the bow into the wind. You still drift, but the bow rides nicely over the waves and it's fairly safe. That is, as long as there is plenty of sea room behind you."

"I can't believe we're moving so fast! This is really cool, Bobby! And so quiet, and peaceful. It's really fun."

Bobby drove the boat to windward easily against a very faint swell. He was using the seat on the port side, with Hali sitting on the side deck next to him as they sailed away from the marina on port tack. The boat was moving to windward at three and a half knots, riding easily over the slight waves. The helm was nicely balanced[21] with just a bit of windward helm. He tacked very slowly though the wind since he had to move the seat to the other side, and Hali was kind of in the way. It would be far easier alone. Finally, the boat accelerated off on starboard tack as they headed back to shore. The boat was obviously fast, but there were no other boats to compare it to. Hali was uncomfortable during the tack, but once the boat settled on the next tack, she was loving it again. They sailed all the way to the shore and tacked again. This time it went better since Hali knew what to expect. She moved the seat across as Bobby turned the boat. Once they got the boat up to speed again to windward, Bobby turned the boat and bore away[22] downwind. Going with the wind felt almost calm. They sat on opposite sides to balance the boat as they cruised slowly back towards the marina. Bobby did his best to surf the swells, but eight knots of breeze barely produces ripples. Hali was just relaxing and enjoying the easy rhythm of the boat as she sailed on slowly. At a little before one, they gybed and turned into the marina fairway in time to meet Gerald standing on the dock.

"How was it, Son?"

"Well, not near enough wind for my taste. But she sails very well to windward. Hali liked it being nice and calm. Helm was nicely balanced. Good day for your first sail. Light and easy."

"I'm looking forward to it. Let me have your dry suit and life jacket and I'll be off."

Bobby peeled them off and handed them to his Dad, who was slightly smaller and could fit into the fleece as well. Bobby was suddenly chilly clad only in his thermals and shorts. So, he hurried Gerald along as much as he could, pushed him off and scurried back to this truck with Hali where he had some more clothes. They watched Gerald sail

---

[21] Balanced Helm – a rudder is balanced when there is little pressure on the tiller. Skippers usually want a bit of windward helm, which means that the boat tends to turn up into the wind if you let go of the tiller. A lot of pressure on the helm means that the rudder is being dragged through the water at a steep angle acting like a brake.

[22] Bear-away – to turn the sailboat away from the direction of the wind

away through the binoculars, making a couple of slow tacks, but sailing well enough. Hali changed in the truck with a little help from Bobby. Getting out of a drysuit presents challenges. Wetsuits are even worse. They finally went for a long walk along the waterfront in the direction Gerald was sailing keeping an eye on him.

"Bobby, I just like being with you, you know that?"

"Mmmm... I do. I like just hangin' with you as well. Did you really like sailing?"

"I did! It was so exciting, but peaceful and quiet at the same time! I love how the boat just glides along serenely."

"Well, it's not always like that. Sometimes it's boring when there's no wind. Sometimes you're hanging on for dear life when there's a lot. I like the high wind stuff, what I call white-knuckle sailing. Screaming along on a plane, with as much water coming over the boat as going under it. Lots of work going to windward, but a blast off the wind. Gybes can be terrifying, and that's what's so fun for me. I love the adrenaline rush. I want to take the boat out for a spin on a heavy wind day just to test it out. That'll tell me more than a light day will. I want to see how she responds to a capsize. Will she right herself? I need to know."

Walking another couple of miles together hand in hand, they eventually made their way back to the truck. They had packed a couple of sandwiches and water, which they ate as they watched his Dad sailing downwind towards the marina. Finishing up their lunch, Bobby cranked up and headed for the ramp. His dad was already at the dock waiting for them with a huge grin on his face. Bobby backed down the ramp and retrieved the keel hoist from the rear. He and Hali folded the sail on the dock as Gerald rigged the keel hoist. Removing the mast was far easier with two people, and the boat was back on the trailer in no time. Gerald was ecstatic. His sail had gone exceptionally well, and he loved the boat.

HALI'S BIG DAY 14

The following weekend, Hali and Courtney were off in Florida for a big beach volleyball tournament, all expenses paid by Gerald's burgeoning sponsorship fund. Of course, Team USA and at least a dozen other professional teams and some colleges would be there, but rumors had it that several European and Asian teams would also be there. This was Hali and Courtney's big chance to prove themselves against international competition. The Team USA coaches would be there scoping out all the teams, *and* the tournament would be televised on ESPN on Sunday evening! The girls flew out on Thursday morning, and would be gone through Monday evening. Annette had taken it upon herself to call Hali's parents, introduce herself and invite them over to watch the tournament. They all gathered at the LaRoche house at a little after two Sunday afternoon and spent a couple of hours chatting and getting to know each other. Annette gushed over Hali and showed off her room with all the new furniture in place. There was no trace of the old furniture Hali had owned for so long. Meanwhile, Bobby and Kellan were outside talking cars. The truck was pulled out and parked next to Kellan's ride, a slammed[23] Civic with a chromaflair paint job that was iridescent purple, pink and green. Both rods glistened in the sun. They later ran over to Frank's shop together to check out the rods over there, and Bobby noticed no trace of Kellan's former attitude. Right before the tournament came on at four, all of them came out to admire the boat. Gerald crowed like a proud parent as they all gushed over her.

The Abaras hadn't been to any of Hali's tournaments since she graduated, and then mostly the indoor tournaments. Annette served finger food for supper while they watched the tournament. The actual tournament was

---

[23] Slammed - lowered

on Friday, Saturday, and Sunday, but it was compressed down to four hours on Sunday for television. Friday was a day for the preliminaries, with the sudden death rounds on Saturday and Sunday. Hali was on strict orders not to call until Monday morning so she wouldn't give away the outcome. The actual tournament was over and decided by the time it aired on the west coast. The preliminary matches on Friday weren't even shown. Hali and Courtney made it to the sudden death rounds easily enough. It wasn't until the third televised match, that they got to see Hali in action. They quietly watched Team USA-A women lose to the Canadians, then the University of Connecticut men lose to the Japanese. Suddenly, the room got loud as Hali and Courtney took the court. With every point, Kellan and Bobby were on their feet screaming and yelling as if Hali could actually hear them. Davie had never watched volleyball before, but he got caught up in the excitement. Hali and Courtney dispatched the team from Brazil in three awfully close games. They won their first game handily, 21 to 15, only to have the Brazilians take the second coming from behind at the last minute. Hali and Courtney gave them no chance in the third game, taking the lead early and keeping it. The final score was 15 to 10. The room got quiet again as they watched Team USA-B women lose very badly to the Germans. It was hard to root against their own country, but this was also a team that Hali and Courtney had to beat out for a place on the national team. Then they watched the Chinese men fall victim to a talented pair from Long Beach. They got a chance to get loud again as Hali and Courtney knocked off an excellent professional team from Santa Clara in two quick games. That put them into the semifinals against the Germans.

One of the German women was a blonde, blue-eyed Amazon, standing well over six feet tall with a totally ripped body. In fact, she was so ripped that she looked more like a male bodybuilder. She'd lost all her feminine curves and smoothness and looked somewhat out of place wearing a bikini. If it weren't for her immense pecs, she would have been completely flat-chested. She consistently played the net, leaving the back court for her brunette partner. The Amazon was the definition of a power player, easily over-powering Hali's power game. They ruled the first game, scoring easily. In fact, it was Courtney's wicked serves and finesse that kept them in the game at all. The Amazon was powerful but limited in her agility and jumping ability. Courtney was able to drop balls behind her several times. The Germans won the first game 21 to 11 without breaking a sweat. Hali and Courtney had things worked out a bit better in the second game and scored the first three hard-earned points. They were working the back court as much as they could and trying to get the Amazon running laterally so they could drop the ball behind her. They were also serving to her, trying to get her running, trying to make her screw up the pass. But the Germans weren't a team to be trifled with. They adjusted their game plan and roared back. With the score at 12 to 10 in favor of the Germans, Courtney served hard right at the Amazon's chest, but she handled it nicely, passing it to the center where her team-mate gave her a perfect set. Hali read the play instantly and was soaring through the air as the Amazon spanked the ball directly at her. Hali didn't try to block the ball. Rather, even before the ball cleared the net, she slammed it right back at her opponent with all her strength. The missile struck the German squarely in the left eye, then bounced off the net and straight to the ground, followed a few milliseconds later by the Amazon. She screamed in anguish and pain, clutching her face and her shattered sunglasses. Hali was there in a heartbeat, apologizing profusely and waving frantically for the coach. The game was stopped. Commercial time. After a long series of commercials, the game resumed. Who knows how long the game was actually delayed since the tournament was compressed for television? The Amazon's eye was swollen and tearing up, but she played on gamely. But she clearly wasn't seeing well. And her left side was suddenly vulnerable. Her partner tried her best to fill that void, but that left the back field unprotected. Courtney was relentless, scoring point after point with her finesse game. Hali occasionally gave them a slam or two just to keep them on their toes, but her primary function was to set the ball up for Courtney. It was a complete role reversal. The rout was on. They won the second game 21 to 16, and the third game 15 to 8.

Courtney's husband, a professional photographer, was shooting the match from the ground level, court side. He took many amazing shots of both Hali and Courtney during the tournament, but one in particular stood out. It featured Hali about to strike the ball. Her light brown skin

and white bikini against an azure sky, the grace and beauty of her feminine form all contrasted with the rippling muscles and the look of fierce
determination and concentration of a world class athlete. Shooting from
ground level upwards, it appeared that she was actually flying, well above
the net. It was her infamous slam back at the Amazon. The photo was the
one money-shot of the bunch and a few months later, Bobby would have
it framed over his dresser where he could see it from his bed every night.
It would be in newspapers all over the country, especially around the
Seattle area, and on the walls of all the LaRoche Autogroup dealerships.
Suddenly, Hali was famous and very quickly became the newest face of
women's beach volleyball. And it brought in tons of sponsorship offers.

The finals featured the Japanese National Team, who had just
knocked off the excellent team from the University of Connecticut.
The Japanese girls were smaller than the giant Germans, more like
Hali. Courtney stood a good three inches taller than either of them.
But they were very quick with an incredible finesse game. It was the
hardest fought battle Bobby had ever witnessed. Long rallies, incredible
blocks, digs, spikes, taps, you name it. Constantly swapping serves. The
first game lasted forty-four minutes and ended up at 36 to 34 in favor
of the Japanese. The second game was the same situation, but Hali and
Courtney eked out a win 29 to 27. The third game wasn't quite as close,
but it was still a long game. Hali's spikes and Courtney's wicked serves
ruled the game and they pulled off a 15 to 13 victory. In the end, it was
conditioning that made the difference. All the players had been playing
for hours in the hot sun and the Florida humidity. The Japanese girls
had begun to wilt, while Hali and Courtney maintained their relentless pressure. Hali and Courtney were the champions, and they'd just
knocked off some of the best teams in the world. Bobby, Kellan, and
Davie were delirious and hoarse. Gerald just smiled quietly and nodded.
He'd backed the right horse. And the LaRoches and the Abaras had
grown closer as the day wore on.

CHANGE OF PLANS

15

Gerald had spent several hours on the previous day sailing the boat in a light to moderate breeze, nothing over ten knots. Bobby didn't bother but used the time to catch up on his homework. Gerald came back ecstatic, though. Sailing the boat, *his* boat, was thrilling. The wind on Monday afternoon after work was more to Bobby's liking. He was looking forward to giving the boat a good thrashing. He launched, pushed off and shot out of the marina. He immediately put the boat into the wind and drove out into the short, steep swells, pinching up into the wind to get over the swells and bearing off as the swell passed. The wind increased as he got further from the shore, and he was finally able to use the trapeze. The hiking stick[24] proved to be a little too short. That would be an easy fix. The first tack didn't go so well as it was the first time Bobby had ever used a trapeze. But the second was slightly better. And the third was even better. He threw a long series of tacks together and when he was done, tacking while on the trapeze was second nature. No need for roll tacking in this breeze. The boat was alive and responsive in the fresh breeze as long as he could keep her flat. But if he let her heel much at all, the rudder loaded up, the boat slid sideways, and she just felt terribly slow.

Without a traveler and a boomvang, the cockpit was completely

---

[24] Hiking Stick – a 'stick' that attaches to the tiller allowing the skipper to steer without having to remain close to the center of the boat. The longer the stick, the further outboard the skipper can sit. They are usually telescoping since long hiking sticks get in the way when the skipper isn't hiking out.

uncluttered, but that didn't mean the skipper had to give up on sail controls. The choker is far more effective than a traditional outhaul[25] at flattening the sail, thereby controlling the power in the sail. The skipper could raise and lower the front of the wishboom which directly affects the curl of the sail. Lower the wishboom, and the leech loosens spilling off excess wind from the sail. Raise it, and you tighten the leech[26]. Leech tension directly affects pressure on the helm as well. Too much tension in higher wind and the rudder starts getting dragged through the water sideways. Awfully slow. Ease the tension by lowering the wishboom until the rudder is balanced and the heel is minimized. The free-standing carbon mast is flexible and therefore self-depowering. It bends with each gust spilling the excess pressure from the sail.

Turning the boat downwind and easing the sheet, she instantly broke into a plane. She was far more stable on a broad reach[27] than dead downwind, especially in waves. And she surfed far easier and longer on a broad reach. With her hard chines, she was faster and far more stable than the Laser. The trapeze was out of the question, as were roll gybes in this wind. Surviving the gybe without capsizing was the goal. And that called for exact timing with the waves. He surfed down the face of one swell, and as the boat sailed through the trough, he put the helm over and snatched the sheets overhead. Then, hiking for all he was worth, he caught the boat as she screamed off on the other gybe down the face of the next wave. Easy. She was also much easier to gybe than the Laser, which has a nasty tendency to have the sheet catch on the corner of the transom as the boom swings over. In a full plane, she was probably

---

[25] Outhaul – a rope on a traditional sailboat that is used to haul the mainsail outwards along the boom, thereby tensioning the sail cloth.

[26] Leech – the trailing edge of the sail

[27] Broad Reach – A course downwind that is at an angle to the wind, keeping the wind on the boat's quarter rather than dead astern. Planing sailboats are usually sailed on a series of broad reaches downwind rather than dead downwind

reaching over ten knots or so, likely twice hull speed[28]. The wind was blowing fifteen to seventeen knots and there was no need to reef at all downwind. And, best of all, she was a dry boat, both upwind and down. Bobby threw gybe after gybe at her and she responded superbly. He turned back into the wind, hauled in the sheet, and beat[29] back to windward against the waves. The full main was a real handful and the trapeze was necessary, but he could keep her flat by feathering into the wind. The next test was reefing. Instead of easing sheets, he tried to do it under sail. He succeeded to a point, but it took a lot of time and he couldn't get enough tension along the luff[30] without letting go of the tiller. He needed the autopilot, which he hadn't brought along. So, he released the sheet and stopped the boat, got the proper luff tension, and even tightened the reef pennants some more, then grabbed the helm and hauled in the sheet. With a single reef, the boat was far more manageable, making the trapeze optional. And she was sailing flatter, she wasn't crashing into the waves and she was just about as fast. Lesson learned. Don't thrash the boat no matter how much fun it is. He retrieved the seat and set it up on the port side, relaxed and drove the boat through the waves at over five knots. She stayed completely dry with her high freeboard. Bobby wanted even more wind, but this was still incredibly exhilarating. She had passed with flying colors.

He turned around and headed back to the marina. With a single reef in this breeze, sailing downwind was simple. She still planed and surfed, but in a very controlled manner. Two long gybes brought her back to the marina where his father awaited. Bobby was pumped! The boat easily outperformed the Laser. Though, with the Laser, he kind of enjoyed living on the cutting edge of disaster. He ripped off his dry

---

[28] Hull speed - the theoretical maximum speed that a displacement hull can travel through the water, limited by the bow wave. Planing hulls can exceed this limitation by traveling over the water rather than through it. Even planing boats operate in displacement mode until they get enough speed to break free.

[29] Beat / Beating – A sailboat that is sailing against the wind is beating, sailing a series of tacks each about 45 degrees off the wind in a zig-zag course

[30] Luff – the leading edge of the sail which, for a mainsail, attaches to the mast with slides or a bolt rope

suit and life jacket and handed them to Gerald, who was impatient to get underway. They left the reef in, and Bobby watched intently as his Dad sailed away. He went to his truck, donned a jacket, and fetched his binoculars. His Dad seemed to be doing okay to windward, though he was heeling too much and there was a lot of spray as he crashed into waves. At least he stayed upright. He sailed only about a couple of miles out, tacking several times. His tacks were tedious. He was obviously fussing with the seat during the tack. Bobby's answer to moving the seat effectively from side to side was to shift his weight to the side deck, take the seat out and place it in the cockpit on the other side. Do all this while still on the old tack. Then he focused on doing a good tack, and when it was complete and the boat was sailing fast again, he installed the seat and shifted his weight into it. Fairly simple, just a lot of things to think about that aren't an issue on a Laser. Bobby watched as his Dad turned the boat downwind. He obviously needed coaching on playing the waves. He was sailing a broad reach well enough. But then he gybed with no consideration of the waves. The first wave almost rolled him. If not for the ballast, he probably would have capsized. He survived only to do it again, and then again. The boat saved him each time. Finally, he returned to the marina looking frustrated. Together, they put the boat away silently. Bobby watched his Dad's reactions and it was obvious that he didn't want to talk about it. Once she was on the trailer, he quietly walked away to his own car. Bobby felt bad as he drove home and tucked the boat back in the shop.

Hali was at home and met him in the back yard with an excited embrace. Bobby held her for a long time and just breathed in her essence. She had only been gone for a few days, but it seemed like an eternity. She could tell that Bobby was troubled, and he told her about his Dad's poor experience on the water. After he finished rinsing off the boat and putting her away, she embraced him again, and together they went in to talk to Gerald. They found him at the dinner table, drinking a glass of wine and obviously in deep contemplation. They both sat down next to him.

"Dad, I watched you struggle out there with the waves. I know you're used to sailing big boats and you're not used to having to play every little wave. Especially on the gybes. You caught the wave wrong on every gybe. I was taught how to play the waves back when I was with the youth sailing team. I don't even think about it anymore. It's second nature. We need to get you some coaching, Dad. We still have time."

"Yeah, I was watching you out there, and you had her dancing over the waves, upwind and down. You were one with the boat and one with the water. And you were going so fast! It was pleasure to see, son. I'd like to learn that."

"I can teach it to you. Or we can get you a coach. We need a motor-boat as a chase boat, though."

"I know I need to learn to play the waves, Bobby. I'm old, but I can still learn a few new tricks. That's not what was really bothering me though. I was only out there for, what? Maybe an hour? And I came back in exhausted. My right forearm is toast. I could barely hang on to the tiller coming back in."

"Really? That's bad. I thought you were almost fully recovered."

"I think I am, but I'm not in shape for dinghy sailing, that's for sure. I haven't been sailing in four years, and that was only in big boats. I want to get in shape and sail her, Bobby. I really do. And I want you to coach me. But I can't do the Race to Alaska. I'm not ready. Maybe next year, after a year of training, but not this year."

Long pause. Bobby nodded slowly. "I understand, Dad. That's wise. I'll help you and we'll get you in shape for next year. Plan on spending a lot of time in the gym."

"I will. I'm sorry, Son. I know you put your heart and soul into building her just so I could compete. And I really love you for doing that. I'll do it next year, that's for sure. She'll make it to Alaska."

"Bobby," Hali broke in "what did you think of the boat?"

"Oh God, Hali! That boat is everything and more than I ever ex-pected. She's amazingly fast, planes easily, is very stable and she sails dry. I'm sure she's faster than the Laser, and she is certainly more stable and controllable off the wind. When I put a reef in today, she became docile and easy as pie to sail and I think she was just as fast! So, as much as I like to thrash a boat and ride the trapeze, that's the wrong answer. Reef early, kick back and enjoy a great relaxing sail to windward. The autopilot would have helped a lot when I reefed her, but we'll work out the bugs. She's a phenomenal boat, Hali."

She placed her hand on his arm. "Bobby, why don't *you* race her this year? Let Gerald do it next year. The boat's ready, you're fit again, and you need some outlet for your competitiveness. I'm serious. You should do it!"

There was a stunned silence in the room, both Gerald and Bobby staring at her. It was Bobby's Mom, who had been listening at the door who broke the silence.

"That's the best idea I've heard all year! If the boat is really that good, she needs to be used for what she was built for. Bobby, you put your heart and soul into building that boat, and you're the only one here capable of sailing her right now. Of course, you should race her this year."

"See, Bobby?" Hali said. "Listen to the women for once. Say you'll do the race."

"You guys have no idea what this race is all about." Bobby protested. "Those are treacherous waters. You've got to go through the Seymour Narrows, which can be deadly. And then there're the gales of Johnston Strait. And Dixon Entrance is notorious for storms and huge waves. It's not to be taken lightly! So many things can go wrong. Hypothermia, for one."

"Bobby," Hali said quietly "you'd let Gerald go do the race. Yet, you're the better sailor, at least in dinghies. And you told me yourself, people have been doing this race since 2015 and no one's gotten hurt yet. And people have done it in kayaks, rowboats and even a paddleboard! You've got a great boat, purpose-built for this race. If they can do it, you can do it. It *is* dangerous, but you recognize those dangers. There are always ways to mitigate the danger. And there are always places you can stop at along the way, either to rest or to quit."

"But Dad's entered, not me."

"That's a lame excuse" his dad finally chimed in. "Of course, you should do the race. I'll bet you anything that Jacob will let you substitute for me. I'll call him if you want, but I think it would be better coming from you."

"Okay... okay... Let me think about this for a while. I haven't even once considered doing the race. It's not something to be taken lightly. It's two weeks of torture, starvation, and sleep deprivation. I've got to talk to Uncle Frank. I don't have that much vacation time accrued. I'd have to take leave without pay. I'll have to get all my schoolwork completed and turned in before the race. And how do we get the boat back home?"

"That's an easy one. I've already thought that out. In fact, I've pondered just about every aspect of this race out in minute detail. I've got lists of supplies, restocking points along the way, even waypoints. I've even bought most of the gear already. You'll need a larger dry suit, but I think I have most everything else. And the answer to getting her home is for me to meet you in Prince Rupert with a trailer. Then we'll just drive home. It's a beautiful drive."

Bobby shook his head. "Oh, God! What have I gotten myself into?" They all laughed.

Later that night, Bobby took Hali out to the hot tub. They undressed and climbed into the hot water. He just held her close and pondered the race. There was so little time to prepare, not even two months. But the boat was perfect for this race. And he was itching to do something wild. Hali's volleyball was stirring his competitive juices. But the Race to Alaska?! That was like learning to swim by jumping into the deep end of the pool. This wasn't just a regatta. This race is huge! It draws world class sailors! God only knows how many world champions have competed so far. And you're on your own out there. You break something, you're stuck. And the shore isn't that friendly either, especially above Seymour Narrows. Much of it is wilderness, full of grizzlies. There are wild currents and eddies, even a military shooting range that you need to avoid. Not to mention the huge ferries, cruise ships and fishing boats plying the waters. He could get run over at night. And with a fixed keel boat, he couldn't just go ashore unless he swam. He caressed Hali and thought about life. She would be off training with the national team for the entire month of June. Maybe longer, especially if she got selected. He would be alone again moping around the house. Yeah... He needed this race. Other people succeeded in lesser boats. He knew he could do it. He had the skills. He just had to focus on the race and figure out all the unknowns. That would bring back his confidence. He made up his mind. He would race.

A NAME

16

It turned out that the Race Boss, Jacob, was very cooperative with Bobby about transferring the entry to his name. He had to fill out a new application in his name, but that's all. Jacob wanted updated pictures of the boat for their website. And the story was very provocative, so he wanted a little write-up about that as well. Jacob made sure that Bobby was aware of all the dangers involved, and even weakly tried to talk him out of taking part. But his warnings only strengthened Bobby's resolve more. The biggest challenge was getting his passport in less than two months. He applied immediately and paid extra for expedited service.

His father had a detailed list of everything he'd need. He couldn't carry enough water, so there were three mandatory stops along the way: Campbell River, Port McNeil, and Bella-Bella. Most of the stuff was already purchased and in the boxes in the garage, but he did need to order a new dry suit and fleece. He decided on a two-piece suit since it was so difficult to get in and out of the one-piece suits, and he needed to be able to add and take off layers as the days warmed up. Not to mention using the toilet, which in this case was a collapsible bucket. He ordered a pair of rather expensive leather sea boots as well.

Bobby and his Dad, and occasionally Hali, went through the boxes and planned out the details of the trip. There were two solar-powered speed pucks that mounted on the mast in clear view of the skipper. These were GPS-based speed and heading displays that resembled a hockey puck. There was the autopilot, which still needed to be mounted and wired up. The two flexible solar panels were already mounted to the cockpit floor with snaps, one aft and a smaller one forward, but needed to be wired up to the battery.

Bobby retrieved his Jet-Boil camp stove, pots and sleeping bag from his bay. His father had ordered a bivvy-sac and a self-inflating sleeping pad. All of this was stowed away under the deck to see how much room there would be. No problem, she was a big boat for a solo sailor. In mid-May, the cockpit dodger and canopy were fitted to the boat, held in place by a series of snaps under the rub rail and along the deck. It used fiberglass battens bent in arches across the cockpit for support and provided an exceptionally large and comfortable sleeping area. The dodger section would remain in place and had two large windows. It was technically possible to pedal the boat with the cockpit completely covered, useful in the rain, but that meant only being able to see dead ahead. Food was going to be a lot of freeze-dried packages which were exceptionally light, plus a bunch of Power Bars and assorted granola bars. Bobby would throw in some carrot sticks as well. They'd keep for a while. There were two five-gallon flexible water bladders, and half a dozen new water bottles with flip up straws for daily use. His father had purchased almost two dozen drybags of all sizes just in case the seals leaked on any of the compartments.

Then there were dozens of paper charts, flares, a bailer, a telescoping paddle, a GPS unit, a hand-held depth sounder, and a small Danforth anchor, chain and a hundred feet of line. A bunch of small rigging parts, sail tape, and line would make up an emergency repair kit for the rig, and some epoxy resin, cloth and mixing cups made up a 'crash kit' in case he hit something and punctured the thin hull. One of the significant risks is hitting a deadhead, a log floating invisibly just at or below the surface. Together, they decided to redesign the rudder attachment so that it would break free without damage if he did hit a log. They replaced the stainless-steel bolts with hollow aluminum bolts designed to shear off on impact. And he'd have plenty of spares and the necessary tools on board.

He decided to order all new clothing just for the race. His base layer would be thin technical thermals. He could change those easy enough, and they'd keep the outer layers fresh for a while. He spent a lot of time perusing online shops with Hali, who insisted on buying him socks, thick thermals, hats, gloves, and a balaclava. Her job was to keep him warm, and if she couldn't be there to do it personally, then at least she'd provide some warm clothes. He also bought several dozen chemical hand warmers. Hygiene would be maintained as much as possible via wet wipes.

The paper charts weren't going to work on a small boat. His Dad's plan was to spend a day at the copy house and make a series of 11x17 laminated charts of just the sections that he would need. But before he could do that, he needed to plan the route and familiarize himself with all the obstacles and course options. Should he take Active Pass into the Straits of Georgia? Or Porlier Pass? Or Gabriola Pass? Or even the Dodd Narrows? For many evenings, while waiting for Hali to get home, they pored over the charts plotting different options. It would all depend on the wind and the current. All options were possible, though Dodd Narrows seemed to be the worst. After a few days, Hali and Bobby spent the better part of a Sunday afternoon in Kinko's making copies of the relevant chart sections. The paper charts would be left behind. Bobby found a GPS app for his phone that offered Canadian charts and down-loaded it. With the charts, it cost less than fifty bucks, much less than the Garmin hand-held GPS unit his father had purchased. He bought a waterproof case for the phone, and a dozen external batteries.

Bobby sailed the boat every opportunity he had. Of course, his schoolwork was suffering, but he was keeping up, barely. Whenever the wind was howling, Bobby would drop everything and launch the boat. Even in thirty knots of wind with a double reef, the boat was dry and perfectly manageable. He could sail her flat and fast through the waves. Going downwind in thirty knots with a double reef was almost boring except for the waves. He couldn't shake a reef going downwind with that much force in the sail, so he would have to turn back head into the wind. With a single reef, she screamed along at over twelve knots surfing from wave to wave. The forward half of the boat all the way back to the keel rose out of the water, and she balanced on the flatter stern sections. This is why planing sailboats are designed with hard chines. She was perfectly manageable, and the gybes, if Bobby timed the waves correctly, were quick and safe. She was a remarkable little boat, but she lacked one thing... a name.

Towards the end of May, with only a week before Hali left for training camp, the family sat around the table at dinner time brainstorming names. All sorts of names were thrown out: *Vixen, Wicked, Nirvana, Dream, Dream Weaver, Quest, Gold Quest, Dream Therapy, Feline, Swan, Swallow, Zephyr, Wind Song, Kitty, Talon, Hawk, Kestrel, Tenacity, Huntress, Grace, Amazing Grace, Wanderlust, Andiamo, Hope, Kismet, Lunacy, Namaste, Zen, and Second Chance.* Bobby favored *Vixen.* Hali was okay with that one, though she was pushing for something like *Quest* or *Dream Therapy* that spoke of both her and Bobby's journey. Bobby agreed, but his Dad wasn't convinced. Bobby suggested *Roach Coach,* and everyone had a good laugh. Bobby had been serious about it but kept that to himself when everyone laughed at the idea.

Jessie dropped by with her new baby and a fresh baked pie and joined the conversation. She listened to the suggested names and considered each.

"I can understand *Quest,* or *Dream Quest,* because that's why she was built. But, when you look at her, what do you see? I don't see a *Quest* or a *Dream. Vixen* possibly. But what I really see is a work of art. She has a fine sheer line and a powerful yet graceful bow. The mast is raked in a very sensual way. She looks fast just sitting still. Her woodwork is meticulous, and the gleaming cedar is magnificent. I see a fine musical instrument played by a master musician..."

"Stradivarius" whispered Bobby. They were all silent.

"Make it a little more feminine," Hali said. *"Stradivaria".*

"Or *Strad* for short" said Gerald. No one came up with an objection. The name stuck. Bobby had graphics made up for each side of the boat, and while he was at it added the race registration numbers. *Team LaRoche* was entry number one and would proudly wear the number one on each side of her bow.

Hali left for national team training camp on May 25. Bobby drove her and Courtney to SeaTac, knowing he wouldn't be seeing her for at least a month. And if she got selected, their time together would be few and far between. This training camp wasn't covered by the national team, so she was using her sponsorship money. Gerald had come through. There were sixteen companies sponsoring them now and more in the wings. Personal contributions poured in through the GoFundMe account proving Kellan wrong. Hali and Courtney had made numerous appearances and played numerous celebrity volleyball tournaments. They had been on both the radio and television, and signed hundreds of autographs. The cities of Lynnwood, Edmonds and Everett all adopted them as their own local sports heroes. Hali's autographed posters were selling as fast as they could be printed. Their faces were in print in the sports sections of the newspaper. They started drawing crowds to their appearances. Both had recently signed individual lucrative modeling contracts for sportswear that allowed them to quit their jobs and just focus on volleyball. By the middle of May, their sponsorship accounts contained more than eighty-five thousand dollars, and still more was pouring in with no end in sight. Their journey had begun. Bobby let her go and told her not to worry about him. "Focus on volleyball. Focus on making the team. Don't worry about me. I'll be here when you get back, whenever that is." They kissed and embraced at the departures curbside area and she was gone. Bobby felt completely empty on the way home. A big part of him had just gone missing. That afternoon, he launched *Strad* and sailed off by himself to mope. The wind was light, which didn't help lighten his mood. Getting hungry, he turned back downwind for the marina and, losing patience, put in the pedal drive unit and pedaled all the way back. It was the first time that he had ever used the pedal drive system and he was pleasantly surprised at how easily she moved along. With almost no help from the sails, he was able to pedal at three knots effortlessly. That little tidbit of info lifted his spirits a bit, but he knew that he would be very lonely tonight.

TRIAL RUN

17

With the race just two weeks away, Bobby decided that he needed a trial run. So, he took a couple of days off work, loaded up *Strad* with everything that he would be taking to Alaska and set an upwind course for Olympia about sixty miles away to the south. The dodger was in place, but the cockpit cover was rolled up and stored away. In the light wind, *Strad* lacked the responsiveness she had when she was empty. Leaving the dock at eight in the morning, he pedaled and sailed south hugging the eastern shore and staying out of the shipping channels. There was a light fog on the water as he started, which began to burn off towards noon as the day warmed up. The water was mostly flat with a slight swell and no vessels in sight.

He pedaled until noon and was happy to discover only a mild fatigue in his muscles. The wind had finally built to a mild southerly as the fog gradually disappeared, maybe five to six knots, and *Strad* glided along at over three knots silently. Bobby was able to relax in the seat and just think of Hali and their wonderful times together over the last three months. There was no doubt in his mind that he was hopelessly in love with her. She was the one for him. *Strad* cruised south silently for several hours, and in the process passed two Lasers, and several assorted other dinghies in Elliot Bay. The sun was out and that brought out all the summertime boaters. The light wind kept the temperature bearable since he was wearing his lifejacket and safety harness. It was way too warm for his dry suit. *Strad* had proven exccedingly difficult to capsize, so he felt safe enough without the drysuit. The horizon was now full of boats, commercial and pleasure, and their wakes dwarfed any sea swells or wind chop. As he approached Des Moines, a two-person Laser II sailboat came out of the marina with a couple about his age aboard. He changed course and sailed over.

"Ahoy there!" The girl called out. "What kind of boat is that?"

"Oh, she's home built" Bobby replied. "My Dad designed her, and I built her. I'm doing the Race to Alaska in her in a couple of weeks and this is my trial run. I'm loaded with all the stuff I'll be taking to Alaska so she's a bit heavy. I'm heading down to Olympia and back for a trial run."

"She's beautiful! You're going to sail her to Alaska? She's really small for that...."

"Yep. All the way. Sleeping on deck under the cockpit cover."

Strad was gradually pulling away from them.

"That's incredible! She's really fast."

"She would be a lot faster if she weren't so loaded. You should see her in a blow. That's when she really scoots."

"That's a really interesting rig also... I've never seen one like it."

"It's designed to be easy to sail for long journeys. You can't hike all the way to Alaska. It's like a windsurfer rig. Quite simple. No traveler and no boomvang."

Strad was now several boat lengths ahead, and they had to yell at each other, so the conversation lagged. The wind came up a bit and both boats sped up, but the Laser II was no match for *Strad*. Maybe off the wind with the spinnaker in light winds, but not to windward even though the Laser II had a small jib. Even fully loaded, *Strad* and Bobby together were probably fifty pounds lighter than the Laser II with two crew. And *Strad* had about twenty-five percent more sail area assuming that the Laser II wasn't using her spinnaker.

The current was still ebbing for at least three more hours, which was robbing him of about a knot of forward progress. Didn't matter that much. He didn't want to show up at the Narrows too early without a push. The current runs four knots under the Tacoma Narrows Bridge. Bucking the current isn't very prudent. Leaving the eastern shore, he crossed the shipping channels towards Vashon and Maury Islands, and rounded Robinson Point right at low tide at close to six o'clock. The breeze was still light, under ten knots, and Bobby decided to see if he could cook supper under sail.

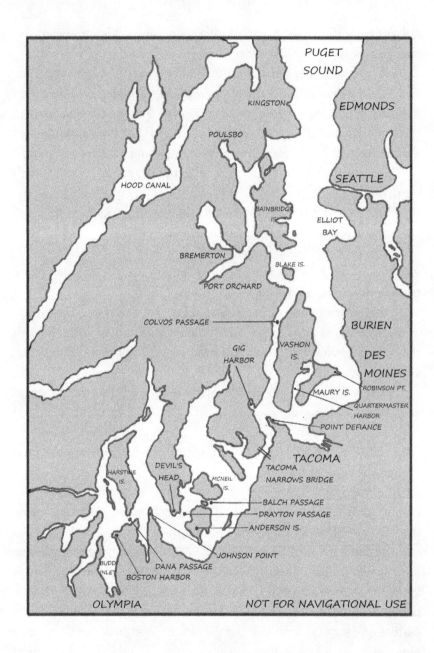

He connected the autopilot and set a course along the shore that would take him across the entrance to Quartermaster Harbor. The cooking gear was in a stern compartment, and the food was in one of the side decks. It took him several minutes to get everything set up, but his little camping stove boiled the water in less than a minute. He needed to get some sort of non-slip mat, so he didn't have to hold the stove continuously. It took almost ten minutes for the freeze-dried food to rehydrate to a state that it was even slightly edible. He preferred the teriyaki sticks and Power Bars that he'd been nibbling on all day. Theoretically, the meal was nutritious, but its primary contribution is that it would be warm. Even though the Race to Alaska is held in June, it still gets cold at night and any day that the sun doesn't come out. Hypothermia is a very real danger.

By the time that Bobby had eaten, cleaned up and stowed his gear, he was ready to round Point Defiance. Even though the currents were theoretically at a minimum, severe current eddies remained across the narrows all the way over to the opening into Gig Harbor. Bobby studied the current lines trying to get a read on which side he needed to be on. It seemed that the newly flooding current was building along the far shore but getting there meant having to cross at least two dangerous eddies. He finally decided to avoid the eddies altogether and cross directly over well to the east of Gig Harbor. From there he could work his way down the coast and into the flood safely.

The wind built considerably as he rounded Point Defiance and *Strad* responded immediately. Her speed jumped up to five and a half knots with about a two-knot push. Staying in the flood required numerous short tacks, so Bobby stowed the seat up forward. His tacks were less than a minute long apiece. Once well inside the Narrows and approaching the bridge, the eddies disappeared, and he was able to make some long boards[31]. His speed puck was showing eight plus knots as he was swept under the bridge. He had some decisions to make once he got well south of the bridge. Should he go south of Anderson Island? Or take Balch Passage? It was dusk now, and he still had eighteen miles to go according to his Garmin GPS. There would be more current south

---

[31] Boards – Sailor lingo for distance spent on one tack

of Anderson Island, but that way was longer. Considering possible anchoring sites, he selected Balch Passage. It was slightly shorter and recommended by the GPS. But it could mean sailing into sheltered areas. At nine-thirty, he was swept into the pass between Anderson Island and McNeil Island with a three-knot push and ejected out into the still, dark waters of Drayton Passage. There was a marina on the northern shore that he had noted as a stop-over spot, but he was not yet tired.

He sailed on slowly into the fading light. He had to make it through Dana Pass before the current turned, or he'd have to anchor and wait it out. That might not actually be such a bad idea since he'd been afloat for over twelve hours already. At peak flow, Dana Pass flows at two to three knots. Though there are plenty of back eddies to take advantage of, he'd need a good stiff breeze to buck the current at full flow. Bobby rounded Johnson Point after eleven on a dying current and a dying wind. The night air was significantly cooler making him eventually pause to don his dry suit. He pedaled lethargically all the way down the passage with the sail hanging limp. He was tempted to stop at Boston Harbor Marina since he was so exhausted. But he was now within five miles of his destination, so he continued slowly into the blackness of Budd Inlet. There were few navigation markers at the north end, and those at the south end were completely obscured by the background glow of the city. Bobby had to rely mainly on his GPS, though if he just continued due south, he'd get there eventually. The only navigational hazard in Budd Inlet was Olympia Shoal, and it was safely submerged by the high tide. He pedaled on numbly, his mind barely awake. He kept nodding off and catching himself before he fell out of his seat. If his destination weren't dead ahead, he'd have anchored long ago.

The streetlights of the Fourth Street Bridge slowly became visible as the early morning wore on. The seas were dead calm now, so the bridge lights reflected perfectly. His destination, West Bay Marina, was somewhere along the western shore ahead. Bobby worked over to the west side, dodged an unlighted buoy, and crossed the shipping channel searching for the marina. All the lights along the shore looked about the same, nothing remarkable that could be the marina. Suddenly an anchored sailboat showing no anchor light loomed out of the blackness ahead of him, requiring him to turn sharply to avoid a collision. It was anchored directly in front of the marina, a complete hazard to navigation. Bobby turned *Strad* shoreward and found a spot south of the marina to anchor in twenty-five feet of water. Turning off his running lights, and turning on his anchor light, he dropped the anchor using all one hundred feet of anchor rode[32]. Setting up his cockpit cover and mattress, he finally drifted off to sleep around four-thirty.

A wake from a passing boat awoke Bobby from a deep slumber. *Strad* had been gently bobbing in the light breeze, which only served to lull him into a deeper sleep. The sun was high in the sky as Bobby unfastened the cockpit cover and stowed it neatly. The City was abuzz on a Saturday morning. There were numerous boats on the water, including several kayaks nearby. There were two large ships at the shipping terminal, both loading logs. Inserting the pedal drive unit, Bobby weighed anchor and pedaled slowly into West Bay Marina. His legs were still complaining a little from all the pedaling that he'd done yesterday. But he was pleased that he'd been able to pedal effectively for so long. The ergonomic seat was a lifesaver, but his butt was still slightly tender from all that sitting.

He found the guest dock near the pump-out station, and moored *Strad*, making sure she wouldn't get banged up against the decrepit dock. His entire body was stiff as he climbed onto the dock and headed towards Tugboat Annie's Restaurant. He reached the top of the ramp before he realized that he was still wearing his dry suit. So back he went and shed it and his fleece on the boat. In the restaurant, he was just in time to order off the breakfast menu. Five more minutes and he'd have had to order lunch. Eggs Benedict and black coffee would wake him up. The sixty-mile voyage down to Olympia had taken him just over nineteen hours, and he'd made it straight through without stopping. He'd get underway on the return trip at noon, but there was no way he'd make it back through the Narrows without stopping.

He looked down upon *Strad* from his window table as she waited patiently for his return. There were several people standing on the dock

---

[32] Anchor rode – the combination of the anchor line and a length of chain

admiring her. She was quite a sight gleaming in the morning sun. The wind had risen steadily as the morning warmed up. By the time Bobby returned to the dock, the crowd had dispersed, and the wind was blowing a steady eight to ten knots. Donning his dry suit and life jacket, he pushed off and pedaled out of the marina under the watchful eyes of several boat owners. It's not every day you see a pedal-powered sailboat, especially not one as gorgeous as *Strad*.

Bobby sailed past Boston Harbor at one o'clock, leaving him an hour before slack water. He was beating easily against the wind, logging about four and a half knots with a half knot push, enjoying the sunshine. His mind was kind of blank with fatigue, but the sailing was gentle and pleasant. He shed his dry suit as the day warmed up and stowed it below the cockpit with his sleeping bag. A small flotilla of tribal fishing boats lined the southern shore of Dana Pass, and several other boats were plying the waters in the distance. It was Saturday, and a gorgeous boating day, so he was surprised there weren't a lot more boats out. He sailed the length of Dana Pass in four long tacks, staying mostly to the north shore to take advantage of what little current remained. But as he rounded Johnson Point, he could see current slightly moving past the daymark in the wrong direction. Decision time. He could go into Zittle's Marina and wait it out sitting on the dock, or maybe make it down Drayton Pass to Long Branch Marina. Needing more sleep, he decided that Long Branch Marina offered some quiet anchorages offshore. Once around Devil's Head Bluff, he easily made headway against the flood, since the current in Drayton Pass is negligible. He was again anchored by four-thirty and asleep by five o'clock under the cockpit cover. *Strad* gently rocked to the wind ripples slapping her sides.

When he awoke at nine, the seas were flat. Dead calm. Groaning, he stowed the cockpit cover and his mattress, and fixed another freeze-dried supper. He was tempted to just stay put for the whole night since the sailing would suck. But the ebb current was beginning and soon he'd be able to ride a three-knot push all the way through the Narrows. If he didn't go now, he'd have to wait almost twelve more hours for the next ebb. His brain still a fog, he found it hard to focus on the options ahead. Maybe he could rest in Gig Harbor, or maybe Quartermaster Harbor. He was eventually underway by ten, pedaling methodically at about two knots, which increased dramatically as he entered Balch Pass. The speed puck jumped to five plus knots. The half-moon was bright to the east lighting his way. He pedaled on for three more hours and was swept under the bridge at over seven knots. He could see the lights on the bridge, and hear the traffic, but the only glimpse he got was when it blocked out the moon. He picked Gig Harbor only because that was the first option available to him and he was totally exhausted. At a little after two o'clock in the morning, he dropped his anchor right behind the sandbar at the entrance.

The next day was much more to his liking. A southerly wind cranked up a little after he awoke at seven-forty and continued to build as the sun rose. By the time *Strad* was underway at nine, the wind had increased to a brisk fifteen to seventeen knots. Bobby had her planing northward at ten knots, gybing up Colvos Passage with the current. This was more like it. Both Bobby and *Strad* felt alive and excited. He passed several larger sailboats also heading north, waving to the crews as he passed. Colvos Passage is about ten miles long, and in just over an hour *Strad* was in open water again. The wind increased further once out in the open, and the seas picked up. With the speed puck reading twelve as he surfed the swells, Bobby guided *Strad* north to Blakely Rock, then gybed and crossed the shipping channels and sailed into Elliot Bay. There were numerous sailboats of all sizes out on Elliot Bay, but Bobby ignored them and held a northerly course towards Ballard. There, he found dozens of small boats out sailing, so he changed course to take a peek. There was a gaggle of Lasers out getting ready for a race, the others were a mixed bag including several 505s, Harpoons, a couple of Lightnings and some other random dinghies. *Strad* planed through their midst and several turned to join him but didn't stand a chance. There was one 505 who popped open his spinnaker and sailed with him for a few minutes, chatting about the boat and the upcoming Race to Alaska. As that boat finally peeled off to get back to his starting line, Bobby gybed cleanly back to port and headed offshore. One more long gybe and he'd be back to Edmonds, less than six miles away. He moored *Strad* at close to two o'clock and slowly put her away. She had passed her first real test with flying colors. So had Bobby. He was stiff and tired, but that was expected. He could take a lot more.

That evening, after giving the full report to his Dad, Bobby went outside to soak in the hot tub. Slipping out of his clothes and into the hot water, he instantly thought of Hali. He could almost feel her skin against his. Her first few days in training camp had been successful. She felt like she had a good chance to make the team. Courtney wasn't quite as driven and might not make it. The coaches wanted to mix up the players and find the best combinations. When they played together, they always won. When they played against each other, Hali always won. Hali was training with the beach volleyball teams since it was summer season, but the indoor coaches had noticed her also. It was early yet, but she felt that she was making a good impression. Bobby missed her, and the hot tub wasn't helping so he finally got out and went to bed. In his own room.

THE RACE TO ALASKA

18

The 2018 Race to Alaska was a week away, starting on June 14. Technically, the real race starts on June 17. The first leg is just a thirty-five-mile qualifier, a 'dash' from Port Townsend to Victoria, BC. Some people just do this leg and call it good. Thirty-five miles across the Strait of Juan de Fuca is no piece of cake. There are several heavily trafficked shipping lanes to cross, and the currents generally rip along at three to four knots easily. Plus, the Strait is known for some severe gales even in the calmer summer months. There's no place to hide or take cover. Once you commit, you're on your own. The qualifier section is really to make the competitors prove that they can move their vessels manually. No motors are allowed, and in Victoria Harbor, no sails are allowed. Competitors must propel their boats the last two miles into the harbor manually. And the same for coming back out. This rule is strictly enforced by the RCMP[33]. For many boats like *Strad* and the rowing shells and the kayaks, this would present no problem. But there were some big heavy boats entered this year, most notably a forty-four-foot-long IOR[34] race boat from the seventies, and a heavy wooden thirty-eight-foot gaff-rigged wooden prawner that was 115 years old. How do you possibly propel a boat like that manually? The racers that survived stage one, would live on to party for two days in Victoria before departing somewhat sober at

---

[33] RCMP – Royal Canadian Mounted Police
[34] IOR – International Offshore Racing Rules, an obsolete set of rules from the 1970s that resulted in a generation of oddly shaped sailboats built to take advantage of the ratings rather than being designed for sea kindliness.

high noon on Sunday, June 17. The start was LeMans-style, with all the boats moored and the crews up on the landing overlooking the docks.

Bobby and Gerald spent that last week poring over the weather reports and the tide charts plotting their strategy. The forecast called for clear weather, which was not a good thing in Bobby's mind. That meant light winds. The lighter the wind, the safer the race. But lighter wind also made for a long and more exhausting race. With a good brisk breeze, especially a southerly, Bobby thought he could break ten days. His real goal was to be the first solo finisher. It's hard to beat teams that could sail for twenty-four hours a day when he would be forced to take sleeping breaks. So, he went through the list of competitors, and basically divided them in two. Those that he wouldn't worry about, and those that he would try to beat. His competitors included a couple of sailboats, a kayaker, a couple of rowers and even two paddle boarders. He also threw in a couple of the beach cats that had no sleeping quarters. Some of these would be very stiff competition if they sailed well and rested little. In heavy winds approaching gale force, he was confident that he could take them, especially since they didn't seem to be equipped with reefing gear. And in drifters, he was confident in his pedal drive system compared to their paddles. Anything in between, and the cats would rule the day in his class.

Gerald and Annette took their big RV to Port Townsend on the 12th and set up at the Fairgrounds. Bobby drove up later after he got off work at two-thirty driving the *Escalade*. Taking the Whidbey Island ferry, it was after six that he finally launched *Strad* at the Port of Port Townsend Harbor. Leaving the trailer at the launch ramp, he picked up his parents to see him off and so they'd have the *Escalade*. Back aboard *Strad*, the breeze was too light for sailing, so Bobby just decided to pedal the boat over to Port Hudson Harbor where the race boats were staging. He opted not to don his dry suit or fleece. The evening temperature was still over seventy degrees. The run to Port Hudson was short, at just over a mile, but the setting sun was in his eyes the whole way. As he neared the Northwest Maritime Center, he heard cheering and a horn sounded. There was quite a crowd on the docks and the breakwater, and at that moment he was the center of their attention. Energized, he pedaled harder bringing *Strad* up to three knots as he rounded the breakwater and entered the harbor. The R2AK boats were all staged on his right, but he circled the harbor once to the sound of many horns welcoming him to the race. He found a spot on the main walk between two finger piers, put out his fenders and cruised over. One problem with his pedal-drive unit is that it didn't have a reverse. But he got close and used his paddle to get in all the way, along with some help from fellow sailors. Immediately, the main walk was crowded with people admiring *Strad* and asking all sorts of questions all at once. Was he going all the way to Alaska? Did he build *Strad* himself? How fast does she pedal? How fast does she sail? How many people will be going on her? And the questions went on and on. He was intending to spend the night on her, mainly just so he wouldn't have to unload all her gear for safe keeping. None of her compartments were lockable. He still hadn't eaten, and his parents were getting antsy to get to a restaurant, so he finally stowed the speed pucks and covered the cockpit and went off to eat. He was a little relieved to put *Strad* and the crowd she attracted behind him for a few hours. The questions were getting tiresome. Tomorrow, he'd be ready for them all. But tonight, he just wanted to get something to eat, then maybe crawl off to bed. It was already approaching eight.

They found a restaurant on Water Street that was still serving dinner this late. It was more of a bar than a restaurant, and was crowded and loud, but options were few. They found a table out on the balcony where it was a bit quieter and a lot cooler and sat down. Within moments, a tall, skinny man with tousled black hair and dark eyes approached them at the table. His appearance was that of someone who had lived on the rough side of life. Bobby was immediately on guard, expecting him to ask for money.

"Greetings, folks. M'name's Damon. You the dude who brought in that sweet cedar dinghy, right?"

"Yep." Bobby replied loudly over the crowd noise.

"Beautiful boat. Are you going all the way?"

"I intend to."

"Sailing solo?" He was hard to hear, and harder to understand with his slurred speech.

"Yep." Bobby wished he'd go away and leave them in peace and wasn't about to engage him in conversation.

"I'm racing, too. Sailing a Flying Dutchman solo. Want to make a bet on the outcome of the race? Thousand bucks to the first solo finisher? Waddya think?"

Bobby didn't answer for a few minutes. He just wanted to be left alone. But he'd love to beat this guy. A Flying Dutchman? Really? It was one of his all-time favorite boats and one of the fastest monohulled sailboats ever designed. It would plane going *against* the wind! At twenty feet long with no ballast, it was a handful for two very stout, athletic sailors.

"Can you really sail a Flying Dutchman solo?" He reluctantly asked.

"Sure, been doin' it for twenny years. Countin' on light winds."

"How are you going to propel her manually?"

"I got me a sweet propeller drive system."

"You goin' ashore to sleep?"

"Yeah. I got a tent an' stuff."

"I'm interested. Talk to me tomorrow. Or in Victoria."

"In Victoria, Satiday at high noon. I got some others interested. If I can get five, it'll be two hundred each. Winner takes it all. We give the money to Jacob on Satiday. He awards the money to the winner."

"Cool" Bobby replied. "Count me in, Damon. I'll see you on Saturday."

He stood up and shook hands with the guy and sent him away. They selected and ordered food.

"What do you think of his chances?" His Dad asked.

"I don't know" Bobby replied. "I can't imagine how he could sail a Flying Dutchman solo. That's a gnarly boat for two big guys. Assuming he can sail as effectively as he says, he would be unbeatable in light winds. I'll have to go check out his boat tomorrow. I have faith in *Strad* under manual power and in a real blow. He might be just as good in a drifter if his propeller unit works. But if there's some real wind, he'll be over-powered real soon. I doubt if he can sail her in fifteen knots of wind unless he could really reef her down. Flying Dutchmen don't usually have reefing gear. They're delicate, complicated boats. I prefer *Strad's* simplicity."

"I agree." His Dad said. "He could get lucky and have light winds all the way. But *Strad* is a better all-round boat for this purpose. I'd put money on you and *Strad*."

"I'll have to check the other entries for solo sailors. See who I might be racing against."

Wednesday was Safety Day. Every boat had to be inspected for proper safety equipment. It was also the day that all the skippers had to check in and get their race packages. Bobby and his parents spent the early morning before the skipper's meeting walking the docks and looking at all the other racers. The bigger boats were moored at the docks while the kayaks, beach cats and rowing shells were on the grass by the NW Maritime Center. The various approaches to manual propulsion were fascinating. Some were extremely well engineered. Others not quite so. Bobby and Gerald were sure a few would fail under any load. They spent an hour at the Maritime Center as well, looking at the various projects in the shop and the completed projects parked outside. The Flying Dutchman was on a trailer by the beach. It looked as old and worn-out as its skipper. The propeller drive system looked potent enough if it held together. Workmanship obviously wasn't a high priority with Damon. The Flying Dutchman is one of the most complicated sailboats ever assembled, and this one was no exception. But the running rigging[35] was old and worn. Bobby noticed several broken blocks[36] and the tip of the rudder was badly chipped. The boom did feature reefing gear, so that question was answered. The mast looked sound, but the sails were well worn. Bobby came away feeling a bit more confident in his chances.

One of the more interesting race boats parked on the beach featured a highly efficient propeller drive system designed by Rick Willoughby in

---

[35] Running rigging – any rigging on a sailboat that is soft and intended to run through blocks. As opposed to standing rigging which is fixed and intended to keep the mast up.

[36] Blocks - pulleys

Australia, the designer of several world record breaking human-powered boats. The hull was a lightweight plywood canoe painted lime green, completely decked over except for a small cockpit complete with a Plexiglas canopy and two small outriggers for stability. Bobby was sure that it would be the boat to beat in a drifter. Alongside it was a more traditional two-person rowing wherry fitted with modern sliding seats and carbon fiber oars. It would be interesting to see how they compared as far as speed. Bobby would put his money on the Green Machine. A few yards away, there was a beautiful purpose-built fiberglass boat that was half rowing shell and half sailboat. It had been built in France just for this race. The skipper, a world-class open-water rower, was the owner of the factory. The other race boats on the beach included several beach cats and a kayak.

At eleven, he attended the skipper's meeting and received a folding sailor's knife from one of the sponsors along with his race packet. They also gave him two R2AK stickers he was expected to put on his boat somewhere. At the meeting, a Canadian Coast Guard officer got up and spoke about all the dangers and informed the racers that help would not be forthcoming if they got into trouble. She stressed that everyone must take extreme care while racing. She also reminded the racers that no sails are allowed in Victoria Harbor and that a patrol boat would be on site to enforce that rule. The U.S. Coast Guard officer was more concerned about the shipping lanes and forbid any racers from entering the turning circles for the shipping lanes. Jacob, the Race Director then talked about the start at five-thirty in the morning, the fun and games in Victoria and the requirements to go through Seymour Narrows and pass by Bella-Bella. By noon, Bobby was back at his boat fielding questions. With a lot of difficulty, since he was laying prone on the dock as people were literally stepping over him, he managed to put the R2AK stickers on each side of the bow right next to the race numbers.

In the early afternoon, a petite, very pretty woman with long reddish-brown hair and a clipboard arrived. She was a race minion. She introduced herself as Susan, and she was performing safety inspections. Together, they went through all the safety requirements. Bobby had to dig everything out, and then convince her that he didn't need a bilge pump since the boat was self-bailing. Any water that came on deck would simply run out through the large ovals cut through the transom. He did have a bucket and a sponge if he had leaking issues. He had the appropriate non-inflatable life jacket, two safety lanyards (one longer one for when he was out on the trapeze), six flares to satisfy Canadian requirements, an anchor and rode, both a whistle and a horn, a hand-held VHF radio and navigational lights. He even had a personal locator beacon. She was obviously taken with the tiny boat, but she was genuinely concerned about safety and comfort in the cold water. Bobby showed her how the cockpit canopy worked and that he would be sleeping on deck. He opened the compartments to show her all the water and food, sleeping bags, stove and more. She, along with everyone else who was looking on was quite impressed. Eventually, Bobby was done with the inspection and he was free to relax and chat with bystanders. He still had to go up and get his official GPS spot tracker before five, which he did when there was a lull in the crowds. The official pre-race party, the Ruckus, wasn't starting until seven, but the partying and craziness had already begun, and the crowds were huge. While he was out fetching the tracker, he came across a tattoo artist who was offering R2AK tattoos for free. Since no one was in line at the time, Bobby sat down and got a new tattoo on his left forearm. Just a little motivation to finish the race.

He went out to eat with his parents at seven, then drifted back alone to the Ruckus later in the evening. The music was loud, the people were drunk, and the venue packed full. It was hot and claustrophobic inside, so half the crowd had taken their beer out to the lawn. Bobby decided to make an early evening of it and get a good night's sleep. Unfortunately, he hadn't brought any earplugs, for the party was going on at the docks as well. Finally, at ten, Bobby had had enough. He pushed off the dock and got underway, and stealthily crept out of the harbor and anchored amongst all the other boats that couldn't fit into the harbor. He could still hear the music, but it was faint. The water was almost flat except for a gentle sea swell and little ripples which would soon lull him to sleep. He set up the cockpit cover and his sleeping gear, then photographed his new tattoo and texted it to Hali. She was dead to the world by that time. But when Bobby awoke the next day, her reply was "Please be careful. I need you." She included lots of heart emoticons.

R2AK STAGE 1

19

Bobby's watch alarm went off at four forty-five. There was a stiff wind blowing and *Strad* was rocking urgently, wanting to be underway. Bobby got dressed and had some breakfast, then stowed his gear and the cockpit cover. A guy was paddling around the anchored fleet on a paddle board giving out free hot oatmeal! So, he accepted and had a second bowl, not quite as hot as the one he prepared himself. At five-fifteen, he raised the sail and then the anchor and he was underway. Amongst the hundreds of anchored spectator boats, he didn't recognize which boat was the committee boat. A growing number of racers mingled with the spectators as they trickled slowly out of the harbor. There were a couple of possibilities, so he decided to pass both boats on the shore side just to make sure. A private helicopter was hovering way too low for safety, creating an incredibly dangerous down-draft just north of the starting line. Bobby stared at it a while wondering what sort of moron would be so inconsiderate as to endanger all the boats with his down draft. Obviously not a sailor.

Competitors were streaming slowly out of the harbor under all sorts of manual propulsion, some efficient, many not so. Looking around, he saw the Flying Dutchman sailing fast among the anchored boats. At five-thirty, a horn sounded, and a flag went up on the nearer of the two large boats. The race was on! Immediately hundreds of horns started sounding and the crowd on the jetty and the myriad of boats started cheering. Bobby had guessed correctly, and he crossed the line on starboard tack alongside the Flying Dutchman and a small crowd of other racers thirty seconds after the horn sounded. The Flying Dutchman was much faster than *Strad*, despite Damon flogging the mainsail and riding the trapeze.

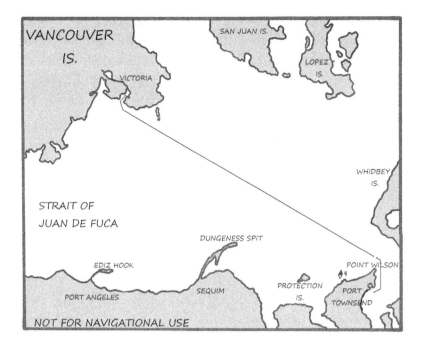

Bobby was beating to windward with a nice gentle sea swell of about two feet, and an ebbing current. The helicopter was to his right, and Bobby steered further to port to avoid the whirlwind. *Strad* was in her element with full sail doing just under five knots, Bobby resting comfortably on his seat on the starboard side. He was heading toward Point Wilson and its notorious tide rips. He had to tack twice to get there. Some of the serious trimarans and a couple of catamarans were passing him now, racers who were sober enough to get to the starting line somewhat close to on time. Half of the racers hadn't even cleared the harbor yet. The tide rips ahead were obvious and, while all the other boats avoided them, Bobby headed right for them. The rip current itself wasn't the major danger if you were going with it. The real danger came where the rip currents re-entered the slower water resulting in large standing, curling waves. He knew that a prudent mariner would avoid the rips completely, but Bobby lived for the thrill of danger. He gleefully watched as his speed puck jumped from four and a quarter knots to ten and a half instantly as she entered the rip. Unfortunately, it was a short ride. He bore away slightly just before he got to the standing waves, avoiding them with only a few quarts of water coming aboard, then bore away on a close reach towards Buoy 4. His plan was to head due west until he got to Dungeness Spit, then turn due north and let the ebb push him to the west. Everyone else seems to have read his playbook, and he was getting tired of bigger boats coming by and stealing his wind. Eventually, he turned north early just before he got to Protection Island. By nine o'clock, he was sailing alone as he crossed the shipping lanes at the prescribed ninety degrees and well clear of the turning circles. Looking back at the other racers, none of them seemed concerned about following the rules, and he didn't see any Coast Guard patrol boats out enforcing them.

The wind died a bit as the sun came up, but *Strad* was still sailing along at four knots. The Flying Dutchman was off in the far distance taking advantage of the lighter wind. The current wasn't setting him west near as much as Bobby had calculated, so he altered course so that *Strad* was heading well to the west of Victoria. It would be a ten plus hour day at this rate, and the flood tide would eventually pull him back to the east. He needed to get well west of Victoria. Looking around at the sails on the horizon, that is exactly what all the race leaders were doing as well. There was no sign of the kayak and rowing shells. They had mostly been late for the start, and Bobby was confident that he had a solid lead on them. The sea swell was larger out here and Bobby was enjoying playing each wave. There was no sign of any shipping, and the AIS[37] app on Bobby's phone didn't show any either, other than the usual Black Ball ferry to the west running between Port Angeles and Victoria Harbor. Bobby and his family had taken that ferry several times growing up. The sun was out, but there were many cumulus clouds as well which Bobby was keeping an eye on. They often had wind associated with them. By noon, the ebb had swept *Strad* far to the west and he rejoined much of the fleet. Cruising along at four knots, Bobby caught

---

[37] AIS – Automatic Information System, an identification system for commercial marine traffic. Each vessel carrying a transponder sends out its identification with its position continuously so that other traffic can 'see' it on their radar or AIS receiver.

sight of the lime-green propeller-powered boat astern of him and holding his own. He dug out some lunch and munched on carrot sticks and
Power Bars washed down with water. The sea breeze continued to drop
as the day warmed up. Eventually, it was time to tack back to port for
the long board to Victoria and the speed had dropped to two knots. He
decided to start peddling to augment the sails, but his forward progress
just backed the sail. He didn't worry about it and just let the sail hang
uselessly as he pedaled on at three knots. *Strad* was catching many of the
bigger boats who were sitting idle, sails barely fluttering. But the Green
Machine was clearly catching all of them, and it wasn't long before she
made her pass and headed off to Victoria on her own. *Strad* was only
about halfway across the Strait. It would be a long, hot day of pedaling
if the wind didn't return. The current was slowly starting to flood, and
by two o'clock, Bobby had to change course to compensate. The current
was far stronger on the north side of the Strait than the south. A few
of his surrounding competitors made the same adjustment, but many
continued their present course without noticing. The Flying Dutchman
was nowhere to be seen. They were all completely out of sight of land,
and there was no point of reference to steer by. Bobby had his GPS on a
tether in his lap was monitoring it every few minutes.

Off in the distance, directly in his path, Bobby noticed a pod of
orcas. Very cool! He had his phone handy in case a picture opportunity
arose. There were maybe six or seven, it was hard to tell since they never
surfaced at the same time. There were two side by side every time they
surfaced, and Bobby guessed it was a mother and calf, though the calf
was certainly not new-born. He watched them intently through his
binoculars as *Strad* approached. They didn't seem to be traveling anywhere, just swimming around in a localized area. Which happened to
be directly in front of *Strad*. They surfaced every four or five minutes.
Could they be feeding? He witnessed one large orca breech off to one
side, jumping three quarters of his body out of the water before crashing back down with a huge splash. They were still half a mile away, and
Bobby was considering changing course to avoid them. He witnessed
another breech, this time with his phone in his hand. He got a picture of

the splash. Suddenly, a huge orca surfaced about fifty feet from him on his port side. He swung around and got the shot, and while looking at the phone's camera view, he realized that it was coming right at him! He shot again, then dropped the phone to hang on, bracing for the collision. At the last moment, when the orca was about ten feet away, it dove under the boat. Bobby could feel the wake on both the keel and the rudder, but there was no contact. The orca surfaced on the other side of the boat about thirty yards away, swimming off to the east quickly. The rest of the pod followed suit. He had never been so close to an orca before in his life, and, while they were spectacular to watch, he was relieved to see them swimming away. They were huge! One careless whack with a tail and *Strad* would be crushed.

Checking his AIS app again, he noticed a larger freighter heading outbound, doing nineteen knots. A second smaller ship was following it. They were still some twenty miles away and not yet visible even with binoculars. The AIS app identified the first as the two-hundred-meter *Apoi Maru* sailing from Vancouver to Japan by way of Hawaii. The second was the one-hundred-twenty-meter Canadian Naval Ship *Bear*. Bobby studied their courses a while, doing mental math to see if it would present a problem. It would be close, but he finally decided that he was safe. They would most likely be well clear by the time he reached the shipping lane. So, that left another question... how would the ships affect all the other racers ahead of him? Would they have to pause to let them pass before heading on across the shipping lane? Bobby hoped that none would be foolish enough to try to cross in front of either. Maybe this was a chance to make up some ground on the leaders.

Bobby pedaled on into the later afternoon, and by four he could see land ahead, and more importantly, a wind line ahead. It turned out to be a westerly, still light, but now an asset. With the wind on the beam, his forward progress through pedaling simply moved the wind forward into a close reach. Still very sailable. The sail filled and drew. Initially, the speed remained at three plus knots but the pressure on the pedals reduced as the sail picked up some of the load. By five, the wind speed had increased, and Bobby put the pedal-drive unit away and blocked up the hole. *Strad* was still doing three knots under sail alone and Bobby was able to rest and have another bite to eat. The bigger boats were starting to gain on him again, and there was nothing to be done about it. The two ships were well clear by the time he reached the shipping lane, and he had in fact gained on some of the fleet. Several boats had been forced to pause by the ships and had been swept east. They now had to claw their way back upstream with only a light wind and a growing flood.

Victoria was getting close now. He could see two cruise ships moored near the entrance, and the seaplanes landing in the harbor. He had played the current well enough and would be entering the harbor without having to fight the current. Not so for many of the other competitors who were fighting their way west against the strong flood. He scanned the boats ahead of him with his binoculars and was very satisfied to see the radically raked mast of the Flying Dutchman amongst the boats that were fighting the strengthening flood trying to get into the harbor.

There were several boats just ahead of *Strad* as they entered the harbor. Several more were deeper into the harbor already creeping along under manual power. An RCMP boat was sitting dead ahead, presumably marking the spot where sails could no longer be used. The light wind died completely once he entered the shelter of the outer harbor, so Bobby went ahead and doused the sail early and installed the pedal unit. Dousing the sail meant simply releasing the halyard. Bobby had rigged lines under the wishboom to catch the sail as it came down all by itself. To a degree, the sail basically folded itself. The bigger boats were taking their time dousing, and were terribly slow under manual power, so *Strad* cruised by four boats in the outer harbor, and another four in the inner harbor. The Flying Dutchman was nowhere to be seen. Once he got to the customs dock, he found a jam-up of boats trying to check in. There was a tiny space at the very end of the dock barely large enough for *Strad's* bow. Bobby took it, jumped ashore and quickly rang the bell officially ending his run. He had rung in before three more boats that were waiting to get to the dock. That's eleven spots he'd moved up in the finishing order since he entered the harbor. That was good enough for fourteenth place out of fifty-four entries. Eventually, thirty-eight entries would finish stage one and qualify for stage two. Bobby had never considered the possibility of winning the whole thing, and still didn't, but the competitor in him always tried to make him beat the next guy up. The real wait was for customs. The boats were piling up and there were only two customs officers on the dock. He waited with growing impatience and hunger for a good hour before one of them turned to him and checked his passport, then required him to call in for the final check. With a confirmation number in hand, he got underway again and vacated the dock. He moored *Strad* to the inside of the docks directly in front of the Empress Hotel just in time to see his parents walking down the ramp.

"Welcome to Victoria, Son. Hungry?"

"Starving! Have you guys already eaten?"

"Oh yes! We found a great Thai restaurant not far from here. We got a take-out meal for you back in the room. And we have a kitchenette, so we can warm it up for you."

"Fantastic! Lead the way. I need to call Hali."

Hali was in good spirits when he called. She had been monitoring his progress online using the GPS tracker that every boat was issued.

"Bobby! Thanks for calling! I just got out of the shower and was about to settle down with a movie. I'm so glad you're safe. How'd the race go?"

"Well, mostly kind of boring actually. Light wind. Long day. I've been on the water all day since five this morning and I did a lot of pedaling. I did see a pod of orcas up close. I witnessed a couple of breeches and one charged me and dove right under the boat at the last second. Scared the hell out of me! I thought he was going to ram me! And then they all swam off."

"Wow, Bobby! That's exciting! I never heard of orcas ramming a boat. Maybe it was just toying with you or trying to scare you off. Maybe you got too close. Or maybe it thought you were a sea lion."

"Yeah, all good guesses. I don't know that much about orcas. That was definitely the closest I've ever been to one. Usually I just see them off in the distance. They're terrifying when you're in a tiny boat and they're so close. They're twice as big as *Strad*."

"I bet! How'd you finish?"

"I don't know, but I know I passed a bunch of bigger boats coming into the harbor. And I jumped in line to get to the finish to ring the bell. There wasn't room for the bigger boats, so they had to wait. Most of the bigger boats are terribly slow under manual power. There's another racer that challenged me to a race within the race. The first solo racer to Ketchikan gets a thousand bucks. Could be four or five participants. I accepted his challenge. I beat him today because he misplayed the current, but his boat is much faster than *Strad* in light winds. I'm hoping for heavy winds. Anyway, *Strad* is safely moored where everyone can see her, and I'm following Mom and Dad to the hotel room. They got me a carryout dinner. Thai."

"I won't keep you then. I just wanted to hear your voice, so I know you're safe."

"Oh, I'm safe. Just very tired. My butt is sore from sitting all day. How's your training coming?"

"Awesome! Too early to tell yet, but the coaches have been giving me lots of attention. There're some world class athletes here. It's a little intimidating, at least until I bounce one of their spikes back at them. Lots of alpha women here."

"Funny. You don't strike me as an alpha woman."

"Oh, I am when I'm in my comfort place, like on the court."

"How's Courtney doing?"

"Pretty good, but I don't think she's good enough. She only plays beach volleyball, and there are probably five to eight women here that are better than her. We keep winning, so far. I suspect that the coaches will split us up at some point, and then she'll flounder. She knows it. Her only chance is for us to stay together. As a team, we've beaten everyone multiple times and the coaches know it. We have great chemistry. I know exactly what she's thinking. She plays above herself when she plays with me. None of these girls have ever beaten the Chinese and Japanese, and we've beaten the Japanese twice. And we've beaten the Brazilians. That's what's keeping us together so far. But she's not as driven as I am. She's married and happy at home. And she dislikes the coach. She thinks the coach already has her team picked out, and no amount of winning on our part will change that. I'm sticking with beach volleyball for the time being to see what happens with her. The coaches want me to train for indoor as well. I'm excited, Bobby. I think I'll get selected. I won't know for a few more weeks, though."

"Hali, I'm really proud of you. You're going to get on that team, I just know it. You just keep on fighting and don't worry about me. I'll always be here for you."

"I know you will, Bobby. I know you will. You can't understand how much that means to me."

"I understand completely, Hali. The feeling is mutual. I'm really missing you right now. But don't worry about me. Focus on your training."

"I will. And I'm missing you right now too. I'm wearing the pajamas you bought me."

"Good! That's why I bought them. There's a girl in you somewhere under all those muscles."

"You bring the girl out in me, Bobby. I can't wait to get back to you."

"Me neither. But keep your mind in the game. We have the rest of our lives to catch up. I love you, Hali. Take care of yourself."

"I love you, Bobby LaRoche. Be safe out there, please. I'll be tracking you."

"I won't be able to call much once the race starts. I'll try to post Facebook updates whenever I get coverage, and I'll text you whenever I can."

"I know. Just promise me that you won't take any unnecessary risks."

"Yeah, I know. And I do promise. I'll get to the finish line safely, don't worry. I'll be waiting for you when you get back. Good night, Sweetheart."

"Good night, Bobby. I love you."

R2AK DAY 1

20

On Friday morning, Bobby and his Dad went down to the boat to roll up the sail and collect Bobby's clothes and other gear. There was quite the crowd on the docks. Many of them were fellow racers and family members, but there were many non-participants as well. All were admiring the boats, swapping sea stories and many were furiously working on their boats. Many of the manual propulsion units did not work out as intended and were being repaired or rebuilt entirely. A lot of people were simply hanging around on their boats waiting for people to come by and chat. Bobby and Gerald did just that for a couple of hours. Some of the propulsion units were incredibly well engineered and complicated. Some were held together by bailing wire and duct tape. Some boats simply had long SUP[38] paddles and that's all. *Strad* was getting a lot of attention. Bobby soon tired of answering the same questions over and over. Next year, they'd make an information poster. Eventually, they made their way back to the hotel, and after lunch enjoyed visiting the town.

The weather forecast was not good. Hot and steamy for the next two days. Winds light and variable. The third day was a maybe. Partly cloudy. That meant there was at least a possibility of wind. Looking at the long-range forecast, there was a front stalled just offshore that was predicted to move inland mid-week. That promised some sort of weather. Hopefully not just rain. Friday afternoon, the temperature soared to eighty-five degrees. In the Pacific northwest, the sun is very direct, when it appears at all, making eighty-five degrees feel closer to ninety-two. Bobby had to reconsider things. He had planned for hypothermia, not heat stroke. While they were out on the town, he

---

[38] SUP – Stand Up Paddleboard

bought a long-sleeve, light and loose white shirt and loose lightweight khaki slacks and a broad rim floppy hat with a built-in neck shade. A bad sunburn could end his race just as fast as hypothermia. He also picked up some Gatorade to augment his water just for the first day or two. Otherwise, his water might not last all the way to Campbell River, requiring an additional stop in Nanaimo.

On Saturday, the temperature only made it up to eighty-two degrees, still sweltering in the direct sun. Bobby and his Dad went down to the boats at noon and were waved over to a group meeting at the landing above the docks. Jacob, the Race Director was there, as were about a dozen others including Damon. In total, there were six teams present, plus some family members. They all agreed to the race within the race and chipped in two hundred each. Twelve hundred dollars all total. The first to Ketchikan wins it all. The Frenchman was in, as was a woman named Claire who was sailing a Hobie 17. The Green Machine was in. The other racer was a former Olympic rower from Canada who had entered a gorgeous wooden wine glass wherry equipped with modern sliding seat rowing gear. Bobby and his Dad went over and checked out his competition. He liked his chances. The Flying Dutchman was his primary concern. The Hobie was extremely fast but was relying on oars with no sliding seat for manual propulsion. Probably not effective for more than an hour or two at the most. The boat itself was old and worn, but at least the sail was new. There was no reefing gear present. They spoke briefly with Claire, who seemed very competent. The wherry would be extremely quick in the hands of an Olympic-caliber athlete, but could he row for eighteen to twenty hours a day? For twelve to fifteen days in a row? Same for the green machine. And its efficient propeller drive system was very delicate, especially for a boat that would be dragged up the beach each night. The Frenchman at least had a sail to give him some rest, but it didn't look fast and had no reefing points. The Flying Dutchman had an effective pedal-drive system but lacked any sort of mounted seat. Rather, he had a cheap plastic chair with the legs sawn off. And when the wind wasn't heavy enough for the trapeze, there was no comfortable seating position. The deck and cockpit sole[39] were covered with cleats and control lines, leaving little room for the crew. All of Bobby's competition would be going ashore at night to rest. Quite possibly, the boats could all get stranded high and dry by the tide. The Hobie was the only one that even had the option of anchoring offshore, but the waterproof gear bags strapped to the trampoline left little room for sleeping.

Bobby spent a few hours down on *Strad* chatting with passersby, but mostly just rested in his room staying out of the sun. He spent a lot of time on the phone with Hali who had the weekend off other than conditioning drills that she and Courtney did on their own. Saturday evening after supper, he and his Dad reviewed the tide charts and tried to calculate what sort of progress he would be making. Should he go for the Strait of Georgia at the first opportunity? Or should he stay within the islands? The stalled weather front held that answer, and it wasn't releasing any clues. If he stayed amongst the islands, there would be far more anchorages available. The current was a known factor, and he'd be fighting it for the first four hours or more of the race. Which posed another question – why not just stay in port until the current changed? If there's no wind, the competitors wouldn't go anywhere fast. The wherry and the green machine would be long gone, but he wasn't too worried about them. He'd overtake them soon enough once the wind came up. It couldn't stay calm forever, could it?

Sunday morning, race day, was more of the same, hot and steamy. The high was predicted to reach eighty. At least the weather was predicted to break tomorrow with the high only reaching seventy-two. But would there be wind? At ten, he moved *Strad* backwards along the dock around the Flying Dutchman and the Green Machine. He didn't want to be in the way. He had decided to stay in port until two. By the time he got out of the harbor, the tide would be nearing slack water. The crews were already gathering and preparing the boats for a swift departure. Each team were talking strategy to get out of dock fast, as if saving fifteen

---

[39] Sole – nautical term for the floor, or bottom of the cockpit, also used in cabin cruisers for the floor below decks.

to twenty seconds really mattered on a 700-mile race. Bobby just tried to stay out of the sun and stay hydrated.

Just before noon, all the crews were called off the docks to the landing. Bobby joined them but stayed to the rear as far away from the mass of hot bodies as possible. He had already loaded up the boat, brought down additional water bottles and mounted the pedal-drive unit. The Race Director was rousing up the energy of the crowd, screaming through his microphone. The crews responded, cheering, and getting worked up and sweaty. Finally, as noon approached, he started a ten-second count down. The crowd counted down with him. Exactly at noon, he sounded a gun and the race was on. The crowd cheered, the crews cheered and the whole hot and sweaty mass swarmed down the ramp to the boats. Thirty-eight boats getting under way at the same time was a sight to behold! Bobby was happy to watch from safely up on the landing with his parents. Boats were fending off from one another and some were in dire danger of being run over. But within half an hour, the docks were mostly empty as the mass of boats moved away slowly. Despite the heat, the Green Machine and the wherry had actually raced out of dock at top speed leaving the fleet far behind. Bobby just smiled. It was a long race. They couldn't keep up that pace for long. But it looked good for the crowd. There were a few remaining boats that only participated in the first stage, and only one other that shared Bobby's strategy. This was an old Cal-20 sailboat, built in the sixties, and sailed by a father-daughter duo.

Once all the boats were clear of the docks, Bobby and his Dad went down and moved *Strad* to the end of the dock in preparation to get underway. A news reporter stopped him.

"Are you racing?"

"Yes, Ma'am."

"Why didn't you start with the others?"

"Well… It's a hot and sunny day. There's no wind and an adverse tide. Why fight the tide in this heat? The tide will sweep half of those guys out to sea."

"Ahh... so this is a strategy move! You think you'll catch the fleet as you come out of the harbor?"

"I do. Most of it. All the bigger boats. Some of the kayaks, and oared boats will just hug the shore and stay out of the current. On a long-distance race like this, especially for solo participants, you really need to conserve your strength. I see no point wasting it fighting the tide unnecessarily."

"That sounds like a wise move. What do you think of your chances?"

"To win it? Just about nil. About a dozen or more boats would have to retire before I have a shot. I'm not here to win the overall race. Solo racers just can't compete with fully crewed boats. But six of us solo racers each put our money where our mouth is. Now we have a race within the race. First solo finisher wins the pot. Twelve hundred dollars to the first solo racer. That's my race."

"Really? We hadn't heard anything about this. What do you think of your chances?"

"This solo race didn't come together until yesterday. And if I were a betting man, I'd bet on me. I think *Strad* here is the best all-around boat of the six entered. The Flying Dutchman will be tough to beat in light winds, but he can't sail in even moderate breezes. I'm impressed with the Hobie 17 also, but her rowing gear is poor at best. If we have long periods of calm, she'll suffer. I like my chances. But it's a long race. Anything can happen."

"Thank you for talking to us. You've given us a whole new aspect to follow on the race trackers. Good luck."

"Thanks."

As it turned out, Bobby waited until two-thirty to depart. The crowds had dispersed, except for a few that had gathered around *Strad*. Their chatter slowed him down.

"Excuse me, folks." Bobby called out "But it's time for me to get underway."

"Oh, I'm sorry." said a woman as she backed away making room for him. "That's a beautiful boat. Did you build it yourself?"

"Thank you, yes I did, just for this race."

"But where's all your gear?"

"Under the deck hatches. I have everything I need for twelve days at sea except water. I'll have to resupply periodically."

"But why didn't you start with the others?"

"Because there's no wind and an adverse tide. No point fighting the tide this early in the race."

"Ahh... good thinking! Well, good luck!"

"Thanks."

Bobby pushed off and settled into his seat. The crowd started murmuring as he pedaled away quickly. They were definitely impressed with *Strad's* ability under power. Bobby had taken the dodger down to allow any breeze created by his forward momentum to reach him. The white clothes and hat were already paying dividends. It was too warm to wear his life jacket, a direct violation of the safety rules that he'd agreed to with Hali and his Mom. The racers were all out of sight, but the harbor was alive with mostly commercial traffic. The water was choppy with all the wakes interacting with each other. Bobby hugged the shore, staying well clear of the traffic lanes.

As he passed the large commercial marina, Fisherman's Wharf, a large ocean-going fishing boat came barreling out of the marina and very nearly ran him over. He swerved hard to starboard to evade, but not nearly enough. The large aluminum boat finally saw him and threw both engines in full reverse, stopping quickly. The two boats missed each other by a mere five or six feet. The tribal crew started screaming at him and the skipper sounded five short blasts on the horn as if it was his fault that they had blasted blindly out of the marina violating several very basic rules of the road and waking all the boats in the marina. Bobby turned back to port after exchanging middle fingers with the fishing boat's crew and pedaled on towards Shoal Point. In a few minutes, the fishing boat passed him close by at full throttle despite being in a no-wake zone. Unfortunately, the RCMP boat wasn't on station as it had been for the trip into the harbor. Bobby had to stop and turn *Strad* into the huge wakes for fear of turning over. What a jackass! He thought about contacting the boat with his radio to chew them out but decided that you can't really argue with morons. Seething, he pedaled on towards Shoal Point and watched the fishing boat get smaller in the distance. Good riddance. Shoal Point marked the limit of the no-sailing zone, but there wasn't a whisper of a breeze, so Bobby continued under manual power.

By three-thirty, *Strad* had finally passed the breakwater and turned east. There was still a sizable ebb, so Bobby hugged the shore. The fleet hadn't gotten far. In fact, half the fleet were anchored close to shore, and most of the rest were creeping very slowly under manual propulsion towards Enterprise Channel. A few had been swept west toward the ocean and were behind him and getting further away. This included Claire on the Hobie. There was no sign of the green machine or the wherry, but the Flying Dutchman and the Frenchie were very slowly inching their way along the shore only a half of a mile from the breakwater. Bobby set an easy pace knowing that he would be pedaling for a long time, and even then, he was easily catching those boats that were still underway. He threaded the needle through the anchored boats exchanging pleasantries with their crews, a much nicer group than the tribal fishermen. He set his sights on the Flying Dutchman and the Frenchie ahead. Even at the easy pace, he was clearly catching them. He reached Enterprise Channel by four-thirty side by side with the Flying Dutchman. His Hobie Mirage drive was proving to be more efficient than the propeller-powered unit on the Flying Dutchman. He chatted with Damon for a little while as they cruised through the channel side by side, but he couldn't get any information out of him as to his plans for the islands.

As the two boats exited Enterprise Channel, he found that the flood had finally begun. So, he abandoned the shoreline and made for deeper water in search of faster current. His intention was to hug the shipping channel and eventually pass Moresby Island to the port. At sixteen miles away, that would normally be five hours of pedaling. Gradually, his speed increased with the current until at six-thirty the speed puck was showing almost seven knots!

The sun was still intense, and Bobby had worked up quite a sweat. He still had on his white shirt and hat, but he'd shed the pants a couple of hours ago. Except for the residual chop from boat wakes, the water was like glass. Much of the fleet was still behind him. A double rowing wherry had passed him in the channel, and the Green Machine and single wherry were still ahead somewhere. Bobby had now been pedaling for over four hours, but his legs were still going strong and he felt like he could go for another three or four hours. His butt was the limiting factor. It was already reminding him that he was reaching the limit.

Since his hands were free, Bobby was able to make a cold supper of carrot sticks, an apple, a couple of teriyaki sticks and a couple of Power Bars, all washed down with Gatorade. The Flying Dutchman and the Frenchie had hugged the shore and were out of sight. As the sun went down, the temperature dropped making for a delightful evening cruise. The sky glowed orange and pink in the distance over the mountains. Somewhere on the west coast of Vancouver Island, people were enjoying a spectacular sunset. He reached Moresby Island at nine as the sun went down and he turned on his running lights. Could he get to Active Pass before the current changed? He still had eight miles to go and the current was lessening as he left the main channel. As the speed on his GPS reduced slowly, he decided that he wasn't going to make it. Slack water was in an hour. The ebb would have begun by the time he got there, and he couldn't buck that six-knot current. The fleet had scattered in all directions. Several were close by, some in front of and most behind him, probably making similar calculations. Well up ahead were a couple of boats that could make it through Active Pass should they choose to do so. That option was another question entirely. Was there wind in the Strait? After considering this for a while, Bobby decided that it was unlikely, so he set a course for Porlier Pass some twenty-two miles off. Amongst the islands there were several stopping points along the way.

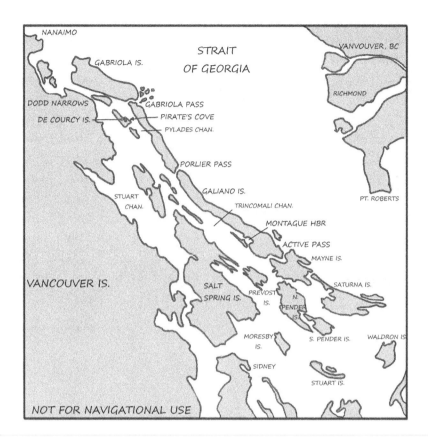

Bobby's legs were starting to complain, and he couldn't even feel his butt any longer. But he pedaled on looking for possible camping spots. Could he make it Montague Harbor? That might be pushing it a little. Had he not been pedaling all day he'd go for it. Maybe Prevost Island, some six miles away would be a better solution. His speed was still four plus knots, so he still had some push. A bit over an hour and a half, he thought his legs could take it, though they were just about done. So, Prevost it would be. There were several sheltered coves on the east side that he could hide in. With that decision made, the fatigue quickly set in. The last couple of miles were a real strain. His speed was reducing further, down to three knots, then two and a half as the ebb gained strength. By the time he reached the island, he was barely making headway against the current. He ended up in Ellen Bay, though he had intended on Diver Bay. He went deep into the bay to find shallow enough water and dropped his anchor close to midnight. He had been rowing for almost ten hours straight, and his legs were done. He could go no further even if he had to. Standing up to lower the anchor was much riskier than usual on his rubbery legs, but at least his butt was no longer complaining. Switching on his anchor light, and turning off his running lights, he remembered to update his Facebook with his position. He barely had cell service. Certainly not good enough to check the tracker to find out where his competition was. He gave himself a cursory wipe over with the wet wipes to remove some of the remaining saltiness from his skin. He yearned for a nice long shower, especially one with Hali in it. But that day would come. It was a crystal-clear night, so he didn't bother with the cockpit cover. And within minutes of rolling out his mattress and sleeping bag, he was sound asleep.

R2AK DAY 2 21

Bobby awoke just before dawn to the restless stirrings of *Strad* and the slapping of little ripples against the hull. Wind! She was itching to be underway. Wiping the sleep from his eyes, he scanned the sky, which was gray. His pocket barometer was down significantly from yesterday. All good signs. It was a chilly fifty degrees, so he donned the fleece bottoms and tops, then listened for the local weather forecast on the radio as he stowed his sleeping gear and turned off his anchor light. It seemed that they were broadcasting every area except where Bobby was. But finally, it came on. Winds light and variable in the morning, building to ten to fifteen in the late afternoon. Looking out to open water, beyond the mouth of the bay he could see the tell-tale carpet of ripples on the water that indicate breeze. Active Pass would be open this morning. Now was his chance to escape the islands and head out into open water. But was that the wise thing to do? It was looking like he would have wind here amongst the islands. Would there be wind offshore as well? He did know that the ebb would be much stronger offshore than here in the islands. The ebb was set to start around ten. So, Porlier Passage, fourteen miles away, would be closed. That only left Gabriola Pass, twenty-five miles away. He did some quick calculations. Assuming he could sail at three knots all day, he would get there in eight hours. He might have to wait an hour or two to make it through, or maybe the wind would be sufficient in the afternoon to allow him to overcome the remnants of the flood. At peak flow, the current moved at about six knots through each of the passages.

Bobby raised the sail for the first time on this part of the voyage, tweaked on it until he was satisfied, then raised the anchor. He donned his life jacket for the first time also and fastened his tether to the lifting eye on the keel. His parents and Hali had discussed safety rules with him before he left. Rule number one was to always wear his lifejacket. Bobby knew better than to try to reason with women, but he had no intention of wearing it when it was hot and there was no wind and no chance of falling overboard. His Mom had wanted him to promise to always wear the dry suit because the water is so cold in the Pacific northwest. His Dad came to his rescue on that one. Way too hot on warm days. But one rule that he did agree on was to use his safety lanyard whenever the sail was up. Downwind, *Strad* would sail along happily if he fell over, maybe even happier without his extra weight. A Laser would simply flip over if the skipper fell over. But *Strad* had a ballasted keel and would stay upright. Now, she ghosted along silently heading for the wind line. Once clear of the headland and into the breeze, Bobby turned her northwest towards Active Pass. The breeze was a southerly, blowing about four to six knots. Perfect for the Flying Dutchman. Bobby wondered if Damon could fly the spinnaker single-handed. The tide was still flooding, so *Strad* moved along downwind at a nice leisurely three knots. In about forty-five minutes, they were in front of Active Pass. Bobby stood up with his binoculars searching the water on the other side for signs of wind. He couldn't determine for sure, but he didn't see anything promising. The decision was made. He would stay amongst the islands where he knew what he had to work with. As he turned *Strad* westwards down the Trincomali Channel, the winds slowly began to increase to six to eight knots, as if to say, 'you made the right choice.'

The hiking stick was telescoping and had some velcro around it which mated to a strip of velcro on both sides of the cockpit. So, sailing downwind, Bobby could simply press the stick to the velcro, and *Strad* would sail herself quite nicely leaving Bobby's hands free. He could also use his autopilot, but that sucked down battery life. Rummaging through the storage compartments, he dug out his stove and pots and selected a freeze-dried breakfast of eggs, sausage, mushrooms, and onions. It sounded good, but he'd had these meals before. Survival is the best description. Plenty of calories, though. It would keep him alive. He also dug out an oatmeal package. Much more appetizing. Even with the fleece, he was looking forward to a hot meal. While he was waiting for the meal to rehydrate, his bladder called out for release. His Dad had come up with this rule: never, ever pee over the side of a little boat. Too many male sailors and fishermen fall over and drown with their zippers down. He had set aside one of the Gatorade bottles just for this purpose. He peed in that, then dumped it over the side while keeping his weight safely centered. The eggs were as awful as he remembered, but they were digestible and theoretically nutritious. They barely made a dent in his appetite though. That's why he brought along so much oatmeal. Very filling and very tasty. After the eggs, it was like a decadent dessert. Maple syrup and brown sugar flavor. That was his favorite. He used powdered milk to sop up all the extra water and sat back in his seat and relaxed with his oatmeal. Life was good! Nice breeze, beautiful boat, gorgeous terrain... what more could he ever desire? The answer came shortly as he started to feel a familiar pressure in his bowels. Great!

He took his time and finished the oatmeal, cleaned the dishes then stowed his gear and dug out the little collapsible bucket. This was a first. He had been hoping to be able to hold off until he made it to his first stop at Campbell River. That obviously wasn't going to happen. At least there were no other boats around, and he was far enough away from any prying eyes ashore. He filled the bucket half-way with seawater, then tried to balance his butt over the bucket with his dry suit bottoms and fleece around his ankles. After a few seconds, he decided this just wasn't going to work. *Strad* seemed to delight in his discomfort by rocking and bouncing even more than usual making it impossible to balance himself. He finally kicked off his boots, followed by his fleece and dry suit bottoms so he could actually spread his feet apart for balance, used his hands on the side decks to support his weight and finally accomplished the deed. Crap goes over the side and paper goes in the garbage bag to be disposed of in the next marina. That was his most difficult travail so far. He got dressed again, washed out the bucket and stowed it, and settled down for the long haul to Gabriola Passage. With a good four hours of solid sleep, a full belly and an empty bowel, Bobby felt like a king. And *Strad* was clicking off a good four and a half knots with a little push from the flood. He spent a few minutes updating his Facebook page with his present status. His Dad had created a special Facebook page for *Team LaRoche*, and it was linked to the R2AK website. So, if anyone were tracking him, they could click on his icon on the screen and the Facebook page would pop up. He had already posted all the pictures of *Strad's* construction, which were very well received.

As Bobby sailed past Salt Spring Island, he found a decent cellular signal and went online to the R2AK tracker site. Even with a strong signal, it took over fifteen minutes for the site to load. Patiently, he watched the icons slowly fill in as the page loaded and tried to make out which ones were his competitors. Overall, more than two-thirds of the fleet were still behind him! He finally found the Green Machine and the wherry still racing on the other side of Salt Spring Island. They were obviously heading for Dodd Narrows near Nanaimo. Both were about even with *Strad* but on opposite sides of the island. So, Bobby had made up time on them, presumably by taking less resting time. He finally found the Flying Dutchman out in the Strait of Georgia. She had gone through Active Pass, probably an hour before Bobby had reached it. She was making a steady five knots, a bit faster than *Strad*, but sailing very deep gybe angles. The additional distance didn't seem to be paying off at the moment. She was no closer to Ketchikan than *Strad*. Claire on the Hobie was making a nice recovery from yesterday's disaster and was slowly gaining on *Strad*. She was still more than twenty miles behind but moving along downwind at five knots compared to *Strad's* four. There was no sign of the Frenchie. Many of the larger boats had gone through Active Pass, but none were going fast. Bobby liked the winds inshore.

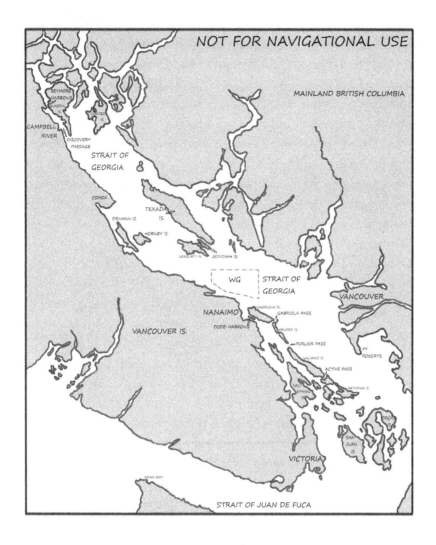

He relaxed and let *Strad* sail herself for a while as he stood up and stretched, trying to force the remaining lactic acid out of his over-worked muscles. This was one big advantage he had over the Green Machine and the wherry. He could stand up and change positions. The seat was wonderfully comfortable, but one could only remain seated for so long. The broken clouds were keeping the temperature in the low sixties, just delightful sailing. The water was flat with an occasional wake, and a steady eight knot breeze. Bobby was sailing shallow gybe angles, not so much for speed, but for stability so he could let *Strad* sail herself. When you sail dead downwind, any deviation of course could cause an unexpected gybe. Things get interesting quickly when the boat gybes without warning. *Strad's* rig allowed the sail to rotate out beyond ninety degrees which helped prevent these. But she was far more stable on a broad reach, so Bobby usually didn't sail dead downwind.

So far, no other boats had come anywhere close to *Strad* except for the jackasses on the fishing boat in Victoria. There were numerous cruising yachts plying the waters mostly in the distance but an occasional one passing nearby. Usually, if a large yacht passes near *Strad*, or any other small boat, they will slow down to make sure their wake didn't disturb the smaller boat. It's not just courtesy. A skipper is legally responsible for any damage done by his wake. But not everyone knows that or cares. As he sailed along the northeast side of Saltspring Island, a large dark-blue motor yacht came ripping out of Montague Harbor heading north west along Galiano Island. Their courses were slowly converging. The international rules of the road gave sailboats the right of way over power boats. Bobby studied her course for quite a while until he finally decided that she wasn't going to give him any sea room, so he turned west to avoid her. The yacht roared by about fifty feet away at full throttle generating a huge wake at least four feet high. A pretty blond woman clad in a tiny bathing suit waved to him gaily from the fantail totally oblivious to the chaos their wake was about to cause. Bobby could only steer the boat into the steep, curling waves and they stopped her dead. The violent rocking could have caused a capsize of an unballasted boat, but *Strad* survived with just the loss of all her momentum. Bobby grabbed the radio and yelled at the skipper, and thankfully got no response. You can't argue with morons, even rich ones. It took a good five to six minutes to regain his momentum.

By ten thirty, Bobby was approaching Porlier Passage. The ebb had just begun, and a part of him wanted to make a run for open water before the passage really got flowing. But he reminded himself that the adverse current off-shore would be stronger than what he would face in-shore. And to reinforce that thought, there was already a debris field formed by the current coming through the passage. The gate was closed. Bobby peered forward at it through his binoculars. There was a solid line of branches, trees and logs marking the current line. The channel was clear well over to the west, and there were several breaks along the line. He studied the line again thinking that he should change course to the west and just avoid the debris field altogether when he suddenly spotted motion on the debris. It had to be an otter. There were millions of river otters in these waters. So many in fact, that they were considered a pest by boaters due to the mess they make on the docks. Cute to be sure, but still a pest. Bobby searched for the movement again but saw nothing. Sighing, he changed course to the west, then picked up the glasses one more time.

Finally, he saw it. A tiny little furry head peering straight at him. Must be a baby otter. But as he sailed closer, he suddenly realized that this was no otter. He stared again to make sure. It was a kitten! What the hell?! How did a kitten get all the way out here? Surely, it couldn't survive out here. He was halfway tempted to let nature take its course. He had no way to care for a kitten. And he was in a race, for God's sake! But as he stared at it, he could see the kitten's mouth opening, though he couldn't hear the faint mew. It was desperately walking towards him balancing precariously on the flotsam and mewing for him. "Damn it!" Bobby cursed himself out loud for being so weak, as he changed course yet again. He swung around the far side of the logs, then turned up into the wind and cruised up towards the log, taking a picture of the kitty on the log as he approached. He reached out and scooped it up, then veered off and let the sails fill once more. He did scan the logs as thoroughly as he could to see if there were any more cats, then set a course for Gabriola Passage. He hadn't gotten as far west as he had intended, but the swift current flowing through Porlier Passage took care of that for him. He stroked the little cat in his lap until he was well clear of the current and eddies, then settled down to examine his new shipmate. It was emaciated, just skin and bones, dirty and likely wouldn't have survived the day had he not come along. He gave it a small capful of fresh water, which the kitty lapped up greedily. He gave it another, then a third before it was satisfied. Bobby was in a quandary. How could he care for a cat? He had no cat food and no litter box. There really wasn't any place he could take the kitty until he got to either Nanaimo or Campbell River. And that could set him back hours. Had he rescued the kitty just to let it die in his lap? He couldn't allow that to happen. Once he had made the commitment to save the kitty, he now felt obliged to care for it. It was a little girl kitty, not quite a cat, but older than a kitten. She was gray tiger stripe with white paws, belly, and chin, maybe six months old, if that. So, what could he give her to eat? He ran down the list of his meals, knowing that he had precious little to spare. But he did have oatmeal, and plenty of that. Would she eat that? The answer was yes, very much so. Bobby made up half a package of oatmeal, let it cool, then sprinkled powdered milk all over it. He used the spoon to feed the kitty who gobbled it up as fast as Bobby could feed it to her. When he was done feeding her, he gave her more water, and then just let her settle down in his lap. She started purring contentedly, and Bobby's heart melted. He took a picture of her and posted it on Facebook under the caption RESCUE AT SEA, just to capture people's attention. He described the rescue and contemplated the possibilities of how she had gotten out there and how long had she been there. He wouldn't know it for some time, but the post went viral. Within a week, it had been viewed by over a hundred thousand people, and shared thousands of times. There was an extremely long string of comments, including from Hali and his parents. They were both supportive of his decision to save the kitty. Hali wanted to keep it for herself. He would never see her post. The family had had cats and dogs when Bobby was growing up, but they hadn't had any pets in several years. Until now.

The wind was freshening as the afternoon wore on and Bobby would soon have to put the kitty down somewhere safe while he drove the boat through the passage to open water. He pondered that, and the puzzle of a litter box. He thought about what he had on board that he could possibly use. Sailors are a creative, industrious breed and Bobbie was no exception. Not having any kind of suitable boxes, he settled on duct tape. One could do just about anything with duct tape. He put the kitty down in the cockpit and dug out the duct tape. He carefully laid ten strips out on the cockpit floor sticky side up, then laid five additional strips across them sticky side down. Each strip overlapped the edges by three inches to form the sides of the box. Carefully, peeling the mass off the deck, he folded up the sides and ran another strip down the length of the loose ends and around the corners. It took a few extra layers to seal the edges and reinforce the bottom. It ended up being a little floppy, but that wouldn't be a problem until he tried to pick it up full of sand. Now if he could just find some sand. With a fixed keel, he couldn't just go ashore. Looking ahead on the GPS, he found Pirate's Cove up ahead and was pleased to see that there was a dinghy dock there. Maybe that problem would be solved. But what should he do with the kitty when things got hairy and he was busy driving the boat? Another puzzle. But soon he came up with an answer. He rummaged through the compartments until he found a whole box of chemical hand warmers. He opened the box and pulled all the hand warmers out and stashed them in a dry bag with his gloves. Now he had a small box. Cats love boxes. He found some duct tape, made some tape loops which he fastened to the bottom of the box, then fastened the box to the deck up forward under the dodger and well clear of the pedals. The kitty was interested in what he was doing, and immediately climbed into the box when Bobby backed away. He had intended to cut the top off, but the kitty simply nosed the top up and climbed in letting the top close on top of her leaving only her tail hanging out. Problem solved. He changed course for Pylades Channel, which led not only to Gabriola Passage, but also right past Pirates Cove. He was early for the flood and had time to kill, so he ducked into the cove. The entry, with a long, submerged shoal, was a bit of a challenge for a sailboat under sail only. He had to follow a crude pair of ranges close to shore, then beat to windward up a very narrow channel. Several tiny tacks later and he was in the cove amongst several dozen anchored cruising boats. A couple more longer tacks and he found himself tied up at the dinghy dock on the port side of the entrance. He grabbed his collapsible bucket and went ashore looking for sand. The shore was mostly rock, but he found enough coarse sand here and there to fill the bucket adequately. The litter box was stowed in the stern against the transom covering part of his solar panel. He took a picture of the duct tape litter box, and the box up front containing a sleeping kitty and updated his Facebook post. He didn't know it at the time, but it again almost went viral. He took a short walk to stretch his legs, chatted with a few people who noticed that he was a competitor, and a few more who were just admiring *Strad*, then eventually got underway.

Sailing out the narrow channel was a simple task going down wind. The wind had risen to over ten knots and *Strad* was coming alive. Not planing yet, but with the wind came some small waves which were almost surfable. Bobby went to work and made the most of it, catching every little wave he could. They reached Gabriola Passage in mid-afternoon. The ebb was still barely flowing, but Bobby went for it. The wind was accelerated through the pass, and he made good about two knots against a two or three knot knock. The passage was short and in half an hour he was in open water. Immediately he saw the Flying Dutchman about a mile or two north. Damon wasn't flying his spinnaker, nor was he out on the trapeze. He was just sailing placidly along dead downwind, with his huge genoa poled out opposite the mainsail. There was a good sized but gentle swell, that Bobby was able to surf a little. He sailed clear of the land for a while, then gybed over to port and headed northwest. Even sailing shallow gybes and getting a few pushes from the waves, *Strad* was not able to keep up with the Flying Dutchman.

Somewhere offshore was the Canadian military's firing range labeled, in typical military fashion, Whiskey-Golf. If it was active, then it would be off limits to all boat traffic and there would be frequent warnings on the VHF radio. Bobby decided that he didn't really need to go out that far and would just hug the shore far enough off to stay in the breeze. He didn't want to use up any more battery life on the radio than he needed.

As it turns out, it was active judging by the military helicopter flying back and forth towing some sort of hydrofoil device. It was probably used for mine sweeping or sonar detection of submarines. Bobby watched, fascinated as the helicopter made pass after pass at probably thirty or forty knots over the water. He took a picture with his phone, and then wondered if posting it would be appropriate. Finally deciding that the military wouldn't be sweeping in plain view if it was classified, he made the Facebook post. He had passed Nanaimo by now but was still some eighty miles south of Campbell River. He would have to find a place to stop for the night. But for the time being, he had a good wind and a flooding tide, and he was running at seven plus knots.

He checked the tracker again as he passed Nanaimo. Both the wherry and the Green Machine were in Nanaimo, apparently at the Port of Nanaimo docks. The Flying Dutchman was due north sailing fast along the shore. The Frenchman was approaching Porlier Pass behind him and was apparently going to go through. The Hobie would likely miss the tide gate for Porlier unless she was ballsy enough to go through at full flow. She could still make Gabriola Pass for the next tide gate. Either way, she was moving fast now with the increased wind. Once offshore, she would very soon be back in the race with Bobby and Damon. The trimarans offshore were finally starting to move out and would soon leave them behind. There was no keeping up with a fully crewed trimaran, so Bobby didn't care.

The forecast called for increasing wind, so he took advantage of the relative calm now and cooked supper. Freeze dried beef stew. Just yummy! Right! But the kitty thought so. She came out of her box as Bobby cooked, watching every move intently. The gentle rocking of the boat didn't faze her. She was focused on the food. Bobby got to eat most of it, but the kitty got her fair share, especially the chunks of meat. She shared his oatmeal dessert as well, then licked her lips contentedly and purred in Bobby's lap. Another Facebook post. He might not be a contender for the ten-thousand-dollar prize, but he was getting a lot of Facebook attention, more so than anyone else. Eventually, Bobby put the kitty in the new litter box so he could clean up the dishes and stow the gear.

The wind had already come up to over fifteen knots, and he needed to focus on playing the waves. For several hours he played the wind and the waves, gybing back and forth, having to shoo the kitty out of his lap with every gybe. This was heaven to him. With the current push, the boat was planing and surfing now and knocking out eleven to twelve knot surges. The Flying Dutchman was out of sight ahead of him by now, but the Hobie was in sight behind him and gaining steadily. Bobby was determined to sail as long as he could keep up this pace. Which was about dusk. As the sun went down, the wind began to die out as well. Searching the GPS for a harbor, Bobby finally settled on Jedediah Island, next to Texada Island, and eventually moored in Long Bay on the north side just before ten. He had to pedal for the last hour. All the coves were full of cruising boats, both sail and motor. But at this time of the evening, all the occupants were below deck and no one paid him any attention. With the sail furled, and the anchor light on, he set up the cockpit cover and his sleeping bag, stripped off his life jacket and dry suit and cleaned up as well as he could with wet wipes. The kitty came over and curled up on the sleeping bag beside him after much kneading to soften it up. Sometime in the night, the kitty decided that being inside the sleeping bag would be even more comfortable and lots warmer and curled up next to Bobby. The kitty had claimed him. Another viral Facebook post.

R2AK DAY 3

22

The run to the head of the Strait of Georgia and up the Discovery Passage to Campbell River was another fifty-six miles, and after that, the infamous Seymour Narrows. There was no wind in the morning at dawn. Flat calm. Glass. The flood was just starting, and Bobby wanted to take advantage of the push. So, he put away his gear and got dressed quickly. Rain was imminent. He could feel it and even smell it. He raised the anchor, turned off his anchor light and pedaled slowly out into the channel. Staying well clear of the traffic lanes, he just let *Strad* drift northwest at one and a half knots as he made breakfast and shared it with the kitty. By seven, the rain set in, so he put up the cockpit cover, stowed his gear and settled into the seat for a long pedal to Campbell River. He was able to make four knots with the push, but at that rate it would take thirteen to fourteen hours, and the flood wouldn't last that long. The current in Discovery Passage leading to Campbell River flows at three knots and often higher. If the wind didn't return, he wouldn't make it on this tide. He crossed over to the western shore near Hornby Island then followed the shore northwards. The rain began in earnest, pelting down in bucket loads. He thought smugly about his competitors racing in the rain while he was warm and dry as he pedaled comfortably with the kitty on his shoulder. A selfie opportunity and another Facebook post. Bobby had wisely moved the litter box forward to make sure it stayed dry.

The cellular reception was spotty at best, and it took half an hour to load the race tracker, but eventually Bobby was able to check on his opponents. The wherry was moving along the coast in the rain at three knots over ten miles behind him, but the Green Machine was still in Nanaimo. Bobby pondered that. Had he had an equipment breakdown?

The Hobie was ashore still as was the Flying Dutchman. They may be staying dry in their tents but they're losing valuable distance. In fact, if the Flying Dutchman didn't get underway soon, Bobby would pass him in twenty minutes. The Frenchie was underway, but he was back near Gabriola Island a long way back.

By noon, the rain abated along with the flood. Bobby stayed as close to the shore as he dared to try to avoid the ebb. The speed dropped off to three knots, then two and a half, then finally two. Bobby left the cockpit cover on until it dried out. While stowing it, he noticed a wind line ahead, so he pedaled in that direction. It came to him before he could reach it. It was directly in his face, but it was wind either way. He raised the dripping sail, stowed the pedal-drive unit, and set off on starboard tack. The wind continued to build and by two was blowing fifteen knots. The kitty was securely in her box up forward, her head sticking out watching him. *Strad* was flying along at three and a half knots despite the ebb tide against her. Bobby was playing the waves beautifully, finally in his element. The other boats were mostly large fishing boats kicking up gigantic wakes. He had to avoid them despite the fact the he was under sail. The unwritten *law of gross tonnage* applies, and they weren't about to change course for a sailboat his size. There were a few other sailboats out sailing in the same general direction as he was, and he was sure some of them were racers. He didn't recognize the Flying Dutchman's unique rig anywhere. A huge ferry went past him at three o'clock heading south. It was so huge that he could see it clearly more than ten miles away. A tug towing a massive barge three decks high above the water was directly behind him and he was keeping a wary eye on it. Eventually it would overtake him, and he'd have to move over.

As the wind continued to rise, he decided that a reef was in order, but he had to get out of the tug's way first. He tacked over to starboard and very nearly drove over a log floating low in the water. He swerved back to windward to avoid the collision and almost went back to port tack, which could have dumped him since he had already moved to the port side. In doing so, he lost his momentum leaving him in irons[40] for the first time since he was fourteen. It took some vigorous pumping of the rudder to get the bow back over to starboard to fill the sail. That shook Bobby. Other than the morons, it was the first unexpected, dangerous hazard that he had encountered. And it was a close call. The broken branches could easily have breached *Strad's* thin cedar hull. The tug was now much closer. He finally got *Strad* going again and sailed quickly out of harm's way. Putting the autopilot in control, Bobby was able to reef without having to dump the wind out of the sail. *Strad* was much happier now with the wind approaching twenty knots. The swells were building to three feet with white caps everywhere. Even with the ebb current, *Strad* was making four knots to windward and riding over the waves smoothly. Bobby was confident that neither the Hobie nor the Flying Dutchman would be out in this wind, so he was happy.

He sailed on for several hours dodging crab pots, flotsam and deadheads hidden in the waves. The wind continued to build reaching probably twenty-five knots judging by the white caps and the steam coming off the waves, requiring a second reef by mid-evening. *Strad* handled the wind and waves nicely with two reefs. The remaining sail looked dinky but was more than adequate and the heeling moment was lowered significantly. Bobby sailed into nightfall playing the waves as best as he could due to the lack of visibility. As complete darkness set in, he had to play them by feel, which he wasn't so good at, but he made the effort. Occasionally, a wave caught *Strad* and slammed her to a shuddering stop, but not very often. Bobby kept *Strad* along the western shore, well clear of the dangerous Wilby Shoals on the south end of Quadra Island.

Discovery Passage had much smoother water, but a lot of commercial traffic even this late at night. The wind didn't abate any, though. If anything, it might even have intensified slightly. Bobby could see the lights of Campbell River a few miles up ahead and was determined to make it. Options for anchoring were slim. He continued to tack up the channel trying to find any back eddies. Despite his great speed through

---

[40] In irons – A sailboat is in irons when it is lying head to wind, sails flapping uselessly, with no momentum to turn in either direction

the water, his speed puck was only reading one knot and sometimes less. It was so frustrating to see his destination so close and be sailing so fast through the water, yet not being able to get there. But slowly, tack after tack, he inched up the channel. He was mostly staying along the western shore. There was a shoal up ahead before he reached Campbell River that he thought might shield him from some of the current. The shoal itself didn't appear to be dangerous, and Bobby couldn't see any eddies or rip currents in the night, so he just sailed on and hoped for the best. The smart sailors and commercial boats were all heading downstream. There were a few high-speed Zodiac boats still zipping around that couldn't care less about the current. The ebb would die soon, but Bobby was afraid that the wind would go with it. He continued sailing hard and by ten, he was able to just sneak inside the breakwater at Campbell River Marina. Inside the breakwater, the water was completely calm. No wind. No current. The shore lights reflected perfectly on the flat water. He drifted over to an open dock and moored *Strad*. It just happened to be in front of the marina office and the showers.

Checking his current charts, slack water was in an hour. The gate was closed at Seymour Narrows. He couldn't get there in time this evening. Campbell River was six miles south of the Narrows, and he had to go through at slack water. Anything else could be deadly for such a small boat. The narrows featured currents that flowed at over nine knots generating huge standing waves and deadly eddies and whirlpools. The next slack water was in six hours. He needed to be underway at three in the morning to make it. He checked the tracker again and found the Hobie ashore just south of Discovery Passage. Clair had made some major gains in the high wind. The Flying Dutchman was ashore further south not too far from the wherry. The Green Machine was still back in Nanaimo. Would they get underway with the flood and try to make the same tide gate at four-thirty? If not, they'd miss two tide gates.

The showers were locked, but he was luckily able to get the code from a couple who were returning to their boat, presumably from a night on the town. The restaurants were calling his name, but it was late, and they were starting to close. Sighing, he stowed the sail properly, turned off the running lights and set up the cockpit cover. He took off his life jacket and lanyard, then dug out his cooking gear. The kitty immediately came over to help. Freeze-dried Chicken Teriyaki. Scrumptious! Maybe not. The kitty didn't even like it. She waited patiently for the oatmeal, leaving Bobby to choke down the chicken. At least it was warm. He ended up having to make two servings of oatmeal since the kitty polished off one all by herself. Later, he emptied his trash and refilled all his water bottles and one five-gallon bladder from the hose bib on the dock.

There were two other racers in the harbor waiting for the tide gate to open. He recognized the monohull as a Santa Cruz 27, and the other, a trimaran, maybe a Corsair 24 or 27. Their exhausted crews were either down below asleep, or up in the bars. After supper, Bobby cleaned up the pots properly for once using fresh water from the dock, then went over to take a shower. It was a coin operated shower and he had stocked up on Loonies just for this occasion. After cleaning himself and shaving, he just lingered in the hot water thinking of Hali and how they used to shower together on the weekends. She was so far away. That whole world seemed so far away. The hot water finally shut off, so he reluctantly dried off using his back-packing super absorbent towel and put on some fresh clothes. He brushed his teeth luxuriously this time. Feeling totally refreshed, he returned to *Strad* and climbed below the cockpit cover throwing his stinking undershirt at the kitty. She immediately claimed it and curled up on it purring.

R2AK DAY 4

23

Bobby's alarm went off at two forty-five, and he very reluctantly got up, shooed the kitty out of his sleeping bag and stowed his gear. It was cold out, so he added thermals under his fleece, and donned the hat and gloves that Hali had bought for him. He made one last trip to the bathroom, then got underway. There was no wind at all, and the marina lights reflected perfectly off the flat water. The Santa Cruz and Corsair still showed no signs of life. He pedaled slowly out of the marina, and into the darkness. It was complete blackness. There was no moon or stars, and once he moved away from the marina, the remaining shore lights were obscured by a light fog or mist. There were no boats at all on the water. At least, none showing lights. If his competition didn't join him now, he'd be able to make some major gains on them. He could barely see *Strad's* bow, and only then because of the running lights on either side. Everything was black. If there were deadheads, he'd never see them. Binoculars didn't help much. He could only trust his GPS to keep him on course. If he weren't looking at it constantly, he'd end up steering in circles. He had the last of the flood behind him adding over a knot to his speed. He signed in to Facebook and made a post "Kitty and I are underway at 3:00 am bound for Seymour Narrows. Everything is Black. No moon. No stars. No lights. Just black. I'm supposed to go through the Narrows in this?! Might not be prudent..."

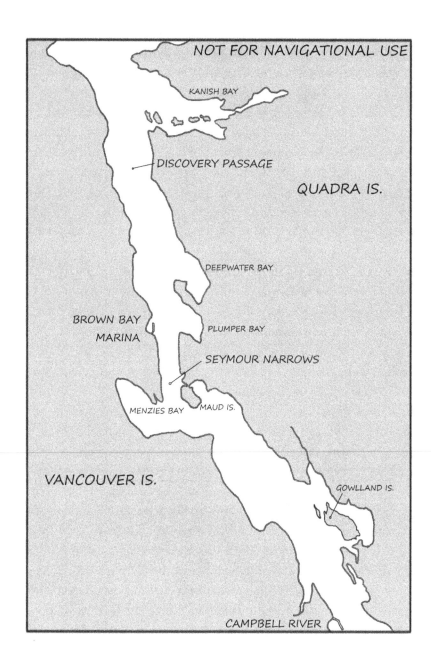

NOT FOR NAVIGATIONAL USE

KANISH BAY

DISCOVERY PASSAGE

QUADRA IS.

DEEPWATER BAY

BROWN BAY
MARINA

PLUMPER BAY

SEYMOUR NARROWS

MENZIES BAY   MAUD IS.

VANCOUVER IS.

GOWLLAND IS.

CAMPBELL RIVER

Actually, the kitty was fast asleep in her little box on Bobby's dirty undershirt and couldn't care less. Bobby pedaled on for an hour with a dying current push. There were no other boats out to chop up the water. He reached the last point before the Narrows at about four-thirty. There was a faint glow along one side of the horizon that indicated that dawn was approaching. Using the binoculars, Bobby tried looking at the water surface for clues, but could discern nothing. He pedaled across towards Maud Island on the east side of the Narrows and the speed puck just read two and half knots. No current push. He was at slack water. It was now or never. He rounded Maud Island and stuck *Strad's* bow out into the channel. There was wind in the channel. Not overly strong, maybe ten knots, but real wind. Bobby was tempted to turn back into shelter and put the sail up. But he couldn't see where he was going, nor could he see the tell-tales on the sail. He needed his hands free to hold the GPS and steer. So, taking a deep breath and trusting the *Ports and Passages Guidebook* that he was here at slack water, he went for it. He'd never be able to see any of the eddies or whirlpools if they were present. He silently recited the Lord's prayer, then asked God for guidance through the Narrows and avoidance of any hazards. He thought that if there were any standing waves, he'd see them. He didn't, even with the binoculars. He pedaled hard and steered up along the east side of the channel. There were still some extraordinarily strong current swirlies that tried to spin *Strad*, but they were manageable. As he pedaled on, the sky got gradually a bit brighter, and both the wind and the adverse current began to intensify. Fortunately, the wind was with the current, or the waves would have built up quickly. He pedaled harder but his speed over ground had dropped to two knots. There was a marina up ahead on the port side, so he gradually worked his way across the Narrows. By six, he was barely making headway. The sky was brighter, and the adverse current was really picking up steam. Another half hour and he'd be swept back through the maelstrom at full flow. That could be deadly. He put *Strad* in shallow water right on the shore trying to avoid the main flow and gradually inched his way towards the little cove occupied by Brown's Bay Marina. He was pedaling as hard as he could to make any headway at all as he entered the cove. He finally relaxed and let his momentum and a bit of back-eddy take him the rest of the way to the marina. The nearest docks were for the larger boats, so he pedaled around the far side where the small boats were. These slips were all full, so he tied alongside a derelict runabout that obviously wasn't going anywhere any time soon.

Updating his Facebook page was a problem since his cold hands were shaking so bad. But eventually he got it done. As tired as he was, setting up the cockpit cover, and retrieving his sleeping gear took several minutes longer than usual. He was back asleep within minutes of stripping off his life jacket and dry suit. He had at least four more hours before the current turned. It took the kitty several more minutes to figure out that a warm body was available, and to join him inside the sleeping bag. They slept soundly until ten o'clock, when a local wake rocked *Strad* violently. Bobby dragged himself out of the bag and slowly got dressed. His head was pounding with fatigue, but it abated slowly once he started moving around. He wandered out and looked at the wind on the water. It was blowing hard. Really hard. There wasn't much wind in the cove, but the channel was nothing but white caps. The wind waves were exceeding a foot high. Nothing breaking though. At least not yet. He estimated the wind was probably over twenty knots.

He wandered over to the marina office and asked the harbormaster if he needed to pay anything for their short stay. He was pleased that there would be no charge. The harbormaster pointed out two other boats that were also participants in the race moored on the far side with the bigger boats. Both were trimarans and both showed signs of life. There was a little store at the marina, but it was mostly fishing stuff. Bobby told the harbormaster the story about saving the kitty and needing some food. His eyes lit up and he wanted to come visit with the kitty. He just happened to be a cat lover. He called his wife and within fifteen minutes she came down with five small cans of wet cat food to give him. He also found a couple of old ashtrays from the restaurant that could be used as water bowl and a food dish.

Bobby taped the water bowl next to the kitty's box up forward and half filled it with water. The kitty immediately drank most of the water.

Fortunately, the cat food cans had a pop top and a resealable lid, so he didn't need a can opener. The kitty ate like she would never see food again. Bobby took his time with his freeze-dried eggs. He was eyeing the restaurant, but they wouldn't open until noon, and he was in a hurry to be off again. He even skipped the oatmeal this time. Cleaning up and using the bathroom one last time, he eyed the wind on the water judging it to about twenty to twenty-five knots. Double reef, but he could handle it. He knew he was violating his own safety rules as well as his promises to avoid unnecessary risks just by going out in this storm. But Bobby was too much of a racer to pass up the opportunity to put some big miles between him and his competition. He battened everything down, including the kitty who wanted to be petted and played with, emptied the cat's water, and raised the sail with two reefs. Anticipating that he would be using the trapeze, he moved the seat to the pedaling location amidships and donned the harness. Pushing out of the slip, he sailed easily around the docks over to the two trimarans. Chatting with them for a few minutes, he discovered that they were staying put until the evening when the wind was expected to die down. So, he wished them good luck and turned towards the breakwater. He left with the feeling that they really didn't believe he would make it much further. It just strengthened his resolve.

His competition was safely behind him and probably wouldn't clear the Narrows for at least five or six more hours. They needed the flood just to get up Discovery Passage, and that was an hour or so away. Could they make it all the way up by the next gate? Bobby assumed so. Hopefully, they would have this same wind where they were and would remain ashore. But he was on his way north to Alaska.

The current was still adverse, but it was weaker, maybe two knots against him. He wanted to get into Johnstone Strait before it turned. He guessed the wind would be less there, though Johnstone Strait is known for its gales and weird current patterns. At least, there were plenty of places to bail out and anchor. He hardened up and braced himself for the onslaught of the wind. It wasn't subtle, more like a sledgehammer. But Bobby eased sheets slightly keeping *Strad* upright until she accelerated to full speed, then hardened up and started beating to weather. Then he eased out onto the trapeze. It felt nice to finally stand up for a while after all that pedaling this morning. The chop looked far worse than it really was. In fact, Bobby even considered shaking out a reef, but decided against it. He had a long way to go. No point in breaking anything. One of Bobby's personal safety rules: when your life depends on the equipment, don't break it.

The kitty wasn't happy with the waves. The bow kept rising and falling under her, making for an uncomfortable ride. She came out to sit in Bobby's lap, but there was none. She even tried crawling up his legs, but Bobby shooed her away. Miffed, she went over and used her litter box, then lay down in the corner adjacent to the litter box and gave Bobby the evil eye. Eventually, she won. Bobby got tired of standing on the trapeze and moved the seat back to the side deck. The kitty had her lap back! She purred contentedly as Bobby stroked her.

From Brown's Bay Marina to Chatham Point, which marks the beginning of Johnstone Strait, is about twelve miles. With an adverse tide, and a strong adverse wind, it took *Strad* over four hours to make it, and the current was beginning to turn when he got there. Bobby knew that the current behind him would clash with the wind against him forming steep, dangerous waves. As expected, the wind did abate very slightly, down to about eighteen to twenty knots. Bobby could easily shake out one of his reefs with this wind, but he decided to play it conservatively. Besides, the kitty was comfortable in his lap and he couldn't bear to disturb her. The speed puck was showing a solid five knots, and he was having a good time playing the waves. *Strad* was happy. Another of Bobby's safety rules: keep the boat happy. That means don't go slamming her into the waves, keep her upright so her foils work properly, and don't strain the rig unnecessarily.

As he drove *Strad* to windward passing Turn Island on the port side, a seaplane came flying over extremely low to the water. Bobby was sure he was trying to land, though he couldn't understand why in the world anyone would want to land out here. But the plane dipped down and circled him several times, then gained elevation and turned away to the south. It must be photographers, Bobby thought. He looked at the rig, and the way *Strad* was sailing through the steep waves and decided satisfactorily that she made a pretty picture. Doubly reefed, the remaining amount of sail is tiny, and the steaming waves effectively told the story of man battling against the elements all by itself. No further words needed. Johnstone Strait. It was enough to strike fear in any prudent sailor considering doing the Inside Passage. The picture eventually showed up on the R2AK Facebook page, and Gerald shared it the Team LaRoche page. It became one of the iconic images of the 2018 Race to Alaska. Much later, it would hang framed in Gerald's office.

The current push was building, and the waves with it. Bobby was working the waves as hard as he could, reluctant to seek shelter and looking for every hole possible. He headed over to the starboard side hoping to find some relief from the waves behind the Walkem Islands. This worked for a bit, but eventually he had to sail out into the chop again. It was too early to stop for the night, and he had at least two hours of push remaining. The speed puck was registering six plus knots. The next possible stopping point was fourteen miles away at Helmcken Island. Dusk would come before he reached it, and the push would be about exhausted by then. Good enough place as any to ride out the adverse current. He had been eating power bars and teriyaki sticks all afternoon since it was too rough for cooking. The kitty nibbled on some Power Bar, but the teriyaki sticks were too spicy. The last thing Bobby needed was a kitty with diarrhea aboard. She would just have to wait. He did offer her some water whenever he drank, which she was happy to accept.

As the sun was setting, both the wind and the current started dying. When he was within two miles, he unreefed the sail completely. The chop remained and was now so random that Bobby had an extremely hard time finding a smooth path through the crests. His speed slowed to four, then three, then two and a half, and both his patience and the push ran out. Dumping the kitty ungracefully into the cockpit, he lowered the sail, installed the pedal-drive unit, and pedaled the rest of the way directly into the remaining chop. The kitty found a comfortable spot on his shoulder and nuzzled his ear telling him that he really should be feeding her right now. There are two bays on Helmcken Island on the north side, Billy Goat Bay and Deer Bay. He picked the first one, which also contained a cruising sailboat. It was dark when he entered, so the other boaters weren't aware of his presence. He anchored, turned off his running lights and turned on his anchor lights, then dug out his pots and stove and freeze-dried food. He had an efficient LED lantern that lit up the whole cockpit which made cooking easier at night. The kitty was a big help selecting his supper. Asian cashew chicken. And she was a big help eating it too, taking care of all the chicken lumps all by herself, leaving Bobby with all the vegetables and noodles. She even ate a good portion of his oatmeal afterwards, and then promptly turned up her nose at her own cat food. Lesson learned. Give the kitty her own food to eat before starting to cook his own supper. Maybe he'd get to eat some of his own that way. He had to cook up one of the Cup-a-Soups to fill himself up.

The night was calm, the sky was clear, and the cove was peaceful. With an adverse current, Bobby didn't really have to worry about the boats behind him for the time being. He had a very weak cell signal, so he made a simple post saying that he was safely moored in Billy Goat Bay awaiting the push. The signal wasn't near strong enough to allow him to check on the progress of his competitors.

As he rigged the cockpit cover, he heard a big splash. Big enough as if someone had done a belly flop in the water. Breaking out the spotlight, he scanned towards the direction the sound came from. Nothing. No animals on shore. No ripples on the water. Nothing at all. He looked over at the cruising sailboat, and their lights were already out for the night. Nothing there. Interesting. It was way too big of a splash to be a fish. He finished putting up the cockpit cover and stowed the spotlight, then heard the splash again. Eerie. He grabbed the spotlight, unzipped the front of the cockpit cover, and again searched the water. Eventually, he saw some ripples that were quickly dissipating. Something big was out there. He searched the water for a long time. Nothing. He went back inside and zipped up the cover. Another unsolved puzzle.

The kitty was waiting somewhat impatiently for him to break out the sleeping gear and warm up her sleeping bag for her. He stroked her for a while thinking that she needed a name. What kind of name would be appropriate to a boat cat? Not just any boat cat, but *Strad's* boat cat. The answer came swiftly. Stradivarius made violins, cellos, violas and even basses. Out of all of those, *Viola* was the only name appropriate for a female kitty. And so, she became Viola and she was *Strad's* boat cat. She was still waiting impatiently for her warm sleeping bag, though. Bobby laughed and dug out his mattress and bag, then stripped off most of his clothes and cleaned up as best he could, then crawled inside the bag wearing a new base layer. He had five hours to sleep before the current changed.

R2AK DAY 5

24

Port McNeil was his next designated stopping spot, and it was over fifty miles away. He was hopeful he could make it in one long day, but the current and wind would have to help. He awoke at four, well before dawn, got dressed and stowed his gear. Breakfast could wait. Viola wasn't pleased to be displaced so early, but she settled in on his dirty undershirt in her box. Raising the anchor was the easy part. Getting out of a harbor surrounded by sharp rocks covered with mussels was more of a challenge. The GPS helped, but Bobby had the spotlight going out ahead of him just in case as he inched out of the bay. Once clear of the harbor, he turned westward and settled down to pedal. The current in Johnstone Strait can do some funny, unpredictable things. He found a weak adverse current on the side of the island that he was on, but later, a push on the other side. Finding and analyzing the current lines is critical on those waters. But for now, the sky was dark, and he was barely able to see the islands and the mainland with the help of the stars. The moon had set long ago. Tide lines and other debris including deadheads, were invisible. Cruising along at an easy gait with a small push at three knots, Bobby got on Facebook and announced Viola's new name and the reason behind it. How many sixteen-foot boats had resident kitties? Now that he had named her, they were bound to each other. But then Viola already knew that. She had claimed him.

At a little before eight, Bobby let *Strad* drift in a one knot current and prepared breakfast. But he fed Viola first and made sure she had water in her little bowl. She ate suspiciously, knowing that Bobby was going to bring out the good stuff later. And he did if you could call freeze-dried eggs with hash browns and sausage 'good-stuff'. She left room for his sausage at least, and even a portion of his oatmeal. She was still a skinny little kitty, but she wasn't looking quite as emaciated. She'd washed herself a few times and was a bit more presentable. There was little sign of the pitiful little kitty that Bobby had rescued. And now that she'd claimed a human as her own, she was quite content. Life was good. With a weak cellular signal, he was eventually able to get an update on his competition. Both the Hobie and the Flying Dutchman had made it through the Narrows along with the trimarans and the Santa Cruz. The wherry was in Campbell River, and both the Frenchie and the Green Machine were approaching the southern opening to Discovery Passage. The Hobie and the Flying Dutchman were in Brown Bay Marina. All the others were giving chase.

The sky had been clear at dawn but was now showing a line of solid cumulus to the west. The barometer was ominously low, even lower than yesterday. Could be a storm coming. A light breeze sprang up at about ten, dead in his face. Bobby pedaled on until the breeze exceeded five knots steady, then set sail. He had been pedaling faster than he was now sailing, but he needed a break. The day had barely begun, and he had been pedaling for almost five hours already. He had covered the first twenty miles, thirty more to go, preferably under sail. *Strad* barely heeled at all in the light breeze for the first hour. By two o'clock, the breeze strengthened to over ten knots and *Strad* was rolling along happily at over four knots. Bobby found almost no push anywhere except along the port shore, so he was short tacking, trying to stay in the current.

On one tack that took him awfully close to shore, Bobby spotted a large tawny-brown grizzly bear on the shore. It didn't look like the bear was aware of him as he sailed by. Bobby extended one tack all the way to the shore so he could get a couple of pictures. The bear was walking along the beach, turning over rocks and eating any crabs hidden beneath them. It was completely oblivious to his presence. Bobby tacked back offshore but returned very soon for a second look. However, the bear was behind him now and Bobby had to focus on sailing. So, the few pictures would have to suffice. Another Facebook post.

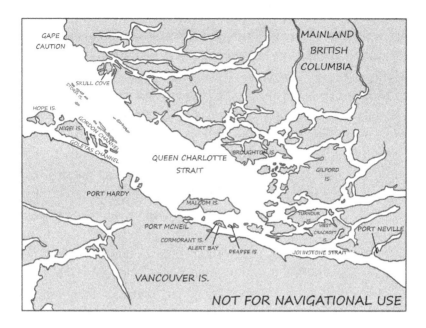

The clouds grew thicker and taller ahead of them. He eyed the clouds warily, hoping that they would blow themselves out before they reached him. By three, Bobby had all the wind he could handle without reefing, but he sailed on enjoying the speed and the wind in his face. The current push had disappeared long ago, but no knock[41] had appeared either. *Strad* was pushing five and a half knots in the flat waters. At one point, Bobby glanced astern and noticed all three trimarans chasing him. There was no way he could stay with them in this wind. At least the Santa Cruz and his competition were still back there out of sight. He sailed on for another hour, then reefed as the wind finally got too much for him. The clouds were getting ominous promising more wind to come. The waves were starting to build, and the surface was covered with small white caps. Bobby worked *Strad* through the waves, steering a sort of S-course and kept the spray out of the cockpit.

Up ahead, he spotted a group of playful little harbor porpoises frolicking in the waves. They appeared to be very dark, almost black.

---

[41] Knock- Adverse current

There could have been a dozen or so playing happily in the growing waves oblivious to the pending storm. They quickly swam over to *Strad* and surrounded her for a few minutes, dashing through the waves and jumping out of the water. Bobby laughed at their obvious exuberance and tried unsuccessfully to get a picture or two. *Strad's* bow-wave and wake weren't large enough to hold their attention for long, though, and they soon lost interest and moved off.

By seven, the clouds ahead had become truly dangerous. They had merged and risen to a true cumulonimbus shape. That meant that extremely strong winds are likely. The lower portions were dark gray, almost black. Lots of rain coming as well. Somewhere to the west, maybe Port Hardy, the folks were about to get slammed. Bobby tried to judge how far off it was and hoped he could still make it to Port McNeil. He took in a second reef in the rising wind and settled in for a long, wet ride. The wind was already over twenty knots, but *Strad* was sailing easily with two reefs. Port McNeil was still ten miles ahead, about two hours away. The sun had already disappeared, and the wind had gotten colder. Bobby had expected the storm to blow out over Port Hardy, but that wasn't the case. The sky just ahead of him was fast turning black. Lightning flashed up ahead striking the sea. The horizon was gone. The waves had abated slightly as he neared Cormorant island, and the wind was being affected by the islands as well. It was no longer consistently in his face but kept shifting wildly from side to side making sailing difficult and frustrating.

Looking astern, he saw no sign of the trimarans. They had either sought shelter or gone north of Malcolm Island. Bobby hoped for their sake that they sought shelter. It was time for him to consider doing the same. Maybe he should seek shelter now. This was not the type of storm to take a small boat out in. It was readily obvious that he wouldn't make it to Port McNeil. He decided to seek shelter in Alert Bay on Cormorant Island instead. It was just ahead on the starboard side, maybe fifteen or twenty minutes at the rate he was sailing. The daredevil in him wanted to try his hand at sailing in the storm since shelter was so close. But he also knew that this storm could pack gusts of well over fifty knots and if he couldn't handle the wind under sail, he wouldn't be able to douse the sail or rig the cockpit cover. It was now or never. But if he stopped now to douse, he would get surely caught up in it. Finally, thinking of Hali and the safety rules that he had agreed to, common sense prevailed. Bobby made the decision to douse sails altogether. It was no easy task in the twenty plus knot winds. *Strad* was in the trough and rocking wildly with the waves. He managed to put on extra lashings around the sail, then fought the cockpit cover for a good ten minutes before succeeding. He remembered to pull the litter box forward away from the open back end of the cover. While this was going on, *Strad* had been swept to the east and was no longer in the shelter of the island. Settling into the seat, Bobby struggled to get her underway in the swells. With a lot of effort, he eventually got her bow into the waves and started to make slow forward progress towards Alert Bay about two miles ahead. Viola approved as she came out of her box and perched on his shoulder.

No sooner had he had passed Gordon Bluff on Cormorant Island when the storm hit with a fury. Even with the sail down, *Strad* was tossed on her side and spun backwards. Rain came down so hard that Bobby couldn't see where he was going, and he thought the canopy might tear off in shreds. Pedaling furiously and timing the waves, he finally got the bow pointed back into the waves. But forward progress was all but impossible. He couldn't see them, but he knew the shoreline on either side were deadly dangerous. He was safe for now in open water, but he was working hard at the pedals. He couldn't keep this up for long. Viola understood the danger from the moment they were tossed on their side. She understood the severity of the storm and how hard Bobby was working to keep them safely pointing into the waves. Instead of hiding in her box, she perched quietly on Bobby's shoulder and listened to the wind and rain. Occasionally, she would let out a low guttural growl at the storm. And occasionally, she would rub her cheek encouragingly against Bobby's ear. There was no helping it, *Strad* was crashing from wave to wave, shuddering with every impact. If Bobby tried to steer anywhere but right into the wind, the bow would be blown right around out of control. The rudder was barely useful at all due to their slow progress. A sea anchor is what he needed, but he didn't have one. They don't sell sea anchors sized for sixteen-foot boats. He had his plastic collapsible bucket, but he was sure the handle would just rip off.

Little by little he was working over to the starboard shore. Ahead lay Alert Bay, though he couldn't see anything. Surely there would be shelter there. As he worked to starboard, the waves became worse and his forward progress was halted. He guessed that the wind was blowing well into the fifty-knot range with gusts into the sixty-knot range. Another rule to add to his list - watch violent storms from the safety of the nice warm living room. Boating in a storm sucks! Everything through the dodger windows was black except for the flashes of lightning. Thankfully, the lightning was still off ahead. GPS was telling him that he was nearing the shoreline. He must at all costs stay off the shore. He had seen the rocks and the steep bluffs on Cormorant Island. He probably would not survive being swept ashore. And Viola kept reminding him of that. His legs were getting tired now, but he kept on pumping the pedals furiously. He tried the spotlight through the dodger, and immediately blinded himself. After letting his eyes recover for a few seconds, he stuck the spotlight under the canopy into the storm and shone it forward. What he saw terrified him! There was a huge section of broken dock bearing down on him dead ahead of *Strad's* bow!

Bobby swerved to port and felt a solid bump which shook *Strad* from end to end as the dock section swept past. They had survived that danger but due to the evasive turn, *Strad* was swept sideways into the trough of the waves and knocked over on her side. Viola wailed and dug all claws in as Bobby struggled to regain control and get *Strad* pointed back into the wind. Just staying in the seat was a challenge. He finally succeeded after several tense moments fearing she would roll over. That little bit of ballast at the end of the four-foot keel had saved her. But they had lost much valuable headway in the process. Bobby again turned on the spotlight, and this time he could see the shore near-by. There was something happening on the beach up ahead, but he couldn't make it out. There were lots of sirens and flashing emergency lights both on the beach and on the water.

Using the light, Bobby could make out flatter spots in the water, and spots where the waves were really roiling. Turning slightly away from the beach, he found a flatter spot and pedaled furiously through it, then turned back to starboard to avoid a rough series of waves. After a few more minutes, he found another flatter area and drove hard through it. Then he was halted by a long series of large waves. All he could do was just ride them out and pray that he didn't lose much ground. Four or five minutes later and he found another flatter spot, so he pedaled hard to make it through that area. This went on for half an hour before he suddenly realized that he was finding more and more flat spots. He pulled in the spotlight and checked the GPS. He was well into Alert Bay. Relief washed over him. His legs and lungs ached, and he was soaking with sweat. It was still incredibly windy, and the waves were still pounding, but not quite as high as in the channel. There were two marinas in the bay. One was behind him now, but he didn't feel safe turning *Strad* downwind. He could let her drift backwards keeping the bow into the wind, or he could just keep on going to the tribal marina up ahead. He decided to keep going forward. The deeper he penetrated the bay, the smaller the waves. And very shortly he was sheltered almost completely from the wind. He pedaled towards the far shore close to the tribal marina, but couldn't make out how to get in. There were no lights at all along the shore, presumably a power failure. So, he abandoned that idea and found a quieter spot in the lee of the bluff and dropped anchor in the somewhat smoother water. He was spent!

He hugged Viola in relief. She understood and started purring immediately. They were safe. The only damage was the litter box which had spilled during the moments spent on their side. Lesson learned. He'd never ride out a storm like that again. He had tried to outrun the storm and make it to Port McNeil before the storm hit, and that was a mistake that had very nearly cost him his life. When he saw the storm approaching, he should have sought refuge in the Pearse Islands. His legs were like rubber, and he was exhausted. And now he was getting cold since he was so sweaty.

Viola reminded him that she had missed her supper. Groaning, he got up and filled her water bowl, then dug out a half open can of cat food and served her royal highness. He got undressed, washed up as much as he could, then donned some dry clothes. He hung his fleece up under the canopy to air out and hopefully dry a bit before tomorrow. He was cold and hungry. He couldn't really stomach the thought of freeze-dried stroganoff, so he went straight for the oatmeal. Quick and hot. And a Power Bar for dessert. The storm continued to rage for another two hours and the seas tossed *Strad* around her anchor line, but Viola was oblivious, snuggled up to her human deep inside her sleeping bag.

R2AK DAY 6

25

Bobby awoke at seven with the sun streaming through the dodger windows. He hadn't set an alarm. Eight hours of solid sleep! It felt decadent! But there was a race to run. He scrambled out of his bag and quickly got dressed. His legs were still sore. He fed Viola and filled her water bowl, then dug out his cooking stuff. Denver omelet. Oh boy! Viola ate her share, then some of the oatmeal as well, before going back to her own food. The day was warming up fast with no sign of any wind. The canopy was dry, so he took it down and rolled it up.

Port McNeil was only six miles away, two hours of pedaling. Bobby's over-used muscles screamed in pain at first, but soon warmed up as the lactic acid from last night was finally flushed out. The seas, which were deadly rough last night, were now calm as a pond. There was debris everywhere though, including several docks and even some semi-swamped boats. A large aluminum fishing trawler, maybe fifty to sixty feet long was high and dry on the beach on the east end of the bay. That must have been what all the emergency lights were all about last night. It would be interesting to see how they refloat that one, but Bobby wasn't going to wait around to find out. He did take a picture and posted his experience to Facebook. He had a decent cellular signal, so he logged into the tracker. The Frenchie and the wherry had made it through the Narrows in the night. The Frenchie was continuing and would soon reach Johnstone Strait. The wherry was in Brown's Bay Marina. The Hobie had made some amazing gains and was now passing Helmcken Island very slowly. With no wind, Claire was rowing along at just over one knot. The Flying Dutchman was behind her but gaining. Both were well over thirty miles behind *Strad*.

As he approached Broad Point, Bobby noticed something white on the shore under a steep bluff. There wasn't much beach there, though at low tide the shore was exposed. It was a wreck. Bobby studied it through his binoculars as he neared. It was a trimaran. Maybe a Corsair or a Farrier 27. The rig was gone. One ama was either gone or submerged. The hull was swamped. There were a couple of people up on the bluff looking down on the wreck, but no sign of life aboard. Bobby checked his tracker and there were no distress signals, and no other competitors anywhere near him, so he was somewhat confident that this wasn't a racer. Probably a boat that had been anchored in Port McNeil before the storm swept it away and crushed it on the rocky shore. He made a close pass and took some photos. The wreck was obviously fresh with a field of debris strewn about the shore for a quarter mile. Bobby silently said a prayer of thanks that he had escaped a similar fate.

As they approached Port McNeil, Bobby was suddenly aware that the pedal-drive unit was no longer making a quiet swish-swish sound. It was creaking with every stroke. He was still cruising along strongly at over two knots, but something was clearly amiss with it. He paused for a few minutes and extracted the unit. The balance cable was broken, and one of the drive cables was severely frayed where it attached to the drive chain. Fortunately, he had all the spare parts and tools to repair the unit, but he decided it could wait until he got into port. He pedaled slowly for the last mile or so contemplating the situation. Obviously, he had strained the unit beyond its limits last night in the storm. But a more somber thought was the revelation that had the unit broken during the storm, he might not be alive today. Once again, fate had been kind to him.

Viola sat on his shoulder and guided him into port at Port McNeil. *Strad* moored close to the fuel dock, right behind a battered trimaran. Bobby walked up to examine her. There was a large hole in her bow and a good three to four feet of one of her amas[42] was torn off and lashed to the netting. She was an extremely high-performance trimaran with a canting mast, lifting foils and rudders on her amas instead of the hull. She wore

---

[42] Ama – a pontoon used for stability of trimarans and proas

an R2AK race number on her battered bow and had probably been the race leader at one point. No one was aboard to talk to. Bobby figured that she had probably hit a dead head at full speed. It certainly did not appear to be storm damage. Returning to *Strad*, Bobby was able to plug in all his chargers at once. Viola took the opportunity to lay out in the sun on the deck forward of the mast. The Hobie Mirage pedal-drive system was easy to repair, taking him only about thirty minutes. And half of that was reading the instructions for tuning it after the cables were replaced. He replaced all three cables, saving the one that was still usable as an emergency repair part. Viola seemed happy lying in the sun on deck and showed no inclination for leaving the boat, so Bobby decided to just leave her and hope she stayed put. He refilled his water bottles and one bladder, emptied his trash, then went off to the opposite side of the harbor to take a shower, shave and put on some clean clothes. Feeling like a king, he ran up to the IGA grocery store. He found the same brand of cat food that Viola was already eating, and a small bag of kitty litter, so she was taken care of. They had no freeze-dried foods, so he bought caribou jerky, carrot sticks, Pop Tarts, and more Power Bars before returning to the boat. Viola had moved into the shade in the cockpit when he returned but was not leaving the boat. This was her new home. He was so tempted to go to the restaurant for a burger, but there was a race to run, and competitors were breathing down his neck. He had little choice but to press on. There was still no wind, but there was an ebb current just starting and he had an ideal opportunity to put some miles between him and his competitors.

As *Strad* was pulling out of dock at eleven thirty, a trimaran entered the harbor under manual power. They were using an elaborate propeller drive system with two pedalers driving a single propeller, but they were only moving at less than two knots. They waved as they passed. Bobby asked about the other trimarans and learned that at least two were heading in this direction. So, for the time being, they were behind him. He moved out of the harbor and set a course for the other side of Queen Charlotte Strait. Skull Cove was over there and looked like a good option if the wind didn't pick up, but that meant pedaling for ten hours. Bobby had done it before, and he knew he could do it again. The pedal-drive system was back to working flawlessly and silently. It was so warm that Bobby was soon down to his undershorts and a T-shirt with Viola sitting approvingly on his shoulder nuzzling his ear.

The speed puck was showing a steady three and a half knots as he cleared Malcolm Island. There was a lot of open water ahead of him and a pod of humpback whales off in the distance in the direction Bobby was heading. He barely took notice of them. They'd be long gone by the time he got there. He pedaled on for hours humming tunes that he didn't know the words for. He had found a good solid push along the southern side of the Strait and his speed exceeded five knots for over two hours. He cleared Dillon Point near Port Hardy and edged northward over towards the Gordon Islands, where he could see a rookery of sea lions ahead. There must have been over a hundred on one rocky isle, but none on the adjacent ones. He pedaled closer and watched them through the binoculars. There were several huge Steller sea lions among the large group of California sea lions.

As he passed the Gordon Islands, he noticed something in the water ahead. At first, he thought it was just flotsam from the storm, but then it moved. And there were others. He peered at them with his binoculars for a few minutes thinking that they were probably sea lions, then suddenly realized that they were sea otters! Bobby had never seen sea otters before. They weren't like the river otters at all. They were almost always on their backs in the water for one thing. And they were much larger with lighter colored coats. As *Strad* approached silently, Bobby could see several were mothers clutching young to their bellies. He pedaled closer and was able to get some good pictures from about fifty feet away. More Facebook fodder. The sea otters didn't seem too overly concerned about his quiet presence. Those directly in his path swam clear, but most of the others just gazed at him lazily. A few were diving for clams, which they whacked at with rocks on their chests when they came back to the surface.

By three o'clock, a faint wind line appeared to the west. Bobby watched it develop, but it was far away and in the wrong direction. He pedaled on but kept an eye on it. It was getting closer, and darker.

Real wind. Bobby took a break and got something to eat and eyed the nearing wind line. It was out of the south, a racer's delight. As it neared, he stowed the pedal drive and raised the sail. The wind came on gently. *Strad* moved out eagerly with the five to six-knot breeze. There was more to come. Within an hour, the wind was up to ten knots and *Strad* was clocking five plus knots on a fast beam reach[43] as he passed Redfern Island. He was still riding a push even though the current chart said he was at slack water.

Now Bobby had a decision to make. Should he attempt Cape Caution at this late hour, or wait until tomorrow? Cape Caution was aptly named. It was exposed to the ocean swell and wasn't to be taken lightly. Prudence would say wait until morning. But this appeared to be the perfect wind for the attempt. If he went for it, he was committing to a long day. He still had options to bail out, but he continued as if he were going for the Cape. The clouds were friendly. Puffy cumulus clouds with blue skies, a sailor's delight. But the wind was freshening. By five, it was up to fifteen knots and *Strad* was planing along at eight knots. Bobby made up his mind – he was going for the Cape. Hali and his Mom might frown on the decision, but he was in a race not a cruise. He cleared the Storm Islands at seven o'clock and veered off on a fast-broad reach. He had swells now to surf and the speed puck was showing consistent spurts of up to ten plus knots. *Strad* was doing what she was built for - planing and surfing, sailing flat and fast. Looking back, Bobby could see two of the trimarans, but they were far from the wind line. And he was putting big miles between him and his real competition.

It was a beautiful evening for sailing and Bobby had the ideal conditions. He was going to milk this dry. He could stop in Smith Sound at Mill Brooke Cove. Or he could continue to Fury Cove. Or maybe he could just sail all night up Fitz Hugh Sound. Prudence pretty much ruled out the latter two, but then prudence should have ruled out even making the attempt on the Cape at this late hour. As he rounded the Cape, he found larger swells coming directly off the Pacific Ocean with

---

[43] Beam Reach – The wind is striking the sailboat on its side, the fastest point of sail

wind waves riding on top from the south. So, he had two different angles that he could surf. The wind was dead astern now and he was playing the waves and sailing shallow gybe angles, keeping the speed up over ten knots.

Bobby had left extra food and water out for Viola and had stuffed his pocket with the last of the Teriyaki sticks and a couple of Power Bars. Viola was in his lap letting him know that she approved of his performance. Every time Bobby gybed, he'd place Viola on the cockpit sole followed by the seat, then he'd gybe over, remount the seat, and settle back down. Viola would wait patiently through this disruption, then retake her throne. That process was repeated every half hour or so as they sped northwards.

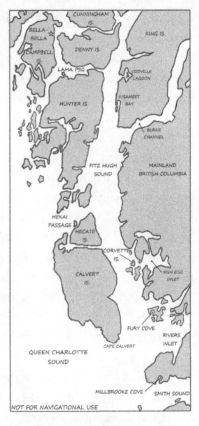

They were finally sailing due north to Alaska. Bobby passed Smith Sound as the sun set at nine thirty and kept on going. There was a brilliant orange, pink and purple sunset that energized him and filled him with wonder. *Red sky at night...* right? He was driving onwards. As he entered Fitz Hugh Sound, the sea swells gradually petered out, but the wind waves remained. Bobby was wide awake after his long sleep the night before. The half-moon rose to the east, and the wind showed no sign of dying. At ten-thirty, he passed Fury Cove. By midnight, Bobby was finally getting tired and Viola was mewing for a place to snuggle up for the night. The wind was still blowing fifteen plus knots within the sound and Bobby hated to give it up, but he had already pushed prudence too far. He found a sheltered cove on Corvette Island and snuck in carefully in the darkness.

The cove was well protected, and by the time Bobby had rolled out his mattress and sleeping bag, he was ready for sleep. There weren't even any ripples to disturb him and he had just nailed down a seventy-mile day, thirty of which was under pedal power. He was happy, and Viola was curled up in her proper place in his sleeping bag.

R2AK DAY 7

26

Early in the morning, as *Strad* cleared Corvette Island and headed out into the open water of Fitz Hugh Sound, Bobby settled down for an hour or so of sailing before preparing breakfast. They suddenly came upon a whole pod of humpback whales just basking on the surface. Bobby didn't see them in the low glow of pre-dawn until he was right on top of them, and then he had to swerve hard to port and put *Strad* in irons to avoid them. He counted six of them. They weren't traveling. They weren't diving. There were no spouts. They were just hanging out on the surface. There was one calf, and it was bigger than *Strad*. Bobby and Viola just stared for several minutes at these behemoths of the deep, reminded of just how puny they really were. He had only ever seen whales from a safe distance and now he was within spitting distance of a couple of them. Their immense size shocked him. They were at least twice if not three times the length of *Strad*. They had barnacles all over them, not the little barnacles you see on the local shores, but huge barnacles two or three inches across from far out at sea. They were peaceful creatures, and more than once they peered up at him curiously. Bobby took some great close-up photos, especially when they raised their heads to look at him. Eventually, Bobby realized that they, like the fishing boats, had no intention of getting out of his way. So, he finally used his telescoping paddle to turn the bow away from the wind, then hauled in the sheet and sailed back in the direction that he'd come. He sailed on for about five minutes in the ten-knot breeze, before tacking back to port hoping to have enough sea room to clear the tail end of the pod. Another rule of prudent sailing – when you're in a small frail boat in frigid waters, stay away from the tail of the whale! And he added humpback whales to the list of things he needed to watch out for.

Sailing downwind comfortably once more, Bobby velcroed the hiking stick in place and just let *Strad* sail herself. She was making a comfortable three knots with tiny little pushes from the wind waves. Far up ahead, Bobby could make out a dark sail that could only be one of the trimarans. They had sailed on through the night and passed him. Oh well, it was bound to happen sooner or later. Bobby had no real expectations of beating any of the trimarans, but it did feel good to have the lead on them for a while. To stay ahead of them, he'd need flat calm and that's the last thing he really wanted. There was no sign of the Flying Dutchman or the Hobie, though he knew that they would have made major gains in that wind. This was his seventh day on the water. The leaders would have finished several days ago, and he still had two hundred miles to go. Probably four more days, three if the wind cooperated.

Sighing and stretching, he finally dug out his stove and pots, then fed Viola. The day was still cold, and the wind chill made it worse. He boiled enough water for his freeze-dried eggs and for a cup of hot chocolate which he savored while waiting patiently for the eggs to rehydrate. Bella-Bella was ahead and was his last planned stop. Prince Rupert was available if he needed another stop, but he planned on only going there after the race was over. He'd meet his Dad there with the trailer. He should top off his water when he stopped in Bella-Bella. The six small bottles had already been used up, and one of his chores this morning was to refill them from the five-gallon bladder. Could he make it to Ketchikan without stopping in Bella-Bella? He'd have to do an inventory after breakfast, but he thought maybe he could. But that would leave him just the Cup-a-Soups in case of an emergency. He thought of yet another rule of prudent sailing – don't sail far from supplies unless you are stocked up adequately. The wind is fickle. If he ended up having to pedal all the way to Ketchikan he could be on the water for another week or ten days. He did not have the supplies for that. Viola was finally starting to prefer her own cat food, and only nibbled a slight bit on some of his eggs. She did enjoy some of his oatmeal but left most of it to Bobby. After cleaning up and stowing his gear, he inventoried his remaining supplies. He had enough breakfasts for four more days after today, and suppers for five more days. Hopefully, that would be enough. If not, he'd be eating Cup-a-Soups for every meal. He was sure he wouldn't be able to find freeze-dried food in Bella-Bella. He was set for lunches, however. Plenty of Power-Bars, carrot sticks and jerky to munch on. And now he had Pop Tarts to boot! Viola had plenty of food and fresh kitty litter, though the box needed repairs. And now he could leave her food out all day so he wouldn't get chastised so severely when she was hungry. He decided just to do a quick stop for water in Bella-Bella but forego the grocery stores. He was still determined to win this solo race. There was a city marina with water in Bella-Bella, and there was another marina at Shearwater Resort, right around the corner a little out of his way. Several people had recommended Shearwater Marina since they had a better store and were more focused on pleasure boaters. The Bella-Bella marina was tribal and commercial and had better water. Either way, they were both thirty-five miles away. With *Strad* happily rolling along at three knots, they'd arrive sometime in the early afternoon. And hopefully, the wind would pick up as the day warmed up.

Bobby did some exercises and stretches trying not to shake the boat, then settled down in the seat amidships where Viola happily settled in his lap, and they cruised north for several hours. Around eleven, the wind increased as did the wind waves, so Bobby moved aft and took the helm. The wind was soon gusting to fifteen knots and *Strad* was pushing five to six knots. When Bobby caught a larger wave, the speed jumped to eight to nine knots. Just before he entered Lama Passage on the port side of the sound, he looked astern and saw a spinnaker in the distance. Could that be the Santa Cruz? He knew in his heart that it was. It was way too big to be the Flying Dutchman. He was severely tempted to skip the stop in Bella-Bella and race the Santa Cruz. But that wouldn't be prudent, and he couldn't drive through the night like they could. He had no realistic chance to beat them to Ketchikan. If the wind held up, they could be there tomorrow.

Lama Passage was sheltered from the wind and his speed dropped back to a leisurely three knots. Up ahead, he suddenly saw a trimaran with tall black carbon sails enter the channel from the port side. They must have come through the cut between Campbell Island and Hunter Island. That was ballsy! The opening on the Queen Charlotte Sound side was blocked by literally hundreds of tiny islets and submerged rocks, and seaweed was everywhere. Definitely a good place to avoid at night. At least they had timed it right. Bobby had considered it during his trip planning and ruled it out as too risky. He had no way of clearing weed off his keel other than sailing backwards, which might be exceedingly difficult to do without a boom to push out. But somehow the trimaran had made it and came sailing fast into Lama Passage ahead of him. They'd be long gone soon, but Bobby had stayed ahead of them until now, two thirds of the way through the race. That should count for something. Within five minutes, the tri had disappeared down Lama Passage heading to Bella-Bella. When Bobby eventually rounded Twilight Point and could finally see Bella-Bella in the distance, the trimaran was nowhere to be seen.

The wind accelerated down this stretch of Lama Passage, and *Strad* was moving steadily at five to six knots again, with surges to eight to nine when Bobby caught a wave exactly right. It was after two o'clock when he finally moored at the city dock in Bella-Bella. He quickly filled his water bladder and four empty bottles, then pushed off the dock again. As he cleared the docks and sailed off, he looked over and saw the Santa Cruz rounding the bend. Maybe he could race them just until he got tired. He had *Strad* back up to speed quickly and sailed off for the lighthouse. Rounding the bend and heading out into Seaforth Channel put *Strad* on a fast beam reach. With the wind now at fifteen knots, he decided to use the trapeze just so he could stand for a while. His knees and butt were getting very sore from sitting so long. *Strad* was sailing along at an easy plane now at over ten knots, but the waves were only barely surfable due to the angle. Bobby had to veer off severely to catch the wave and then come back to course as he surfed. The extra distance wasn't worth the short gains, so Bobby gave it up. As he approached Rithit Island on the starboard side, a runabout came racing over to him and circled him several times shaking him severely with its wake. They finally came along side, where one guy in the bow cupped his hands around his mouth and yelled at him.

"Ahoy, there Team LaRoche! We're working for the Race Director taking pictures and doing interviews. Would you be willing to do an interview with us?"

"Okay," Bobby screamed back at him "as long as I don't have to stop. I'm racing the Santa Cruz behind me!"

"I have a microphone and earpiece for you, so we don't have to yell" he yelled back.

They inched the runabout up to Bobby on the trapeze and handed him a dry bag. Coming off the trapeze and letting the autopilot steer for a few minutes, he put the microphone lanyard around his neck and clipped the battery pack and the mike to his life jacket. Then he placed both earpieces in his ears after fiddling with them to sort out how they went in. He stuffed the drybag under his life jacket. Then he was back on the trapeze and steering effectively again. The runabout had moved to a leeward[44] and slightly astern position where they could film him as he talked. At least *Strad* was strutting her stuff in a consistent full plane. Once the radio check was complete, they were ready for the interview.

"The world wants to know... how's the kitty? Do you still have her with you?"

"Of course. She's adopted me. She's asleep in her box up under the deck forward right now. I named her Viola because the boat's name is Stradivaria. They go together. How many sixteen-foot boats have their own boat cats?"

"Not many. Tell us about her rescue."

---

[44] Leeward – the downwind, sheltered side

"I found her on a debris field back at Porlier Pass. She must have been adrift for several days. She was starved and thirsty, almost dead. I didn't have any cat food or milk. I gave her water which she was desperate for. I gave her some of my oatmeal and she really liked it. She's been sharing my freeze-dried food for a while. I made a litter box for her out of duct tape and stopped at Pirate's Cove for some sand. Then I used a hand warmer box as a bed for her. She loves it, especially with a dirty shirt in it. The Dock Master at Brown's Bay Marina gave us several cans of cat food, so, she's happy and well fed now. She sleeps with me in my sleeping bag, and rides on my shoulder when I pedal the boat. If I weren't on the trapeze right now, she'd be in my lap. I think she's the Captain and I'm just the First Mate."

"Well, you know your Faccbook post has just gone viral, don't you? The two of you have more followers than everyone else put together."

"Great! I didn't know that. I won't get the ten thousand dollars, or the steak knives. But I have my own prize and she's precious. And I'm still in the running for the first solo finisher. And that's worth a grand."

"Tell us about the highlights of the race so far."

"Well, building the boat was huge. I loved it and learned so much. I had no idea how to build a boat when I started. But she came out phenomenally. And she sails beautifully, especially when the wind is up. So, the boat is the main highlight. For the last two days, I've had this great southerly wind finally and the sailing has been fantastic! I'm really enjoying this. So, any time I'm not pedaling, I'm happy."

"Would you describe the pedal system for us?"

"I'm using a Hobie Mirage Drive mounted up forward of the keel. It works incredibly well. I can cruise at two and half to three knots all day. And I've done so. I've pedaled for ten hours straight a few days ago. It's reliable and efficient and fairly simple to build into the boat. I'd recommend it to any future racers. And... I can pedal and sail at the same time if I wanted to."

"What were your low points of the race so far?"

"Ohhh… I tried to outrun a storm when I was close to Port McNeil but got caught out in it. It was a vicious storm and it could have killed us. We survived, barely, by fighting our way into Alert Bay. An awfully close call and foolish in hindsight. We almost crashed into a dock that had broken free. A big aluminum trawler was washed up on shore. That was scary. The lesson learned is to seek shelter before the storm hits."

"Yeah, that one did a lot of damage. Two racers abandoned the race because of that storm. Gear damage. You did a good job just surviving that. Any other low points?"

"Just the long hours pedaling waiting for the wind to come up. Really tiring and tedious, but I've got to admit it kept me ahead of three trimarans and a Santa Cruz 27 for a long time. The tris are past me now, but the Santa Cruz is still astern of me."

"What route are you going to take from here? Inside Passage?"

"No. Not enough wind and too much adverse current. That's a good way to go south, not north. My route will depend on the wind and the waves. I'm planning to go inside Aristazabal Island and Banks Island."

"And after Banks Island?"

"We'll see. Totally weather dependent again. It's shallow up there, so the waves can get rough. Great to surf on if they're behind me. If they're against me, then I need to get inshore. Dixon Entrance will be the big challenge up ahead. I'm praying for smooth seas."

"Okay, then. Thanks for talking with us. Good luck getting to the finish."

It took another fifteen minutes to remove the mike and stow it without dropping anything overboard, then hand it over to them. All the while, *Strad* was happily planing along at over ten knots.

Bobby and Gerald had spent months poring over the charts determining their route north. There were so many options. British Columbia's famous Inside Passage runs from just north of Seattle, all the way up to the border with Alaska. And it continues in Alaska all the way up to Skagway and Glacier Bay National Park. With a few exceptions, a boater could travel all the way from Seattle to Glacier Bay without having to feel the brunt of the Pacific Ocean at any time. The route runs northward on the east side of Vancouver Island up the Strait of Georgia, through Discovery Pass (There are some alternate passages here, but the ferries and cruise ships all go through Seymour Narrows and Discovery Pass.) to Johnstone Passage and finally Queen Charlotte Strait. The first exposed part of the journey is between the mouth of Queen Charlotte Strait and the mouth of Fitz Hugh Sound. This is the infamous Cape Caution area and it can get quite rough. Mariners are advised to stay five miles offshore as they pass the Cape.

After Bella-Bella, the ferries, cruise ships and most boaters go up Princess Royal Channel and then over to Grenville Channel which takes them up a very protected and beautiful fjord through the mountains all the way to Prince Rupert, right on the border of British Columbia and Alaska. For tourists, this is a highly recommended route north. But Bobby and Gerald saw problems. The current flows strongly south, and weakly north. It's a great way to return from Alaska after the race, with as much as a five-knot southerly flow. The northerly flow runs at less than two knots. Furthermore, it's a fjord. The depths are thousands of feet deep and extend all the way to the steep cliffs on either side. There are very few anchorage sites along the way. The steep mountains and cliffs on either side funnel and accelerate the wind down the length one way or another. Murphy's law rules that it will usually be against you. And another big factor on this route is the high volume of both commercial and recreational vessel traffic.

One of the options for Bobby was the direct route from Bella-Bella to Ketchikan that runs for more than two hundred miles straight up Hecate Strait and across Dixon Entrance. Bobby would have to take a couple of breaks. This route is direct but exposed so would be very weather dependent. Dixon Entrance is notorious for bad waves. The full brunt of the Pacific Ocean sweeps in and crashes on to Learmonth Bank and then Celestial Reef forming monstrous waves. Dixon Entrance is a good place for small boats to avoid. Unfortunately, you can't reach Alaska by boat without crossing Dixon Entrance.

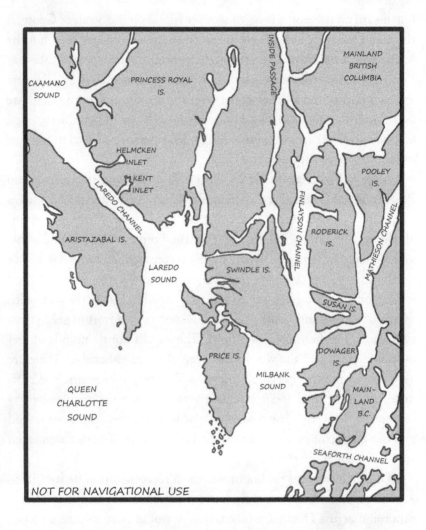

NOT FOR NAVIGATIONAL USE

The protected route that Bobby had chosen as his primary route went behind three large islands, Aristazabal, Banks and Porcher, which would take him close to Prince Rupert. His immediate concern coming out of Seaforth Channel was getting around Price Island which was very exposed to the Pacific swell. Alternatively, he could take the narrows behind the island, but he would have to pedal through that and then only at high tide. As Bobby sailed out of Seaforth Channel heading for open water, he was hoping he could clear Price Island via the open water route and stop overnight in the mouth of Kent Inlet behind Aristazabal Island. The day was getting on and the wind was still blowing fifteen knots as he sailed out of Seaforth Channel and entered Milbanke Sound. He had to harden up to a close reach and play the three to four-foot swells. The speed dropped off to four knots, but the course was good so that Bobby didn't have to swerve through the waves. He was going over them cleanly at about forty-five degrees to the waves. He decided to go for it. If he could make Kent Inlet, he'd be set up for a good long run tomorrow. Viola came out of her box and complained about the waves, so Bobby came off the trapeze, mounted the seat and gave her a nice lap to snuggle in. He was getting tired of standing anyway. One exceptionally long tack that took over two hours took him all the way to the tip of Price Island and the numerous islets and rocks at the tip. Extremely dangerous waters, and the sea foam and crashing waves reminded him just how tenuous his situation was. If he broke a mast right now, he'd be washed ashore and smashed on the rocks. There was just no surviving that. There were no buoys marking the channels up here. You're on your own. Thank God for GPS! He kept going for another twenty minutes after he rounded the point just to make sure he was clear, then bore away and eased the sheet. *Strad* instantly responded, jumping into a plane and a surf all at once with the speed puck jumping to fourteen knots as she screamed down the face of a six-foot roller. He still had twenty-five miles to go to get to Kent Inlet and the sun was getting low. Another gorgeous sunset. But the miles were screaming by as Bobby surfed the swells, which were so large that he couldn't see over them when he was in the trough. He'd eaten little all day since breakfast, and he was ravenous. All he had for lunch back near Belle-Bella was a couple of pieces of jerky and a Pop Tart. Even Viola, who had her own food, was getting restless awaiting her mealtime.

Looking back, the Santa Cruz was also following his path and gaining, though she would likely continue north on the outside of Aristazabal Island. He was more discouraged by the smaller sail astern of the Santa Cruz. Assuming it to be a racer, it could only be either the Flying Dutchman or the Hobie. Whoever it was, they'd made significant gains and were now within ten miles of him. Bobby wondered where they would stop for the night out here. Maybe they wouldn't. Who knows? He couldn't control what they did or didn't do. He was tired and needed to rest.

The sun had set by the time he reached Laredo Channel behind Aristazabal Island. His speed was down to about five knots in the smooth water of the channel, which meant he had over an hour to go before he could anchor. He turned on his running lights and sailed on, letting the autopilot drive for a while as he prepared a late supper. Feeding Viola first, Bobby cooked up the dreaded beef stroganoff. It wasn't really that bad, and between the two of them, they polished it off quickly. He even cooked up one of the Cup-a-Soups to augment the meal. Even then, Bobby needed oatmeal to satisfy his hunger and only let Viola have a few nibbles. She still had food and water in her bowls.

Safely anchored near shore in Kent Inlet by eleven-thirty, Bobby wearily set up his cockpit cover, cleaned himself in preparation for bed and put on his last clean base layer. Not much point in arriving in Ketchikan with unused gear, unless maybe it was his emergency gear. It had been another exceedingly long run, but it was the most fun sailing he'd had since he started the voyage. Speeds of up to fourteen knots surfing down long ocean swells. Viola had slept through most of the excitement, and then had helped by keeping one of Bobby's hands busy stroking her through the rest of the day.

As he rolled out his air mattress and sleeping bag, he suddenly heard a large animal rummaging through the underbrush near-by. Viola fled to her box in a panic. He unzipped the cover and scanned the shoreline with his spotlight. A large pair of yellowish-green eyes peered back, just a few dozen feet away. A bear! Bobby stared at it trying to decide if he should be scared or excited. Could the bear swim out to *Strad*? Definitely. Was it a grizzly or a black bear? He wasn't worried about the black bears, but grizzlies can be unpredictable. He stared at the eyes for a while longer until they disappeared. The bear had looked away. Even with the spotlight, the bear was invisible. It must be black, but that didn't mean it was a black bear. Grizzlies are often black. The eyes returned a few feet from where they had been when they were last visible. It wasn't any closer. It was walking along the beach. Bobby scanned the beach and was satisfied that he had a good thirty to forty feet between *Strad* and the shore. That should be enough to keep him safe. He heard the bear breaking through the underbrush again going inland. Another search and he could find no trace of it with the spotlight.

He finally settled down with Viola, but it took a while to fall to sleep. The bear was on his mind. He was confident that he was safe, but that was the closest that he had ever been to a truly wild bear. He'd seen nuisance bears in the city streets up in the mountains before, but this was the real wilderness. This is where bears were supposed to live. Here, bears ruled and were the top of the food chain. It was most likely a black bear. There were tons of them on these islands. Kent Inlet was on Princess Royal Island. Bobby had heard about 'spirit bears', and this certainly was not one. Spirit bears, or Kermode bears as the scientists call them, are white bears. They're technically black bears that just happen to be white. They aren't albinos, though. Black bears can be any shade from black to brown to blond and very rarely white. Only about one percent of the black bear population is white, but, on this island for some reason, thirty percent are spirit bears. And they tend to live mostly on the west side of the island, precisely where Bobby was anchored. Bobby would love to see a spirit bear, but this one was certainly black. He wasn't too worried about bears since he wasn't going ashore. He'd let his competitors worry about that.

He finally drifted off after checking his cellular signal strength. Nothing. Nothing since he left Port McNeil. He was wondering where his competition was. It was still windy even at night, and *Strad* swung at her anchor all night as ripples slapped her hull. Bobby was oblivious and dead to the world as he labored to keep Viola warm.

R2AK DAY 8

27

They were underway well before dawn after a good five hours much-needed sleep. The wind had abated a bit in the early morning allowing them to sail casually downwind at three plus knots. Bobby rarely used the autopilot in calm water downwind since *Strad* would sail a nice course on her own unless the wind built up beyond about ten knots. Every now and then he'd have to make an adjustment. It worked even better on a broad reach. There were no signs of life on the water, save for plenty of seagulls. Bobby hoped that his competitors were still fast asleep. The sky to the east was a spectacular red and orange with some purple overtones. He pondered if there was any truth to the adage *'Red sky at night, sailors delight. Red sky in morning, sailors take warning.'* His barometer was up slightly, and the southerly breeze that he had been enjoying showed no signs of abating. As in the past few days, he expected it to build later in the morning. Small cumulus clouds dotted the sky to the west, and he assumed that they would enlarge as the day warmed up. But for now, *Strad* was sailing along leisurely allowing him and Viola to just recline in the cockpit and just enjoy the situation, admire the colorful dawn, feel *Strad* happily and easily slipping through the water. Occasionally he'd sit up and make sure there were no logs or boats ahead, tweak the course, then lie back down.

Finally, his bladder got the best of him forcing him out of his reverie. While he was up, he dug out his cooking gear and another freeze-dried dish of scrambled eggs with ham and cheese and hash browns on the side. Besides Hali, his mother's cooking was what he missed the most. If all things went as planned, he'd be in Ketchikan in two more days. He opened a fresh can of cat food and gave Viola half. This was a new flavor, lamb, and she devoured it. Maybe being fresh also had something to do with it. Regardless, Bobby got to eat his eggs all by himself. The hash browns weren't half bad, but the eggs tasted like rubber. Another lesson learned – bring ketchup packages next time. It would make anything taste better. Viola demanded her share of the oatmeal though. After breakfast, they settled back down to contemplate life. There was no cellular service up here, so he was cut off from the world save for his tracker and his VHF radio. And the radio only had a range of three or four miles. He had some music on his phone, and he had ear buds, but that would destroy the feeling of tranquility and serenity that he was feeling right then. He just lay across the cockpit with Viola on his chest until he finally felt *Strad* getting twitchy. The wind had increased to twelve knots and the waves were starting to pick up as well. *Strad* was still in a happy groove, but she wanted Bobby to be alert. Her speed was exceeding four plus knots now and every now and then a little wave would shove her forward for a few seconds. He was hoping to be able to make it to Hodgson Cove behind Banks Island today, but that was sixty miles away. At this rate, it would take fifteen hours. That would get him there at about eight that evening.

They entered Caamaño Sound by mid-morning and felt the large swells from the Pacific rolling in. Unfortunately, they weren't really surfable in the direction they were traveling. *Strad* was sailing broadside to the swells. Clear of the land, the wind moved more to the west putting him on a reach. Suddenly, Bobby was startled when a huge shape splashed in the water directly in front of *Strad*. He yanked the helm to take evasive action, but there was no need. A pod of dolphins appeared all around him and swam with *Strad* for several minutes before moving off fifty feet or so. They were the common Pacific white-sided dolphin and there were several dozens of them including some young ones. They were entertaining to watch as they streaked through the water effortlessly and jumped through the building waves. After half an hour or so, they tired of *Strad* and moved off into the distance.

Bobby glanced over his shoulder and was shocked to see the Hobie on his stern quarter within a few hundred yards. Claire was coming from outside of Aristazabal Island and was screaming along on a broad reach at almost twice *Strad's* speed. And further astern was the Flying Dutchman, also gaining rapidly on a fast reach. Bobby's heart sank, knowing that there was absolutely nothing he could do to prevent them from passing him.

As expected, the puffy white cumulus clouds did get larger as the day warmed up. And with their increased size came more wind. Bobby had to be more assertive on the helm as *Strad* began to plane, the speed building to over six knots with pushes up to eight with a little help from the waves. When the wind hit fifteen knots, Bobby was actively surfing the waves, putting her on broad reaches for speed then turning downwind to ride the waves. The speed was consistently eight knots now, and the miles were racing by. The Hobie was getting smaller in the distance. The Flying Dutchman, with Damon out on the trapeze, was alongside and passing him quickly. He waved bleakly as Damon sailed by. He passed a large Grand Banks trawler heading south, then another similar trawler an hour later. By one o'clock, the clouds had covered the sky blocking out the sun and the wind had increased to just under twenty knots. Assuming the wind would continue to increase, Bobby took in a precautionary reef. Even with the reef, she was still rocketing down the face of the small waves at ten knots and only slowing to eight in the trough.

As Bobby glumly watched the Flying Dutchman growing smaller in the distance, he suddenly saw a white sail pop up a mile or so in front of Damon. It was flapping in the breeze, idle. Bobby stared at it trying to make sense of it for a long time before he finally realized that it must be the Hobie. But it had emerged from nowhere. Had Claire lowered her sail for some reason? Finally, after probably fifteen minutes from the time it emerged, the sail filled, and Claire was on her way again just a little bit ahead of Damon. Bobby suddenly realized what had happened. She had capsized! Righting a catamaran is a real bitch, especially one with deck cargo. Maybe that is why it took her so long. Maybe she had had to release her cargo bags to get the boat back up, then reattach them all. Whatever had happened, it was obvious that she was ok and back in the race.

Damon was really struggling to control the Flying Dutchman in the freshening breeze. One crew was not nearly enough weight since she had no ballast in the centerboard[45]. Bobby watched intently as the Flying Dutchman heeled over wildly and rounded up into the wind. Damon had reefed the mainsail and rolled up a good portion of the genoa, but he still wasn't heavy enough to control the boat in this wind. Once back in control, Damon only sailed on for a few more minutes before losing it again and rounding up into the wind. He was dangerously close to capsizing several times. Bobby kept an eye on him just in case he needed to come to the rescue. But eventually, Damon doused his mainsail and sailed on with only his partially rolled up his genoa[46]. He was better able to control her, but he was still struggling.

Bobby gybed *Strad* back to port without going all the way over to the shore. He wasn't familiar with the shoreline and what effect it would have on the wind, so he just preferred to stay in deep water where he knew what he had to work with. Besides, there were submerged rocks over there somewhere. After a while, he got out on the trapeze to rest his butt. For the most part, the trapeze was quite comfortable, and he loved seeing *Strad* from out over the water. Her lines were so elegant, and he loved seeing her bow rising powerfully out of the water on a plane. Unfortunately, he often got wet with spray out there, but on a warm day he didn't mind.

The wind continued to increase, and by three with the wind exceeding thirty knots, he took in his final reef. The Flying Dutchman had pulled over into a safe harbor. Now he had a chance to make some major gains, but he had to be careful. With no more reef points, any further wind increase could cause him similar problems. He searched his GPS for alternate anchorages and found Port Stevens just ahead. Too close. Bobby felt he would be fine for a while yet. Buchan Inlet was

---

[45] Centerboard – a form of a keel that pivots up into the hull for downwind sailing and trailering

[46] Genoa – a large headsail that overlaps the mast

next, another four miles north. That would be his Plan B. *Strad* was in a
full screaming plane now, consistently hitting twelve knots and surfing
to fourteen. The bow was completely out of the water back to the keel.
Her hard chines gave her stability and control, so Bobby was able to
completely relax and enjoy playing the waves. Gybes were a little scary,
but Bobby executed them flawlessly. This was his cup of tea. *Strad* was
so much easier to control than a Flying Dutchman in a full plane. As he
passed Port Stevens, he saw the Hobie's mast in the anchorage. Another
chance to make some big gains. By four, he had passed Buchan Inlet. The
wind was still manageable but howling. White caps were everywhere,
and the wind waves had built to almost two feet. He knew that he was
violating his promise to Hali and his parents. He should be seeking shelter. And he was risking serious gear failure at a minimum. But he was
racing, and he was loving it and just didn't have it in his heart to quit.
In his mind this wasn't a storm, rather it was just a delightfully blustery
day. He was able to keep her surfing now for several minutes on end.
By six, he had passed his original goal of Hodgson Cove. He still wasn't
ready to quit quite yet. He sailed on and on and the wind continued
to build. He'd just logged a long surf at sixteen knots, his fastest yet.
Another gybe took him back towards Banks Island, and one more and
he was screaming over to Foul Point on Anger Island. The last gybe was
hairy, and he finally realized that maybe, just maybe, he was at the limit
of his abilities. The wind was most likely over thirty-five knots with gusts
even higher at this point. *Strad* shot past Foul Point and was immediately
blanketed from the wind and waves. Bobby sailed on slowly into the
smooth water in the lee of the islands and coves looking for a place to
anchor. He finally doused his sail and pedaled into a small, completely
protected cove on the north side of the island. As he dropped his anchor,
he could hear the wind high overhead, and could see the trees whipping
and leaves and branches flying, but the water around him was as flat
as glass. He had sailed more than seventy miles that day, and now was
even anchoring before dusk for the first time. If not for the gale, he'd
have kept going and maybe made it to Spicer Island. He'd put seventeen
miles on the Hobie and twenty-one on the Flying Dutchman. The race

wasn't over yet, though. He still had one hundred and forty miles to go to the finish line. Two more days if he could log seventy-mile days. More if he couldn't.

As he and Viola cooked a supper of freeze-dried spaghetti and meat balls, he heard another big splash. Peering out in the direction of the noise, he saw nothing. After a while, he sat back down and fixed a cup of hot chocolate. Something big was out there. It was way too big to be a fish, that's for sure. Now that he was out of the wind, the temperature wasn't that bad. But he'd gotten chilled while sailing, and he savored his hot chocolate as he contemplated what sort of creature might be out there. The spaghetti wasn't bad, though Viola turned up her royal nose at it. In fact, it was probably one of the better freeze-dried meals he'd had. As the night darkened and he rigged the cockpit cover, he heard another big splash, a little closer this time. Using the spotlight, he scanned the water again and saw nothing. Eerie. He settled back under the canopy and tried not to think about it. It was too early to go to bed, but Viola managed to convince him otherwise. Just as he settled in, something big thumped against the keel rocking *Strad* severely and throwing Bobby and Viola across the cockpit. Bobby jumped up, grabbed the searchlight, unzipped the cover, and searched the water. Nothing. He was starting to get a little spooked. It was almost black out other than a tiny glow on the horizon to the southwest where the sun had set more than two hours prior. His experience with the orcas came to mind. Even Viola was a little uneasy and sat waiting for him to do his duty and comfort her. He settled back down with Viola, but sleep was slow in coming. He heard the splashes again twice, but further away. Eventually, he dropped off to an uneasy sleep.

R2AK DAY 9

28

Bobby awoke in the very wee hours of morning, took a drink, and tried to settle back down. But he was wide awake and antsy from just sitting idle. The mystery creature didn't help either. Sighing, he got up, turned on his light and put Viola in her little box. It was cold out, probably in the low forties, so he donned his thermals, then his fleece and dry suit and added his hat and gloves. There was a ground fog blocking out any light from the moon or stars. He listened for the wind and could hear none. All was still. He stowed his sleeping gear, and the cockpit cover and raised anchor. Turning on his running lights, he very carefully made his way out of the cove using both the GPS and the spotlight for guidance. Once in the clear water out in Petrel Channel, he found no wind and a thick, blinding fog, so he started pedaling earnestly northwards. He had easily three hours until dawn, but the pedaling would keep him warm. Now was his chance to put some more miles between him and his competition. The foghorn that he sounded every two minutes destroyed any semblance of peace and tranquility. It also kept him awake.

He had thought about making a run across Dixon Entrance directly from Banks Island, but that was eighty miles with no protected options for stopping once he committed. Without wind, it was out of the question. He knew there would be large waves left over from the previous windy days to contend with, so it was not a realistic proposition at this point. But that's what the larger boats would be doing. His plan was to work closer to Prince Rupert and continue north. Once he got past Porcher Island, he was basically committed to just heading north-northwest directly for Ketchikan. He'd have some shelter from the ocean swells behind a string of islands and islets until he got past Dundas Island. Then he was on his own for the twenty miles across Dixon Entrance.

Bobby was pedaling along in the dark sounding his horn as required when suddenly a large fishing boat emerged from the fog ahead of him. No sound signals at all and running lights that didn't pierce the fog at all. They were awfully close, but not quite on a collision course. The boat did slow when they heard Bobby's horn, so their wake wasn't too bad. Then it continued into the mist silently. Bobby could hear other vessels in the distance, but nary a foghorn as required by the international rules of the road. He had a radar reflector fastened to his wishboom, so the bigger boats should be able to detect him on their radars, but it was his foghorn that had saved him from a potential disaster.

Dawn brought no wind and the intense fog continued unabated. He kept pedaling for a while guided only by the GPS until he got into Ogden Channel. There he stopped to make a late breakfast with Viola. She hated the foghorn, so he gave it a rest while they were eating. The morning was quiet though he could hear boats in the distance. If the wind didn't come up, it was going to be a long, long day. But the good news is that he was sure that he was extending his lead. There was still no cellular signal, so he couldn't tell what his competition was doing.

Ogden Channel fed into Arthur Passage which rejoined the Inside Passage. This meant traffic - cruise ships, ferries, lots of pleasure boats, fishing boats and tugs. All in a narrow channel. All in the fog. Bobby munched his eggs saving some for Viola, then had some oatmeal. He was in a hurry to get underway, but not to pedal. As he ate his breakfast, he wished for wind. None was forthcoming. The day got warmer as the sun burned its way very slowly through the fog. In preparation for a long day pedaling, he stripped down and wore only his undershorts and T-shirt and the fleece top. And that would come off once he got going and warmed up. Stowing his gear, he finally got underway again. For the next three hours, he pedaled slowly down Ogden Channel dodging dead heads, crab pots and fishing boats as the fog grew thinner. In his mind, any time he wasn't heading north to Alaska was a waste of time, so he was quite happy to finally turn north into Arthur Passage. The fog was gone now, leaving a blue sky and lots of sunshine. Bobby donned his white shirt and broad-brimmed hat for the first time since day one.

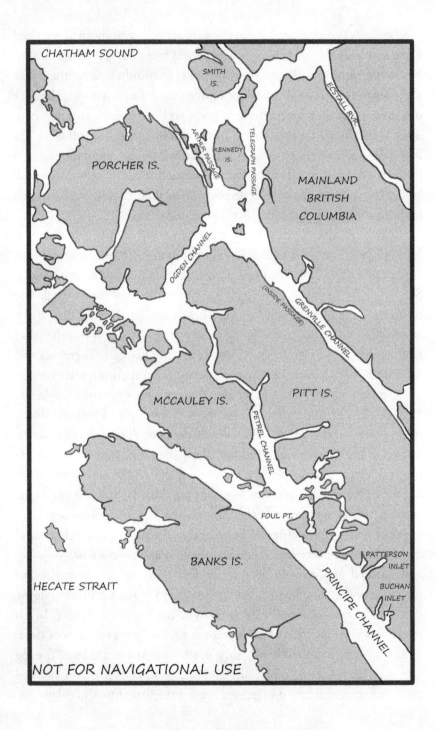

Two monstrous cruise ships steamed by heading south ahead of him as he approached the entrance. He kept *Strad* as close to the port side as he dared. He surprisingly found a small current push which lifted his spirits a bit. Four hours of tedium later and he had just emerged from behind Porcher Island. His legs were tired. His butt was numb. He was tired. Prince Rupert was on his starboard side. He was still pedaling weakly and looking for a place to stop when he noticed a weak wind line on his port side. It was getting closer. Prince Rupert Harbor was crowded with boats and ships of all sizes. There were several cargo ships and a couple of barges anchored offshore. After the solitude and tranquility of the voyage so far, Bobby just wanted to get clear of this crowded place. He eyed the wind line again and decided to put up the sail. It was too early to quit moving north, but his legs were spent.

The wind eventually reached *Strad* and she was underway once more. It was a light westerly, good enough for a steady two plus knots. The light ocean breeze was very cool, so Bobby donned his fleece, along with his life jacket and lanyard. He sailed north for a couple of hours, then put the autopilot on and made supper. Beef stew this time. That was more to Viola's liking. Bobby contemplated his lack of progress as he ate. He'd pedaled for over twelve hours today and his legs were pretty much done. All he had to show for it was a measly thirty miles. But he was sure that he'd extended his lead. They were cruising along with a nice westerly breeze and Bobby was inclined to just keep on going as long as he could. There were anchorages up ahead close to Melville and Dunira Islands, but they were a good three to four hours away. They'd get there after dark unless the wind cooperated.

Bobby turned to scan the busy harbor for dangers, and saw a ferry bearing down on *Strad*. Knowing that ferries don't turn for anyone, he put *Strad* hard into the wind and hauled in the sheet. The speed picked up to a little over three knots which would get him clear in just a few minutes. He double checked their courses and he was satisfied he was clear. About that time a familiar pressure in his bowels let him know he had business to attend to, personal business. The ferry was getting closer. They would pass by much closer than usual, within a quarter mile. He checked again and was sure the bow wave was getting smaller! Were they really slowing? The pressure in his bowels was increasing and the last thing in the world he needed right now was an audience. The ferry did in fact slow down as they passed nearby. There were literally hundreds of people lining the rail watching him and waving and taking pictures. He heard an announcement on the PA system "Keep it up, Team LaRoche! You're almost there." He waved, and the crowd on deck cheered him on, but his personal need was getting urgent and painful. Ever so slowly, the ferry drew ahead and, once clear, accelerated away changing course away from him. Bobby turned *Strad* so that the dodger gave him a tiny bit a privacy and ripped off his fleece pants which he threw over the dodger windows for more privacy, dug out his bucket and did his job as best he could in the ferry's turbulent wake. Hopefully, no one caught that on film.

The evening breeze freshened a bit and *Strad* was making just under four knots on a close reach. At this rate, they could even make the north side of Dundas Island. It might be close to midnight, but that would set him up for the dash to Alaska tomorrow. Alaska would be only twenty miles away and Ketchikan would be sixty plus. If he had a decent breeze, he could finish tomorrow! That was an encouraging thought after the slow going this morning. It would be an exceptionally long day, but if he made it to Dundas Island, he would have made good sixty-five miles. Bobby resumed his supper by cooking up some oatmeal which of course he shared with Viola. He fed her the oatmeal on his spoon, not caring about kitty germs. They were a pair. The wind held and even strengthened a bit when the sun went down. There was no sign of the Hobie or the Flying Dutchman. Bobby passed up the possible anchorages in Melville and Dunira Islands. He was intent on getting to Dundas Island. The moon rose and lit up the seas as best it could through the broken cloud cover. By rights, he should be exhausted after all his pedaling, and his body was. But he was wide awake and excited. Alaska was so close now! He was almost there! And he was confident that he was still leading his competitors! He sailed on through the darkness, occasionally sweeping the water in front of him with the spotlight for dead heads.

For every single one that he'd actually seen, there were probably dozens lurking submerged and semi submerged just below the water. Another rule of prudent sailing – always keep an alert look-out. But look-outs don't stay alert for more than four hours or so. They need to be constantly rotated. Not possible when solo sailing. It was a small miracle he hadn't hit anything yet. But the voyage wasn't over yet. Close, but not yet.

Strad finally entered a small cove on the north side of Dundas Island around midnight and anchored in twenty feet of water. There was another sailboat further out with no lights on, not even an anchor light. Dead to the world, which is where Bobby and Viola would be in less than fifteen minutes.

R2AK DAY 10

29

Strad began dancing around and tugging at her anchor line around five in the morning. She was itching to go. Bobby awoke and listened intently... wind! Real wind! They might be able to make it to the finish today! He got up and got into his fleece, then pulled the canopy back. Dixon Entrance was rough! Three to four-foot swells with two to three-foot wind waves on top of the swells! White caps everywhere. And the wind was out of the west, the direction he'd have to sail. He estimated the wind at twenty knots plus. There was an element of doubt in his mind. He'd sailed many times in twenty knots, but not with a big sea swell against him. Dixon Entrance was not to be trifled with. He pondered whether to go for it. He could always just try it, see how bad it is, then turn around if he couldn't make it. Prudence be damned! He was going to give it a try. He knew the Flying Dutchman and the Hobie wouldn't dare try the crossing in this wind. This was his chance to get across and get to the finish first. It was twenty miles across. He decided on a double reef right off the bat just because he would have a hard time adding a reef once he got out in those waves. The next debate was whether to prepare breakfast. He opted against. He was way too antsy to get underway. He could stop on the other side for a lunch in smooth water.

He heard another big splash as he prepared to get underway. But he was so focused on the task at hand that he barely looked in the general direction the sound came from. It could have been Nessie, the Loch Ness Monster for all he cared right then. Bobby raised the sail with a double reef, and then hauled up the anchor after putting Viola in her box. *Strad* quickly gathered way and headed for open water. Two harbor seals watched him curiously and followed *Strad* until she cleared the harbor. Bobby put her hard on the wind as he cleared the Gnarled Rocks offshore, and immediately started playing the waves. The sea swells were easy and predictable, but the wind waves weren't. *Strad* crashed through waves periodically, killing her forward speed. Bobby sometimes had to choose wave or swell that he would swerve around, sometimes he could swerve and dodge both, but he never missed both. He could tolerate missing a wind wave since they were significantly smaller than the sea swells. Yes, it would slow their progress, but that was much better than getting knocked over into the trough by a big sea swell. The speed puck was reading less than three knots, despite their great speed through the water. There must be a current knock. He hadn't checked the state of the currents since he was in such a hurry to get underway. That might have made a difference to his decision making. But he was still making good almost three solid knots over land. It might take him seven hours to get across at this rate. Bobby checked the course made good on his GPS and was pleased to see that he was easily fetching Cape Fox with plenty of room to spare. If this keeps up, he will end up smack in the middle of Revillagigedo Channel, which was his goal. He was glad that he'd put the second reef in. She was far more manageable, sailing upright and was still making decent forward progress. Viola came out of her box and jumped up in his lap. He was severely deficient in keeping her bed still, and so she found a much better one in his lap. It was going to be a long day, but Bobby was determined. For such a small boat, the waves were enormous! In fact, when he traversed the trough, the swells would block some of the wind, reducing his drive. Swell after swell, Bobby steered a curvy course keeping *Strad* on her feet and making as much speed as possible.

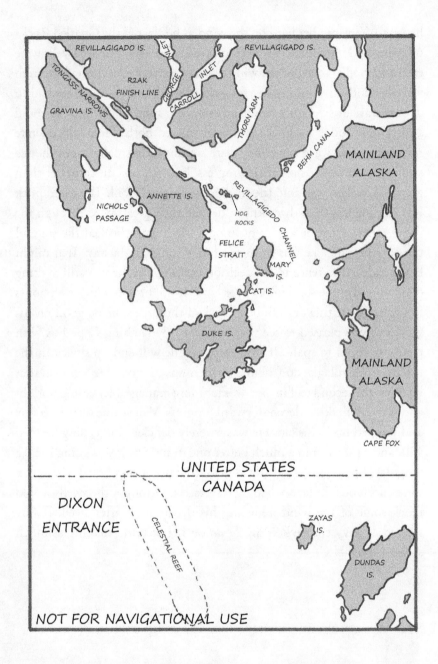

A U.S. Coast Guard aluminum motor surf boat was operating further upwind nearer Celestial Reef, and eventually saw *Strad's* tiny scrap of sail and came over to investigate. They hailed him on the loud hailer as he sailed near. He screamed back at them, but neither could understand each other. Bobby found his radio and turned it on.

"Coast Guard Patrol Boat, this is *Strad*. Over."

"Sailing vessel, this is Coast Guard 47413. Is everything okay with your vessel? Over."

"Coast Guard 47413, Sailing vessel *Strad*. Affirmative. Over."

"Sailing vessel, CG413. This is no place for a boat that small. These waters are treacherous. Over."

"CG413, *Strad*. Concur. But I am within my capabilities, and I've got to get across. Over."

"Sailing vessel, CG413. What is your destination? Over."

"CG413, *Strad*. I am heading for Ketchikan. Over."

"Sailing vessel, CG413. Are you part of the Race to Alaska? Over."

"CG413, *Strad*. Affirmative. Over."

"*Strad*, CG413. Roger that. Good luck. Request that you leave your radio on and monitor channel sixteen. We'll call to check on you every so often until you get across. Over."

"CG413, *Strad*. Roger that and thank you. *Strad* out."

With that, the big patrol boat turned and drove off with a big puff of black diesel smoke through the waves as if they hardly fazed them. Bobby watched them go away and thought about how small they were. Maybe it wasn't such a good idea coming out here. But what options did he have? He had to get across Dixon Entrance. This was the last barrier to Alaska. It was almost as good as a wall. Today wasn't even a storm, just a typical windy day. He'd hate to see this place during a storm. He suddenly had a lot of respect for the Coast Guard men and women who operated out here day to day. The day wore on and by nine Bobby was regretting not having breakfast before he left. The Coast Guard patrol boat had called him twice to check up on him. But by the third check-up, he was out of range to respond. The GPS told him that he had just crossed the international border. Beyond the point of no return! He stared hard out at the horizon but could see nothing. There was a thin mist in the air and his visibility was probably less than two miles. But he'd made it to Alaska! He was in the USA again!

The thought gave him additional energy. A couple of strawberry Pop-Tarts didn't hurt either. He kept on driving focusing only on the waves. Bobby suddenly noticed that the speed puck was reading over four knots. The current must have changed! He was now getting a boost to seaward. He checked the GPS and sure enough now the course made good was pointing directly at Duke Island. He could finally ease sheets slightly and bear off.

With that, the situation immediately improved. He was no longer crashing through any waves at all, and the speed puck climbed to six plus knots. He sighed with relief. He hated thrashing *Strad*, pounding her against the waves. She didn't deserve it. Now she was so much happier. And Viola was happier. And if Viola is happy, then all is right with the world. He searched the horizon in vain. There was land out there somewhere. Noon came and went without a sighting. The GPS showed Duke Island only three miles away, but it wasn't to be seen. They kept on sailing trusting the GPS. Gradually the sea swells lessened. Damn it! They must be able to see land by now! Bobby stood up, dumping Viola into the cockpit. Scanning the horizon, he finally saw something gray and dim in the mist ahead of him. Alaska! The first sighting! He eased the sheet some more and let *Strad* run on a close reach. She responded by jumping into a plane and surfing down the next wave at over ten knots. They had made it! He had to notify the Coast Guard so they could stop worrying about him.

"Coast Guard 413, Coast Guard 413, This is the sailing vessel *Strad*. Over."

No response. After a few minutes, he tried again.

"Coast Guard 413, Coast Guard 413, This is the sailing vessel *Strad*. Over."

He waited. No response. He was about to put his radio down when he heard another hail.

"Station calling for the Coast Guard, this is Coast Guard Station Ketchikan. Over."

"Station Ketchikan, this is sailing vessel *Strad*. Request you relay to Coast Guard 413 that we made it safely across Dixon Entrance. Over."

"*Strad*, Station Ketchikan. Roger. Welcome to Alaska. Are you part of the Race to Alaska? Over"

"Station Ketchikan, *Strad*. Affirmative. Over"

"*Strad*, Station Ketchikan. Welcome back to the USA. Proceed directly to Ketchikan to check in with Customs. Do not set foot ashore anywhere until you have checked in. Over."

"Station Ketchikan, *Strad*. Roger that. Out."

The very same ebb tide that had enabled *Strad* to bear off and run for Revillagigedo Channel was now against them once inside the Channel. Once behind Duke Island, the sea swells disappeared, and the island blocked much of the wind as well. Bobby shook out both reefs and sailed on with a full sail. The speed puck, once proudly displaying ten knots as they entered the channel, dropped to four knots, then three knots, then two and finally to just over one knot as the current checked their headway. Ketchikan was still almost forty miles away. Bobby let the autopilot steer for a while and prepared an extremely late breakfast. It was his last freeze-dried breakfast, though he still had several more packages of oatmeal to go. Scrambled eggs with diced ham and cheese again. One of Viola's favorites. He refilled her water dish and gave her some more food. At least she had plenty to eat. No crisis there. She was much happier now that Bobby had finally started to do his job correctly and kept *Strad* steady.

By the time they finished brunch at three, the wind had died completely, and a light rain set in. They were losing precious ground. Bobby pedaled over to Cat Island and quickly anchored, then set up the cockpit cover. Wiping down the wet cockpit, he and Viola settled down to wait out the current. They had six hours to wait unless the wind came up, but there was no sign of impending wind. The sky was low and gray. Just a light, steady rain for hours. He had a very weak cell signal, so he made a quick post to Facebook adding a picture of Viola cleaning herself on his sleeping bag.

"Forty miles to go to finish line. No wind. Adverse current. Steady rain. Anchored at Cat Island until nine. Resting up for a loooong pedal all night long, but we should arrive in the morning. Plenty of cat food, but people food getting scarce." His cellular signal wasn't quite strong enough to allow him to check the tracker. And at this point, there was nothing he could do about it anyway. He was confident that his competition had yet to cross Dixon Entrance.

R2AK DAY 11

30

Bobby eventually was able to doze off from about five until a little after eight. The sun was setting, but he'd never know it due to the rain. They made supper and used his last freeze-dried meal, chicken teriyaki. He'd held on to this one until last hoping he wouldn't have to eat it. Viola had even turned up her nose at it. At least she had something else to eat. Bobby cooked it, a Cup-a-Soup, and the oatmeal at the same time. The oatmeal was ready first and he savored it, with a little help from Viola. Dessert first tonight. He'd need all the energy he could get. Forty miles of pedaling meant at least ten hours with a push. But the push would only last for four or five hours if that. It was sure to be an awfully long day. He ate the Cup-a-Soup next, avoiding the dreaded chicken teriyaki. It didn't fill him up. He offered Viola a bite of the chicken, and she nibbled a bit, then left the rest to him. But it wasn't quite as bad as he had remembered, and he needed the rice to fill him up. But he wouldn't be buying freeze-dried chicken teriyaki again in the future. Finally sated, he cleaned up and stowed all his gear. He got out a couple of Pop Tarts, the last of the jerky, the last of the carrot sticks and a couple of Power Bars for later and refilled his water bottles. It was time to go. One last long push to the finish.

It was black outside. The rain shielded him from any shore or celestial lights. His running lights on either side of the bow reflecting on the rain was the only hint that there was even a world outside the dodger. Bobby was operating one hundred percent on GPS. He wanted to cut inside Mary Island to save some time, but the pass was aptly called Danger Passage due to all the rocks. He hadn't come this far just to crush poor *Strad* on the rocks at the finish line. So, he set a safe course outside, and searched for a push. Setting a steady cadence for three knots, the current pushed him along at four plus knots. There were no other boats out that he could see. Due to the canopy, he was blind except for straight ahead, and it was so dark out that he wouldn't be able to see anything anyway. For four long and tedious hours, he pedaled on into the inky blackness listening to the steady rain on the canopy and Viola's contented purring on his shoulder and finally passed the Hog Rocks. At least now he was pointed directly at Ketchikan. And his competition wouldn't be gaining on him. About eighteen miles to go, but he was awfully close to exhaustion again.

The push was starting to fade, and his speed was down to three knots. He pedaled on and soon the rain died completely leaving eerie silence. Even Viola stopped purring. Only the quiet swish-swish of his pedals remained. Two o'clock came and went and his speed was down to two knots, but he was still making progress. The current, for or against you, wasn't as strong this deep into the channel. By three-thirty, his speed was down to one and a half knots. Bobby could almost discern a faint lighting in the sky when he felt a light breeze. His legs spent, he drifted for a while and snacked on the Pop Tarts and carrot sticks. Was this a tease? Or was the breeze setting in? Either way, he could pedal no more and he still had ten miles to go. Putting Viola in her box, he took down and stowed the wet canopy. Standing up on rubbery legs was tricky, but it felt good to get out of the seat. He raised the dripping sail, which barely filled, and sat on the leeward side to heel the boat slightly. *Strad* very gradually and very grudgingly began to move, ghosting along silently in the faint pre-dawn light. The speed puck was reading less than half a knot, but they were moving in the right direction and Bobby was able to rest.

What little headway they were making disappeared with the change of current. The speed puck read zero knots from five until seven, but at least they weren't losing ground. At a little past eight, the wind freshened to a whopping three knots and they were making forward progress again. As he finally reached the crossing for Nichols Passage, he could see a strong wind line ahead. It was a westerly coming straight down

Tongass Narrows. But he could also see a small sail off in the distance, maybe four or five miles away. The radically raked mast could only be the Flying Dutchman. Damon had made the crossing over the night and was now sailing slowly up Nichols Passage in the lee of Gravina Island against the slow ebb. But slow as it was, Damon was sailing and making decent headway while *Strad* was ghosting along at maybe a knot. The Flying Dutchman was awfully good in a light breeze. In a panic, Bobby quickly mounted the pedal-drive system and pedaled as hard as his spent legs would allow towards the wind line. As he pedaled, he broke out his binoculars to study his opponent, and spied Clair on the Hobie out in the open water. He could tell by the angle of the mast that she had a fresh breeze and would be sailing extremely fast. But she'd eventually sail into the same dead zone that Damon was now sailing through. Damon was closing faster now. His breeze had increased. Finally, the wind freshened a bit more as *Strad* neared the wind line and she slowly picked up speed. Bobby put away the pedal-drive unit and got ready to sail hard for the last dash to the finish. The Flying Dutchman was closing fast. The speed puck was reading two knots as they crossed the line and within moments, they had all the wind Bobby could handle with a full sail.

Strad leapt forward like a thoroughbred racehorse, the speed puck jumping to five knots within seconds. Bobby decided that he'd been sitting in the seat long enough, so he stowed it, donned his harness, and got out on the trapeze. The wind was easily blowing fifteen knots with gusts to eighteen. The Flying Dutchman was maybe two miles astern, with the Hobie another mile astern of her. They all had the same breeze now and Damon and Claire were both going much faster than *Strad*. It was truly a race to the finish. The Flying Dutchman was now flogging the mainsail since Damon didn't want to waste time in reefing. Bobby was beating to windward nervously with Ketchikan dead ahead. He could see a cruise ship and buildings lining the shore and hill ahead. He witnessed a commercial airliner flying at a low altitude directly overhead on approach to the international airport on the island off the left. Only five miles to go, maybe an hour. Suddenly he realized that he had absolutely no idea where the finish line was! Somewhere in his gear, he had the race instructions and he vaguely remembered a drawing of the finishing area. It was at a marina, but he didn't see one anywhere up ahead. He could see the cruise ship in port ahead of him and, not seeing any sign of a marina, assumed that it was beyond it. He was no longer alone on the water. Fishing boats were plying the waters on both sides oblivious to his adventure. Cruisers were also plentiful, and behind him was another huge ferry. He had no idea where the ferry terminal was and was just hoping to get to the finish line before he had to take evasive action. But it was coming on quickly.

He was suddenly aware of a small runabout motoring alongside him. When he looked over, he saw a photographer and a videographer in the bow. He looked back at *Strad* and was pleased that she was giving them such a good show. As usual, the sail was perfect. *Strad* was sailing beautifully to windward and towards the finish so near. He looked back at the ferry. They were getting closer. The ferries normally move at seventeen or eighteen knots, though they slow in congested waters and when they approach their terminal. It appeared that it had reduced speed but was still coming on too fast. And Damon was now within a mile astern. As he looked forward again, he suddenly realized that he was surrounded by small motorboats, from aluminum skiffs to runabouts and they were all cheering him on. Some were in his way since he had to tack. He did so, scattering the boats as he spun *Strad* efficiently without losing much speed. He was heading towards the cruise ship at a fast clip, looking back at the ferry who was closing fast. Would he have room to tack between the moored cruise ship and the ferry? Yes, but it looked tight. A better solution would be to stop and wait until it passed. But that meant letting the Flying Dutchman catch up. As he was pondering this, he heard a familiar voice screaming at him. He looked over to see Hali standing in the bow of a runabout with his parents cheering and taking pictures with their phones. What the hell was she doing here? Could that mean she didn't make the team? Shit! He hoped not, but his heart leapt to see her again. He waved, then turned his focus to sailing again.

Strad was nearing a big concrete pier with many people on it cheering him on and blowing air horns, so he tacked back out on starboard towards the center of the channel. The ferry wasn't going to give him much space to sail. The Flying Dutchman had closed to within half a mile and was gaining quickly. The Hobie was within a mile now also. All three sailors were out on the trapeze and driving their boats as hard as they possibly could. Breaking their equipment wasn't a consideration anymore. The Flying Dutchman was planing against the wind, an impossible feat for just about any other sailboat. Bobby realized that he wouldn't hold the lead much longer and it pained him to think that he could get so close and lose the race just shy of the finish line. He studied Damon who was out on the trapeze staring directly back at him. How was it possible for one man to sail a Flying Dutchman seven hundred and fifty miles solo? Through all sorts of currents and winds. It just didn't seem plausible, yet there he was right on *Strad's* stern. He deserved the win for that super-human effort.

Bobby glanced back towards the big pier and his heart leapt! There was the marina! Tucked back behind the concrete pier totally invisible from the direction he'd been sailing! Some of his welcoming fleet were already turning in to the marina; the rest had gone on to welcome in the other two boats. He did a quick tack and within seconds cruised into the sheltered marina maybe a hundred yards ahead of the Flying Dutchman. He looked around for the finish line and the famous bell. On the left, he saw a dock full of cheering people and assumed that was where he had to go though there was no sign of a bell. He sailed beyond it almost all the way to the docks, then spun *Strad* into the wind, dropped the sail and drifted all the way over to the dock. He came in a little too fast, but the crowd caught *Strad* and kept her from bumping. He leapt gracefully ashore only to be yanked back to the cockpit sole by his lanyard. Scrambling up and unfastening his lanyard, he stepped ashore looking for the bell and found it at the end of the dock. He ran over and rang it as loud as he could, and kept ringing it, and ringing it and ringing it. His race was finally over. The Flying Dutchman had moored at the dock only minutes after him, followed by the Hobie another five minutes later. There must have been forty or fifty people crowding the dock and the landing above it cheering the three of them on. Finally, he stopped ringing the bell to give Damon a chance and looked around for Hali and his parents. No sign of them, but there was a customs officer waiting for him at the end of the dock. He went back to *Strad* and found his passport and took care of that little business which took maybe five minutes. No, he had nothing to declare other than a sore butt, exhaustion, and an empty stomach. And a new kitty. The crowd had tied up *Strad* adequately enough and even put out his fenders for him. The sail could wait. The Hobie had come in and was busily rafting up next the Flying Dutchman.

Once the customs agent moved on to Damon, the crowd swarmed him, slapping him on the back and congratulating him. What a close finish by the solo sailors! They were thrilled. Many were racers, still hanging around after finishing earlier. The Santa Cruz 27 had finished just before him by four hours. One of the trimarans had come in just six hours before him. Their whole crews had turned out for his finish. And several other crews had stayed in Ketchikan just to welcome the solo racers in. The finishing dock and the landing above were packed. And what a finish it was! Seven hundred miles and only a minute separated him from Damon and another four minutes from Claire. They had swapped the lead three or four times. The crowd included a couple of reporters and Jacob, the Race Director. Jacob came over to shake their hands and gave them each a six pack of Alaskan Amber Ale. Bobby immediately popped open a beer and chugged it to the delight of the crowd. He shook hands with Damon and gave him a man-hug. Then they both hugged Claire who was far more attractive but stunk just as bad as either of them. The crowd all wanted to know about Viola, so he went back to *Strad* and found her hiding from the chaos in her little box. He fetched her out and the crowd closed in to pet her. She clung to Bobby but let everyone pet her. After a while, she started purring.

Questions were being thrown at him from every direction and he did his best to answer as he searched for Hali. Half the crowd was admiring *Strad*.

"Congratulations on winning the solo race! That was a hell of a finish after seven hundred miles! How's it feel to be the first one in?"

"Oh, man... I'm just so happy to be done. I'm so exhausted I can hardly think straight! I thought I was way out ahead until the last five miles. Those guys came out of nowhere. It's a miracle that I was able to hold them off to the finish. They're both much faster than me."

"Bobby, how much sleep have you been getting?"

"Not nearly enough. I'm beat! I pedaled all night since nine. The wind came up just in time for my finish. I might have gotten three, four hours sleep each night."

"What motivated you to keep pushing so hard?"

"Those guys. And they gave me one hell of a race. Swapped the lead at least three times. I wanted that grand for being the first solo finisher."

"And you accomplished that. The first solo finisher this year, and the record for the fastest solo finisher ever. And sixteenth place overall. Congratulations!"

Finally, Jacob came over and waved the other skippers over. The crowd moved in closer if that was even possible. Dozens of cameras and video cameras were pointed at them recording the awards.

"You guys put on a hell of a race! Far more exciting than the first-place overall finisher. Congratulations to all of you. It was utterly amazing to see such small boats finish the race at all, and to have you three racing head-to-head all the way was just frickin' awesome! And a special congratulations to Damon. To see one guy man-handling a Flying Dutchman for seven hundred miles is unreal. And Claire, you too. You sailed a hell of a race. And both of you almost prevailed. But there can only be one winner. And by the skin of his teeth, the winner is Bobby LaRoche in *Stradivaria*! Congratulations, Bobby. You win the twelve hundred dollars for being the first solo sailor." The crowd roared as he handed Bobby the wad of cash. Handshakes all around. More hugs all around. Lots of chatter, then the reporters moved in again.

"Would you do the race again next year?"

"Probably not. Next year will be my Dad's turn. I built the boat for him to race."

"Are you going to keep the kitty?"

"Well, she's claimed me. So, I guess I don't have any choice. We've been through a lot together these last ten days."

"Did you know that you have the most Facebook followers ever because of her? More than the R2AK Facebook site itself?"

Bobby grinned. "I heard something to that effect. But it was a special moment and she was such a great companion. She deserves the attention."

"You built the boat yourself. Did she perform up to your expectations?"

"Oh, hell yeah! She was perfect! I think she's probably the ideal boat to do this race with solo. She excels in heavy air, and she does superbly under manual power also. My Dad designed her. I think he should market the plans."

"I understand that he was intending to race the boat himself but had a stroke and couldn't race. So, you went instead. Is that right?

"Yeah. He had a stroke about a year ago. I built his boat for him so that he'd still be able to race this year. It was done in secret. I showed it to him on April Fool's Day when it was done. Brought tears to his eyes. But it turns out that he hadn't recovered enough to race this year. So, I stepped up at the last minute and entered the race. And here I am."

He looked around for Hali and found her in the crowd on the landing above him watching the interviews.

"Hali! Get down here!"

In moments, Hali was in his arms. He lifted her off the ground and embraced her. She wrapped her legs around him, and they held each for a long time. Bobby just wanted to hold her and obviously the feeling was mutual. The crowd cheered. Viola jumped down and ran back to *Strad* and hid in her box. After many minutes, he let her down and kissed her deeply. Then he offered her a beer and took another for himself. In a few minutes, Gerald and Annette were there and they were hugging again. All of them, including Hali. Bobby had tears streaming down his face.

Everyone was talking at once, and suddenly Bobby was very tired. He sat down at the picnic table, and Hali sat with him holding his hand.

"Are you okay, Bobby?"

"I'm just so damn tired. I can't even stand up."

"Let's get you back to the hotel. C'mon, Bobby. Stand up."

"Nahhh... not yet. I've still got to put *Strad* away. She can't stay here. And I need to roll up the sail. And then there's Viola..."

"No, you're done, here, Bobby. Let's get you to the hotel. It's a short walk. Gerald can take care of *Strad*. And Annette will bring Viola over."

She wouldn't listen to any more arguments. She physically dragged him to his feet and dragged him over to his Dad.

"Gerald, I'm taking Bobby to the hotel. He's exhausted. Can you put the boat away?"

"Sure. Okay. Don't worry about it."

"And Viola... can you bring Viola over afterwards?"

"Uhh... sure... I guess. Where is she?"

"I'm sure she's in her box up forward." Bobby said, finally peeling off his life jacket. "That's her safe spot. I'll need her litter box as well. Did you bring my duffle bag?"

"Yeah, Hali has it in the hotel."

"Cool, thanks, Dad. Take care of *Strad*. She's one hell of a little boat."

He laughed. "Go get cleaned up and take a nap, Son. You look like crap. We'll talk tonight at supper."

Hali led him three blocks down the front street, and up to their hotel room. She pulled off his dry suit and boots, then undressed him and led him straight to the shower. She didn't join him, but she made sure he was clean and freshly shaven before leading him to bed. Then she peeled off her outer clothes and joined him in bed clad in her underwear, lacy feminine underwear that she had bought just for this occasion. She cuddled with him and he was asleep in minutes. And she stayed with him, holding him, for another hour until Gerald and Annette came up with Viola and a brand-new litter box. They released Viola onto the bed, and she immediately went over to Bobby and curled up next to him. They all three chuckled and went out for the afternoon in town.

A PROPOSAL

31

Hali returned to the hotel room at a little before five with all of Bobby's cleaned laundry and found Bobby still fast asleep. Slipping out of her clothes, she climbed in and snuggled up with him. He groaned and rolled over allowing Hali to rest her head on his shoulder and throw her leg over his waist. Viola stalked off. Bobby kissed her, then kissed her again with far more passion.

"Hold that thought, Baby" she whispered. "We're meeting your folks for supper in less than an hour."

"That's okay... this won't take that long..."

Hali laughed. "Oh no you don't! When we make love, I want the full treatment! No quickies!"

"I've been looking forward to making love to you for a month."

"So have I, Baby. So have I. You do such a good job at it. I really hit the jackpot finding you. But we can wait a little while longer. We all want to hear about your race."

"Yeah... okay. Where are we going to eat? I'm starving."

"I don't know. There's a couple of nice restaurants this part of town. And a couple of rowdy pubs. I'm just supposed to be getting you up."

"Hmmm.... well, you've done a rather good job of that."

Hali giggled. "Yeah, I noticed." She ran her fingernails down the length of his erection. "I'll take care of this now if you promise that you'll make love to me tonight."

Bobby kissed her passionately. "That'll be my pleasure!"

"Well," Hali replied slyly "I think it'll be my pleasure..."

They met Bobby's parents in the lobby on time at six and left in search of a restaurant. They ended up in Annabelle's Famous Keg and

Chowder House in the historic Gilmore Hotel on Front Street. No visit to Ketchikan is complete without a stop at Annabelle's. There was a loud crowd near the bar, so they waited until a table in the rear was available. The Hostess assured Bobby that they had no freeze-dried food on the menu. In the meantime, they all got started with a round of beer. And finally, they were seated.

"Bobby, you've lost a lot of weight" his Mom noted. Hali nodded in agreement.

"Probably" he replied. "Sailing is hard work. I was working for about eighteen to twenty hours per day, probably burning twice the calories I'd normally burn in a day. And I only had two meals a day, plus some snacks for lunch. Probably not nearly enough calories. And Viola insisted on helping me with my dinners. After Hali, the one thing I missed the most out there was your cooking."

She laughed. "I'm glad to hear that, Bobby. I'll fatten you up again pronto."

"Bobby, I still can't get over that finish" his Dad said. "That was just so damn exciting! After seven hundred miles, to see you three actually racing to the finish line together was incredible! And *Strad* was so beautiful this morning in the morning sun! We got some phenomenal pictures! You were sailing her so well. Very impressive!"

"Thanks. Maybe I won't tell you how lucky I was" Bobby replied. "I almost gave the race away at the end."

"Really? How so?"

"Ohhh... Well, I feel like an idiot admitting it" Bobby said sheepishly. "But I didn't know where the finish line was. I knew it was at a marina, but I didn't see one anywhere. I thought I had to sail past the cruise ships, and then the ferry was going to be a big problem. I had already concluded that I couldn't hold off either boat, that I'd finish third, and then I look over and there's the marina and the finish line! So, I tacked and ducked in just ahead of Damon. I probably gave him another hundred feet or so before I figured it out. Just pure dumb luck that I realized my error at the last possible moment. I was heading down the river past the cruise ships!"

"Oh crap! I didn't know that!" His Dad said. "It would have been a shame to lose it after all that distance."

"Damon did a phenomenal job sailing that boat" Bobby said. "I never would have thought it possible. If he'd had another person on board, he'd have beaten me by days. That boat is incredibly fast. And Claire... the girl on the Hobie... she did a phenomenal job also."

"Yeah, they both did" his Dad said. "I didn't think either would finish, especially not the Flying Dutchman. It's ludicrous to think that one man could sail that boat seven hundred miles to Alaska and still be competitive!"

"Did you see us on the ferry?" Hali broke in.

"No... the one in Prince Rupert Harbor?"

"Yes" his Mom piped in. "Hali and I had a wonderful cruise up the Inside Passage. We shared a cabin and we really got to know each other. I had her all to myself for two days. I really love Hali. You picked a fine girl, Bobby."

"Thanks, Annette. You're so sweet! I love you guys, too" Hali replied. "We were tracking you all the way. I don't think an hour passed without one of us checking your progress. Especially last night. It seemed like you just never stopped to rest. We were so afraid that we'd miss you when you went outside, and we went inside. If we hadn't stopped in Prince Rupert, we would have gone right past you without seeing you."

"I got on the ferry and joined the girls in Prince Rupert" Gerald said. "I drove the trailer up and left it ready for the return trip."

"We toured the bridge and mentioned to the Officer in Charge that you were right ahead of us and in the Race to Alaska" Hali said. "He made an announcement over the PA about the race and that you were right ahead. Everyone came over to the rail to see you and cheer you on. You looked so tiny out there! Everyone, and I mean everyone was amazed that you had sailed so far in such a tiny boat. We were screaming at you as loud as we could. It's a shame you didn't hear us. But I'm so glad to have seen you out there."

Bobby grinned. "Uhhh... I had other things on my mind at the time."

"Yes?" His Dad asked.

"You really want to know?"

"Yes" Hali said. "Spill it, Bobby."

"Well, since you insist... I had to take a crap super bad and then you guys show up and slow way down and I'm stuck with an audience. I was in pain waiting for you guys to leave! If anyone took my picture, they'd see me grimacing with pain as I clenched as hard as I could. And I didn't have any clean underwear left, either. If you had stayed for another five minutes, I would've crapped in my pants!"

They all roared with laughter. Gerald and Hali had tears in their eyes. Only his Mom looked sympathetic. They laughed until their meals were brought out. And even then, they would burst out chuckling from time to time.

"Viola is a great kitty, Bobby" Annette finally spoke up to change the subject. "She warmed right up to me when we retrieved her from *Strad*. I haven't had a kitty in years. Of course, we'll keep her, right Gerald?"

"I'm out voted, so I'll just go along with the majority. Sure, Viola is welcome."

"Good" said Bobby. "That means I get to stay as well. I'm staying with Viola. We've been through a lot together."

"Tell me about the low points of the race" his Dad chimed in. "Try to scare me away from doing it next year."

"The worst was getting caught out in a really severe storm in Queen Charlotte Strait. Really stupid of me. I totally misjudged its intensity. I was sure it would expend itself over Port Hardy. But it didn't let go until it got to Port McNeil. I tried to outrun the storm and get to Port McNeil first, but I was going right at it and it was coming right at me. Right before it broke, I'd given up on Port McNeil and was just trying to get to shelter in Alert Bay. I didn't make it. I doused the sail, put up the cockpit cover and just pedaled against the wind. I only had to go a couple of miles to Alert Bay, but I was making almost no forward progress against huge waves. It was terrifying and dangerous. Pitch black out. Almost got run over by broken piece of dock. Then I almost got rolled when I evaded it. Must have been over fifty knot winds and gusts over sixty with huge waves. Wrecked two boats that I could see. I finally made it into shelter and anchored for the night. I was peddling so hard that I strained the pedal-drive. I had to replace all the drive cables the next day."

Gerald nodded slowly. "And your decision-making ability was undoubtedly impaired due to exhaustion."

"Very probably. I was racing. I was going to sail as long as I possibly could. I sought shelter, but a little too late. When *you* sail, you won't be pushing so hard. You'll take shelter earlier. I guess the next low point was all the pedaling I had to do. I did ten hours straight twice and twelve hours once. Go to the gym and start training, Dad. She pedals like a dream, but that's still a long time sitting in the seat. Of course, I was motivated to get to the finish as fast as possible. You could probably pedal only half as much as I did and still finish before the sweep boat. I pedaled through the night several times. It's pitch-black out on the water at night. The GPS and the compass are all that kept me going straight."

"How do you think the pedal-drive system compared to the other drive systems?"

"Far better and simpler. Little to go wrong and easy to repair if you break a cable. Far more efficient than rowing and you can see where you're going. I was going faster than most of the high-tech propeller driven boats. And they're all just way too complicated. A problem waiting to happen. *AND*... I could pedal with the cockpit canopy on and stay dry. Not to mention that Viola loved to ride on my shoulder and tell me what to do as I pedaled. Thank Ralph for that idea. Dixon Entrance was another challenge. I probably should have waited for a calmer day, but that could have been days waiting. And I had Damon and Claire breathing down my neck. It was rough and very windy. But *Strad* handled it simply fine with a double reef. The Coast Guard came over to check on me. They must have thought I was crazy!"

Bobby suddenly looked at Hali. "Hali, what the hell are you doing here? You're supposed to be training right now."

"You don't know?" His Mom asked. "Tell him, Hali."

"I made the team!" She screamed before Bobby hugged her joyfully. Now she was tearing up. "I'm on the national team!"

"Congratulations, Hali!" Bobby gushed. "I'm so proud of you! Did Courtney make it as well?"

"Probably. Not yet, though. She may yet make it. She withdrew. She was getting really pissed off at the coach. After what we did in Florida, she still ranked me as number six of the twenty-two girls trying out, and her as number fourteen. Only eight girls are on the team. And that's after we beat everyone at the training camp soundly multiple times. As a team, we're ranked higher than all the others. It was only the men's A team that gave us any competition. They're the two-time defending national champions. They beat us two matches out of three on the men's court, but it was a hard fought, close battle each time. Courtney and I are a great combo. We feed off each other. We know exactly what each other is thinking and about to do. We almost don't even need to signal each other. She's a finesse player with a great serve. I'm a power player. The coaches know it. They saw us beat the Japanese. They saw us beat all their players. I don't think there's a team in the world that can beat us. I think there's still a lot of unspoken bias against black volleyball players. Especially beach volleyball. I'm the only black girl on the beach ball squad. There's a few more trying out for the indoor squad. Karch invited us, not the coach. So, Courtney had it out with the coach. Karch had to step in. The coach argued that skin color had nothing to do with it. She tried to quantify every player's attributes and rank them accordingly without any consideration to the court chemistry. Doesn't work. Karch knows it. He's been observing us for over a year. He put me on the team over the coach's objections. The coach ended up getting fired and an assistant quit over it. Good riddance! They ended the women's camp early until they can get a new coach, so here I am. Courtney has a spot if she wants it. She may skip the next training camp, but I'm betting she'll be back in August."

"Beach volleyball or team volleyball?

"Beach ball, especially if Courtney comes back. But they were looking at me seriously for the indoor team as well. There's some real world-class talent on that team, so I'm flattered that they want me to play for them. But, one way or another, I'm in! Oh God! It feels so good! I've been wanting this for such a long time!"

"Well, congratulations again, Hali! I'm so incredibly proud of you. Thank God for Karch! I'm so glad that talent finally prevailed over skin color. How long do I have you for?"

Hali looked at Bobby. "Baby, as long as you want me, I'm yours."

He kissed her. "Yeah, I think I know that. But when do you have to go back?"

"Oh, in about three weeks. Then again in August. And we have tournaments all summer as well that I'll be traveling to. I'm playing with Courtney even though she's not on the team yet. The Nationals are next month, and the Worlds the month after that. Then in fall, the indoor season starts, if I choose to go that route. And even if I stay with beach ball, I'll be doing a lot of international travel. I'll be away a lot. But you knew that."

Bobby sighed. "Yeah... I know. You go conquer the world. I'll always be here for you. I'll go with you to some of your tournaments this summer, but I'll miss you a lot when you're gone."

Hali kissed him. "Don't worry, Baby. You're my guy. Never doubt that. I'll always come home to you. And while I'm gone, you go to school and get that degree. You've got a bright future to consider."

"True. And I'll do exactly that. And after the Olympics?"

"I really have no idea. You're so lucky. You have a great career all laid out for you. Just get your degree and start down that golden path. I look into your future and I see you taking over your Dad's business, maybe adding a Ford dealership, maybe even living in the same house, driving nice cars, being a successful businessman. I don't have a vision like that. Before I met you, I'd look off into my future beyond the Olympics and I'd see... well, just a blank screen. I mean, there's law school and all that, then nothing. It's all blank. But now that I've met you, when I look into my future now beyond law school, all I see is you."

Bobby locked eyes with her for a long time. Taking her in his arms, he asked "Hali, would you marry me?"

His Mom gasped audibly on the other side of the table. Hali's jaw dropped. There was silence for a few moments, then she grabbed him in a big embrace and, with tears flowing down her cheeks, she screamed "Yes! Oh Yes! A thousand times Yes! Oh God, Bobby! I would so love to be your wife! YESSS!" They were crying and laughing at the same time as they embraced. The other diners, having overheard her response, clapped, and cheered. Eventually, they calmed down, and both Gerald and Annette came over and hugged them both. Gerald even kissed Hali.

"Bobby, that was so beautiful!" Annette gushed, tears flowing freely now. "I'm so happy that I got to see that... You've made me incredibly happy!"

"Congratulations, both of you. I couldn't be prouder of you, Bobby. You've picked a wonderful girl. She's already part of the family. Annette and I both love her like a daughter. When do you think you'll get married?"

"Oh, I don't know. I hadn't planned this. It just came out. No rush. I just want to get a ring on her before some other guy steals her away."

"Yeah, I'm in no hurry. And no guy is going to steal me away, Bobby. I have some say in that matter, don't I? I'm all yours. Now that I know you'll marry me we can take our time. Maybe after the Olympics? And after you graduate? But I would like to go shopping for a ring. That would be so special for me."

"Bobby, if you'd allow me," his Dad chimed in. "I'd like to help out with the cost of a nice ring. Get her something she'll still appreciate twenty years from now rather than just a small stone."

"Thanks, Dad. But no thanks. This is from me, and only me. I have money, thanks to not having to pay rent. Well... maybe that's how you can consider that you contributed to the ring, by giving me free room and board. *And*... as of yesterday, I happen to have an additional twelve hundred dollars to put towards a ring. I can't think of a better use for my winnings than putting a ring on Hali's finger. If we buy a small ring, well, it will always be special because that's the ring that we got married with. But I think I can afford a nice one."

"I don't want anything extravagant" Hali said. "I'm not into jewelry too much, and I don't want to be afraid to wear it out. Just something small and simple, that's what I want. Something that I can look at when I'm away that will always remind me of Bobby. As if I really need anything to remind me of him. I dream about him constantly. And this is what I've been dreaming about for the last month. I was so hoping that he'd ask me."

"I suppose I'm not doing a very good job of not being a distraction to your training, Hali."

"Oh, you're a hell of a distraction, Bobby! But, when I get out on the court, I'm totally focused. Occasionally, I still think of you and the guys cheering me on and then picking me up and parading me around the court after I won, and that motivates me and cheers me up. You make me happy, Bobby. And when I'm happy, I play better. When we first met, I was trying to impress you just as much as the national team coaches. I still like to think that you're watching me and so I play harder. You inspire me, Bobby. Especially after this race. That was one hell of an accomplishment, Bobby! I never quite realized how much of an accomplishment it was until I saw you from the ferry. *Strad* was just a tiny speck on the water. And you sailed her all the way from Port Townsend! That's so insane! But I'm so incredibly proud of you."

The waitress brought out a complimentary bottle of champagne and glasses all around. She'd over-heard the proposal. They finished their supper and the champagne.

"Here's to the happy couple, may they live long and prosper!" Gerald said raising his glass.

"Here, here!" said Annette. "And produce plenty of grandchildren!"

They all laughed. "Not yet though," warned Gerald "don't you go getting pregnant, now."

"Don't worry, Gerald" said Hali slyly. "We've got it under wraps, don't we, Baby?"

They all laughed again for a long time as they polished off the champagne. But Bobby and Hali had unfinished business, so they skipped dessert and were back at their room by eight-thirty.

EPILOG

Bobby fought through the hordes of people trailed by his parents, trying to get to Shiokaze Park. The subways in Tokyo are notoriously crowded and adding a few million extra visitors for the Olympics hadn't helped the situation. The Olympic Committee had added extra trains and extra shuttle busses, but it was still a chore getting anywhere. Gerald had not been able to get tickets to the opening ceremonies, closing ceremonies or to most of the more popular events. They were sold out more than a year in advance. But they *were* able to score tickets to the beach volleyball venue at Shiokaze Park. It was general seating on hard metal temporary bleachers, so the girl's families tried to get there an hour in advance. Even that often didn't work since there were other games playing all the time. But somehow, with a lot of patience, they were able to get to each of Team USA's games. They found a dinner theater in town that had the opening ceremonies on the movie screen, so they could comfortably watch the show, hear the commentary, and dine in peace without the hassle of the crowd.

There were forty-eight teams that eventually qualified for the Olympics, delayed as it was, and Bobby presumed that all of them would be here. Three teams were from the USA, the maximum allowed. The first week of competition was the preliminary pool-play. The top two teams from each pool went on to the sudden-death bracket play. Team USA-1 (Hali and Courtney) was in Pool A, along with the Canadians, the Japanese, the Netherlands, Mexico, and the Italians. Of these, the Canadians were undoubtably the team to beat, but the Italians, the Japanese and the Netherlands were also top teams. It was one of the toughest pools in the tournament. Hali and Courtney had played against all these teams over the last two years and were familiar with their abilities and style of play.

Before the Olympics were delayed due to that damn global pandemic, they'd spent the whole year on the international circuit starting back in August of 2018 at the Nationals followed by the World Championships in Yokohama, Japan the following month. The women's national team did not attend the Worlds or the Nationals in 2018 due to the coaching dilemma, but Hali and Courtney went as individuals. They successfully defended their title at the Nationals, locking Courtney and Hali together as a team. At the Worlds the following month, they did well in the preliminaries and won their first two rounds in the sudden death bracket. But the same Canadian team that they would meet in the Olympics ended their run. They ended up ranked tenth overall.

The highlight of the tournament was playing the German team, the very same women that they defeated in Florida. This time, they had the Amazon figured out. They often served to her, mostly on the outside, trying to get her running, trying to take advantage of her sub-par agility. It usually worked, causing her to make sloppy passes that her team-mate would just have to clear rather than set, if at all. They also often served deep to the brunette, who was a good all-around player, so she would have to do the hitting. Her attacks were very manageable and easily blocked. Courtney had also perfected the open-hand roll-block, setting the ball as part of the block allowing Hali to slam the ball back on the second touch before the Amazon could get set to receive it. The match was never close. Hali and Courtney beat them 21 to 16 in the first and 21 to 14 in the second.

Over the course of 2019, they traveled the world on the FIVB professional circuit and did well enough to more than cover their expenses. They won a tournament in New Zealand, followed by another in Australia a few weeks later. Over the entire year, they never finished worse than tenth, playing against the absolute best teams in the world. Mostly, they were on the podium. They often traveled and trained with the two top Canadian teams, as they had all become close. At least off the court. The Canadians trained in Florida most of the year, and Hali and Courtney sparred with them numerous times. By the time the 2019 World Championships came around in Hamburg, Germany in June, Hali and Courtney were ranked number four internationally. They had beaten every team ahead of them at least once. Unfortunately, they had also been beaten by all those ahead of them and behind them in the top twenty. The closest other team from the USA in the rankings was a team out of Long Beach, CA who were ranked twelfth. Hali and Courtney dominated the preliminaries at the World Championships without losing a game, and then cruised through the sudden death bracket into the finals looking like they'd win it all. Then they ran into a brick wall called the Canucks. The Canadian A-Team was unstoppable. The games were all remarkably close, and Hali and Courtney won the second game before succumbing in an exceptionally long third game. They took home the silver and forty-five grand for their troubles but left unsatisfied.

As the whole world knows, 2020 was a disaster in every possible way. It started in late December when a new form of coronavirus was discovered in Wuhan, China. Hali and Courtney were traveling in January on a world tour ramping up for the Olympics in July. They repeated their victory in New Zealand, then took a silver in Sidney. In doing so, they beat the Canadian A-team twice. Their tour would take them to Brazil, Mexico, Greece, Italy, Spain, and France by the end of March. Then they'd have two months of intensive training to recover from the tour to prepare for the Olympics. Even though the U.S. Olympic Committee wouldn't select the team until April, they didn't have to worry about selection. They were by far the best U.S. team and ranked fourth internationally. They had beaten all the teams ranked higher than themselves several times, so they were confident in their chances.

And then the COVID-19 pandemic started in January. Annette had been following the news of the virus diligently from the start. Gerald and Bobby weren't particularly interested until borders started to close. Annette, the compulsive worrier, had already started stockpiling food and supplies at the beginning of the year. Bobby and Jessie had teased her mercilessly as they unloaded cases and cases of toilet paper and disinfectant, not to mention huge amounts of food enough to feed an army. The chest freezer in the pantry was completely full for the first time in Bobby's memory. By the middle of January, Bobby and Gerald were finally paying attention with increasing concern. When it came to protecting her brood, Annette was the Field Marshall. Bobby remembered a phone conversation that he overheard between Annette and Hali.

"Hali? Annette. I need you to cancel your tour and come home. Yes. Now. Immediately. I want you on the very next plane home. And make sure Courtney comes with you." Pause "I'm serious, Hali. I don't care about your schedule. You need to come home now! They're gonna close the borders soon! Then you won't be able to come home. I want you here right now." Long pause. "Hali, I don't give a damn about the Olympics, but I do care about you very, very much! They're saying the Olympics may get delayed or even canceled. Hali, this isn't a request! Get your ass on a plane right now! No more talk. Call me with your schedule. And tell your Canadian friends to get home also. Your friends can always crash with us. We have plenty of room and supplies."

By the time Hali and Courtney returned on January 21, the U.S. borders were closed to Europe and China, and they were talking of closing the borders to Canada and Mexico as well. The death rates were growing exponentially. Since their flight from Australia took them through Japan with a day layover, they were required to self-quarantine for fourteen days when they returned, completely isolated for five days, then socially distancing themselves for another nine days if they tested negative. Courtney and Hali both hung out together, watching TV mostly, in Hali's room for those five days, then passed their tests and were allowed downstairs. By that time, Governor Jay Inslee had shut down all public gatherings, closed all unnecessary businesses and asked everyone to stay home except for essential travel. Anticipated that move, Gerald and Bobby had converted the carports on both sides of the garage into home gyms so Courtney and Hali could at least work on conditioning. Brand new aerobic equipment was on one end, free weights, and weight machines on the other. Hali and Courtney would be training hard right there at home. After fourteen days, Hali was finally free of quarantine and Bobby rushed into her arms and straight into her bed. Courtney moved into Bobby's room with her husband Dillan.

The social distancing got worse as the global death count grew, and eventually turned into social confinement. Bobby's classwork was now all online. Gerald had shut down his dealerships except for a skeleton staff and put everyone on half-pay. He even allowed all customers who had loans out through the Autogroup to postpone payments for three months. Jessie and Ralph kept their two kids to themselves much to Annette's dismay. She kept the rest of her brood locked down well into June, then made sure everyone got into the habit of using hand sanitizer continuously and staying away from any close encounters with other people for the rest of the summer. She was thrilled to have so many mouths to feed, and Courtney and Dillan were a big help in the kitchen. Despite the global contagion, the LaRoche house was full of laughter. Games and puzzles that hadn't come out of the closet for twenty years saw new life. Hali and Courtney thrashed the work-out equipment for as much as six to eight hours every day. Bobby joined them and marveled at their strength and endurance. About an hour of intense effort was all that he could muster. He loved watching the girls workout and spent hours with them cheering their efforts. Gerald and Dillan even started working out daily with the girls coaching them. The Olympics were eventually postponed to 2021, though it was still called the 2020 Olympic Games. The social lock-down lasted for over three months before the pandemic in the U.S.A. finally began to wane. In July, in addition to the conditioning, they finally went back to the courts for training. All national and international tournaments were canceled through the summer, along with the national team training camps. The Nationals were finally held in September, even though all the qualifying events had been canceled. They accepted applications based on team's prior records. Of course, Hali and Courtney were accepted, and easily defended their title for the second time. There wasn't much competition domestically at their level. When the training camps were finally held in October, they were paired with the Men's teams. By this time, they were competing head to head with the men and winning at least as much as they lost.

By the end of the year, the disease had faded away in the U.S.A. and most of Europe and China. Borders began to open worldwide, though the disease still raged in high density populations zones such Indonesia, India, Rio de Janeiro, Mexica City and Ecuador. The toll was breath-taking, not just on the population but also on the global economy as well. Sponsorship money was non-existent, even from the National Team. Hali and Courtney could only focus on those few remaining tournaments that offered any prize money at all. They still had their modeling contracts, though those had been put on ice for a while. They also had over a hundred thousand in previous winnings, donations and sponsorships banked, plus their personal accounts that contained their modeling proceeds. Unlike most of their competition, they had enough to continue in their quest. Fortunately, flights and hotels were all at a steep discount in the post pandemic year. They wore masks everywhere. The Brazilian championships only drew twenty-eight teams, the tournament in France drew thirty-four, and a tournament in Japan drew twenty-two. Forty-eight teams were typical for these tournaments. The teams that were still active were the best, so the competition was stiff. Hali and Courtney did very well, winning in both Brazil and Japan and taking a silver in France. They dominated all the events in the U.S.

Bobby didn't get to see any of these games. He graduated from the University of Washington in June of 2020 with a degree in business management, and immediately started work on his MBA. That summer, he entered into negotiations with Ford to open a dealership. The sticking point was location. There were plenty of dealerships already in the Everett, Edmonds, and Lynnwood market area. The market was saturated. He was offered a heavy truck dealership in Mount Vernon, which he considered for a while. Bobby didn't really want to go all the way up to Mount Vernon or Bellingham, where Ford suggested. And then one day in early 2021 he was notified that a dealership in Lynnwood would be available. The owner of an existing successful dealership had succumbed to the pandemic and his heirs had decided to liquidate his assets. Bobby had the opportunity to buy it all, lock, stock, and barrel. Jessie, Gerald, and Bobby spent all winter going over their books to determine a true value so he could make an educated offer. Gerald had already agreed to cosign a loan and had arranged a business loan through his long-time bank. If the numbers worked, Bobby wasn't going to bicker.

In early 2021, Hali and Courtney resumed their global tour starting in New Zealand and Australia. After victories in New Zealand for the third year in a row, and again in Australia, their global rankings moved up a notch to number three. Their tour took them to Greece, France, and Brazil, before landing them back in the U.S. for two tournaments and their long conditioning training camp. They didn't win any of these international tournaments, taking a silver and two bronzes. But they dominated the domestic tournaments even with the Canadians present. They were ranked number two internationally behind the Canadians going into their last training camp.

Back at the Olympics, the LaRoches had to wait for over thirty minutes for a match between Mexico and the Netherlands to finish and the bleachers to clear out, before they could find a seat. Courtney's family and later Asha and Zane Abara joined them as the bleachers slowly filled. Kellan was working now for Frank and couldn't make the trip. After the first game, Bobby had purchased bleacher seats for them all. Gerald sponsored Courtney's parent's travel and hotel costs since her father barely survived on a disability pension, and her mother worked for a publisher editing manuscripts for not much more than a living wage. Missing these Olympics was not an option. Courtney's husband, Dillan, was here as well, though he had to leave all his camera equipment at the hotel since the Olympic Committee owned the copyright for all commercial photographs taken.

There were eight courts set up end to end, four for the women and four for the men. The net is a little higher on the men's courts. Each court was surrounded by temporary aluminum bleachers that allowed several hundred spectators to watch each game. The only standing room was on the ends where you couldn't really see the whole game. But, if you didn't get there early, that's where you would end up. Between eight courts and five games per day, over ten thousand people got to attend one or more games per day. There was a delay between matches of about half an hour to forty-five minutes as they raked the sand and changed judges. When Hali and Courtney emerged on the court sporting their red, white, and blue Team USA bikinis, Asha's mother let out a high pitch scream that Hali instantly recognized. Her face lit up with delight as she saw her cheering section all standing up yelling her name. The girls had decided to remain in the Athlete's Village and not meet up with their families at all until their games were over so they could focus. Bobby had a few telephone conversations with Hali over the last few weeks, but mostly let her focus on the task at hand. He hadn't held her in three weeks now. Hali and Courtney had already dispatched the Italians in two quick games, the Mexicans in three surprisingly long games, and the Netherlands in three long games. The Mexicans were a real shocker, because they were ranked seventeenth internationally, and Hali and Courtney had beaten them soundly all three times they had met previously. They learned a lesson from that close call about not taking their victory for granted, and that enabled them to scrape by a determined Netherlands team the following day. And today they faced the Canucks. This was still the preliminaries, so they didn't need to be perfect, but try to tell that to an elite athlete.

The Canadians served first, a hard shot directly to Hali at chest level. She easily stepped sideways and passed it to Courtney on the left side. The set was for a shot down the middle, but Hali hit it cross-court catching the Canuck's by surprise. The receiver lunged for the ball and only succeeded in knocking it out of bounds. That would be the theme all afternoon. Hali had mastered the finesse game. In fact, she had mastered the art of misinformation. Every player unconsciously telegraphs their intentions as they attack the ball, but Hali had learned to telegraph something completely different from what she was intending. Against the Canucks, the skill paid dividends. They frustrated their opponents over and over as they played. And Courtney had improved tremendously since Bobby had last seen her play as well. She was now an excellent blocker and hitter and played the net as confidently as Hali. Hali was incredibly quick with lightning reflexes, so she played the back court as well if not better than the net. When she received, she could expect Courtney to give her a great set enabling her to attack effectively. Sometimes she would slam the ball, and sometimes she would do something completely different. A light tap into an open area, a spike at the net or a hard drive right at her opponent. They never knew what was coming. And Courtney's open-handed roll-block set, enabling Hali to slam the ball back at the opponent on the second touch, was very difficult to defend against, and if they succeeded, they were drawn completely out of position leaving them vulnerable for a quick shot to an open area. Both girls had gained muscle and lost any remaining body fat and had acclimated themselves to the high humidity. They were fit. Hali and Courtney scored quickly and cruised to a moderately easy victory in game one, 21 to 14. The second game was closer as the Canucks became more aggressive, but now Hali was good on defense, easily as good as Courtney. They withstood the assault and scored point for point with the Canadians. The final score was 24 to 22. Bobby got a quick hug and a kiss from Hali as she departed, but that was all. The crowd wasn't allowed to contact the athletes, and there were plenty of officials to enforce that rule.

Hali and Courtney defeated the Japanese two days later to remain perfect in the preliminaries. The Japanese team was the same team that they had faced back in 2018 in Florida, and they hadn't changed their game at all. They were still a finesse team rather than a power team and were exceptionally agile and accurate with their shots. But they had a hard time withstanding either Hali's or Courtney's attacks, and Hali's misinformation had them consistently opening areas for shots. They cruised to a 21 to 11 victory in game one and 21 to 12 victory in game two.

In the sudden death rounds, Team USA-1 cruised to two quick victories over France and then Portugal. Brazil put up a great battle, but finally succumbed. Three games and all went to match point many times. In the quarter-finals round, they met a team from Serbia that they had never played before. They were ranked number five internationally, so Hali and Courtney weren't going to give them any leeway. They attacked fiercely, but the Serbs responded just as fiercely. It turns out that

that they were very evenly matched and had many of the same skills. They traded serves, and occasionally points, as the games dragged on. After an hour, they were still on the first game with the score at 26-25 favoring the Serbs. Team USA scored the next two points, then they swapped serves and points until the score reached 33-32 favoring Team USA. Courtney finally put the game away with her curveball serve to the outside near court. They had been playing for one hour and twenty-two minutes. And they had just finished one game. The second game was just as long, and the Serbians came out ahead 41 to 39. Almost three hours of extreme effort left both teams dragging but dragging about equally. The attacks were not as intense, the passes were sloppier, the attacks less accurate. Many times, both teams found themselves just having to clear the ball without getting a decent set. And they again traded serves, and eventually points. The minutes crept by a lot faster than the points accumulated. No amount of encouragement from their supporters could revive the athletes. An hour into the third match and the score was 16 to 15, Serbia's favor. But Team USA fought back, and they kept swapping points for another ten minutes. Hali finally got the spike to end the game 24 to 22, after a great set from Courtney as she dove out of bounds after an errant pass. The entire match had lasted four hours and forty-two minutes, a new Olympic record. And another record for the most total points scored in a match. All four athletes almost had to be carried off the court. Team USA-1 had made it to the semifinals.

There was to be no rest for the weary. The semifinals matches were the very next day. The girls soaked in a hot tub in the evening, went to bed early and even got massages first thing in the morning before their match. They were well rested, but their muscles still reminded them of the previous abuse. Their opponents were Team USA-3. Hali and Courtney had played these women many times over the past two years, especially at the national training camps, and had never lost. But they hadn't played them in the last six months, and somehow this pair had upped their game and made it into the semi-finals. They knew better than to under-estimate their opponent. And Hali's typical strategy was to attack, attack, attack. Why change now?

It only took a light jog and some calisthenics to warm up and push out any remaining lactic acid. They entered the court ready to rock. The stands were packed with very loud and obnoxious Americans, including the LaRoches, the Abaras and Courtney's folks. They were probably the most obnoxious of all. The game started slowly with both teams swapping serves several times before Courtney scored the first point. They were still feeling out their opponents, who hadn't really changed much since their last meeting. They settled into a routine with Courtney playing the net and Hali receiving as much as possible. That enabled Hali to attack, which she did very efficiently. But when the opponents started serving to Courtney instead, they discovered that her attack was almost as strong. And both girls were good passers and setters as well. Little by little, Hali and Courtney over-whelmed them. They traded points for the first dozen or so points, then Hali and Courtney upped the pressure and started scoring two points for every one that their opponents scored. The final score for game one was 21 to 16. The second game wasn't as close. Hali and Courtney were in the groove and scoring at will. The final score was 21 to 11. They'd made it to the gold medal round. Team USA-3 would play one more game for the bronze.

There was a one-day delay before the finals as the courts were re-aligned to allow for much larger bleachers all around the court. The eight courts were reduced to two, one for the men and one for the women, separated by several hundred yards. There were four games in the medal round. The bronze medal game was at nine, followed soon after by the gold medal game. The men played at the same time. The awards ceremony would be immediately after the last match ended. In the women's medal chase, Team USA-1 would be facing the Canucks again for the gold medal. Team USA-3 would be facing Argentina for the bronze. Hali and Courtney spent their lay day by themselves, resting, reading, eating good food, soaking in the hot tub, and even doing a light workout in the Athletes Village gym. They didn't discuss volleyball much. There wasn't much left to talk about. They knew what they had to do.

The bronze medal match lasted less than two hours. The Argentinians won in two games that weren't as close as the score suggested. The final score was 21 to 18 in the first game and 21 to 16 in the second, but the Argentinians were comfortably in control the entire match. Their Olympics were over. At eleven forty-five, Hali and Courtney took the court to thunderous applause. Most of the fans were sporting USA flags and clothing, but there was a sizable number of Canucks as well. All were cheering loudly. Hali basked in the adoration that she'd been craving for so long. Skin color was no longer an issue. She and Courtney were America's sweethearts.

The game got underway at twelve-fifteen with Courtney serving. It very soon became apparent that the Canadians had changed their game plan since their last meeting. They were playing much more of a finesse game, but Hali and Courtney were good with that. They swapped serves for a while, occasionally scoring points, and kept the score within one or two points until they were approaching game point forty-five minutes later. As the end approached, Hali and Courtney began to attack aggressively. But the Canadians withstood the assault and stayed with their game plan. They reached game point first, then won the first game with an ace served to Hali on the outside that hit the top of the net then dropped to the ground in bounds as Hali dove to intercept its original trajectory. It was a lucky shot, but it won the game.

Hali and Courtney kept to the same strategy with Hali playing back and Courtney playing the net in the second game. But they were playing more aggressively now. They scored first and for a while it looked like they were the dominant team. The Canadians were struggling, but they somehow managed to keep the score close. They were tied at 10 to 10, then the Canadians went on a streak and scored three unanswered points. Hali and Courtney fought back swapping points with them, but the Canadians maintained their three-point lead all the way to the end. The Canadians were the gold medal winners. Hali and Courtney had to settle for the silver.

The awards ceremony later that afternoon was a somewhat subdued affair compared to those in the main arenas. Most of the crowd had left. Only the beach volleyball medals were presented, the men first then the women. It took much longer to play the anthems through the tinny speakers than it took to award the medals. Hali and Courtney were exhausted and just wanted to be alone, but their families were all over them. Eventually, the crowd dispersed, and Hali and Courtney made their way back to their room in the Athlete's Village. They had an hour to commiserate and clean up before meeting their families for supper, their first time together. Tomorrow, they were all going to flee the crowds of Tokyo and fly down to Hiroshima for a day, then a couple of days in Osaka before heading back to Tokyo for the closing ceremonies. Again, the tickets to the ceremonies had been long sold out, so the families would watch at the dinner theater. Of course, Hali and Courtney would participate. They wouldn't miss it for the world.

They met at the hotel restaurant at seven o'clock. A little late to be eating, but the girls had needed some down time to themselves. They proudly wore their silver medals over their Team USA polo shirts as they entered. Asha jumped up and wrapped both girls in her huge bear hug, followed by Courtney's Mom.

"Hali, Courtney, I am so proud of you two!" Asha gushed. "I've never been prouder. I can die happy now! To see you two out there playing so hard and looking so beautiful... well, I don't know where you got it from, certainly not me!"

Bobby finally got his turn to hug Hali, and they embraced for a long time. He had tears in his eyes when they finally let go and sat down. But he kept his arm around her, and she held his hand. Drinks were served then the dinner order was placed as the families chattered about the things they saw in Tokyo.

"So, Hali, Courtney... What now?" Gerald asked, whose left forearm was now proudly displaying his own R2AK tattoo.

The girls looked at each other for a while, then Hali looked down at her silver medal and toyed with it.

"I don't know" she said after a long pause. "I feel like we came so close, but we came up short. The gold is all I've been thinking about for years. We were second best at the worlds, and now we're second best here at the Olympics. I just feel that I didn't train this hard to be second best."

Courtney nodded. "I think I'd like to keep competing for a little while yet. Maybe take a little break for a few days. The World Championships are in September this year. Maybe we can finally get our gold."

Hali broke in. "I'm all in for the worlds, but I want to get married first! I've been waiting three years for this!"

Everyone cheered to that, especially Bobby. He hugged her for a long time. Both were crying.

"We'll do that as soon as we get back, Sweetheart" Bobby said. "We can start planning it while we travel. It's a long flight back to the US and I'm sure Mom and Asha will want to sit next to you and help plan. I'm sure they can put something special together quickly. Getting your dress on time will be the highest priority."

"I don't care about a dress! I just want to get married, Bobby. I've been waiting so long! I don't care if we even have a ceremony."

"Oh Honey! You're going to have a ceremony!" Asha chimed in. "Don't even think about skipping that. Annette and I are on it. You just show up at the right place and the right time. We'll get you married in fine style!"

Hali laughed. "Deal! Courtney and I'll focus on training and I'll show up when you tell me to. I don't even want to think about it. But here're my requirements: it'll be in a church; it'll be informal; and it'll be fun for everyone."

Asha and Annette both laughed. "You just leave it to us, Baby. We'll make you proud. This will be so much fun for us!"

"So, after the world championships are you going back to school?" Gerald asked.

"I don't know" Hali responded. "I don't think so. Somehow, I'm not even thinking of being a lawyer anymore. I never really was… It was just the only option for a decent career that I came up with. I might just go into coaching. With an Olympic medal, I'm probably pretty damn marketable. We'll see how I feel after the Worlds. Maybe Courtney and I will just keep playing professionally. We were making tons of money before the economy died. It'll come back and we'll make lots more with our endorsements and sponsors, plus our winnings."

"I was hoping you'd say that" Courtney spoke up. "I feel like we spent all that time training and we're now... well, like the best in the world. It would be a waste to stop now that we just got here. I have no desire to enter the corporate world at all. Let's keep playing for a while. Who knows? Maybe we'll get another shot at the Olympics."

"Well, now that you mention it," Dillan spoke up for the first time tonight. "I heard that snow volleyball was a demonstration sport in 2018 and is being considered for next year in 2022. Three on three. Maybe you won't have to wait three more years."

"Snow volleyball?" Hali asked. "I'm not so sure about that. Sounds cold to me. But maybe. We'll see. What do you think, Baby? What would you think if I kept competing? I'll be on the road a lot. It's not really fair to you to keep on waiting for me."

"Sweetheart," Bobby replied, kissing her. "I promise you that you will never, ever resent me for holding you back from your goals. I will support you whatever you decide. I'm just incredibly proud of you right now, and I'd be proud to support you if you continue competing. You go on competing with my complete blessing. As far as being away all the time, well, military families do it all the time and they survive. I'll miss you, sure, but I'll give you a great homecoming when you get back."

"Well said, Bobby! I feel the same way" Dillan spoke up. "You two girls need to keep on competing. It's obvious that's what you were meant for. And you're only just now reaching your potential. You've got great careers ahead of you as professionals."

Hali jumped up and gave Courtney a high five, then a quick hug. "Okay, Partner... we're on! I feel sooo good to get that decided. I wasn't looking forward to school, anyway."

CPSIA information can be obtained
at www.ICGtesting.com
Printed in the USA
BVHW031457240720
584534BV00001B/18